Soldiers Three by Rudyard Kipling

Rudyard Kipling: A great Victorian, a great writer of Empire, a great man.

Rudyard Kipling was one of the most popular writers of prose and poetry in the late 19th and 20th Century and awarded the Noble Prize for Literature in 1907.

Born in Bombay on 30th December 1865, as was the custom in those days, he and his sister were sent back to England when he was 5. The ill-treatment and cruelty by the couple who they boarded with in Portsmouth, Kipling himself suggested, contributed to the onset of his literary life. This was further enhanced by his return to India at age 16 to work on a local paper, as not only did this result in him writing constantly but also made him explore issues of identity and national allegiance which pervade much of his work.

Whilst he is best remembered for his classic children's stories and his popular poem 'If..'. He is also regarded as a major innovator in the art of the short story and of course the novels and other works that have seen him acknowledged as a writer of the first rank.

Index of Contents

THE GOD FROM THE MACHINE

Hit a man an' help a woman, an' ye can't be far wrong anyways.—Maxims of Private Mulvaney.

The Inexpressibles gave a ball. They borrowed a seven-pounder from the Gunners, and wreathed it with laurels, and made the dancing-floor plate-glass, and provided a supper, the like of which had never been eaten before, and set two sentries at the door of the room to hold the trays of programme-cards. My friend, Private Mulvaney, was one of the sentries, because he was the tallest man in the regiment. When the dance was fairly started the sentries were released, and Private Mulvaney went to curry favour with the Mess Sergeant in charge of the supper. Whether the Mess Sergeant gave or Mulvaney took, I cannot say. All that I am certain of is that, at supper-time, I found Mulvaney with Private Ortheris, two-thirds of a ham, a loaf of bread, half a pate-de-foie-gras, and two magnums of champagne, sitting on the roof of my carriage. As I came up I heard him saying—

'Praise be a danst doesn't come as often as Ord'ly-room, or, by this an' that, Orth'ris, me son, I wud be the dishgrace av the rig'mint instid av the brightest jool in uts crown.'

'Hand the Colonel's pet noosance,' said Ortheris. 'But wot makes you curse your rations? This 'ere fizzy stuff's good enough.'

'Stuff, ye oncivilised pagin! 'Tis champagne we're dhrinkin' now. 'Tisn't that I am set ag'in. 'Tis this quare stuff wid the little bits av black leather in it. I misdoubt I will be distressin'ly sick wid it in the mornin'. Fwhat is ut?'

'Goose liver,' I said, climbing on the top of the carriage, for I knew that it was better to sit out with Mulvaney than to dance many dances.

'Goose liver is ut?' said Mulvaney. 'Faith, I'm thinkin' thim that makes it wud do betther to cut up the Colonel. He carries a power av liver undher his right arrum whin the days are warm an' the nights chill. He wud give thim tons an' tons av liver. 'Tis he sez so. "I'm all liver to-day," sez he; an' wid that he ordhers me ten days C. B. for as moild a dhrink as iver a good sodger tuk betune his teeth.'

'That was when 'e wanted for to wash 'isself in the Fort Ditch,' Ortheris explained. 'Said there was too much beer in the Barrack water-butts for a God-fearing man. You was lucky in gettin' orf with wot you did, Mulvaney.'

'Say you so? Now I'm pershuaded I was cruel hard trated, seein' fwhat I've done for the likes av him in the days whin my eyes were wider opin than they are now. Man alive, for the Colonel to whip me on the peg in that way! Me that have saved the repitation av a ten times better man than him! 'Twas ne-farious—an' that manes a power av evil!'

'Never mind the nefariousness,' I said. 'Whose reputation did you save?'

'More's the pity, 'twasn't my own, but I tuk more trouble wid ut than av ut was. 'Twas just my way, messin' wid fwhat was no business av mine. Hear now!' He settled himself at ease on the top of the carriage. 'I'll tell you all about ut. Av coorse I will name no names, for there's wan that's an orf'cer's lady now, that was in ut, and no more will I name places, for a man is thracked by a place.'

'Eyah!' said Ortheris lazily, 'but this is a mixed story wot's comin'.'

'Wanst upon a time, as the childer-books say, I was a recruity.'

'Was you though?' said Ortheris; 'now that's extry-ordinary!'

'Orth'ris,' said Mulvaney, 'av you opin thim lips av yours again, I will, savin' your presince, Sorr, take you by the slack av your trousers an' heave you.'

'I'm mum,' said Ortheris. 'Wot 'appened when you was a recruity?'

'I was a betther recruity than you iver was or will be, but that's neither here nor there. Thin I became a man, an' the divil of a man I was fifteen years ago. They called me Buck Mulvaney in thim days, an', begad, I tuk a woman's eye. I did that! Ortheris, ye scrub, fwhat are ye sniggerin' at? Do you misdoubt me?'

'Devil a doubt!' said Ortheris; 'but I've 'eard summat like that before!'

Mulvaney dismissed the impertinence with a lofty wave of his hand and continued—

'An' the orf'cers av the rig'mint I was in in thim days was orf'cers—gran' men, wid a manner on 'em, an' a way wid 'em such as is not made these days—all but wan—wan o' the capt'ns. A bad dhrill, a wake voice, an' a limp leg—thim three things are the signs av a bad man. You bear that in your mind, Orth'ris, me son.

'An' the Colonel av the rig'mint had a daughter—wan av thim lamblike, bleatin', pick-me-up-an'-carry-me-or-I'll-die gurls such as was made for the natural prey av men like the Capt'n, who was iverlastin' payin' coort to her, though the Colonel he said time an' over, "Kape out av the brute's way, my dear." But he niver had the heart for to send her away from the throuble, bein' as he was a widower, an' she their wan child.'

'Stop a minute, Mulvaney,' said I; 'how in the world did you come to know these things?'

'How did I come?' said Mulvaney, with a scornful grunt; 'bekase I'm turned durin' the Quane's pleasure to a lump av wood, lookin' out straight forninst me, wid a—a—candelabbrum in my hand, for you to pick your cards out av, must I not see nor feel? Av coorse I du! Up my back, an' in my boots, an' in the short hair av the neck—that's where I kape my eyes whin I'm on duty an' the reg'lar wans are fixed. Know! Take my word for it, Sorr, ivrything an' a great dale more is known in a rig'mint; or fwhat wud be the use av a Mess Sargint, or a Sargint's wife doin' wet-nurse to the Major's baby? To reshume. He was a bad dhrill was this Capt'n—a rotten bad dhrill—an' whin first I ran me eye over him, I sez to myself: "My Militia bantam!" I sez, "My cock av a Gosport dunghill"—'twas from Portsmouth he came to us— "there's combs to be cut," sez I, "an' by the grace av God, 'tis Terence Mulvaney will cut thim."

'So he wint menowderin', and minanderin', an' blandandherin' roun' an' about the Colonel's daughter, an' she, poor innocint, lookin' at him like a Comm'ssariat bullock looks at the Comp'ny cook. He'd a dhirty little scrub av a black moustache, an' he twisted an' turned ivry wurrd he used as av he found ut too sweet for to spit out. Eyah! He was a tricky man an' a liar by natur'. Some are born so. He was wan. I knew he was over his belt in money borrowed from natives; besides a lot av other matthers which, in regard for your presince, Sorr, I will oblitherate. A little av fwhat I knew, the Colonel knew, for he wud have none av him, an' that, I'm thinkin', by fwhat happened aftherwards, the Capt'n knew.

'Wan day, bein' mortial idle, or they wud never ha' thried ut, the rig'mint gave amshure theatricals—orf'cers an' orf'cers' ladies. You've seen the likes time an' agin, Sorr, an' poor fun 'tis for them that sit in the back row an' stamp wid their boots for the honour av the rig'mint. I was told off for to shif' the scenes, haulin' up this an' draggin' down that. Light work ut was, wid lashins av beer and the gurl that dhressed the orf'cers' ladies—but she died in Aggra twelve years gone, an' my tongue's gettin' the betther av me. They was actin' a play thing called Sweethearts, which you may ha' heard av, an' the Colonel's daughter she was a lady's maid. The Capt'n was a boy called Broom—Spread Broom was his name in the play. Thin I saw —ut come out in the actin'—fwhat I niver saw before, an' that was that he was no gentleman. They was too much together, thim two, a-whishperin' behind the scenes I shifted, an' some av what they said I heard; for I was death—blue death an' ivy—on the comb-cuttin'. He was iverlastin'ly oppressing her to fall in wid some sneakin' schame av his, an' she was thryin' to stand out against him, but not as though she was set in her will. I wonder now in thim days that my ears did not grow a yard on me head wid list'nin'. But I looked straight forninst me an' hauled up this an' dragged down that, such as was my duty, an' the orf'cers' ladies sez one to another, thinkin' I was out av listen-reach: "Fwhat an obligin' young man is this Corp'ril Mulvaney!" I was a Corp'ril then. I was rejuced aftherwards, but, no matther, I was a Corp'ril wanst.

'Well, this Sweethearts" business wint on like most amshure theatricals, an' barrin' fwhat I suspicioned, 'twasn't till the dhress-rehearsal that I saw for certain that thim two—he the blackguard, an' she no wiser than she should ha' been—had put up an evasion.'

'A what?' said I.

'E-vasion! Fwhat you call an elopemint. E-vasion I calls it, bekaze, exceptin' whin 'tis right an' natural an' proper, 'tis wrong an' dhirty to steal a man's wan child she not knowin' her own mind. There was a Sargint in the Comm'ssariat who set my face upon e-vasions. I'll tell you about that—'

'Stick to the bloomin' Captains, Mulvaney,' said Ortheris; 'Comm'ssariat Sargints is low.'

Mulvaney accepted the amendment and went on:—

'Now I knew that the Colonel was no fool, any more than me, for I was hild the smartest man in the rig'mint, an' the Colonel was the best orf'cer commandin' in Asia; so fwhat he said an' I said was a mortial truth. We knew that the Capt'n was bad, but, for reasons which I have already oblitherated, I knew more than me Colonel. I wud ha' rolled out his face wid the butt av my gun before permittin' av him to steal the gurl. Saints knew av he wud ha' married her, and av he didn't she wud be in great tormint, an' the divil av a "scandal." But I niver sthruck, niver raised me hand on my shuperior orf'cer; an' that was a merricle now I come to considher it.'

'Mulvaney, the dawn's risin',' said Ortheris, 'an' we're no nearer 'ome than we was at the beginnin'. Lend me your pouch. Mine's all dust.'

Mulvaney pitched his pouch over, and filled his pipe afresh.

'So the dhress-rehearsal came to an end, an', bekaze I was curious, I stayed behind whin the scene-shiftin' was ended, an' I shud ha' been in barricks, lyin' as flat as a toad under a painted cottage thing. They was talkin' in whispers, an' she was shiverin' an' gaspin' like a fresh-hukked fish. "Are you sure you've got the hang av the manewvers?" sez he, or wurrds to that effec', as the coort-martial sez. "Sure as death," sez she, "but I misdoubt 'tis cruel hard on my father." "Damn your father," sez he, or anyways 'twas fwhat he thought, "the arrangement is as clear as mud. Jungi will drive the carr'ge afther all's over, an' you come to the station, cool an' aisy, in time for the two o'clock thrain, where I'll be wid your kit." "Faith," thinks I to myself, "thin there's a ayah in the business tu!"

'A powerful bad thing is a ayah. Don't you niver have any thruck wid wan. Thin he began sootherin' her, an' all the orf'cers an' orf'cers' ladies left, an' they put out the lights. To explain the theory av the flight, as they say at Muskthry, you must understand that afther this Sweethearts'' nonsinse was ended, there was another little bit av a play called Couples—some kind av couple or another. The gurl was actin' in this, but not the man. I suspicioned he'd go to the station wid the gurl's kit at the end av the first piece. 'Twas the kit that flusthered me, for I knew for a Capt'n to go trapesing about the impire wid the Lord knew what av a truso on his arrum was nefarious, an' wud be worse than easin' the flag, so far as the talk afterwards wint.'

"Old on, Mulvaney. Wot's truso?' said Ortheris.

'You're an oncivilised man, me son. Whin a gurl's married, all her kit an' 'coutrements are truso, which manes weddin'-portion. An' 'tis the same whin she's runnin' away, even wid the biggest blackguard on the Arrmy List.

'So I made my plan av campaign. The Colonel's house was a good two miles away. "Dennis," sez I to my colour-sargint, "av you love me lend me your kyart, for me heart is bruk an' me feet is sore wid trampin' to and from this foolishness at the Gaff." An' Dennis lent ut, wid a rampin', stampin' red stallion in the shafts. Whin they was all settled down to their Sweethearts for the first scene, which was a long wan, I slips outside and into the kyart. Mother av Hivin! but I made that horse walk, an' we came into the Colonel's compound as the divil wint through Athlone—in standin' leps. There was no one there excipt the servints, an' I wint round to the back an' found the girl's ayah.

'"Ye black brazen Jezebel," sez I, "sellin' your masther's honour for five rupees—pack up all the Miss Sahib's kit an' look slippy! Capt'n Sahib's order," sez I. "Going to the station we are," I sez, an' wid that I laid my finger to my nose an' looked the schamin' sinner I was.

'"Bote acchy," says she; so I knew she was in the business, an' I piled up all the sweet talk I'd iver learnt in the bazars on to this she-bullock, an' prayed av her to put all the quick she knew into the thing. While she packed, I stud outside an' sweated, for I was wanted for to shif the second scene. I tell you, a young gurl's e-vasion manes as much baggage as a rig'mint on the line av march! "Saints help Dennis's springs," thinks I, as I bundled the stuff into the thrap, "for I'll have no mercy!"

'"I'm comin' too," says the ayah.

'"No, you don't," sez I, "later—pechy! You baito where you are. I'll pechy come an' bring you sart, along with me, you maraudin'"-niver mind fwhat I called her.

'Thin I wint for the Gaff, an' by the special ordher av Providence, for I was doin' a good work you will ondersthand, Dennis's springs hild toight. "Now, whin the Capt'n goes for that kit," thinks I, "he'll be throubled." At the end av Sweethearts off the Capt'n runs in his kyart to the Colonel's house, an' I sits down on the steps and laughs. Wanst an' again I slipped in to see how the little piece was goin', an' whin ut was near endin' I stepped out all among the carr'ges an' sings out very softly, "Jungi!" Wid that a carr'ge began to move, an' I waved to the dhriver. "Hitherao!" sez I, an' he hitheraoed till I judged he was at proper distance, an' thin I tuk him, fair an' square betune the eyes, all I knew for good or bad, an' he dhropped wid a guggle like the canteen beer-engine whin ut's runnin' low. Thin I ran to the kyart an' tuk out all the kit an' piled it into the carr'ge, the sweat runnin' down my face in dhrops. "Go home," sez I, to the sais; "you'll find a man close here. Very sick he is. Take him away, an' av you iver say wan wurrd about fwhat you've dekkoed, I'll marrow you till your own wife won't sumjao who you are!" Thin I heard the stampin' av feet at the ind av the play, an' I ran in to let down the curtain. Whin they all came out the gurl thried to hide herself behind wan av the pillars, an' sez "Jungi" in a voice that wouldn't ha' scared a hare. I run over to Jungi's carr'ge an' tuk up the lousy old horse-blanket on the box, wrapped my head an' the rest av me in ut, an' dhrove up to where she was.

'"Miss Sahib," sez I; "going to the station? Captain Sahib's order!" an' widout a sign she jumped in all among her own kit.

'I laid to an' dhruv like steam to the Colonel's house before the Colonel was there, an' she screamed an' I thought she was goin' off. Out comes the ayah, saying all sorts av things about the Capt'n havin' come for the kit an' gone to the station.

'"Take out the luggage, you divil," sez I, "or I'll murther you!"

'The lights av the thraps people comin' from the Gaff was showin' across the parade ground, an', by this an' that, the way thim two women worked at the bundles an' thrunks was a caution! I was dyin' to help, but, seein' I didn't want to be known, I sat wid the blanket roun' me an' coughed an' thanked the Saints there was no moon that night.

'Whin all was in the house again, I niver asked for bukshish but dhruv tremenjus in the opp'site way from the other carr'ge an' put out my lights. Presintly, I saw a naygur man wallowin' in the road. I slipped down before I got to him, for I suspicioned Providence was wid me all through that night. 'Twas Jungi, his nose smashed in flat, all dumb sick as you please. Dennis's man must have tilted him out av the thrap. Whin he came to, "Hutt!" sez I, but he began to howl.

'"You black lump av dirt," I sez, "is this the way you dhrive your gharri? That tikka has been owin" an' fere-owin" all over the bloomin' country this whole bloomin' night, an' you as mut-walla as Davey's sow. Get up, you hog!" sez I, louder, for I heard the wheels av a thrap in the dark; "get up an' light your lamps, or you'll be run into!" This was on the road to the Railway Station.

'"Fwhat the divil's this?" sez the Capt'n's voice in the dhark, an' I could judge he was in a lather av rage.

'"Gharri dhriver here, dhrunk, Sorr," sez I; "I've found his gharri sthrayin' about cantonmints, an' now I've found him."

'"Oh!" sez the Capt'n; "fwhat's his name?" I stooped down an' pretended to listen.

'"He sez his name's Jungi, Sorr," sez I.

'"Hould my harse," sez the Capt'n to his man, an' wid that he gets down wid the whip an' lays into Jungi, just mad wid rage an' swearin' like the scutt he was.

'I thought, afther a while, he wud kill the man, so I sez:—"Stop, Sorr, or you'll, murdher him!" That dhrew all his fire on me, an' he cursed me into Blazes, an' out again. I stud to attenshin an' saluted:— "Sorr," sez I, "av ivry man in this wurruld had his rights, I'm thinkin' that more than wan wud be beaten to a jelly for this night's work—that niver came off at all, Sorr, as you see?" "Now," thinks I to myself, "Terence Mulvaney, you've cut your own throat, for he'll sthrike, an' you'll knock him down for the good av his sowl an' your own iverlastin' dishgrace!"

'But the Capt'n niver said a single wurrd. He choked where he stud, an' thin he went into his thrap widout sayin' good-night, an' I wint back to barricks.'

'And then?' said Ortheris and I together.

'That was all,' said Mulvaney; 'niver another word did I hear av the whole thing. All I know was that there was no e-vasion, an' that was fwhat I wanted. Now, I put ut to you, Sorr, is ten days' C. B. a fit an' a proper tratement for a man who has behaved as me?'

'Well, any'ow,' said Ortheris, 'tweren't this 'ere Colonel's daughter, an' you was blazin' copped when you tried to wash in the Fort Ditch.'

'That,' said Mulvaney, finishing the champagne, 'is a shuparfluous an' impert'nint observation.'

OF THOSE CALLED

We were wallowing through the China Seas in a dense fog, the horn blowing every two minutes for the benefit of the fishery craft that crowded the waterways. From the bridge the fo'c'sle was invisible; from the hand-wheel at the stern the captain's cabin. The fog held possession of everything—the pearly white fog. Once or twice when it tried to lift, we saw a glimpse of the oily sea, the flitting vision of a junk's sail spread in the vain hope of catching the breeze, or the buoys of a line of nets. Somewhere close to us lay the land, but it might have been the Kurile Islands for aught we knew. Very early in the morning there passed us, not a cable's-length away, but as unseen as the spirits of the dead, a steamer of the same line as ours. She howled melodiously in answer to our bellowing, and passed on.

Suppose she had hit us,' said a man from Saigon. 'Then we should have gone down,' answered the chief officer sweetly. 'Beastly thing to go down in a fog,' said a young gentleman who was travelling for pleasure. 'Chokes a man both ways, y' know.' We were comfortably gathered in the smoking-room, the weather being too cold to venture on the deck. Conversation naturally turned upon accidents of fog, the horn tooting significantly in the pauses between the tales. I heard of the wreck of the Eric, the cutting down of the Strathnairn within half a mile of harbour, and the carrying away of the bow plates of the Sigismund outside Sandy Hook.

'It is astonishing,' said the man from Saigon, 'how many true stories are put down as sea yarns. It makes a man almost shrink from telling an anecdote.'

'Oh, please don't shrink on our account,' said the smoking-room with one voice.

'It's not my own story,' said the man from Saigon. 'A fellow on a Massageries boat told it me. He had been third officer of a sort on a Geordie tramp—one of those lumbering, dish-bottomed coal-barges where the machinery is tied up with a string and the plates are rivetted with putty. The way he told his tale was this. The tramp had been creeping along some sea or other with a chart ten years old and the haziest sort of chronometers when she got into a fog—just such a fog as we have now.'

Here the smoking-room turned round as one man, and looked through the windows.

'In the man's own words, "just when the fog was thickest, the engines broke down. They had been doing this for some weeks, and we were too weary to care. I went forward of the bridge, and leaned over the side, wondering where I should ever get something that I could call a ship, and whether the old hulk would fall to pieces as she lay. The fog was as thick as any London one, but as white as steam. While they were tinkering at the engines below, I heard a voice in the fog about twenty yards from the ship's side, calling out, 'Can you climb on board if we throw you a rope?' That startled me, because I fancied we were going to be run down the next minute by a ship engaged in rescuing a man overboard. I shouted for the engine-room whistle; and it whistled about five minutes, but never the sound of a ship could we hear. The ship's boy came forward with some biscuit for me. As he put it into my hand, I heard the voice in the fog, crying out about throwing us a rope. This time it was the boy that yelled, 'Ship on us!' and off went the whistle again, while the men in the engine-room—it generally took the ship's crew to repair the Hespa's engines—tumbled upon deck to know what we were doing. I told them about the hail, and we listened in the smother of the fog for the sound of a screw. We listened for ten minutes, then we blew the whistle for another ten. Then the crew began to call the ship's boy a fool, meaning that the third mate was no better. When they were going down below, I heard the hail the third time, so did the ship's boy. 'There you are,' I said, 'it is not twenty yards from us.' The engineer sings out, 'I heard it too! Are you all asleep?' Then the crew began to swear at the engineer; and what with discussion, argument, and a little swearing,—for there is not much discipline on board a tramp,—we raised such a row that our skipper came aft to enquire. I, the engineer, and the ship's boy stuck to our tale. 'Voices or no voices,' said the captain, 'you'd better patch the old engines up, and see if you've got enough steam to whistle with. I've a notion that we've got into rather too crowded ways."

'"The engineer stayed on deck while the men went down below. The skipper hadn't got back to the chart-room before I saw thirty feet of bowsprit hanging over the break of the fo'c'sle. Thirty feet of bowsprit, sir, doesn't belong to anything that sails the seas except a sailing-ship or a man-of-war. I speculated quite a long time, with my hands on the bulwarks, as to whether our friend was soft wood or steel plated. It would not have made much difference to us, anyway; but I felt there was more honour in being rammed, you know. Then I knew all about it. It was a ram. We opened out. I am not exaggerating—we opened out, sir, like a cardboard box. The other ship cut us two-thirds through, a little behind the break of the fo'c'sle. Our decks split up lengthways. The mizzen-mast bounded out of its place, and we heeled over. Then the other ship blew a fog-horn. I remember thinking, as I took water from the port bulwark, that this was rather ostentatious after she had done all the mischief. After that, I was a mile and a half under sea, trying to go to sleep as hard as I could. Some one caught hold of my hair, and waked me up. I was hanging to what was left of one of our boats under the lee of a large English ironclad. There were two men with me; the three of us began to yell. A man on the ship sings out, 'Can you climb on board if we throw you a rope?' They weren't going to let down a fine new man-of-war's boat to pick up three half-drowned rats. We accepted the invitation. We climbed—I, the engineer, and the ship's boy. About half an hour later the fog cleared entirely; except for the half of the boat away in the offing, there was neither stick nor string on the sea to show that the Hespa had been cut down."

'And what do you think of that now?' said the man from Saigon.

PRIVATE LEAROYD'S STORY

And he told a tale.—Chronicles of Gautama Buddha.

Far from the haunts of Company Officers who insist upon kit-inspections, far from keen-nosed Sergeants who sniff the pipe stuffed into the bedding-roll, two miles from the tumult of the barracks, lies the Trap. It is an old dry well, shadowed by a twisted pipal tree and fenced with high grass. Here, in the years gone by, did Private Ortheris establish his depot and menagerie for such possessions, dead and living, as could not safely be introduced to the barrack-room. Here were gathered Houdin pullets, and fox-terriers of undoubted pedigree and more than doubtful ownership, for Ortheris was an inveterate poacher and pre-eminent among a regiment of neat-handed dog-stealers.

Never again will the long lazy evenings return wherein Ortheris, whistling softly, moved surgeon-wise among the captives of his craft at the bottom of the well; when Learoyd sat in the niche, giving sage counsel on the management of 'tykes,' and Mulvaney, from the crook of the overhanging pipal, waved his enormous boots in benediction above our heads, delighting us with tales of Love and War, and strange experiences of cities and men.

Ortheris—landed at last in the 'little stuff bird-shop' for which your soul longed; Learoyd—back again in the smoky, stone-ribbed North, amid the clang of the Bradford looms; Mulvaney—grizzled, tender, and very wise Ulysses, sweltering on the earthwork of a Central India line—judge if I have forgotten old days in the Trap!

Orth'ris, as allus thinks he knaws more than other foaks, said she wasn't a real laady, but nobbut a Hewrasian. I don't gainsay as her culler was a bit doosky like. But she was a laady. Why, she rode iv a carriage, an' good 'osses, too, an' her 'air was that oiled as you could see your faice in it, an' she wore dimond rings an' a goold chain, an' silk an' satin dresses as mun 'a' cost a deal, for it isn't a cheap shop as keeps enough o' one pattern to fit a figure like hers. Her name was Mrs. DeSussa, an't' waay I coom to be acquainted wi' her was along of our Colonel's Laady's dog Rip.

I've seen a vast o' dogs, but Rip was t' prettiest picter of a cliver fox-tarrier 'at iver I set eyes on. He could do owt you like but speeak, an' t' Colonel's Laady set more store by him than if he hed been a Christian. She hed bairns of her awn, but they was i' England, and Rip seemed to get all t' coodlin' and pettin' as belonged to a bairn by good right.

But Rip were a bit on a rover, an' hed a habit o' breakin' out o' barricks like, and trottin' round t' plaice as if he were t' Cantonment Magistrate coom round inspectin'. The Colonel leathers him once or twice, but Rip didn't care an' kept on gooin' his rounds, wi' his taail a-waggin' as if he were flag-signallin' to t' world at large 'at he was 'gettin' on nicely, thank yo', and how's yo'sen?' An' then t' Colonel, as was noa sort of a hand wi' a dog, tees him oop. A real clipper of a dog, an' it's noa wonder yon laady, Mrs. DeSussa, should tek a fancy tiv him. Theer's one o' t' Ten Commandments says yo' maun't cuwet your neebor's ox nor his jackass, but it doesn't say nowt about his tarrier dogs, an' happen thot's t' reason why Mrs. DeSussa cuvveted Rip, tho' she went to church reg'lar along wi' her husband who was so mich darker 'at if he hedn't such a good coaat tiv his back yo' might ha' called him a black man and nut tell a lee nawther. They said he addled his brass i' jute, an' he'd a rare lot on it.

Well, you seen, when they teed Rip up, t' poor awd lad didn't enjoy very good 'elth. So t' Colonel's Laady sends for me as 'ad a naame for bein' knowledgeable about a dog, an' axes what's ailin' wi' him.

'Why,' says I, 'he's getten t' mopes, an' what he wants is his libbaty an' coompany like t' rest on us, wal happen a rat or two 'ud liven him oop. It's low, mum,' says I, 'is rats, but it's t' nature of a dog; an' soa's cuttin' round an' meetin' another dog or two an' passin' t' time o' day, an' hevvin' a bit of a turn-up wi' him like a Christian.'

So she says her dog maunt niver fight an' noa Christians iver fought.

'Then what's a soldier for?' says I; an' I explains to her t' contrairy qualities of a dog, 'at, when yo' coom to think on't, is one o't' curusest things as is. For they larn to behave theirsens like gentlemen born, fit for t' fost o' coompany—they tell me t' Widdy herself is fond of a good dog and knaws one when she sees it as well as onny body: then on t' other hand a-tewin' round after cats an' gettin' mixed oop i' all manners o' blackguardly street-rows, an' killin' rats, an' fightin' like divils.

T' Colonel's Laady says:—'Well, Learoyd, I doan't agree wi' you, but you're right in a way o' speeakin', an' I should like yo' to tek Rip out a-walkin' wi' you sometimes; but yo' maun't let him fight, nor chase cats, nor do nowt 'orrid': an them was her very wods.

Soa Rip an' me goes out a-walkin' o' evenin's, he bein' a dog as did credit tiv a man, an' I catches a lot o' rats an we hed a bit of a match on in an awd dry swimmin'-bath at back o't' cantonments, an' it was none so long afore he was as bright as a button again. He hed a way o' flyin' at them big yaller pariah dogs as if he was a harrow offan a bow, an' though his weight were nowt, he tuk 'em so suddint-like they rolled over like skittles in a halley, an' when they coot he stretched after 'em as if he were rabbit-runnin'. Saame with cats when he cud get t' cat agaate o' runnin'.

One evenin', him an' me was trespassin' ovver a compound wall after one of them mongooses 'at he'd started, an' we was busy grubbin' round a prickle-bush, an' when we looks up there was Mrs. DeSussa wi' a parasel ovver her shoulder, a-watchin' us. 'Oh my!' she sings out; 'there's that lovelee dog! Would he let me stroke him, Mister Soldier?'

'Ay, he would, mum,' sez I, 'for he's fond o' laady's coompany. Coom here, Rip, an' speeak to this kind laady.' An'Rip, seein' 'at t'mongoose hed getten clean awaay, cooms up like t' gentleman he was, nivver a hauporth shy or okkord.

'Oh, you beautiful—you prettee dog!' she says, clippin' an' chantin' her speech in a way them sooart has o' their awn; 'I would like a dog like you. You are so verree lovelee—so awfullee prettee,' an' all thot sort o' talk, 'at a dog o' sense mebbe thinks nowt on, tho' he bides it by reason o' his breedin'.

An' then I meks him joomp ovver my swagger-cane, an' shek hands, an' beg, an' lie dead, an' a lot o' them tricks as laadies teeaches dogs, though I doan't haud with it mysen, for it's makin' a fool o' a good dog to do such like.

An' at lung length it cooms out 'at she'd been thrawin' sheep's eyes, as t' sayin' is, at Rip for many a day. Yo' see, her childer was grown up, an' she'd nowt mich to do, an' were allus fond of a dog. Soa she axes me if I'd tek somethin' to dhrink. An' we goes into t' drawn-room wheer her husband was a-settin'. They meks a gurt fuss ower t' dog an' I has a bottle o' aale, an' he gave me a handful o' cigars.

Soa I coomed away, but t' awd lass sings out—'Oh, Mister Soldier, please coom again and bring that prettee dog.'

I didn't let on to t' Colonel's Laady about Mrs. DeSussa, and Rip, he says nowt nawther; an' I gooes again, an' ivry time there was a good dhrink an' a handful o' good smooaks. An' I telled t' awd lass a heeap more about Rip than I'd ever heeared; how he tuk t' fost prize at Lunnon dog-show and cost thotty-three pounds fower shillin' from t' man as bred him; 'at his own brother was t' propputty o' t' Prince o' Wailes, an' 'at he had a pedigree as long as a Dook's. An' she lapped it all oop an' were niver tired o' admirin' him. But when t' awed lass took to givin' me money an' I seed 'at she were gettin' fair fond about t' dog, I began to suspicion summat. Onny body may give a soldier t' price of a pint in a friendly way an' theer's no 'arm done, but when it cooms to five rupees slipt into your hand, sly like, why, it's what t' 'lectioneerin' fellows calls bribery an' corruption. Specially when Mrs. DeSussa threwed hints how t' cold weather would soon be ower an' she was goin' to Munsooree Pahar an' we was goin' to Rawalpindi, an' she would niver see Rip any more onless somebody she knowed on would be kind tiv her.

Soa I tells Mulvaney an' Ortheris all t' taale thro', beginnin' to end.

"'Tis larceny that wicked ould laady manes,' says t' Irishman, ''tis felony she is sejuicin' ye into, my frind Learoyd, but I'll purtect your innocence. I'll save ye from the wicked wiles av that wealthy ould woman, an' I'll go wid ye this evenin' and spake to her the wurrds av truth an' honesty. But Jock,' says he, waggin' his heead, ''twas not like ye to kape all that good dhrink an' thim fine cigars to yerself, while Orth'ris here an' me have been prowlin' round wid throats as dry as lime-kilns, and nothin' to smoke but Canteen plug. 'Twas a dhirty thrick to play on a comrade, for why should you, Learoyd, be balancin' yourself on the butt av a satin chair, as if Terence Mulvaney was not the aquil av anybody who thrades in jute!'

'Let alone me sticks in Orth'ris, 'but that's like life. Them wot's really fitted to decorate society get no show while a blunderin' Yorkshireman like you—'

'Nay,' says I, 'it's none o' t' blunderin' Yorkshireman she wants; it's Rip. He's the gentleman this journey.'

Soa t' next day, Mulvaney an' Rip an' me goes to Mrs. DeSussa's, an' t' Irishman bein' a strainger she wor a bit shy at fost. But you've heeard Mulvaney talk, an' yo' may believe as he fairly bewitched t' awd lass wal she let out 'at she wanted to tek Rip away wi' her to Munsooree Pahar. Then Mulvaney changes his tune an' axes her solemn-like if she'd thought o' t' consequences o' gettin' two poor but honest soldiers sent t' Andamning Islands. Mrs. DeSussa began to cry, so Mulvaney turns round oppen t' other tack and smooths her down, allowin' 'at Rip ud be a vast better off in t' Hills than down i' Bengal, and 'twas a pity he shouldn't go wheer he was so well beliked. And soa he went on, backin' an' fillin' an' workin' up t' awd lass wal she felt as if her life warn't worth nowt if she didn't hev t' dog.

Then all of a suddint he says:—'But ye shall have him, marm, for I've a feelin' heart, not like this could-blooded Yorkshireman; but 'twill cost ye not a penny less than three hundher rupees.'

'Don't yo' believe him, mum,' says I; 't' Colonel's Laady wouldn't tek five hundred for him.'

'Who said she would?' says Mulvaney; 'it's not buyin' him I mane, but for the sake o' this kind, good laady, I'll do what I never dreamt to do in my life. I'll stale him!'

'Don't say steal,' says Mrs. DeSussa; 'he shall have the happiest home. Dogs often get lost, you know, and then they stray, an' he likes me and I like him as I niver liked a dog yet, an' I must hev him. If I got him at t' last minute I could carry him off to Munsooree Pahar and nobody would niver knaw.'

Now an' again Mulvaney looked acrost at me, an' though I could mak nowt o' what he was after, I concluded to take his leead.

'Well, mum,' I says, 'I never thowt to coom down to dog-steealin', but if my comrade sees how it could be done to oblige a laady like yo'sen, I'm nut t' man to hod back, tho' it's a bad business I'm thinkin', an' three hundred rupees is a poor set-off again t' chance of them Damning Islands as Mulvaney talks on.'

'I'll mek it three fifty,' says Mrs. DeSussa; 'only let me hev t'dog!'

So we let her persuade us, an' she teks Rip's measure theer an' then, an' sent to Hamilton's to order a silver collar again t' time when he was to be her awn, which was to be t' day she set off for Munsooree Pahar.

'Sitha, Mulvaney,' says I, when we was outside, 'you're niver goin' to let her hev Rip!'

'An' would ye disappoint a poor old woman?' says he; 'she shall have a Rip.'

'An' wheer's he to come through?' says I.

'Learoyd, my man,' he sings out, 'you're a pretty man av your inches an' a good comrade, but your head is made av duff. Isn't our friend Orth'ris a Taxidermist, an' a rale artist wid his nimble white fingers? An' what's a Taxidermist but a man who can thrate shkins? Do ye mind the white dog that belongs to the Canteen Sargint, bad cess to him—he that's lost half his time an' snarlin' the rest? He shall be lost for good now; an' do ye mind that he's the very spit in shape an' size av the Colonel's, barrin' that his tail is an inch too long, an' he has none av the colour that diversifies the rale Rip, an' his timper is that av his masther an' worse. But fwhat is an inch on a dog's tail? An' fwhat to a professional like Orth'ris is a few ringstraked shpots av black, brown, an' white? Nothin' at all, at all.'

Then we meets Orth'ris, an' that little man, bein' sharp as a needle, seed his way through t' business in a minute. An' he went to work a-practisin' 'air-dyes the very next day, beginnin' on some white rabbits he had, an' then he drored all Rip's markin's on t' back of a white Commissariat bullock, so as to get his 'and in an' be sure of his colours; shadin' off brown into black as nateral as life. If Rip hed a fault it was too mich markin', but it was straingely reg'lar an' Orth'ris settled himself to make a fost-rate job on it when he got haud o' t' Canteen Sargint's dog. Theer niver was sich a dog as thot for bad timper, an' it did nut get no better when his tail hed to be fettled an inch an' a half shorter. But they may talk o' theer Royal Academies as they like. I niver seed a bit o' animal paintin' to beat t' copy as Orth'ris made of Rip's marks, wal t' picter itself was snarlin' all t' time an' tryin' to get at Rip standin' theer to be copied as good as goold.

Orth'ris allus hed as mich conceit on himsen as would lift a balloon, an' he wor so pleeased wi' his sham Rip he wor for tekking him to Mrs. DeSussa before she went away. But Mulvaney an' me stopped thot, knowin' Orth'ris's work, though niver so cliver, was nobut skin-deep.

An' at last Mrs. DeSussa fixed t' day for startin' to Munsooree Pahar. We was to tek Rip to t' stayshun i' a basket an' hand him ovver just when they was ready to start, an' then she'd give us t' brass—as was agreed upon.

An' my wod! It were high time she were off, for them 'air-dyes upon t' cur's back took a vast of paintin' to keep t' reet culler, tho' Orth'ris spent a matter o' seven rupees six annas i' t' best drooggist shops i' Calcutta.

An' t' Canteen Sargint was lookin' for 'is dog everywheer; an', wi' bein' tied up, t' beast's timper got waur nor ever.

It wor i' t' evenin' when t' train started thro' Howrah, an' we 'elped Mrs. DeSussa wi' about sixty boxes, an' then we gave her t' basket. Orth'ris, for pride av his work, axed us to let him coom along wi' us, an' he couldn't help liftin' t' lid an' showin' t' cur as he lay coiled oop.

'Oh!' says t' awd lass; 'the beautee! How sweet he looks!' An' just then t' beauty snarled an' showed his teeth, so Mulvaney shuts down t' lid and says: 'Ye'll be careful, marm, whin ye tek him out. He's disaccustomed to travelling by t' railway, an' he'll be sure to want his rale mistress an' his friend Learoyd, so ye'll make allowance for his feelings at fost.'

She would do all thot an' more for the dear, good Rip, an' she would nut oppen t' basket till they were miles away, for fear anybody should recognise him, an' we were real good and kind soldier-men, we were, an' she bonds me a bundle o' notes, an' then cooms up a few of her relations an' friends to say good-by—not more than seventy-five there wasn't—an' we cuts away.

What coom to t' three hundred and fifty rupees? Thot's what I can scarcelins tell yo', but we melted it— we melted it. It was share an' share alike, for Mulvaney said: 'If Learoyd got hold of Mrs. DeSussa first, sure 'twas I that renumbered the Sargint's dog just in the nick av time, an' Orth'ris was the artist av anius that made a work av art out av that ugly piece av ill-nature. Yet, by way av a thank-offerin' that I was not led into felony by that wicked ould woman, I'll send a thrifle to Father Victor for the poor people he's always beggin' for.'

But me an' Orth'ris, he bein' Cockney an' I bein' pretty far north, did nut see it i' t' saame way. We'd getten t' brass, an' we meaned to keep it. An' soa we did—for a short time.

Noa, noa, we niver heered a wod more o' t' awd lass. Our rig'mint went to Pindi, an' t' Canteen Sargint he got himself another tyke insteead o' t' one 'at got lost so reg'lar, an' was lost for good at last.

THE BIG DRUNK DRAF'

We're goin' 'ome, we're goin' 'ome—
Our ship is at the shore,
An' you mus' pack your 'aversack,
For we won't come back no more.
Ho, don't you grieve for me,
My lovely Mary Ann,
For I'll many you yet on a fourp'ny bit,
As a time expired ma-a-an!
Barrack-room Ballad.

An awful thing has happened! My friend, Private Mulvaney, who went home in the Serapis, time-expired, not very long ago, has come back to India as a civilian! It was all Dinah Shadd's fault. She could not stand the poky little lodgings, and she missed her servant Abdullah more than words could tell. The fact was that the Mulvaneys had been out here too long, and had lost touch of England.

Mulvaney knew a contractor on one of the new Central India lines, and wrote to him for some sort of work. The contractor said that if Mulvaney could pay the passage he would give him command of a gang of coolies for old sake's sake. The pay was eighty-five rupees a month, and Dinah Shadd said that if Terence did not accept she would make his life a 'basted purgathory.' Therefore the Mulvaneys came out as 'civilians,' which was a great and terrible fall; though Mulvaney tried to disguise it, by saying that he was 'Ker'nel on the railway line, an' a consequinshal man.'

He wrote me an invitation, on a tool-indent form, to visit him; and I came down to the funny little 'construction' bungalow at the side of the line. Dinah Shadd had planted peas about and about, and nature had spread all manner of green stuff round the place. There was no change in Mulvaney except the change of clothing, which was deplorable, but could not be helped. He was standing upon his trolly, haranguing a gangman, and his shoulders were as well drilled, and his big, thick chin was as clean-shaven as ever.

'I'm a civilian now,' said Mulvaney. 'Cud you tell that I was iver a martial man? Don't answer, Sorr, av you're strainin' betune a compliment an' a lie. There's no houldin' Dinah Shadd now she's got a house av her own. Go inside, an' dhrink tay out av chiny in the drrrrawin'-room, an' thin we'll dhrink like Christians undher the tree here. Scutt, ye naygur-folk! There's a Sahib come to call on me, an' that's more than he'll iver do for you onless you run! Get out, an' go on pilin' up the earth, quick, till sundown.'

When we three were comfortably settled under the big sisham in front of the bungalow, and the first rush of questions and answers about Privates Ortheris and Learoyd and old times and places had died away, Mulvaney said, reflectively—'Glory be there's no p'rade to-morrow, an' no bun-headed Corp'ril-bhoy to give you his lip. An' yit I don't know. 'Tis harrd to be something ye niver were an' niver meant to be, an' all the ould days shut up along wid your papers. Eyah! I'm growin' rusty, an' 'tis the will av God that a man mustn't serve his Quane for time an' all.'

He helped himself to a fresh peg, and sighed furiously.

'Let your beard grow, Mulvaney,' said I, 'and then you won't be troubled with those notions. You'll be a real civilian.'

Dinah Shadd had told me in the drawing-room of her desire to coax Mulvaney into letting his beard grow. 'Twas so civilian-like,' said poor Dinah, who hated her husband's hankering for his old life.

'Dinah Shadd, you're a dishgrace to an honust, clanescraped man!' said Mulvaney, without replying to me. 'Grow a beard on your own chin, darlint, and lave my razors alone. They're all that stand betune me and dis-ris-pect-ability. Av I didn't shave, I wud be torminted wid an outrajis thurrst; for there's nothin' so dhryin' to the throat as a big billy-goat beard waggin' undher the chin. Ye wudn't have me dhrink ALWAYS, Dinah Shadd? By the same token, you're kapin' me crool dhry now. Let me look at that whiskey.'

The whiskey was lent and returned, but Dinah Shadd, who had been just as eager as her husband in asking after old friends, rent me with—

'I take shame for you, Sorr, coming down here—though the Saints know you're as welkim as the daylight whin you DO come—an' upsettin' Terence's head wid your nonsense about—about fwhat's much better forgotten. He bein' a civilian now, an' you niver was aught else. Can you not let the Arrmy rest? 'Tis not good for Terence.'

I took refuge by Mulvaney, for Dinah Shadd has a temper of her own.

'Let be—let be,' said Mulvaney. ''Tis only wanst in a way I can talk about the ould days.' Then to me:—'Ye say Dhrumshticks is well, an' his lady tu? I niver knew how I liked the gray garron till I was shut av him an' Asia.'—'Dhrumshticks' was the nickname of the Colonel commanding Mulvaney's old regiment.— 'Will you be seein' him again? You will. Thin tell him'—Mulvaney's eyes began to twinkle—'tell him wid Privit—'

'MISTER, Terence,' interrupted Dinah Shadd.

'Now the Divil an' all his angils an' the Firmament av Hiven fly away wid the "Mister," an' the sin av making me swear be on your confession, Dinah Shadd! Privit, I tell ye. Wid Privit Mulvaney's best obedience, that but for me the last time-expired wud be still pullin' hair on their way to the sea.'

He threw himself back in the chair, chuckled, and was silent.

'Mrs. Mulvaney,' I said, 'please take up the whiskey, and don't let him have it until he has told the story.'

Dinah Shadd dexterously whipped the bottle away, saying at the same time, ''Tis nothing to be proud av,' and thus captured by the enemy, Mulvaney spake:—

''Twas on Chuseday week. I was behaderin' round wid the gangs on the 'bankmint—I've taught the hoppers how to kape step an' stop screechin'—whin a head-gangman comes up to me, wid two inches av shirt-tail hanging round his neck an' a disthressful light in his oi. "Sahib," sez he, "there's a rig'mint an' a half av soldiers up at the junction, knockin' red cinders out av ivrything an' ivrybody! They thried to hang me in my cloth," he sez, "an' there will be murder an' ruin an' rape in the place before nightfall! They say they're comin' down here to wake us up. What will we do wid our women-folk?"

'"Fetch my throlly!" sez I; "my heart's sick in my ribs for a wink at anything wid the Quane's uniform on ut. Fetch my throlly, an' six av the jildiest men, and run me up in shtyle."'

'He tuk his best coat,' said Dinah Shadd reproachfully.

"'Twas to do honour to the Widdy. I cud ha' done no less, Dinah Shadd. You and your digresshins interfere wid the coorse av the narrative. Have you iver considhered fwhat I wud look like wid me head shaved as well as me chin? You bear that in your mind, Dinah darlin'.

'I was throllied up six miles, all to get a shquint at that draf'. I knew 'twas a spring draf' goin' home, for there's no rig'mint hereabouts, more's the pity.'

'Praise the Virgin!' murmured Dinah Shadd. But Mulvaney did not hear.

'Whin I was about three-quarters av a mile off the rest-camp, powtherin' along fit to burrst, I heard the noise av the men an', on my sowl, Sorr, I cud catch the voice av Peg Barney bellowin' like a bison wid the belly-ache. You remimber Peg Barney that was in D Comp'ny—a red, hairy scraun, wid a scar on his jaw? Peg Barney that cleared out the Blue Lights' Jubilee meeting wid the cook-room mop last year?

'Thin I knew ut was a draf of the ould rig'mint, an' I was conshumed wid sorrow for the bhoy that was in charge. We was harrd scrapin's at any time. Did I iver tell you how Horker Kelley went into clink nakid as Phoebus Apollonius, wid the shirts av the Corp'ril an' file undher his arrum? An' he was a moild man! But I'm digreshin'. 'Tis a shame both to the rig'mints and the Arrmy sendin' down little orf'cer bhoys wid a draf av strong men mad wid liquor an' the chanst av gettin' shut av India, an' niver a punishment that's fit to be given right down an' away from cantonmints to the dock! 'Tis this nonsince. Whin I am servin' my time, I'm undher the Articles av War, an' can be whipped on the peg for thim. But whin I've served my time, I'm a Reserve man, an' the Articles av War haven't any hould on me. An orf'cer can't do anythin' to a time-expired savin' confinin' him to barricks. 'Tis a wise rig'lation bekaze a time-expired does not have any barricks; bein' on the move all the time. 'Tis a Solomon av a rig'lation, is that. I wud like to be introduced to the man that made ut. 'Tis easier to get colts from a Kibbereen horse-fair into Galway than to take a bad draf' over ten miles av country. Consiquintly that rig'lation—for fear that the men wud be hurt by the little orf'cer bhoy. No matther. The nearer my throlly came to the rest-camp, the woilder was the shine, an' the louder was the voice av Peg Barney. "'Tis good I am here," thinks I to myself, "for Peg alone is employmint for two or three." He bein', I well knew, as copped as a dhrover.

'Faith, that rest-camp was a sight! The tent-ropes was all skew-nosed, an' the pegs looked as dhrunk as the men—fifty av thim—the scourin's, an' rinsin's, an' Divil's lavin's av the Ould Rig'mint. I tell you, Sorr, they were dhrunker than any men you've ever seen in your mortial life. How does a draf' get dhrunk? How does a frog get fat? They suk ut in through their shkins.

'There was Peg Barney sittin' on the groun' in his shirt—wan shoe off an' wan shoe on—whackin' a tent-peg over the head wid his boot, an singin' fit to wake the dead. 'Twas no clane song that he sung, though. 'Twas the Divil's Mass.'

'What's that? 'I asked.

'Whin a bad egg is shut av the Arrmy, he sings the Divil's Mass for a good riddance; an' that manes swearin' at ivrything from the Commandher-in-Chief down to the Room-Corp'ril, such as you niver in your days heard. Some men can swear so as to make green turf crack! Have you iver heard the Curse in an Orange Lodge? The Divil's Mass is ten times worse, an' Peg Barney was singin' ut, whackin' the tent-peg on the head wid his boot for each man that he cursed. A powerful big voice had Peg Barney, an' a hard swearer he was whin sober. I stood forninst him, an' 'twas not me oi alone that cud tell Peg was dhrunk as a coot.

'"Good mornin' Peg," I sez, whin he dhrew breath afther cursin' the Adj'tint Gen'ral; "I've put on my best coat to see you, Peg Barney," sez I.

'"Thin take ut off again," sez Peg Barney, latherin' away wid the boot; "take ut off an' dance, ye lousy civilian!"

'Wid that he begins cursin' ould Dhrumshticks, being so full he clean disremimbers the Brigade-Major an' the Judge Advokit Gen'ral.

'"Do you know me, Peg?" sez I, though me blood was hot in me wid being called a civilian.'

'An' him a decent married man!' wailed Dinah Shadd.

'"I do not," sez Peg, "but dhrunk or sober I'll tear the hide off your back wid a shovel whin I've stopped singin'."

'"Say you so, Peg Barney?" sez I. "'Tis clear as mud you've forgotten me. I'll assist your autobiography." Wid that I stretched Peg Barney, boot an' all, an' wint into the camp. An awful sight ut was!

'"Where's the orf'cer in charge av the detachment?" sez I to Scrub Greene—the manest little worm that ever walked.

'"There's no orf'cer, ye ould cook," sez Scrub; "we're a bloomin' Republic."

'"Are you that?" sez I; "thin I'm O'Connell the Dictator, an' by this you will larn to kape a civil tongue in your rag-box."

'Wid that I stretched Scrub Greene an' wint to the orf'cer's tent. 'Twas a new little bhoy—not wan I'd iver seen before. He was sittin' in his tent, purtendin' not to 'ave ear av the racket.

'I saluted—but for the life av me I mint to shake hands whin I went in. 'Twas the sword hangin' on the tentpole changed my will.

'"Can't I help, Sorr?" sez I; "'tis a strong man's job they've given you, an' you'll be wantin' help by sundown." He was a bhoy wid bowils, that child, an' a rale gintleman.

'"Sit down," sez he.

'"Not before my orf'cer," sez I; an' I tould him fwhat my service was.

'"I've heard av you," sez he. "You tuk the town av Lungtungpen nakid."

'"Faith," thinks I, "that's Honour an' Glory"; for 'twas Lift'nint Brazenose did that job. "I'm wid ye, Sorr," sez I, "if I'm av use. They shud niver ha' sent you down wid the draf'. Savin' your presince, Sorr," I sez, "'tis only Lift'nint Hackerston in the Ould Rig'mint can manage a Home draf'."

'"I've niver had charge of men like this before," sez he, playin' wid the pens on the table; "an' I see by the Rig'lations—"

'"Shut your oi to the Rig'lations, Sorr," I sez, "till the throoper's into blue wather. By the Rig'lations you've got to tuck thim up for the night, or they'll be runnin' foul av my coolies an' makin' a shiverarium half through the country. Can you trust your non-coms, Sorr?"

'"Yes," sez he.

'"Good," sez I; "there'll be throuble before the night. Are you marchin', Sorr?"

'"To the next station," sez he.

'"Better still," sez I; "there'll be big throuble."

'"Can't be too hard on a Home draf'," sez he; "the great thing is to get thim in-ship."

'"Faith you've larnt the half av your lesson, Sorr," sez I, "but av you shtick to the Rig'lations you'll niver get thim in-ship at all, at all. Or there won't be a rag av kit betune thim whin you do."

'"Twas a dear little orf'cer bhoy, an' by way av kapin' his heart up, I tould him fwhat I saw wanst in a draf' in Egypt.'

'What was that, Mulvaney?' said I.

'Sivin an' fifty men sittin' on the bank av a canal, laughin' at a poor little squidgereen av an orf'cer that they'd made wade into the slush an' pitch the things out av the boats for their Lord High Mightinesses. That made me orf'cer bhoy woild with indignation.

'"Soft an' aisy, Sorr," sez I; "you've niver had your draf' in hand since you left cantonmints. Wait till the night, an' your work will be ready to you. Wid your permission, Sorr, I will investigate the camp, an' talk to my ould frinds. 'Tis no manner av use thryin' to shtop the divilment now."

'Wid that I wint out into the camp an' inthrojuced mysilf to ivry man sober enough to remimber me. I was some wan in the ould days, an' the bhoys was glad to see me—all excipt Peg Barney wid a eye like a tomata five days in the bazar, an' a nose to match. They come round me an' shuk me, an' I tould thim I was in privit employ wid an income av me own, an' a drrrawin'-room fit to bate the Quane's; an' wid me lies an' me shtories an' nonsinse gin'rally, I kept 'em quiet in wan way an' another, knockin' roun' the camp. 'Twas bad even thin whin I was the Angil av Peace.

'I talked to me ould non-coms—they was sober—an' betune me an' thim we wore the draf' over into their tents at the proper time. The little orf'cer bhoy he comes round, decint an' civil-spoken as might be.

'"Rough quarters, men," sez he, "but you can't look to be as comfortable as in barricks. We must make the best av things. I've shut my eyes to a dale av dog's tricks today, an' now there must be no more av ut."

'"No more we will. Come an' have a dhrink, me son," sez Peg Barney, staggerin' where he stud. Me little orf'cer bhoy kep' his timper.

'"You're a sulky swine, you are," sez Peg Barney, an' at that the men in the tent began to laugh.

'I tould you me orf'cer bhoy had bowils. He cut Peg Barney as near as might be on the oi that I'd squshed whin we first met. Peg wint spinnin' acrost the tent.

'"Peg him out, Sorr," sez I, in a whishper.

'"Peg him out!" sez me orf'cer bhoy, up loud, just as if 'twas battalion-p'rade an' he pickin' his wurrds from the Sargint.

'The non-coms tuk Peg Barney—a howlin' handful he was—an' in three minutes he was pegged out—chin down, tight-dhrawn—on his stummick, a tent-peg to each arm an' leg, swearin' fit to turn a naygur white.

'I tuk a peg an' jammed ut into his ugly jaw.—"Bite on that, Peg Barney," I sez; "the night is settin' frosty, an' you'll be wantin' divarsion before the mornin'. But for the Rig'lations you'd be bitin' on a bullet now at the thriangles, Peg Barney," sez I.

'All the draf' was out av their tents watchin' Barney bein' pegged.

'"'Tis agin the Rig'lations! He strook him!" screeches out Scrub Greene, who was always a lawyer; an' some of the men tuk up the shoutin'.

'"Peg out that man!" sez my orf'cer bhoy, niver losin' his timper; an' the non-coms wint in and pegged out Scrub Greene by the side av Peg Barney.

'I cud see that the draf' was comin' roun'. The men stud not knowin' fwhat to do.

'"Get to your tents!" sez me orf'cer bhoy. "Sargint, put a sintry over these two men."

'The men wint back into the tents like jackals, an' the rest av the night there was no noise at all excipt the stip av the sintry over the two, an' Scrub Greene blubberin' like a child. 'Twas a chilly night, an' faith, ut sobered Peg Barney.

'Just before Revelly, my orf'cer bhoy comes out an' sez: "Loose those men an' send thim to their tents!" Scrub Greene wint away widout a word, but Peg Barney, stiff wid the cowld, stud like a sheep, thryin' to make his orf'cer understhand he was sorry for playin' the goat.

'There was no tucker in the draf' whin ut fell in for the march, an' divil a wurrd about "illegality" cud I hear.

'I wint to the ould Colour Sargint and I sez:—"Let me die in glory," sez I. "I've seen a man this day!"

'"A man he is," sez ould Hother; "the draf's as sick as a herrin'. They'll all go down to the sea like lambs. That bhoy has the bowils av a cantonmint av Gin'rals."

'"Amin," sez I, "an' good luck go wid him, wheriver he be, by land or by sea. Let me know how the draf gets clear."

'An' do you know how they did? That bhoy, so I was tould by letter from Bombay, bullydamned 'em down to the dock, till they cudn't call their sowls their own. From the time they left me oi till they was 'tween decks, not wan av thim was more than dacintly dhrunk. An', by the Holy Articles av War, whin they wint aboard they cheered him till they cudn't spake, an' that, mark you, has not come about wid a draf in the mim'ry av livin' man! You look to that little orf'cer bhoy. He has bowils. 'Tis not ivry child that wud chuck the Rig'lations to Flanders an' stretch Peg Barney on a wink from a brokin an' dilapidated ould carkiss like mesilf. I'd be proud to serve—'

'Terence, you're a civilian,' said Dinah Shadd warningly.

'So I am—so I am. Is ut likely I wud forget ut? But he was a gran' bhoy all the same, an' I'm only a mud-tipper wid a hod on my shoulthers. The whiskey's in the heel av your hand, Sorr. Wid your good lave we'll dhrink to the Ould Rig'mint—three fingers—standin' up!'

And we drank.

THE WRECK OF THE VISIGOTH

'Eternal Father, strong to save,
Whose arm hath bound the restless wave,
Who bidst the mighty ocean keep
Its own appointed limits deep.'

The lady passengers were trying the wheezy old harmonium in front of the cuddy, because it was Sunday night. In the patch of darkness near the wheel-grating sat the Captain, and the end of his cheroot burned like a head-lamp. There was neither breath nor motion upon the waters through which the screw was thudding. They spread, dull silver, under the haze of the moonlight till they joined the low coast of Malacca away to the eastward. The voices of the singers at the harmonium were held down by the awnings, and came to us with force.

'Oh, hear us when we cry to Thee,
For those in peril on the sea.'

It was as though the little congregation were afraid of the vastness of the sea. But a laugh followed, and some one said, 'Shall we take it through again a little quicker?' Then the Captain told the story of just such a night, lowering his voice for fear of disturbing the music and the minds of the passengers.

'She was the Visigoth,—five hundred tons, or it may have been six,—in the coasting trade; one of the best steamers and best found on the Kutch-Kasauli line. She wasn't six years old when the thing happened: on just such a night as this, with an oily smooth sea, under brilliant starlight, about a hundred miles from land. To this day no one knows really what the matter was. She was so small that she could not have struck even a log in the water without every soul on board feeling the jar; and even if she had struck something, it wouldn't have made her go down as she did. I was fourth officer then; we had about seven saloon passengers, including the Captain's wife and another woman, and perhaps five hundred deck-passengers going up the coast to a shrine, on just such a night as this, when she was ripping through the level sea at a level nine knots an hour. The man on the bridge, whoever it was, saw that she was sinking at the head. Sinking by the head as she went along. That was the only warning we got. She began to sink as she went along. Of course the Captain was told, and he sent me to wake up the saloon passengers and tell them to come on deck. 'Sounds a curious sort of message that to deliver on a dead still night. The people tumbled up in their dressing-gowns and pyjamas, and wouldn't believe me. We were just sinking as fast as we could, and I had to tell 'em that. Then the deck-passengers got wind of it, and all Hell woke up along the decks.

'The rule in these little affairs is to get your saloon passengers off first, then to fill the boats with the balance, and afterwards—God help the extras, that's all. I was getting the starboard stern boat—the mail-boat—away. It hung as it might be over yonder, and as I came along from the cuddy, the deck-passengers hung round me, shoving their money-belts into my hand, taking off their nose-rings and earrings, and thrusting 'em upon me to buy just one chance for life. If I hadn't been so desperately busy, I should have thought it horrible. I put biscuits and water into the boat, and got the two ladies in. One of 'em was the Captain's wife. She had to be put in by main force. You've no notion how women can struggle. The other woman was the wife of an officer going to meet her husband; and there were a couple of passengers beside the lascars. The Captain said he was going to stay with the ship. You see the rule in these affairs, I believe, is that the Captain has to bow gracefully from the bridge and go down. I haven't had a ship under my charge wrecked yet. When that comes, I'll have to do like the others. After the boats were away, and I saw that there was nothing to be got by waiting, I jumped overboard exactly as I might have vaulted over into a flat green field, and struck out for the mail-boat. Another officer did the same thing, but he went for a boat full of natives, and they whacked him on the chest with oars, so he had some difficulty in climbing in.

'It was as well that I reached the mail-boat. There was a compass in it, but the idiots had managed to fill the boat half full of water somehow or another, and none of the crew seemed to know what was required of them. Then the Visigoth went down and took every one with her—ships generally do that; the corpses don't cumber the sea for some time.

'What did I do? I kept all the boats together, and headed into the track of the coasting steamers. The aggravating thing was the thought that we were close to land as far as a big steamer was concerned, and in the middle of eternity as far as regarded a little boat. The sea looks hugeous big from a boat at night.'

'Oh, Christ, whose voice the waters heard
And hushed their ravings at Thy word,
Who walkedst on the foaming deep

And calm amidst its rage did keep,—
Oh, hear us when we cry to Thee,
For those in peril on the sea!'
sang the passengers cheerily.

'That harmonium is disgracefully out of tune,' said the Captain. 'The sea air affects their insides. Well, as I was saying, we settled down in the boat. The Captain's wife was unconscious; she lay in the bottom of the boat and moaned. I was glad she wasn't threshing about the boat: but what I did think was wrong, was the way the two men passengers behaved. They were useless with funk—out and out fear. They lay in the boat and did nothing. Fetched a groan now and again to show they were alive; but that was all. But the other woman was a jewel. Damn it, it was worth being shipwrecked to have that woman in the boat; she was awfully handsome, and as brave as she was lovely. She helped me bail out the boat, and she worked like a man.

'So we kicked about the sea from midnight till seven the next evening, and then we saw a steamer. "I'll—I'll give you anything I'm wearing to hoist as a signal of distress," said the woman; but I had no need to ask her, for the steamer picked us up and took us back to Bombay. I forgot to tell you that, when the day broke, I couldn't recognise the Captain's wife—widow, I mean. She had changed in the night as if fire had gone over her. I met her a long time afterwards, and even then she hadn't forgiven me for putting her into the boat and obeying the Captain's orders. But the husband of the other woman—he's in the Army—wrote me no end of a letter of thanks. I don't suppose he considered that the way his wife behaved was enough to make any decent man do all he could. The other fellows, who lay in the bottom of the boat and groaned, I've never met. Don't want to. Shouldn't be civil to 'em if I did. And that's how the Visigoth went down, for no assignable reason, with eighty bags of mail, five hundred souls, and not a single packet insured, on just such a night as this.'

'Oh, Trinity of love and power,
Our brethren shield in that dread hour,
From rock and tempest, fire and foe,
Protect them whereso'er they go.
Thus evermore shall rise to Thee
Glad hymns of praise by land and sea.'

'Strikes me they'll go on singing that hymn all night. Imperfect sort of doctrine in the last lines, don't you think? They might have run in an extra verse specifying sudden collapse—like the Visigoth's. I'm going on to the bridge, now. Good-night,' said the Captain.

And I was left alone with the steady thud, thud, of the screw and the gentle creaking of the boats at the davits.

That made me shudder.

THE SOLID MULDOON

Did ye see John Malone, wid his shinin', brand-new hat?
Did ye see how he walked like a grand aristocrat?

There was flags an' banners wavin' high, an' dhress and shtyle were shown,
But the best av all the company was Misther John Malone.
John Malone.

There had been a royal dog-fight in the ravine at the back of the rifle-butts, between Learoyd's Jock and Ortheris's Blue Rot—both mongrel Rampur hounds, chiefly ribs and teeth. It lasted for twenty happy, howling minutes, and then Blue Rot collapsed and Ortheris paid Learoyd three rupees, and we were all very thirsty. A dog-fight is a most heating entertainment, quite apart from the shouting, because Rampurs fight over a couple of acres of ground. Later, when the sound of belt-badges clicking against the necks of beer-bottles had died away, conversation drifted from dog to man-fights of all kinds. Humans resemble red-deer in some respects. Any talk of fighting seems to wake up a sort of imp in their breasts, and they bell one to the other, exactly like challenging bucks. This is noticeable even in men who consider themselves superior to Privates of the Line: it shows the Refining Influence of Civilisation and the March of Progress.

Tale provoked tale, and each tale more beer. Even dreamy Learoyd's eyes began to brighten, and he unburdened himself of a long history in which a trip to Malham Cove, a girl at Pateley Brigg, a ganger, himself and a pair of clogs were mixed in drawling tangle.

'An' so Ah coot's yead oppen from t' chin to t' hair, an' he was abed for t' matter o' a month,' concluded Learoyd pensively.

Mulvaney came out of a reverie—he was lying down—and flourished his heels in the air. 'You're a man, Learoyd,' said he critically, 'but you've only fought wid men, an' that's an ivry-day expayrience; but I've stud up to a ghost, an' that was not an ivry-day expayrience.'

'No?' said Ortheris, throwing a cork at him. 'You git up an' address the 'ouse—you an' yer expayriences. Is it a bigger one nor usual?'

"Twas the livin' trut'!' answered Mulvaney, stretching out a huge arm and catching Ortheris by the collar. 'Now where are ye, me son? Will ye take the wurrud av the Lorrd out av my mouth another time?' He shook him to emphasise the question.

'No, somethin' else, though,' said Ortheris, making a dash at Mulvaney's pipe, capturing it and holding it at arm's length; 'I'll chuck it acrost the ditch if you don't let me go!'

'You maraudin' hathen! 'Tis the only cutty I iver loved. Handle her tinder, or I'll chuck you acrost the nullah. If that poipe was bruk—Ah! Give her back to me, Sorr!'

Ortheris had passed the treasure to my hand. It was an absolutely perfect clay, as shiny as the black ball at Pool. I took it reverently, but I was firm.

'Will you tell us about the ghost-fight if I do?' I said.

'Is ut the shtory that's troublin' you? Av course I will. I mint to all along. I was only gettin' at ut my own way, as Popp Doggle said whin they found him thrying to ram a cartridge down the muzzle. Orth'ris, fall away!'

He released the little Londoner, took back his pipe, filled it, and his eyes twinkled. He has the most eloquent eyes of any one that I know.

'Did I iver tell you,' he began, 'that I was wanst the divil av a man?'

'You did,' said Learoyd with a childish gravity that made Ortheris yell with laughter, for Mulvaney was always impressing upon us his great merits in the old days.

'Did I iver tell you,' Mulvaney continued calmly, 'that I was wanst more av a divil than I am now?'

'Mer—ria! You don't mean it?' said Ortheris.

'Whin I was Corp'ril—I was rejuced aftherwards—but, as I say, whin I was Corp'ril, I was a divil of a man.'

He was silent for nearly a minute, while his mind rummaged among old memories and his eye glowed. He bit upon the pipe-stem and charged into his tale.

'Eyah! They was great times. I'm ould now; me hide's wore off in patches; sinthrygo has disconceited me, an' I'm a married man tu. But I've had my day—I've had my day, an' nothin' can take away the taste av that! Oh my time past, whin I put me fut through ivry livin' wan av the Tin Commandmints between Revelly and Lights Out, blew the froth off a pewter, wiped me moustache wid the back av me hand, an' slept on ut all as quiet as a little child! But ut's over—ut's over, an' 'twill niver come back to me; not though I prayed for a week av Sundays. Was there any wan in the Ould Rig'mint to touch Corp'ril Terence Mulvaney whin that same was turned out for sedukshin? I niver met him. Ivry woman that was not a witch was worth the runnin' afther in those days, an' ivry man was my dearest frind or—I had stripped to him an' we knew which was the betther av the tu.

'Whin I was Corp'ril I wud not ha' changed wid the Colonel—no, nor yet the Commandher-in-Chief. I wud be a Sargint. There was nothin' I wud not be! Mother av Hivin, look at me! Fwhat am I now?

'We was quartered in a big cantonmint—'tis no manner av use namin' names, for ut might give the barricks disrepitation—an' I was the Imperor av the Earth to my own mind, an' wan or tu women thought the same. Small blame to thim. Afther we had lain there a year, Bragin, the Colour Sargint av E Comp'ny, wint an' took a wife that was lady's maid to some big lady in the Station. She's dead now is Annie Bragin—died in child-bed at Kirpa Tal, or ut may ha' been Almorah—seven—nine years gone, an' Bragin he married agin. But she was a pretty woman whin Bragin inthrojuced her to cantonmint society. She had eyes like the brown av a buttherfly's wing whin the sun catches ut, an' a waist no thicker than my arm, an' a little sof' button av a mouth I would ha' gone through all Asia bristlin' wid bay'nits to get the kiss av. An' her hair was as long as the tail av the Colonel's charger—forgive me mentionin' that blunderin' baste in the same mouthful with Annie Bragin—but'twas all shpun gold, an' time was when a lock av ut was more than di'monds to me. There was niver pretty woman yet, an' I've had thruck wid a few, cud open the door to Annie Bragin.

''Twas in the Cath'lic Chapel I saw her first, me oi rolling round as usual to see fwhat was to be seen.

"You're too good for Bragin, my love," thinks I to mesilf, "but that's a mistake I can put straight, or my name is not Terence Mulvaney."

'Now take my wurrd for ut, you Orth'ris there an' Learoyd, an' kape out av the Married Quarters—as I did not. No good iver comes av ut, an' there's always the chance av your bein' found wid your face in the dirt, a long picket in the back av your head, an' your hands playing the fifes on the tread av another man's doorstep. 'Twas so we found O'Hara, he that Rafferty killed six years gone, when he wint to his death wid his hair oiled, whistlin' Larry O'Rourke betune his teeth. Kape out av the Married Quarters, I say, as I did not. 'Tis onwholesim, 'tis dangerous, an' 'tis ivrything else that's bad, but—O my sowl, 'tis swate while ut lasts!

'I was always hangin' about there whin I was off duty an' Bragin wasn't, but niver a sweet word beyon' ordinar' did I get from Annie Bragin. "'Tis the pervarsity av the sect," sez I to mesilf, an' gave my cap another cock on my head an' straightened my back—'twas the back av a Dhrum Major in those days— an' wint off as tho' I did not care, wid all the women in the Married Quarters laughin', I was pershuaded—most bhoys are I'm thinkin'—that no woman born av woman cud stand against me av I hild up my little finger. I had reason fer thinkin' that way—till I met Annie Bragin.

'Time an' agin whin I was blandandherin' in the dusk a man wud go past me as quiet as a cat. "That's quare," thinks I, "for I am, or I should be, the only man in these parts. Now what divilment can Annie be up to?" Thin I called myself a blayguard for thinkin' such things; but I thought thim all the same. An' that, mark you, is the way av a man.

'Wan evenin' I said:—"Mrs. Bragin, manin' no disrespect to you, who is that Corp'ril man"—I had seen the stripes though I cud niver get sight av his face—"who is that Corp'ril man that comes in always whin I'm goin' away?"

'"Mother av God!" sez she, turnin' as white as my belt, "have you seen him too?"

'"Seen him!" sez I; "av coorse I have. Did ye want me not to see him, for"—we were standin' talkin' in the dhark, outside the veranda av Bragin's quarters—"you'd betther tell me to shut me eyes. Onless I'm mistaken, he's come now."

'An', sure enough, the Corp'ril was walkin' to us, hangin' his head down as though he was ashamed av himsilf.

'"Good-night, Mrs. Bragin," sez I, very cool; "'tis not for me to interfere wid your a-moors; but you might manage things wid more dacincy. I'm off to canteen," I sez.

'I turned on my heel an' wint away, swearin' I wud give that man a dhressin' that wud shtop him messin' about the Married Quarters for a month an' a week. I had not tuk ten paces before Annie Bragin was hangin' on to my arm, an' I cud feel that she was shakin' all over.

'"Stay wid me, Mister Mulvaney," sez she; "you're flesh an' blood, at the least—are ye not?"

'"I'm all that," sez I, an' my anger wint away in a flash. "Will I want to be asked twice, Annie?"

'Wid that I slipped my arm round her waist, for, begad, I fancied she had surrindered at discretion, an' the honours av war were mine.

'"Fwhat nonsinse is this?" sez she, dhrawin' hersilf up on the tips av her dear little toes. "Wid the mother's milk not dhry on your impident mouth? Let go!" she sez.

'"Did ye not say just now that I was flesh an' blood?" sez I. "I have not changed since," I sez; an' I kep' my arm where ut was.

'"Your arms to yoursilf!" sez she, an' her eyes sparkild.

'"Sure, 'tis only human nature," sez I, an' I kep' my arm where ut was.

'"Nature or no nature," sez she, "you take your arm away or I'll tell Bragin, an' he'll alter the nature av your head. Fwhat d'you take me for?" she sez.

'"A woman," sez I; "the prettiest in barricks."

'"A wife," sez she; "the straightest in cantonmints!"

'Wid that I dropped my arm, fell back tu paces, an' saluted, for I saw that she mint fwhat she said.'

'Then you know something that some men would give a good deal to be certain of. How could you tell?' I demanded in the interests of Science.

'"Watch the hand," said Mulvaney; "av she shuts her hand tight, thumb down over the knuckle, take up your hat an' go. You'll only make a fool av yoursilf av you shtay. But av the hand lies opin on the lap, or av you see her thryin' to shut ut, an' she can't,—go on! She's not past reasonin' wid."

'Well, as I was sayin', I fell back, saluted, an' was goin' away.

'"Shtay wid me," she sez. "Look! He's comin' again."

'She pointed to the veranda, an' by the Hoight av Impart'nince, the Corp'ril man was comin' out av Bragin's quarters.

'"He's done that these five evenin's past," sez Annie Bragin. "Oh, fwhat will I do!"

"He'll not do ut again," sez I, for I was fightin' mad.

'Kape away from a man that has been a thrifle crossed in love till the fever's died down. He rages like a brute beast.

'I wint up to the man in the veranda, manin', as sure as I sit, to knock the life out av him. He slipped into the open. "Fwhat are you doin' philanderin' about here, ye scum av the gutter?" sez I polite, to give him his warnin', for I wanted him ready.

'He niver lifted his head, but sez, all mournful an' melancolius, as if he thought I wud be sorry for him: "I can't find her," sez he.

'"My troth," sez I, "you've lived too long—you an' your seekin's an' findin's in a dacint married woman's quarters! Hould up your head, ye frozen thief av Genesis," sez I, "an' you'll find all you want an' more!"

'But he niver hild up, an' I let go from the shoulther to where the hair is short over the eyebrows.

'"That'll do your business," sez I, but it nearly did mine instid. I put my bodyweight behind the blow, but I hit nothing at all, an' near put my shoulther out. The Corp'ril man was not there, an' Annie Bragin, who had been watchin' from the veranda, throws up her heels, an' carries on like a cock whin his neck's wrung by the dhrummer-bhoy. I wint back to her, for a livin' woman, an' a woman like Annie Bragin, is more than a p'rade-groun' full av ghosts. I'd niver seen a woman faint before, an' I stud like a shtuck calf, askin' her whether she was dead, an' prayin' her for the love av me, an' the love av her husband, an' the love av the Virgin, to opin her blessed eyes again, an' callin' mesilf all the names undher the canopy av Hivin for plaguin' her wid my miserable a-moors whin I ought to ha' stud betune her an' this Corp'ril man that had lost the number av his mess.

'I misremimber fwhat nonsinse I said, but I was not so far gone that I cud not hear a fut on the dirt outside. 'Twas Bragin comin' in, an' by the same token Annie was comin' to. I jumped to the far end av the veranda an' looked as if butter wudn't melt in my mouth. But Mrs. Quinn, the Quarter-Master's wife that was, had tould Bragin about my hangin' round Annie.

'"I'm not pleased wid you, Mulvaney," sez Bragin, unbucklin' his sword, for he had been on duty.

'"That's bad hearin'," I sez, an' I knew that the pickets were dhriven in. "What for, Sargint?" sez I.

'"Come outside," sez he, "an' I'll show you why."

'"I'm willin'," I sez; "but my stripes are none so ould that I can afford to loses him. Tell me now, who do I go out wid?" sez I.

'He was a quick man an' a just, an' saw fwhat I wud be afther. "Wid Mrs. Bragin's husband," sez he. He might ha' known by me askin' that favour that I had done him no wrong.

'We wint to the back av the arsenal an' I stripped to him, an' for ten minutes 'twas all I cud do to prevent him killin' himself against my fistes. He was mad as a dumb dog—just frothing wid rage; but he had no chanst wid me in reach, or learnin', or anything else.

'"Will ye hear reason?" sez I, whin his first wind was run out.

'"Not whoile I can see," sez he. Wid that I gave him both, one after the other, smash through the low gyard that he'd been taught whin he was a boy, an' the eyebrow shut down on the cheek-bone like the wing av a sick crow.

'"Will ye hear reason now, ye brave man?" sez I.

'"Not whoile I can speak," sez he, staggerin' up blind as a stump. I was loath to do ut, but I wint round an' swung into the jaw side-on an' shifted ut a half pace to the lef'.

'"Will ye hear reason now?" sez I; "I can't keep my timper much longer, an' 'tis like I will hurt you."

'"Not whoile I can stand," he mumbles out av one corner av his mouth. So I closed an' threw him—blind, dumb, an' sick, an' jammed the jaw straight.

'"You're an ould fool, Mister Bragin," sez I.

'"You're a young thief," sez he, "an' you've bruk my heart, you an' Annie betune you!"

'Thin he began cryin' like a child as he lay. I was sorry as I had niver been before. 'Tis an awful thing to see a strong man cry.

'"I'll swear on the Cross!" sez I.

'"I care for none av your oaths," sez he.

'"Come back to your quarters," sez I, "an' if you don't believe the livin', begad, you shall listen to the dead," I sez.

'I hoisted him an' tuk him back to his quarters. "Mrs. Bragin," sez I, "here's a man that you can cure quicker than me."

'"You've shamed me before my wife," he whimpers.

'"Have I so?" sez I. "By the look on Mrs. Bragin's face I think I'm for a dhressin'-down worse than I gave you."

'An' I was! Annie Bragin was woild wid indignation. There was not a name that a dacint woman cud use that was not given my way. I've had my Colonel walk roun' me like a cooper roun' a cask for fifteen minutes in Ord'ly Room, bekaze I wint into the Corner Shop an' unstrapped lewnatic; but all I iver tuk from his rasp av a tongue was ginger-pop to fwhat Annie tould me. An' that, mark you, is the way av a woman.

'Whin ut was done for want av breath, an' Annie was bendin' over her husband, I sez: "'Tis all thrue, an' I'm a blayguard an' you're an honest woman; but will you tell him of wan service that I did you?"

'As I finished speakin' the Corp'ril man came up to the veranda, an' Annie Bragin shqualed. The moon was up, an' we cud see his face.

'"I can't find her," sez the Corp'ril man, an' wint out like the puff av a candle.

'"Saints stand betune us an' evil!" sez Bragin, crossin' himself; "that's Flahy av the Tyrone."

'"Who was he?" I sez, "for he has given me a dale av fightin' this day."

'Bragin tould us that Flahy was a Corp'ril who lost his wife av cholera in those quarters three years gone, an' wint mad, an' walked afther they buried him, huntin' for her.

'"Well," sez I to Bragin, "he's been hookin' out av Purgathory to kape company wid Mrs. Bragin ivry evenin' for the last fortnight. You may tell Mrs. Quinn, wid my love, for I know that she's been talkin' to you, an' you've been listenin', that she ought to ondherstand the differ 'twixt a man an' a ghost. She's had three husbands," sez I, "an' you've got a wife too good for you. Instid av which you lave her to be boddered by ghosts an'—an' all manner av evil spirruts. I'll niver go talkin' in the way av politeness to a man's wife again. Good-night to you both," sez I; an' wid that I wint away, havin' fought wid woman, man and Divil all in the heart av an hour. By the same token I gave Father Victor wan rupee to say a mass for Flahy's soul, me havin' discommoded him by shticking my fist into his systim.'

'Your ideas of politeness seem rather large, Mulvaney,' I said.

'That's as you look at ut,' said Mulvaney calmly; 'Annie Bragin niver cared for me. For all that, I did not want to leave anything behin' me that Bragin could take hould av to be angry wid her about—whin an honust wurrd cud ha' cleared all up. There's nothing like opin-speakin'. Orth'ris, ye scutt, let me put me oi to that bottle, for my throat's as dhry as whin I thought I wud get a kiss from Annie Bragin. An' that's fourteen years gone! Eyah! Cork's own city an' the blue sky above ut—an' the times that was—the times that was!'

WITH THE MAIN GUARD

Der jungere Uhlanen
Sit round mit open mouth
While Breitmann tell dem stdories
Of fightin' in the South;
Und gif dem moral lessons,
How before der battle pops,
Take a little prayer to Himmel
Und a goot long drink of Schnapps.
Hans Breitmann's Ballads.

'Mary, Mother av Mercy, fwhat the divil possist us to take an' kape this melancolious counthry? Answer me that, Sorr.'

It was Mulvaney who was speaking. The time was one o'clock of a stifling June night, and the place was the main gate of Fort Amara, most desolate and least desirable of all fortresses in India. What I was doing there at that hour is a question which only concerns M'Grath, the Sergeant of the Guard, and the men on the gate.

'Slape,' said Mulvaney, 'is a shuparfluous necessity. This gyard'll shtay lively till relieved.' He himself was stripped to the waist; Learoyd on the next bedstead was dripping from the skinful of water which Ortheris, clad only in white trousers, had just sluiced over his shoulders; and a fourth private was muttering uneasily as he dozed open-mouthed in the glare of the great guard-lantern. The heat under the bricked archway was terrifying.

'The worrst night that iver I remimber. Eyah! Is all Hell loose this tide?' said Mulvaney. A puff of burning wind lashed through the wicket-gate like a wave of the sea, and Ortheris swore.

'Are ye more heasy, Jock?' he said to Learoyd. 'Put yer 'ead between your legs. It'll go orf in a minute.'

'Ah don't care. Ah would not care, but ma heart is plaayin' tivvy-tivvy on ma ribs. Let me die! Oh, leave me die!' groaned the huge Yorkshireman, who was feeling the heat acutely, being of fleshly build.

The sleeper under the lantern roused for a moment and raised himself on his elbow.—'Die and be damned then!' he said. 'I'm damned and I can't die!'

'Who's that?' I whispered, for the voice was new to me.

'Gentleman born,' said Mulvaney; 'Corp'ril wan year, Sargint nex'. Red-hot on his C'mission, but dhrinks like a fish. He'll be gone before the cowld weather's here. So!'

He slipped his boot, and with the naked toe just touched the trigger of his Martini. Ortheris misunderstood the movement, and the next instant the Irishman's rifle was dashed aside, while Ortheris stood before him, his eyes blazing with reproof.

'You!' said Ortheris. 'My Gawd, you! If it was you wot would we do?'

'Kape quiet, little man,' said Mulvaney, putting him aside, but very gently; 'tis not me, nor will ut be me whoile Dinah Shadd's here. I was but showin' something.'

Learoyd, bowed on his bedstead, groaned, and the gentleman-ranker sighed in his sleep. Ortheris took Mulvaney's tendered pouch and we three smoked gravely for a space while the dust-devils danced on the glacis and scoured the red-hot plain.

'Pop?' said Ortheris, wiping his forehead.

'Don't tantalise wid talkin' av dhrink, or I'll shtuff you into your own breech-block an'—fire you off!' grunted Mulvaney.

Ortheris chuckled, and from a niche in the veranda produced six bottles of gingerade.

'Where did ye get ut, ye Machiavel?' said Mulvaney. ''Tis no bazar pop.'

''Ow do Hi know wot the Orf'cers drink?' answered Ortheris. 'Arst the mess-man.'

'Ye'll have a Disthrict Coort-martial settin' on ye yet, me son,' said Mulvaney, 'but'—he opened a bottle—'I will not report ye this time. Fwhat's in the mess-kid is mint for the belly, as they say, 'specially whin that mate is dhrink. Here's luck! A bloody war or a—no, we've got the sickly season. War, thin!'— he waved the innocent 'pop' to the four quarters of Heaven. 'Bloody war! North, East, South, an' West! Jock, ye quakin' hayrick, come an' dhrink.'

But Learoyd, half mad with the fear of death presaged in the swelling veins in his neck, was begging his Maker to strike him dead, and fighting for more air between his prayers. A second time Ortheris drenched the quivering body with water, and the giant revived.

'An' Ah divn't see thot a mon is i' fettle for gooin' on to live; an' Ah divn't see thot there is owt for t' livin' for. Hear now, lads! Ah'm tired—tired. There's nobbut watter i' ma bones. Let me die!'

The hollow of the arch gave back Learoyd's broken whisper in a bass boom. Mulvaney looked at me hopelessly, but I remembered how the madness of despair had once fallen upon Ortheris, that weary, weary afternoon on the banks of the Khemi River, and how it had been exorcised by the skilful magician Mulvaney.

'Talk, Terence!' I said, 'or we shall have Learoyd slinging loose, and he'll be worse than Ortheris was. Talk! He'll answer to your voice.'

Almost before Ortheris had deftly thrown all the rifles of the Guard on Mulvaney's bedstead, the Irishman's voice was uplifted as that of one in the middle of a story, and, turning to me, he said—

'In barricks or out of it, as you say, Sorr, an Oirish rig'mint is the divil an' more. 'Tis only fit for a young man wid eddicated fisteses. Oh the crame av disruption is an Oirish rig'mint, an' rippin', tearin', ragin' scattherers in the field av war! My first rig'mint was Oirish—Faynians an' rebils to the heart av their marrow was they, an' so they fought for the Widdy betther than most, bein' contrairy—Oirish. They was the Black Tyrone. You've heard av thim, Sorr?'

Heard of them! I knew the Black Tyrone for the choicest collection of unmitigated blackguards, dog-stealers, robbers of hen-roosts, assaulters of innocent citizens, and recklessly daring heroes in the Army List. Half Europe and half Asia has had cause to know the Black Tyrone—good luck be with their tattered Colours as Glory has ever been!

'They was hot pickils an' ginger! I cut a man's head tu deep wid my belt in the days av my youth, an', afther some circumstances which I will obliterate, I came to the Ould Rig'mint, bearin' the character av a man wid hands an' feet. But, as I was goin' to tell you, I fell acrost the Black Tyrone agin wan day whin we wanted thim powerful bad. Orth'ris, me son, fwhat was the name av that place where they sint wan comp'ny av us an' wan av the Tyrone roun' a hill an' down again, all for to tache the Paythans something they'd niver learned before? Afther Ghunzi 'twas.'

'Don't know what the bloomin' Paythans called it. We called it Silver's Theayter. You know that, sure!'

'Silver's Theatre—so 'twas. A gut betune two hills, as black as a bucket, an' as thin as a girl's waist. There was over-many Paythans for our convaynience in the gut, an' begad they called thimselves a Reserve—bein' impident by nature! Our Scotchies an' lashins av Gurkeys was poundin' into some Paythan rig'mints, I think 'twas. Scotchies an' Gurkeys are twins bekaze they're so onlike an' they get dhrunk together whin God plazes. As I was sayin', they sint wan comp'ny av the Ould an' wan of the Tyrone to double up the hill an' clane out the Paythan Reserve. Orf'cers was scarce in thim days, fwhat with dysintry an' not takin' care av thimselves, an' we was sint out wid only wan orf'cer for the comp'ny; but he was a Man that had his feet beneath him, an' all his teeth in their sockuts.'

'Who was he?' I asked.

'Captain O'Neil—Old Crook—Cruikna-bulleen—him that I tould ye that tale av whin he was in Burma.

[Footnote:

Now first of the foemen of Boh Da Thone
Was Captain O'Neil of the Black Tyrone.
The Ballad of Boh Da Thone.]

Hah!

He was a Man! The Tyrone tuk a little orf'cer bhoy, but divil a bit was he in command, as I'll dimonstrate presintly. We an' they came over the brow av the hill, wan on each side av the gut, an' there was that ondacint Reserve waitin' down below like rats in a pit.

'"Howld on, men," sez Crook, who tuk a mother's care av us always. "Rowl some rocks on thim by way av visitin' kyards." We hadn't rowled more than twinty bowlders, an' the Paythans was beginnin' to swear tremenjus, whin the little orf'cer bhoy av the Tyrone shqueaks out acrost the valley:—"Fwhat the devil an' all are you doin', shpoilin' the fun for my men? Do ye not see they'll stand?"

'"Faith, that's a rare pluckt wan!" sez Crook. "Niver mind the rocks, men. Come along down an' take tay wid thim!"

'"There's damned little sugar in ut!" sez my rear-rank man; but Crook heard.

'"Have ye not all got spoons?" he sez, laughin', an' down we wint as fast as we cud. Learoyd bein' sick at the Base, he, av coorse, was not there.

'Thot's a lie!' said Learoyd, dragging his bedstead nearer. 'Ah gotten thot theer, an' you knaw it, Mulvaney.' He threw up his arms, and from the right armpit ran, diagonally through the fell of his chest, a thin white line terminating near the fourth left rib.

'My mind's goin',' said Mulvaney, the unabashed. 'Ye were there. Fwhat I was thinkin' of! 'Twas another man, av coorse. Will, you'll remember thin, Jack, how we an' the Tyrone met wid a bang at the bottom an' got jammed past all movin' among the Paythans.'

'Ow! It was a tight 'ole. I was squeezed till I thought I'd bloomin' well bust,' said Ortheris, rubbing his stomach meditatively.

'"Twas no place for a little man, but wan little man'—Mulvaney put his hand on Ortheris's shoulder—'saved the life av me. There we shtuck, for divil a bit did the Paythans flinch, an' divil a bit dare we; our business bein' to clear 'em out. An' the most exthryordinar' thing av all was that we an' they just rushed into each other's arrums, an' there was no firing for a long time. Nothin' but knife an' bay'nit when we cud get our hands free: an' that was not often. We was breast-on to thim, an' the Tyrone was yelpin' behind av us in a way I didn't see the lean av at first. But I knew later, an' so did the Paythans.

'"Knee to knee!" sings out Crook, wid a laugh whin the rush av our comin' into the gut shtopped, an' he was huggin' a hairy great Paythan, neither bein' able to do anything to the other, tho' both was wishful.

'"Breast to breast!" he sez, as the Tyrone was pushin' us forward closer an' closer.

'"An' hand over back!" sez a Sargint that was behin'. I saw a sword lick out past Crook's ear, an' the Paythan was tuk in the apple av his throat like a pig at Dromeen fair.

'"Thank ye, Brother Inner Guard," sez Crook, cool as a cucumber widout salt. "I wanted that room." An' he wint forward by the thickness av a man's body, havin' turned the Paythan undher him. The man bit the heel off Crook's boot in his death-bite.

'"Push, men!" sez Crook. "Push, ye paper-backed beggars!" he sez. "Am I to pull ye through?" So we pushed, an' we kicked, an' we swung, an' we swore, an' the grass bein' slippery, our heels wouldn't bite, an' God help the front-rank man that wint down that day!'

"Ave you ever bin in the Pit hentrance o' the Vic, on a thick night?' interrupted Ortheris. 'It was worse nor that, for they was goin' one way an' we wouldn't 'ave it. Leastways, I 'adn't much to say.'

'Faith, me son, ye said ut, thin. I kep' the little man betune my knees as long as I cud, but he was pokin' roun' wid his bay'nit, blindin' an' stiffin' feroshus. The devil of a man is Orth'ris in a ruction—aren't ye?' said Mulvaney.

'Don't make game!' said the Cockney. 'I knowed I wasn't no good then, but I guv 'em compot from the lef' flank when we opened out. No!' he said, bringing down his hand with a thump on the bedstead, 'a bay'nit ain't no good to a little man—might as well 'ave a bloomin' fishin'-rod! I 'ate a clawin', maulin' mess, but gimme a breech that's wore out a bit, an' hamminition one year in store, to let the powder kiss the bullet, an' put me somewheres where I ain't trod on by 'ulkin swine like you, an' s'elp me Gawd, I could bowl you over five times outer seven at height 'undred. Would yer try, you lumberin' Hirishman.'

'No, ye wasp. I've seen ye do ut. I say there's nothin' better than the bay'nit, wid a long reach, a double twist av ye can, an' a slow recover.'

'Dom the bay'nit,' said Learoyd, who had been listening intently. 'Look a-here!' He picked up a rifle an inch below the foresight with an underhand action, and used it exactly as a man would use a dagger.

'Sitha,' said he softly, 'thot's better than owt, for a mon can bash t' faace wi' thot, an', if he divn't, he can breeak t' forearm o' t' gaard.' 'Tis not i' t' books, though. Gie me t' butt.'

'Each does ut his own way, like makin' love,' said Mulvaney quietly; 'the butt or the bay'nit or the bullet accordin' to the natur' av the man. Well, as I was sayin', we shtuck there breathin' in each other's faces and swearin' powerful; Orth'ris cursin' the mother that bore him bekaze he was not three inches taller.

'Prisintly he sez:—"Duck, ye lump, an' I can get at a man over your shouldher!"

'"You'll blow me head off," I sez, throwin' my arm clear; "go through under my arm-pit, ye bloodthirsty little scutt," sez I, "but don't shtick me or I'll wring your ears round."

'Fwhat was ut ye gave the Paythan man forninst me, him that cut at me whin I cudn't move hand or foot? Hot or cowld was ut?'

'Cold,' said Ortheris, 'up an' under the rib-jint. 'E come down flat. Best for you 'e did.'

'Thrue, my son! This jam thing that I'm talkin' about lasted for five minutes good, an' thin we got our arms clear an' wint in. I misremimber exactly fwhat I did, but I didn't want Dinah to be a widdy at the

Depot. Thin, after some promishkuous hackin' we shtuck again, an' the Tyrone behin' was callin' us dogs an' cowards an' all manner av names; we barrin' their way.

'"Fwhat ails the Tyrone?" thinks I; "they've the makin's av a most convanient fight here."

'A man behind me sez beseechful an' in a whisper:—"Let me get at thim! For the Love av Mary give me room beside ye, ye tall man!"

'"An' who are you that's so anxious to be kilt?" sez I, widout turnin' my head, for the long knives was dancin' in front like the sun on Donegal Bay whin ut's rough.

'"We've seen our dead," he sez, squeezin' into me; "our dead that was men two days gone! An' me that was his cousin by blood could not bring Tim Coulan off! Let me get on," he sez, "let me get to thim or I'll run ye through the back!"

'"My troth," thinks I, "if the Tyrone have seen their dead, God help the Paythans this day!" An' thin I knew why the Oirish was ragin' behind us as they was.

'I gave room to the man, an' he ran forward wid the Haymaker's Lift on his bay'nit an' swung a Paythan clear off his feet by the belly-band av the brute, an' the iron bruk at the lockin'-ring.

'"Tim Coulan'll slape easy to-night," sez he wid a grin; an' the next minut his head was in two halves and he wint down grinnin' by sections.

'The Tyrone was pushin' an' pushin' in, an' our men was swearin' at thim, an' Crook was workin' away in front av us all, his sword-arm swingin' like a pump-handle an' his revolver spittin' like a cat. But the strange thing av ut was the quiet that lay upon. 'Twas like a fight in a drame—except for thim that was dead.

'Whin I gave room to the Oirishman I was expinded an' forlorn in my inside. 'Tis a way I have, savin' your presince, Sorr, in action. "Let me out, bhoys," sez I, backin' in among thim. "I'm going to be onwell!" Faith they gave me room at the wurrud, though they would not ha' givin room for all Hell wid the chill off. When I got clear, I was, savin' your presince, Sorr, outragis sick bekaze I had dhrunk heavy that day.

'Well an' far out av harm was a Sargint av the Tyrone sittin' on the little orf'cer bhoy who had stopped Crook from rowlin' the rocks. Oh, he was a beautiful bhoy, an' the long black curses was slidin' out av his innocint mouth like mornin'-jew from a rose!

'"Fwhat have you got there?" sez I to the Sargint.

'"Wan av Her Majesty's bantams wid his spurs up," sez he. "He's goin' to Coort-martial me."

'"Let me go!" sez the little orf'cer bhoy. "Let me go and command my men!" manin' thereby the Black Tyrone which was beyond any command—ay, even av they had made the Divil a Field-orf'cer.

'"His father howlds my mother's cow-feed in Clonmel," sez the man that was sittin' on him. "Will I go back to his mother an' tell her that I've let him throw himself away? Lie still, ye little pinch av dynamite, an' Coort-martial me afterwards."

"Good," sez I; "'tis the likes av him makes the likes av the Commandher-in-Chief, but we must presarve thim. Fwhat d'you want to do, Sorr?" sez I, very politeful.

'"Kill the beggars—kill the beggars!" he shqueaks; his big blue eyes brimmin' wid tears.

'"An' how'll ye do that?" sez I. "You've shquibbed off your revolver like a child wid a cracker; you can make no play wid that fine large sword av yours; an' your hand's shakin' like an asp on a leaf. Lie still an' grow," sez I.

'"Get back to your comp'ny," sez he; "you're insolint!"

'"All in good time," sez I, "but I'll have a dhrink first."

'Just thin Crook comes up, blue an' white all over where he wasn't red.

'"Wather!" sez he; "I'm dead wid drouth! Oh, but it's a gran' day!"

'He dhrank half a skinful, and the rest he tilts into his chest, an' it fair hissed on the hairy hide av him. He sees the little orf'cer bhoy undher the Sargint.

'"Fwhat's yonder?" sez he.

'"Mutiny, Sorr," sez the Sargint, an' the orf'cer bhoy begins pleadin' pitiful to Crook to be let go: but divil a bit wud Crook budge.

'"Kape him there," he sez, "'tis no child's work this day. By the same token," sez he, "I'll confishcate that iligant nickel-plated scent-sprinkler av yours, for my own has been vomitin' dishgraceful!"

'The fork av his hand was black wid the backspit av the machine. So he tuk the orf'cer bhoy's revolver. Ye may look, Sorr, by my faith, there's a dale more done in the field than iver gets into Field Ordhers!

'"Come on, Mulvaney," sez Crook; "is this a Coort-martial?" The two av us wint back together into the mess an' the Paythans were still standin' up. They was not too impart'nint though, for the Tyrone was callin' wan to another to remimber Tim Coulan.

'Crook stopped outside av the strife an' looked anxious, his eyes rowlin' roun'.

'"Fwhat is ut, Sorr?" sez I; "can I get ye anything?"

'"Where's a bugler?" sez he.

'I wint into the crowd—our men was dhrawin' breath behin' the Tyrone who was fightin' like sowls in tormint—an' prisintly I came acrost little Frehan, our bugler bhoy, pokin' roun' among the best wid a rifle an' bay'nit.

'"Is amusin' yoursilf fwhat you're paid for, ye limb?" sez I, catchin' him by the scruff. "Come out av that an' attind to your duty," I sez; but the bhoy was not pleased.

'"I've got wan," sez he, grinnin', "big as you, Mulvaney, an' fair half as ugly. Let me go get another."

'I was dishplease dat the personability av that remark, so I tucks him under my arm an' carries him to Crook who was watchin' how the fight wint. Crook cuffs him till the bhoy cries, an' thin sez nothin' for a whoile.

'The Paythans began to flicker onaisy, an' our men roared. "Opin ordher! Double!" sez Crook. "Blow, child, blow for the honour of the British Arrmy!"

'That bhoy blew like a typhoon, an' the Tyrone an' we opined out as the Paythans broke, an' I saw that fwhat had gone before wud be kissin' an' huggin' to fwhat was to come. We'd dhruv thim into a broad part av the gut whin they gave, an' thin we opined out an' fair danced down the valley, dhrivin' thim before us. Oh, 'twas lovely, an' stiddy, too! There was the Sargints on the flanks av what was left av us, kapin' touch, an' the fire was runnin' from flank to flank, an' the Paythans was dhroppin'. We opined out wid the widenin' av the valley, an' whin the valley narrowed we closed again like the shticks on a lady's fan, an' at the far ind av the gut where they thried to stand, we fair blew them off their feet, for we had expinded very little ammunition by reason av the knife work.'

'Hi used thirty rounds goin' down that valley,' said Ortheris, 'an' it was gentleman's work. Might 'a' done it in a white 'andkerchief an' pink silk stockin's, that part. Hi was on in that piece.'

'You could ha' heard the Tyrone yellin' a mile away,' said Mulvaney, 'an' 'twas all their Sargints cud do to get thim off. They was mad—mad—mad! Crook sits down in the quiet that fell whin we had gone down the valley, an' covers his face wid his hands. Prisintly we all came back again accordin' to our natures and disposishins, for they, mark you, show through the hide av a man in that hour.

'"Bhoys! bhoys!" sez Crook to himself. "I misdoubt we could ha' engaged at long range an' saved betther men than me." He looked at our dead an' said no more.

'"Captain dear," sez a man av the Tyrone, comin' up wid his mouth bigger than iver his mother kissed ut, spittin' blood like a whale; "Captain dear," sez he, "if wan or two in the shtalls have been discommoded, the gallery enjoyed the performinces av a Roshus."

'Thin I knew that man for the Dublin dock-rat he was—wan av the bhoys that made the lessee av Silver's Theatre gray before his time wid tearin' out the bowils av the benches an' t'rowin' thim into the pit. So I passed the wurrud that I knew when I was in the Tyrone an' we lay in Dublin. "I don't know who 'twas," I whispers, "an' I don't care, but anyways I'll knock the face av you, Tim Kelly."

'"Eyah!" sez the man, "was you there too? We'll call ut Silver's Theatre." Half the Tyrone, knowin' the ould place, tuk it up: so we called ut Silver's Theatre.

'The little orf'cer bhoy av the Tyrone was thremblin' an' cryin'. He had no heart for the Coort-martials that he talked so big upon. "Ye'll do well later," sez Crook, very quiet, "for not bein' allowed to kill yourself for amusemint."

'"I'm a dishgraced man!" sez the little orf'cer bhoy.

'"Put me undher arrest, Sorr, if you will, but, by my sowl, I'd do ut again sooner than face your mother wid you dead," sez the Sargint that had sat on his head, standin' to attention an' salutin'. But the young wan only cried as tho' his little heart was breakin'.

'Thin another man av the Tyrone came up, wid the fog av fightin' on him.'

'The what, Mulvaney?'

'Fog av fightin'. You know, Sorr, that, like makin' love, ut takes each man diff'rint. Now I can't help bein' powerful sick whin I'm in action. Orth'ris, here, niver stops swearin' from ind to ind, an' the only time that Learoyd opins his mouth to sing is whin he is messin' wid other people's heads; for he's a dhirty fighter is Jock. Recruities sometime cry, an' sometime they don't know fwhat they do, an' sometime they are all for cuttin' throats an' such like dirtiness; but some men get heavy-dead-dhrunk on the fightin'. This man was. He was staggerin', an' his eyes were half shut, an' we cud hear him dhraw breath twinty yards away. He sees the little orf'cer bhoy, an' comes up, talkin' thick an' drowsy to himsilf. "Blood the young whelp!" he sez; "blood the young whelp"; an' wid that he threw up his arms, shpun roun', an' dropped at our feet, dead as a Paythan, an' there was niver sign or scratch on him. They said 'twas his heart was rotten, but oh, 'twas a quare thing to see!

'Thin we wint to bury our dead, for we wud not lave thim to the Paythans, an' in movin' among the haythen we nearly lost that little orf'cer bhoy. He was for givin' wan divil wather and layin' him aisy against a rock. "Be careful, Sorr," sez I; "a wounded Paythan's worse than a live wan." My troth, before the words was out of my mouth, the man on the ground fires at the orf'cer bhoy lanin' over him, an' I saw the helmit fly. I dropped the butt on the face av the man an' tuk his pistol. The little orf'cer bhoy turned very white, for the hair av half his head was singed away.

'"I tould you so, Sorr!" sez I; an', afther that, whin he wanted to help a Paythan I stud wid the muzzle contagious to the ear. They dare not do anythin' but curse. The Tyrone was growlin' like dogs over a bone that had been taken away too soon, for they had seen their dead an' they wanted to kill ivry sowl on the ground. Crook tould thim that he'd blow the hide off any man that misconducted himself; but, seeing that ut was the first time the Tyrone had iver seen their dead, I do not wondher they were on the sharp. 'Tis a shameful sight! Whin I first saw ut I wud niver ha' given quarter to any man north of the Khaibar—no, nor woman either, for the women used to come out afther dhark—Auggrh!

'Well, evenshually we buried our dead an' tuk away our wounded, an' come over the brow av the hills to see the Scotchies an' the Gurkeys taking tay with the Paythans in bucketsfuls. We were a gang av dissolute ruffians, for the blood had caked the dust, an' the sweat had cut the cake, an' our bay'nits was hangin' like butchers' steels betune ur legs, an' most av us were marked one way or another.

'A Staff Orf'cer man, clean as a new rifle, rides up an' sez: "What damned scarecrows are you?"

'"A comp'ny av Her Majesty's Black Tyrone an' wan av the Ould Rig'mint," sez Crook very quiet, givin' our visitors the flure as 'twas.

'"Oh!" sez the Staff Orf'cer; "did you dislodge that Reserve?"

'"No!" sez Crook, an' the Tyrone laughed.

'"Thin fwhat the divil have ye done?"

'"Disthroyed ut," sez Crook, an' he took us on, but not before Toomey that was in the Tyrone sez aloud, his voice somewhere in his stummick: "Fwhat in the name av misfortune does this parrit widout a tail mane by shtoppin' the road av his betthers?"

'The Staff Orf'cer wint blue, an' Toomey makes him pink by changin' to the voice av a minowderin' woman an' sayin': "Come an' kiss me, Major dear, for me husband's at the wars an' I'm all alone at the Depot."

'The Staff Orf'cer wint away, an' I cud see Crook's shoulthers shakin'.

'His Corp'ril checks Toomey. "Lave me alone," sez Toomey, widout a wink. "I was his batman before he was married an' he knows fwhat I mane, av you don't. There's nothin' like livin' in the hoight av society." D'you remimber that, Orth'ris!'

'Hi do. Toomey, 'e died in 'orspital, next week it was, 'cause I bought 'arf his kit; an' I remember after that—'

'GUARRD, TURN OUT!'

The Relief had come; it was four o'clock. 'I'll catch a kyart for you, Sorr,' said Mulvaney, diving hastily into his accoutrements. 'Come up to the top av the Fort an' we'll pershue our invistigations into M'Grath's shtable.' The relieved Guard strolled round the main bastion on its way to the swimming-bath, and Learoyd grew almost talkative. Ortheris looked into the Fort ditch and across the plain. 'Ho! it's weary waitin' for Ma-ary!' he hummed; 'but I'd like to kill some more bloomin' Paythans before my time's up. War! Bloody war! North, East, South, and West.'

'Amen,' said Learoyd slowly.

'Fwhat's here?' said Mulvaney, checking at a blur of white by the foot of the old sentry-box. He stooped and touched it. 'It's Norah—Norah M'Taggart! Why, Nonie darlin', fwhat are ye doin' out av your mother's bed at this time?'

The two-year-old child of Sergeant M'Taggart must have wandered for a breath of cool air to the very verge of the parapet of the Fort ditch. Her tiny night-shift was gathered into a wisp round her neck and she moaned in her sleep. 'See there!' said Mulvaney; 'poor lamb! Look at the heat-rash on the innocint skin av her. 'Tis hard—crool hard even for us. Fwhat must it be for these? Wake up, Nonie, your mother will be woild about you. Begad, the child might ha' fallen into the ditch!'

He picked her up in the growing light, and set her on his shoulder, and her fair curls touched the grizzled stubble of his temples. Ortheris and Learoyd followed snapping their fingers, while Norah smiled at them a sleepy smile. Then carolled Mulvaney, clear as a lark, dancing the baby on his arm—

'If any young man should marry you,
Say nothin' about the joke;
That iver ye slep' in a sinthry-box,
Wrapped up in a soldier's cloak.'

'Though, on my sowl, Nonie,' he said gravely, 'there was not much cloak about you. Niver mind, you won't dhress like this ten years to come. Kiss your friends an' run along to your mother.'

Nonie, set down close to the Married Quarters, nodded with the quiet obedience of the soldier's child, but, ere she pattered off over the flagged path, held up her lips to be kissed by the Three Musketeers. Ortheris wiped his mouth with the back of his hand and swore sentimentally; Learoyd turned pink; and the two walked away together. The Yorkshireman lifted up his voice and gave in thunder the chorus of The Sentry-Box, while Ortheris piped at his side.

"Bin to a bloomin' sing-song, you two?' said the Artilleryman, who was taking his cartridge down to the Morning Gun. 'You're over merry for these dashed days.'

'I bid ye take care o' the brat, said he,
For it comes of a noble race,'

Learoyd bellowed. The voices died out in the swimming-bath.

'Oh, Terence!' I said, dropping into Mulvaney's speech, when we were alone, 'it's you that have the Tongue!'

He looked at me wearily; his eyes were sunk in his head, and his face was drawn and white. 'Eyah!' said he; 'I've blandandhered thim through the night somehow, but can thim that helps others help thimselves? Answer me that, Sorr!'

And over the bastions of Fort Amara broke the pitiless day.

IN THE MATTER OF A PRIVATE

Hurrah! hurrah! a soldier's life for me!
Shout, boys, shout! for it makes you jolly and free.
The Ramrod Corps.

People who have seen, say that one of the quaintest spectacles of human frailty is an outbreak of hysterics in a girls' school. It starts without warning, generally on a hot afternoon, among the elder pupils. A girl giggles till the giggle gets beyond control. Then she throws up her head, and cries, 'Honk, honk, honk,' like a wild goose, and tears mix with the laughter. If the mistress be wise, she will rap out something severe at this point to check matters. If she be tender-hearted, and send for a drink of water, the chances are largely in favour of another girl laughing at the afflicted one and herself collapsing. Thus the trouble spreads, and may end in half of what answers to the Lower Sixth of a boys' school rocking and whooping together. Given a week of warm weather, two stately promenades per diem, a heavy mutton and rice meal in the middle of the day, a certain amount of nagging from the teachers, and a few other things, some amazing effects develop. At least, this is what folk say who have had experience.

Now, the Mother Superior of a Convent and the Colonel of a British Infantry Regiment would be justly shocked at any comparison being made between their respective charges. But it is a fact that, under certain circumstances, Thomas in bulk can be worked up into dithering, rippling hysteria. He does not weep, but he shows his trouble unmistakably, and the consequences get into the newspapers, and all the good people who hardly know a Martini from a Snider say: 'Take away the brute's ammunition!'

Thomas isn't a brute, and his business, which is to look after the virtuous people, demands that he shall have his ammunition to his hand. He doesn't wear silk stockings, and he really ought to be supplied with a new Adjective to help him to express his opinions: but, for all that, he is a great man. If you call him 'the heroic defender of the national honour' one day, and a 'brutal and licentious soldiery' the next, you naturally bewilder him, and he looks upon you with suspicion. There is nobody to speak for Thomas except people who have theories to work off on him; and nobody understands Thomas except Thomas, and he does not always know what is the matter with himself.

That is the prologue. This is the story:—

Corporal Slane was engaged to be married to Miss Jhansi M'Kenna, whose history is well known in the regiment and elsewhere. He had his Colonel's permission, and, being popular with the men, every arrangement had been made to give the wedding what Private Ortheris called 'eeklar.' It fell in the heart of the hot weather, and, after the wedding, Slane was going up to the Hills with the bride. None the less, Slane's grievance was that the affair would be only a hired-carriage wedding, and he felt that the 'eeklar' of that was meagre. Miss M'Kenna did not care so much. The Sergeant's wife was helping her to make her wedding-dress, and she was very busy. Slane was, just then, the only moderately contented man in barracks. All the rest were more or less miserable.

And they had so much to make them happy, too. All their work was over at eight in the morning, and for the rest of the day they could lie on their backs and smoke Canteen-plug and swear at the punkah-coolies. They enjoyed a fine, full flesh meal in the middle of the day, and then threw themselves down on their cots and sweated and slept till it was cool enough to go out with their 'towny,' whose vocabulary contained less than six hundred words, and the Adjective, and whose views on every conceivable question they had heard many times before.

There was the Canteen, of course, and there was the Temperance Room with the second-hand papers in it; but a man of any profession cannot read for eight hours a day in a temperature of 96 degrees or 98 degrees in the shade, running up sometimes to 103 degrees at midnight. Very few men, even though they get a pannikin of flat, stale, muddy beer and hide it under their cots, can continue drinking for six hours a day. One man tried, but he died, and nearly the whole regiment went to his funeral because it gave them something to do. It was too early for the excitement of fever or cholera. The men could only wait and wait and wait, and watch the shadow of the barrack creeping across the blinding white dust. That was a gay life.

They lounged about cantonments—it was too hot for any sort of game, and almost too hot for vice—and fuddled themselves in the evening, and filled themselves to distension with the healthy nitrogenous food provided for them, and the more they stoked the less exercise they took and more explosive they grew. Then tempers began to wear away, and men fell a-brooding over insults real or imaginary, for they had nothing else to think of. The tone of the repartees changed and instead of saying light-heartedly: 'I'll knock your silly face in.' men grew laboriously polite and hinted that the cantonments were not big enough for themselves and their enemy, and that there would be more space for one of the two in another Place.

It may have been the Devil who arranged the thing, but the fact of the case is that Losson had for a long time been worrying Simmons in an aimless way. It gave him occupation. The two had their cots side by side, and would sometimes spend a long afternoon swearing at each other; but Simmons was afraid of Losson and dared not challenge him to a fight. He thought over the words in the hot still nights, and half the hate he felt towards Losson he vented on the wretched punkah-coolie.

Losson bought a parrot in the bazar, and put it into a little cage, and lowered the cage into the cool darkness of a well, and sat on the well-curb, shouting bad language down to the parrot. He taught it to say: 'Simmons, ye so-oor,' which means swine, and several other things entirely unfit for publication. He was a big gross man, and he shook like a jelly when the parrot had the sentence correctly. Simmons, however, shook with rage, for all the room were laughing at him—the parrot was such a disreputable puff of green feathers and it looked so human when it chattered. Losson used to sit, swinging his fat legs, on the side of the cot, and ask the parrot what it thought of Simmons. The parrot would answer: 'Simmons, ye so-oor.' 'Good boy,' Losson used to say, scratching the parrot's head; 'ye 'ear that, Sim?' And Simmons used to turn over on his stomach and make answer: 'I 'ear. Take 'eed you don't 'ear something one of these days.'

In the restless nights, after he had been asleep all day, fits of blind rage came upon Simmons and held him till he trembled all over, while he thought in how many different ways he would slay Losson. Sometimes he would picture himself trampling the life out of the man, with heavy ammunition-boots, and at others smashing in his face with the butt, and at others jumping on his shoulders and dragging the head back till the neckbone cracked. Then his mouth would feel hot and fevered, and he would reach out for another sup of the beer in the pannikin.

But the fancy that came to him most frequently and stayed with him longest was one connected with the great roll of fat under Lesson's right ear. He noticed it first on a moonlight night, and thereafter it was always before his eyes. It was a fascinating roll of fat. A man could get his hand upon it and tear away one side of the neck; or he could place the muzzle of a rifle on it and blow away all the head in a flash. Losson had no right to be sleek and contented and well-to-do, when he, Simmons, was the butt of the room. Some day, perhaps, he would show those who laughed at the 'Simmons, ye so-oor' joke, that he was as good as the rest, and held a man's life in the crook of his forefinger. When Losson snored, Simmons hated him more bitterly than ever. Why should Losson be able to sleep when Simmons had to stay awake hour after hour, tossing and turning on the tapes, with the dull liver pain gnawing into his right side and his head throbbing and aching after Canteen? He thought over this for many many nights, and the world became unprofitable to him. He even blunted his naturally fine appetite with beer and tobacco; and all the while the parrot talked at and made a mock of him.

The heat continued and the tempers wore away more quickly than before. A Sergeant's wife died of heat-apoplexy in the night, and the rumour ran abroad that it was cholera. Men rejoiced openly, hoping that it would spread and send them into camp. But that was a false alarm.

It was late on a Tuesday evening, and the men were waiting in the deep double verandas for 'Last Posts,' when Simmons went to the box at the foot of his bed, took out his pipe, and slammed the lid down with a bang that echoed through the deserted barrack like the crack of a rifle. Ordinarily speaking, the men would have taken no notice; but their nerves were fretted to fiddle-strings. They jumped up, and three or four clattered into the barrack-room only to find Simmons kneeling by his box.

'Ow! It's you, is it?' they said and laughed foolishly. 'We thought 'twas—'

Simmons rose slowly. If the accident had so shaken his fellows, what would not the reality do?

'You thought it was—did you? And what makes you think?' he said, lashing himself into madness as he went on; 'to Hell with your thinking, ye dirty spies.'

'Simmons, ye so-oor,' chuckled the parrot in the veranda sleepily, recognising a well-known voice. Now that was absolutely all.

The tension snapped. Simmons fell back on the arm-rack deliberately,—the men were at the far end of the room,—and took out his rifle and packet of ammunition. 'Don't go playing the goat, Sim!' said Losson. 'Put it down,' but there was a quaver in his voice. Another man stooped, slipped his boot and hurled it at Simmons's head. The prompt answer was a shot which, fired at random, found its billet in Losson's throat. Losson fell forward without a word, and the others scattered.

'You thought it was!' yelled Simmons. 'You're drivin' me to it! I tell you you're drivin' me to it! Get up, Losson, an' don't lie shammin' there—you an' your blasted parrit that druv me to it!'

But there was an unaffected reality about Losson's pose that showed Simmons what he had done. The men were still clamouring in the veranda. Simmons appropriated two more packets of ammunition and ran into the moonlight, muttering: 'I'll make a night of it. Thirty roun's, an' the last for myself. Take you that, you dogs!'

He dropped on one knee and fired into the brown of the men on the veranda, but the bullet flew high, and landed in the brickwork with a vicious phwit that made some of the younger ones turn pale. It is, as musketry theorists observe, one thing to fire and another to be fired at.

Then the instinct of the chase flared up. The news spread from barrack to barrack, and the men doubled out intent on the capture of Simmons, the wild beast, who was heading for the Cavalry parade-ground, stopping now and again to send back a shot and a curse in the direction of his pursuers.

'I'll learn you to spy on me!' he shouted; 'I'll learn you to give me dorg's names! Come on, the 'ole lot o' you! Colonel John Anthony Deever, C. B.!'—he turned towards the Infantry Mess and shook his rifle— 'you think yourself the devil of a man—but I tell you that if you put your ugly old carcass outside o' that door, I'll make you the poorest-lookin' man in the army. Come out, Colonel John Anthony Deever, C. B.! Come out and see me practiss on the rainge. I'm the crack shot of the 'ole bloomin' battalion.' In proof of which statement Simmons fired at the lighted windows of the mess-house.

'Private Simmons, E Comp'ny, on the Cavalry p'rade-ground, Sir, with thirty rounds,' said a Sergeant breathlessly to the Colonel. 'Shootin' right and lef', Sir. Shot Private Losson. What's to be done, Sir?'

Colonel John Anthony Deever, C. B., sallied out, only to be saluted by a spurt of dust at his feet.

'Pull up!' said the Second in Command; 'I don't want my step in that way, Colonel. He's as dangerous as a mad dog.'

'Shoot him like one, then,' said the Colonel bitterly, 'if he won't take his chance. My regiment, too! If it had been the Towheads I could have understood.'

Private Simmons had occupied a strong position near a well on the edge of the parade-ground, and was defying the regiment to come on. The regiment was not anxious to comply, for there is small honour in being shot by a fellow-private. Only Corporal Slane, rifle in hand, threw himself down on the ground, and wormed his way towards the well.

'Don't shoot,' said he to the men round him; 'like as not you'll 'it me. I'll catch the beggar, livin'.'

Simmons ceased shouting for a while, and the noise of trap-wheels could be heard across the plain. Major Oldyne, Commanding the Horse Battery, was coming back from a dinner in the Civil Lines; was driving after his usual custom—that is to say, as fast as the horse could go.

'A orf'cer! A blooming spangled orf'cer!' shrieked Simmons; 'I'll make a scarecrow of that orf'cer!' The trap stopped.

'What's this?' demanded the Major of Gunners. 'You there, drop your rifle.'

'Why, it's Jerry Blazes! I ain't got no quarrel with you, Jerry Blazes. Pass frien', an' all's well!'

But Jerry Blazes had not the faintest intention of passing a dangerous murderer. He was, as his adoring Battery swore long and fervently, without knowledge of fear, and they were surely the best judges, for Jerry Blazes, it was notorious, had done his possible to kill a man each time the Battery went out.

He walked towards Simmons, with the intention of rushing him, and knocking him down.

'Don't make me do it, Sir,' said Simmons; 'I ain't got nothing agin you. Ah! you would?'—the Major broke into a run—'Take that then!'

The Major dropped with a bullet through his shoulder, and Simmons stood over him. He had lost the satisfaction of killing Losson in the desired way: but here was a helpless body to his hand. Should he slip in another cartridge, and blow off the head, or with the butt smash in the white face? He stopped to consider, and a cry went up from the far side of the parade-ground: 'He's killed Jerry Blazes!' But in the shelter of the well-pillars Simmons was safe, except when he stepped out to fire. 'I'll blow yer 'andsome 'ead off, Jerry Blazes,' said Simmons reflectively. 'Six an' three is nine an' one is ten, an' that leaves me another nineteen, an' one for myself.' He tugged at the string of the second packet of ammunition. Corporal Slane crawled out of the shadow of a bank into the moonlight.

'I see you!' said Simmons. 'Come a bit furder on an' I'll do for you.'

'I'm comin',' said Corporal Slane briefly; 'you've done a bad day's work, Sim. Come out 'ere an' come back with me.'

'Come to—,' laughed Simmons, sending a cartridge home with his thumb. 'Not before I've settled you an' Jerry Blazes.'

The Corporal was lying at full length in the dust of the parade-ground, a rifle under him. Some of the less-cautious men in the distance shouted: 'Shoot 'im! Shoot 'im, Slane!'

'You move 'and or foot, Slane,' said Simmons, 'an' I'll kick Jerry Blazes' 'ead in, and shoot you after.'

'I ain't movin',' said the Corporal, raising his head; 'you daren't 'it a man on 'is legs. Let go o' Jerry Blazes an' come out o' that with your fistes. Come an' 'it me. You daren't, you bloomin' dog-shooter!'

'I dare.'

'You lie, you man-sticker. You sneakin' Sheeny butcher, you lie. See there!' Slane kicked the rifle away, and stood up in the peril of his life. 'Come on, now!'

The temptation was more than Simmons could resist, for the Corporal in his white clothes offered a perfect mark.

'Don't misname me,' shouted Simmons, firing as he spoke. The shot missed, and the shooter, blind with rage, threw his rifle down and rushed at Slane from the protection of the well. Within striking distance, he kicked savagely at Slane's stomach, but the weedy Corporal knew something of Simmons's weakness, and knew, too, the deadly guard for that kick. Bowing forward and drawing up his right leg till the heel of the right foot was set some three inches above the inside of the left knee-cap, he met the blow standing on one leg—exactly as Gonds stand when they meditate—and ready for the fall that would follow. There was an oath, the Corporal fell over to his own left as shinbone met shinbone, and the Private collapsed, his right leg broken an inch above the ankle.

"Pity you don't know that guard, Sim,' said Slane, spitting out the dust as he rose. Then raising his voice—'Come an' take him orf. I've bruk 'is leg.' This was not strictly true, for the Private had accomplished his own downfall, since it is the special merit of that leg-guard that the harder the kick the greater the kicker's discomfiture.

Slane walked to Jerry Blazes and hung over him with ostentatious anxiety, while Simmons, weeping with pain, was carried away. "Ope you ain't 'urt badly, Sir,' said Slane. The Major had fainted, and there was an ugly, ragged hole through the top of his arm. Slane knelt down and murmured: 'S'elp me, I believe 'e's dead. Well, if that ain't my blooming luck all over!'

But the Major was destined to lead his Battery afield for many a long day with unshaken nerve. He was removed, and nursed and petted into convalescence, while the Battery discussed the wisdom of capturing Simmons, and blowing him from a gun. They idolised their Major, and his reappearance on parade brought about a scene nowhere provided for in the Army Regulations.

Great, too, was the glory that fell to Slane's share. The Gunners would have made him drunk thrice a day for at least a fortnight. Even the Colonel of his own regiment complimented him upon his coolness, and the local paper called him a hero. These things did not puff him up. When the Major offered him money and thanks, the virtuous Corporal took the one and put aside the other. But he had a request to make and prefaced it with many a 'Beg y' pardon, Sir.' Could the Major see his way to letting the Slane-M'Kenna wedding be adorned by the presence of four Battery horses to pull a hired barouche? The Major could, and so could the Battery. Excessively so. It was a gorgeous wedding.

'Wot did I do it for?' said Corporal Slane. 'For the 'orses o' course. Jhansi ain't a beauty to look at, but I wasn't goin' to 'ave a hired turn-out. Jerry Blazes? If I 'adn't 'a' wanted something, Sim might ha' blowed Jerry Blazes' blooming 'ead into Hirish stew for aught I'd 'a' cared.'

And they hanged Private Simmons—hanged him as high as Haman in hollow square of the regiment; and the Colonel said it was Drink; and the Chaplain was sure it was the Devil; and Simmons fancied it was both, but he didn't know, and only hoped his fate would be a warning to his companions; and half a dozen 'intelligent publicists' wrote six beautiful leading articles on 'The Prevalence of Crime in the Army.'

But not a soul thought of comparing the 'bloody-minded Simmons' to the squawking, gaping schoolgirl with which this story opens.

BLACK JACK

To the wake av Tim O'Hara
Came company,
All St. Patrick's Alley
Was there to see.
Robert Buchanan.

As the Three Musketeers share their silver, tobacco, and liquor together, as they protect each other in barracks or camp, and as they rejoice together over the joy of one, so do they divide their sorrows. When Ortheris's irrepressible tongue has brought him into cells for a season, or Learoyd has run amok through his kit and accoutrements, or Mulvaney has indulged in strong waters, and under their influence reproved his Commanding Officer, you can see the trouble in the faces of the untouched two. And the rest of the regiment know that comment or jest is unsafe. Generally the three avoid Orderly Room and the Corner Shop that follows, leaving both to the young bloods who have not sown their wild oats; but there are occasions—

For instance, Ortheris was sitting on the drawbridge of the main gate of Fort Amara, with his hands in his pockets and his pipe, bowl down, in his mouth. Learoyd was lying at full length on the turf of the glacis, kicking his heels in the air, and I came round the corner and asked for Mulvaney.

Ortheris spat into the ditch and shook his head. 'No good seein' 'im now,' said Ortheris; "e's a bloomin' camel. Listen.'

I heard on the flags of the veranda opposite to the cells, which are close to the Guard-Room, a measured step that I could have identified in the tramp of an army. There were twenty paces crescendo, a pause, and then twenty diminuendo.

'That's 'im,' said Ortheris; 'my Gawd, that's 'im! All for a bloomin' button you could see your face in an' a bit o' lip that a bloomin' Harkangel would 'a' guv back.'

Mulvaney was doing pack-drill—was compelled, that is to say, to walk up and down for certain hours in full marching order, with rifle, bayonet, ammunition, knapsack, and overcoat. And his offence was being dirty on parade! I nearly fell into the Fort Ditch with astonishment and wrath, for Mulvaney is the smartest man that ever mounted guard, and would as soon think of turning out uncleanly as of dispensing with his trousers.

'Who was the Sergeant that checked him?' I asked.

'Mullins, o' course,' said Ortheris. 'There ain't no other man would whip 'im on the peg so. But Mullins ain't a man.' E's a dirty little pigscraper, that's wot 'e is.'

'What did Mulvaney say? He's not the make of man to take that quietly.'

'Said! Bin better for 'im if 'e'd shut 'is mouth. Lord, ow we laughed! "Sargint," 'e sez, "ye say I'm dirty. Well," sez 'e, "when your wife lets you blow your own nose for yourself, perhaps you'll know wot dirt is. You're himperfectly eddicated, Sargint," sez 'e, an' then we fell in. But after p'rade, 'e was up an' Mullins was swearin' 'imself black in the face at Ord'ly Room that Mulvaney 'ad called 'im a swine an' Lord knows wot all. You know Mullins. 'E'll 'ave 'is 'ead broke in one o' these days. 'E's too big a bloomin' liar for ord'nary consumption. "Three hours' can an' kit," sez the Colonel; "not for bein' dirty on p'rade, but for 'avin' said somethin' to Mullins, tho' I do not believe," sez 'e, "you said wot 'e said you said." An' Mulvaney fell away sayin' nothin'. You know 'e never speaks to the Colonel for fear o' gettin' 'imself fresh copped.'

Mullins, a very young and very much married Sergeant, whose manners were partly the result of innate depravity and partly of imperfectly digested Board School, came over the bridge, and most rudely asked Ortheris what he was doing.

'Me?' said Ortheris. 'Ow! I'm waiting for my C'mission. 'Seed it comin' along yit?'

Mullins turned purple and passed on. There was the sound of a gentle chuckle from the glacis where Learoyd lay.

''E expects to get 'is C'mission some day,' explained Ortheris;' Gawd 'elp the Mess that 'ave to put their 'ands into the same kiddy as 'im! Wot time d'you make it, Sir? Fower! Mulvaney'll be out in 'arf an hour. You don't want to buy a dorg, Sir, do you? A pup you can trust—'arf Rampore by the Colonel's grey-'ound.'

'Ortheris,' I answered sternly, for I knew what was in his mind, 'do you mean to say that—'

'I didn't mean to arx money o' you, any'ow,' said Ortheris; 'I'd 'a' sold you the dorg good an' cheap, but—but—I know Mulvaney'll want somethin' after we've walked 'im orf, an' I ain't got nothin', nor 'e 'asn't neither. I'd sooner sell you the dorg, Sir. 'S trewth I would!'

A shadow fell on the drawbridge, and Ortheris began to rise into the air, lifted by a huge hand upon his collar.

'Onything but t' braass,' said Learoyd quietly, as he held the Londoner over the ditch. 'Onything but t' braass, Orth'ris, ma son! Ah've got one rupee eight annas of ma own.' He showed two coins, and replaced Ortheris on the drawbridge rail.

'Very good,' I said;' where are you going to?'

'Goin' to walk 'im orf wen 'e comes out—two miles or three or fower,' said Ortheris.

The footsteps within ceased. I heard the dull thud of a knapsack falling on a bedstead, followed by the rattle of arms. Ten minutes later, Mulvaney, faultlessly dressed, his lips tight and his face as black as a thunderstorm, stalked into the sunshine on the drawbridge. Learoyd and Ortheris sprang from my side and closed in upon him, both leaning towards as horses lean upon the pole. In an instant they had disappeared down the sunken road to the cantonments, and I was left alone. Mulvaney had not seen fit to recognise me; so I knew that his trouble must be heavy upon him.

I climbed one of the bastions and watched the figures of the Three Musketeers grow smaller and smaller across the plain. They were walking as fast as they could put foot to the ground, and their heads were bowed. They fetched a great compass round the parade-ground, skirted the Cavalry lines, and vanished in the belt of trees that fringes the low land by the river.

I followed slowly, and sighted them—dusty, sweating, but still keeping up their long, swinging tramp—on the river bank. They crashed through the Forest Reserve, headed towards the Bridge of Boats, and presently established themselves on the bow of one of the pontoons. I rode cautiously till I saw three puffs of white smoke rise and die out in the clear evening air, and knew that peace had come again. At the bridge-head they waved me forward with gestures of welcome.

'Tie up your 'orse,' shouted Ortheris, 'an' come on, Sir. We're all goin' 'home in this 'ere bloomin' boat.'

From the bridge-head to the Forest Officer's bungalow is but a step. The mess-man was there, and would see that a man held my horse. Did the Sahib require aught else—a peg, or beer? Ritchie Sahib had left half a dozen bottles of the latter, but since the Sahib was a friend of Ritchie Sahib, and he, the mess-man, was a poor man—

I gave my order quietly, and returned to the bridge. Mulvaney had taken off his boots, and was dabbling his toes in the water; Learoyd was lying on his back on the pontoon; and Ortheris was pretending to row with a big bamboo.

'I'm an ould fool,' said Mulvaney, reflectively, 'dhrag-gin' you two out here bekaze I was undher the Black Dog—sulkin' like a child. Me that was soldierin' when Mullins, an' be damned to him, was shqueal in' on a counterpin for five shillin' a week—an' that not paid! Bhoys, I've took you five miles out av natural pevarsity. Phew!'

'Wot's the odds so long as you're 'appy?' said Ortheris, applying himself afresh to the bamboo. 'As well 'ere as anywhere else.'

Learoyd held up a rupee and an eight-anna bit, and shook his head sorrowfully. 'Five mile from t' Canteen, all along o' Mulvaney's blaasted pride.'

'I know ut,' said Mulvaney penitently. 'Why will ye come wid me? An' yet I wud be mortial sorry if ye did not—any time—though I am ould enough to know betther. But I will do penance. I will take a dhrink av wather.'

Ortheris squeaked shrilly. The butler of the Forest bungalow was standing near the railings with a basket, uncertain how to clamber down to the pontoon. 'Might 'a' know'd you'd 'a' got liquor out o' bloomin' desert, Sir,' said Ortheris, gracefully, to me. Then to the mess-man: 'Easy with them there bottles. They're worth their weight in gold. Jock, ye long-armed beggar, get out o' that an' hike 'em down.'

Learoyd had the basket on the pontoon in an instant, and the Three Musketeers gathered round it with dry lips. They drank my health in due and ancient form, and thereafter tobacco tasted sweeter than ever. They absorbed all the beer, and disposed themselves in picturesque attitudes to admire the setting sun—no man speaking for a while.

Mulvaney's head dropped upon his chest, and we thought that he was asleep.

'What on earth did you come so far for?' I whispered to Ortheris.

'To walk 'im orf, o' course. When 'e's been checked we allus walks 'im orf. 'E ain't fit to be spoke to those times—nor 'e ain't fit to leave alone neither. So we takes 'im till 'e is.'

Mulvaney raised his head, and stared straight into the sunset. 'I had my rifle,' said he dreamily, 'an' I had my bay'nit, an' Mullins came round the corner, an' he looked in my face an' grinned dishpiteful. "You can't blow your own nose," sez he. Now, I cannot tell fwhat Mullins's expayrience may ha' been, but, Mother av God, he was nearer to his death that minut' than I have iver been to mine—and that's less than the thicknuss av a hair!'

'Yes,' said Ortheris calmly, 'you'd look fine with all your buttons took orf, an' the Band in front o' you, walkin' roun' slow time. We're both front-rank men, me an' Jock, when the rig'mint's in 'ollow square. Bloomin' fine you'd look. "The Lord giveth an' the Lord taketh awai,—Heasy with that there drop!—Blessed be the naime o' the Lord,"' he gulped in a quaint and suggestive fashion.

'Mullins! Wot's Mullins?' said Learoyd slowly. 'Ah'd take a coomp'ny o' Mullinses-ma hand behind me. Sitha, Mulvaney, don't be a fool.'

'You were not checked for fwhat you did not do, an' made a mock av afther. 'Twas for less than that the Tyrone wud ha' sent O'Hara to hell, instid av lettin' him go by his own choosin', whin Rafferty shot him,' retorted Mulvaney.

'And who stopped the Tyrone from doing it?' I asked.

'That ould fool who's sorry he didn't stick the pig Mullins.' His head dropped again. When he raised it he shivered and put his hands on the shoulders of his two companions.

'Ye've walked the Divil out av me, bhoys,' said he.

Ortheris shot out the red-hot dottel of his pipe on the back of the hairy fist. 'They say 'Ell's 'otter than that,' said he, as Mulvaney swore aloud. 'You be warned so. Look yonder!'—he pointed across the river to a ruined temple—'Me an' you an' 'im'—he indicated me by a jerk of his head—'was there one day when Hi made a bloomin' show o' myself. You an' 'im stopped me doin' such—an' Hi was on'y wishful for to desert. You are makin' a bigger bloomin' show o' yourself now.'

'Don't mind him, Mulvaney,' I said; 'Dinah Shadd won't let you hang yourself yet awhile, and you don't intend to try it either. Let's hear about the Tyrone and O'Hara. Rafferty shot him for fooling with his wife. What happened before that?'

'There's no fool like an ould fool. You know you can do anythin' wid me whin I'm talkin'. Did I say I wud like to cut Mullins's liver out? I deny the imputashin, for fear that Orth'ris here wud report me—Ah! You wud tip me into the river, wud you? Sit quiet, little man. Anyways, Mullins is not worth the trouble av an extry p'rade, an' I will trate him wid outrajis contimpt. The Tyrone an' O'Hara! O'Hara an' the Tyrone, begad! Ould days are hard to bring back into the mouth, but they're always inside the head.'

Followed a long pause.

'O'Hara was a Divil. Though I saved him, for the honour av the rig'mint, from his death that time, I say it now. He was a Divil—a long, bould, black-haired Divil.'

'Which way?' asked Ortheris.

'Women.'

'Thin I know another.'

'Not more than in reason, if you mane me, ye warped walkin'-shtick. I have been young, an' for why should I not have tuk what I cud? Did I iver, whin I was Corp'ril, use the rise av my rank—wan step an' that taken away, more's the sorrow an' the fault av me!—to prosecute a nefarious inthrigue, as O'Hara did? Did I, whin I was Corp'ril, lay my spite upon a man an' make his life a dog's life from day to day? Did I lie, as O'Hara lied, till the young wans in the Tyrone turned white wid the fear av the Judgment av God killin' thim all in a lump, as ut killed the woman at Devizes? I did not! I have sinned my sins an' I have made my confesshin, an' Father Victor knows the worst av me. O'Hara was tuk, before he cud spake, on Rafferty's doorstep, an' no man knows the worst av him. But this much I know!

'The Tyrone was recruited any fashion in the ould days. A draf from Connemara—a draf' from Portsmouth—a draf' from Kerry, an' that was a blazin' bad draf'—here, there and iverywhere—but the large av thim was Oirish—Black Oirish. Now there are Oirish an' Oirish. The good are good as the best, but the bad are wurrst than the wurrst. 'Tis this way. They clog together in pieces as fast as thieves, an' no wan knows fwhat they will do till wan turns informer an' the gang is bruk. But ut begins again, a day later, meetin' in holes an' corners an' swearin' bloody oaths an' shtickin' a man in the back an' runnin' away, an' thin waitin' for the blood-money on the reward papers—to see if ut's worth enough. Those are the Black Oirish, an' 'tis they that bring dishgrace upon the name av Oireland, an' thim I wud kill—as I nearly killed wan wanst.

'But to reshume. My room—'twas before I was married—was wid twelve av the scum av the earth—the pickin's av the gutter—mane men that wud neither laugh nor talk nor yet get dhrunk as a man shud. They thried some av their dog's thricks on me, but I dhrew a line round my cot, an' the man that thransgressed ut wint into hospital for three days good.

'O'Hara had put his spite on the room—he was my Colour Sargint—an' nothin' cud we do to plaze him. I was younger than I am now, an' I tuk what I got in the way av dressing down and punishment-dhrill wid my tongue in my cheek. But it was diff'rint wid the others, an' why I cannot say, excipt that some men are borrun mane an' go to dhirty murdher where a fist is more than enough. Afther a whoile, they changed their chune to me an' was desp'rit frien'ly—all twelve av thim cursin' O'Hara in chorus.

'"Eyah," sez I, "O'Hara's a divil an' I'm not for denyin' ut, but is he the only man in the wurruld? Let him go. He'll get tired av findin' our kit foul an' our 'coutrements onproperly kep'."

'"We will not let him go," sez they.

'"Thin take him," sez I, "an' a dashed poor yield you will get for your throuble."

'"Is he not misconductin' himself wid Slimmy's wife?" sez another.

'"She's common to the rig'mint," sez I. "Fwhat has made ye this partic'lar on a suddint?"

'"Has he not put his spite on the roomful av us? Can we do anythin' that he will not check us for?" sez another.

'"That's thrue," sez I.

'"Will ye not help us to do aught," sez another—"a big bould man like you."

'"I will break his head upon his shoulthers av he puts hand on me," sez I. "I will give him the lie av he says that I'm dhirty, an' I wud not mind duckin' him in the Artillery troughs if ut was not that I'm thryin' for my shtripes."

'"Is that all ye will do?" sez another. "Have ye no more spunk than that, ye blood-dhrawn calf?"

'"Blood-dhrawn I may be," sez I, gettin' back to my cot an' makin' my line round ut; "but ye know that the man who comes acrost this mark will be more blood-dhrawn than me. No man gives me the name in my mouth," I sez. "Ondersthand, I will have no part wid you in anythin' ye do, nor will I raise my fist to my shuperior. Is any wan comin' on?" sez I.

'They made no move, tho' I gave them full time, but stud growlin' an' snarlin' together at wan ind av the room. I tuk up my cap and wint out to Canteen, thinkin' no little av mesilf, and there I grew most ondacintly dhrunk in my legs. My head was all reasonable.

'"Houligan," I sez to a man in E Comp'ny that was by way av bein' a frind av mine; "I'm overtuk from the belt down. Do you give me the touch av your shoulther to presarve my formation an' march me acrost the ground into the high grass. I'll sleep ut off there," sez I; an' Houligan—he's dead now, but good he was while he lasted—walked wid me, givin' me the touch whin I wint wide, ontil we came to the high grass, an', my faith, the sky an' the earth was fair rowlin' undher me. I made for where the grass was thickust, an' there I slep' off my liquor wid an easy conscience. I did not desire to come on books too frequent; my charachter havin' been shpotless for the good half av a year.

'Whin I roused, the dhrink was dyin' out in me, an' I felt as though a she-cat had littered in my mouth. I had not learned to hould my liquor wid comfort in thim days. 'Tis little betther I am now. "I will get Houligan to pour a bucket over my head," thinks I, an' I wud ha' risen, but I heard some wan say: "Mulvaney can take the blame av ut for the backslidin' hound he is."

'"Oho!" sez I, an' my head rang like a guard-room gong: "fwhat is the blame that this young man must take to oblige Tim Vulmea?" For 'twas Tim Vulmea that shpoke.

'I turned on my belly an' crawled through the grass, a bit at a time, to where the spache came from. There was the twelve av my room sittin' down in a little patch, the dhry grass wavin' above their heads an' the sin av black murdher in their hearts. I put the stuff aside to get a clear view.

'"Fwhat's that?" sez wan man, jumpin' up.

'"A dog," says Vulmea. "You're a nice hand to this job! As I said, Mulvaney will take the blame—av ut comes to a pinch."

'"'Tis harrd to swear a man's life away," sez a young wan.

'"Thank ye for that," thinks I. "Now, fwhat the divil are you paragins conthrivin' against me?"

'"'Tis as easy as dhrinkin' your quart," sez Vulmea. "At seven or thereon, O'Hara will come acrost to the Married Quarters, goin' to call on Slimmy's wife, the swine! Wan av us'll pass the wurrd to the room an' we shtart the divil an' all av a shine—laughin' an' crackin' on an' t'rowin' our boots about. Thin O'Hara will come to give us the ordher to be quiet, the more by token bekaze the room-lamp will be knocked over in the larkin'. He will take the straight road to the ind door where there's the lamp in the veranda, an' that'll bring him clear against the light as he shtands. He will not be able to look into the dhark. Wan av us will loose off, an' a close shot ut will be, an' shame to the man that misses. 'Twill be Mulvaney's rifle, she that is at the head av the rack—there's no mistakin' that long-shtocked, cross-eyed bitch even in the dhark."

'The thief misnamed my ould firin'-piece out av jealousy—I was pershuaded av that—an' ut made me more angry than all.

'But Vulmea goes on: "O'Hara will dhrop, an' by the time the light's lit again, there'll be some six av us on the chest av Mulvaney, cryin' murdher an' rape. Mulvaney's cot is near the ind door, an' the shmokin' rifle will be lyin' undher him whin we've knocked him over. We know, an' all the rig'mint knows, that Mulvaney has given O'Hara more lip than any man av us. Will there be any doubt at the Coort-Martial? Wud twelve honust sodger-bhoys swear away the life av a dear, quiet, swate-timpered man such as is Mulvaney—wid his line av pipe-clay roun' his cot, threatenin' us wid murdher av we overshtepped ut, as we can truthful testify?"

'"Mary, Mother av Mercy!" thinks I to mesilf; "it is this to have an unruly mimber an' fistes fit to use! Oh the sneakin' hounds!"

'The big dhrops ran down my face, for I was wake wid the liquor an' had not the full av my wits about me. I laid shtill an' heard thim workin' themselves up to swear my life by tellin' tales av ivry time I had put my mark on wan or another; an' my faith, they was few that was not so dishtinguished. 'Twas all in the way av fair fight, though, for niver did I raise my hand excipt whin they had provoked me to ut.

'"'Tis all well," sez wan av thim, "but who's to do this shootin'?"

'"Fwhat matther?" sez Vulmea. "'Tis Mulvaney will do that—at the Coort-Martial."

'"He will so," sez the man, "but whose hand is put to the trigger—in the room?"

'"Who'll do ut?" sez Vulmea, lookin' round, but divil a man answeared. They began to dishpute till Kiss, that was always playin' Shpoil Five, sez: "Thry the kyards!" Wid that he opined his tunic an' tuk out the greasy palammers, an' they all fell in wid the notion.

'"Deal on!" sez Vulmea, wid a big rattlin' oath, "an' the Black Curse av Shielygh come to the man that will not do his duty as the kyards say. Amin!"

'"Black Jack is the masther," sez Kiss, dealin'. Black Jack, Sorr, I shud expaytiate to you, is the Ace av Shpades which from time immimorial has been intimately connect wid battle, murdher an' suddin death.

'Wanst Kiss dealt an' there was no sign, but the men was whoite wid the workin's av their sowls. Twice Kiss dealt an' there was a gray shine on their cheeks like the mess av an egg. Three times Kiss dealt an' they was blue. "Have ye not lost him?" sez Vulmea, wipin' the sweat on him; "Let's ha' done quick!" "Quick ut is," sez Kiss, t'rowin' him the kyard; an' ut fell face up on his knee—Black Jack!

'Thin they all cackled wid laughin'. "Duty thrippence," sez wan av thim, "an' damned cheap at that price!" But I cud see they all dhrew a little away from Vulmea an' lef' him sittin' playin' wid the kyard. Vulmea sez no word for a whoile but licked his lips—cat-ways. Thin he threw up his head an' made the men swear by ivry oath known to stand by him not alone in the room but at the Coort-Martial that was to set on me! He tould off five av the biggest to stretch me on my cot whin the shot was fired, an' another man he tould off to put out the light, an' yet another to load my rifle. He wud not do that himself; an' that was quare, for 'twas but a little thing considerin'.

'Thin they swore over again that they wud not bethray wan another, an' crep' out av the grass in diff'rint ways, two by two. A mercy ut was that they did not come on me. I was sick wid fear in the pit av my stummick—sick, sick, sick! Afther they was all gone, I wint back to Canteen an' called for a quart to put a thought in me. Vulmea was there, dhrinkin' heavy, an' politeful to me beyond reason. "Fwhat will I do—fwhat will I do?" thinks I to mesilf whin Vulmea wint away.

'Presintly the Arm'rer Sargint comes in stiffin' an' crackin' on, not pleased wid any wan, bekaze the Martini Henri bein' new to the rig'mint in those days we used to play the mischief wid her arrangements. 'Twas a long time before I cud get out av the way av thryin' to pull back the back-sight an' turnin' her over afther firin'—as if she was a Snider.

'"Fwhat tailor-men do they give me to work wid?" sez the Arm'rer Sargint. "Here's Hogan, his nose flat as a table, laid by for a week, an' ivry Comp'ny sendin' their arrums in knocked to small shivreens."

'"Fwhat's wrong wid Hogan, Sargint?" sez I.

'"Wrong!" sez the Arm'rer Sargint; "I showed him, as though I had been his mother, the way av shtrippin' a 'Tini, an' he shtrup her clane an' easy. I tould him to put her to again an' fire a blank into the blow-pit to show how the dirt hung on the groovin'. He did that, but he did not put in the pin av the fallin'-block, an' av coorse whin he fired he was strook by the block jumpin' clear. Well for him 'twas but a blank—a full charge wud ha' cut his oi out."

'I looked a thrifle wiser than a boiled sheep's head. "How's that, Sargint?" sez I.

'"This way, ye blundherin' man, an' don't you be doin' ut," sez he. Wid that he shows me a Waster action—the breech av her all cut away to show the inside—an' so plazed he was to grumble that he dimonstrated fwhat Hogan had done twice over. "An' that comes av not knowin' the wepping you're purvided wid," sez he.

'"Thank ye, Sargint," sez I; "I will come to you again for further information."

'"Ye will not," sez he. "Kape your clanin'-rod away from the breech-pin or you will get into throuble."

'I wint outside an' I could ha' danced wid delight for the grandeur av ut. "They will load my rifle, good luck to thim, whoile I'm away," thinks I, and back I wint to the Canteen to give them their clear chanst.

'The Canteen was fillin' wid men at the ind av the day. I made feign to be far gone in dhrink, an', wan by wan, all my roomful came in wid Vulmea. I wint away, walkin' thick an' heavy, but not so thick an' heavy that any wan cud ha' tuk me. Sure and thrue, there was a kyartridge gone from my pouch an' lyin' snug in my rifle. I was hot wid rage against thim all, an' I worried the bullet out wid my teeth as fast as I cud, the room bein' empty. Then I tuk my boot an' the clanin'-rod and knocked out the pin av the fallin'-block. Oh, 'twas music when that pin rowled on the flure! I put ut into my pouch an' stuck a dab av dirt on the holes in the plate, puttin' the fallin'-block back. "That'll do your business, Vulmea," sez I, lyin' easy on the cot. "Come an' sit on my chest the whole room av you, an' I will take you to my bosom for the biggest divils that iver cheated halter." I wud have no mercy on Vulmea. His oi or his life—little I cared!

'At dusk they came back, the twelve av thim, an' they had all been dhrinkin'. I was shammin' sleep on the cot. Wan man wint outside in the veranda. Whin he whishtled they began to rage roun' the room an' carry on tremenjus. But I niver want to hear men laugh as they did—skylarkin' too! 'Twas like mad jackals.

'"Shtop that blasted noise!" sez O'Hara in the dark, an' pop goes the room-lamp. I cud hear O'Hara runnin' up an' the rattlin' av my rifle in the rack an' the men breathin' heavy as they stud roun' my cot. I cud see O'Hara in the light av the veranda lamp, an' thin I heard the crack av my rifle. She cried loud, poor darlint, bein' mishandled. Next minut' five men were holdin' me down. "Go easy," I sez; "fwhat's ut all about?"

'Thin Vulmea, on the flure, raised a howl you cud hear from wan ind av cantonmints to the other. "I'm dead, I'm butchered, I'm blind!" sez he. "Saints have mercy on my sinful sowl! Sind for Father Constant! Oh sind for Father Constant an' let me go clean!" By that I knew he was not so dead as I cud ha' wished.

'O'Hara picks up the lamp in the veranda wid a hand as stiddy as a rest. "Fwhat damned dog's thrick is this av yours?" sez he, an turns the light on Tim Vulmea that was shwimmin' in blood from top to toe. The fallin'-block had sprung free behin' a full charge av powther—good care I tuk to bite down the brass af ther takin' out the bullet that there might be somethin' to give ut full worth—an' had cut Tim from the lip to the corner av the right eye, lavin' the eyelid in tatthers, an' so up an' along by the forehead to the hair. 'Twas more av a rakin' plough, if you will ondherstand, than a clean cut; an' niver did I see a man bleed as Vulmea did. The dhrink an' the stew that he was in pumped the blood strong. The minut' the men sittin' on my chest heard O'Hara spakin' they scatthered each wan to his cot, an' cried out very politeful: "Fwhat is ut, Sargint?"

'"Fwhat is ut!" sez O'Hara, shakin' Tim. "Well an' good do you know fwhat ut is, ye skulkin' ditch-lurkin' dogs! Get a doolie, an' take this whimperin' scutt away. There will be more heard av ut than any av you will care for."

'Vulmea sat up rockin' his head in his hand an' moanin' for Father Constant.

'"Be done!" sez O'Hara, dhraggin' him up by the hair. "You're none so dead that you cannot go fifteen years for thryin' to shoot me."

'"I did not," sez Vulmea; "I was shootin' mesilf."

'"That's quare," sez O'Hara, "for the front av my jackut is black wid your powther." He tuk up the rifle that was still warm an' began to laugh. "I'll make your life Hell to you," sez he, "for attempted murdher an' kapin' your rifle onproperly. You'll be hanged first an' thin put undher stoppages for four fifteen. The rifle's done for," sez he.

'"Why, 'tis my rifle!" sez I, comin' up to look; "Vulmea, ye divil, fwhat were you doin' wid her—answer me that?"

'"Lave me alone," sez Vulmea; "I'm dyin'!"

'"I'll wait till you're betther," sez I, "an' thin we two will talk ut out umbrageous."

'O'Hara pitched Tim into the doolie, none too tinder, but all the bhoys kep' by their cots, which was not the sign av innocint men. I was huntin' ivrywhere for my fallin'-block, but not findin' ut at all. I niver found ut.

'"Now fwhat will I do?" sez O'Hara, swinging the veranda light in his hand an' lookin' down the room. I had hate and contimpt av O'Hara an' I have now, dead tho' he is, but, for all that, will I say he was a brave man. He is baskin' in Purgathory this tide, but I wish he cud hear that, whin he stud lookin' down the room an' the bhoys shivered before the oi av him, I knew him for a brave man an' I liked him so.

'"Fwhat will I do?" sez O'Hara agin, an' we heard the voice av a woman low an' sof' in the veranda. 'Twas Slimmy's wife, come over at the shot, sittin' on wan av the benches an' scarce able to walk.

'"O Denny!—Denny, dear," sez she, "have they kilt you?"

'O'Hara looked down the room again an' showed his teeth to the gum. Then he spat on the flure.

'"You're not worth ut," sez he. "Light that lamp, ye dogs," an' wid that he turned away, an' I saw him walkin' off wid Slimmy's wife; she thryin' to wipe off the powther-black on the front av his jackut wid her handkerchief. "A brave man you are," thinks I—"a brave man an' a bad woman."

'No wan said a word for a time. They was all ashamed, past spache.

'"Fwhat d'you think he will do?" sez wan av thim at last. "He knows we're all in ut."

'"Are we so?" sez I from my cot. "The man that sez that to me will be hurt. I do not know," sez I, "fwhat onderhand divilmint you have conthrived, but by what I've seen I know that you cannot commit murdher wid another man's rifle—such shakin' cowards you are. I'm goin' to slape," I sez, "an' you can blow my head off whoile I lay." I did not slape, though, for a long time. Can ye wonder?

'Next morn the news was through all the rig'mint, an' there was nothin' that the men did not tell. O'Hara reports, fair an' easy, that Vulmea was come to grief through tamperin' wid his rifle in barricks, all for to show the mechanism. An' by my sowl, he had the impart'nince to say that he was on the shpot at the time an' cud certify that ut was an accident! You might ha' knocked my roomful down wid a straw whin they heard that. 'Twas lucky for thim that the bhoys were always thryin' to find out how the new rifle was made, an' a lot av thim had come up for easin' the pull by shtickin' bits av grass an' such in the part av the lock that showed near the thrigger. The first issues of the 'Tinis was not covered in, an' I mesilf have eased the pull av mine time an' agin. A light pull is ten points on the range to me.

'"I will not have this foolishness!" sez the Colonel. "I will twist the tail off Vulmea!" sez he; but whin he saw him, all tied up an' groanin' in hospital, he changed his will. "Make him an early convalescint," sez he to the Doctor, an' Vulmea was made so for a warnin'. His big bloody bandages an' face puckered up to wan side did more to kape the bhoys from messin' wid the insides av their rifles than any punishmint.

'O'Hara gave no reason for fwhat he'd said, an' all my roomful were too glad to inquire, tho' he put his spite upon thim more wearin' than before. Wan day, howiver, he tuk me apart very polite, for he cud be that at the choosin'.

'"You're a good sodger, tho' you're a damned insolint man," sez he.

'"Fair words, Sargint," sez I, "or I may be insolint again."

'"'Tis not like you," sez he, "to lave your rifle in the rack widout the breech-pin, for widout the breech-pin she was whin Vulmea fired. I should ha' found the break av ut in the eyes av the holes, else," he sez.

'"Sargint," sez I, "fwhat wud your life ha' been worth av the breech-pin had been in place, for, on my sowl, my life wud be worth just as much to me av I tould you whether ut was or was not. Be thankful the bullet was not there," I sez.

'"That's thrue," sez he, pulling his moustache; "but I do not believe that you, for all your lip, was in that business."

'"Sargint," I sez, "I cud hammer the life out av a man in ten minuts wid my fistes if that man dishpleased me; for I am a good sodger, an' I will be threated as such, an' whoile my fistes are my own they're strong enough for all work I have to do. They do not fly back towards me!" sez I, lookin' him betune the eyes.

'"You're a good man," sez he, lookin' me betune the eyes—an' oh he was a gran'-built man to see!— "you're a good man," he sez, "an' I cud wish, for the pure frolic av ut, that I was not a Sargint, or that you were not a Privit; an' you will think me no coward whin I say this thing."

'"I do not," sez I. "I saw you whin Vulmea mishandled the rifle. But, Sargint," I sez, "take the wurrd from me now, spakin' as man to man wid the shtripes off, tho' 'tis little right I have to talk, me being fwhat I am by natur'. This time ye tuk no harm, an' next time ye may not, but, in the ind, so sure as Slimmy's wife came into the veranda, so sure will ye take harm—an' bad harm. Have thought, Sargint," sez I. "Is ut worth ut?"

'"Ye're a bould man," sez he, breathin' harrd. "A very bould man. But I am a bould man tu. Do you go your way, Privit Mulvaney, an' I will go mine."

'We had no further spache thin or afther, but, wan by another, he drafted the twelve av my room out into other rooms an' got thim spread among the Comp'nies, for they was not a good breed to live together, an' the Comp 'ny orf'cers saw ut. They wud ha' shot me in the night av they had known fwhat I knew; but that they did not.

'An', in the ind, as I said, O'Hara met his death from Rafferty for foolin' wid his wife. He wint his own way too well—Eyah, too well! Shtraight to that affair, widout turnin' to the right or to the lef', he wint, an' may the Lord have mercy on his sowl. Amin!'

"'Ear! 'Ear!' said Ortheris, pointing the moral with a wave of his pipe. 'An' this is 'im 'oo would be a bloomin' Vulmea all for the sake of Mullins an' a bloomin' button! Mullins never went after a woman in his life. Mrs. Mullins, she saw 'im one day—'

'Ortheris,' I said, hastily, for the romances of Private Ortheris are all too daring for publication, 'look at the sun. It's a quarter past six!'

'O Lord! Three quarters of an hour for five an' a 'arf miles! We'll 'ave to run like Jimmy O.'

The Three Musketeers clambered on to the bridge, and departed hastily in the direction of the cantonment road. When I overtook them I offered them two stirrups and a tail, which they accepted enthusiastically. Ortheris held the tail, and in this manner we trotted steadily through the shadows by an unfrequented road.

At the turn into the cantonments we heard carriage wheels. It was the Colonel's barouche, and in it sat the Colonel's wife and daughter. I caught a suppressed chuckle, and my beast sprang forward with a lighter step.

The Three Musketeers had vanished into the night.

L'ENVOI

And they were stronger hands than mine
That digged the Ruby from the earth—
More cunning brains that made it worth
The large desire of a King;
And bolder hearts that through the brine
Went down the Perfect Pearl to bring.

Lo, I have made in common clay
Rude figures of a rough-hewn race;
For Pearls strew not the market-place
In this my town of banishment,
Where with the shifting dust I play
And eat the bread of Discontent.

Yet is there life in that I make,—
Oh Thou who knowest, turn and see,
As Thou hast power over me,
So I have power over these,
Because I wrought them for Thy sake,
And breathed in them mine agonies.

Small mirth was in the making. Now
I lift the cloth that clokes the clay,
And, wearied, at Thy feet I lay
My wares ere I go forth to sell.
The long bazar will praise—but Thou—
Heart of my heart, have I done well?

POOR DEAR MAMMA

The wild hawk to the wind-swept sky,
The deer to the wholesome wold,
And the heart of a man to the heart of a maid,
As it was in the days of old.
                                        Gypsy Song.

SCENE.—Interior of MISS MINNIE THREEGAN'S bedroom at Simla. MISS THREEGAN, in window-seat, turning over a drawerful of things. MISS EMMA DEERCOURT, bosom-friend, who has come to spend the day, sitting on the bed, manipulating the bodice of a ballroom frock and a bunch of artificial lilies of the valley. Time, 5.30 P. M. on a hot May afternoon.

MISS DEERCOURT. And he said: 'I shall never forget this dance,' and, of course, I said: 'Oh! how can you be so silly!' Do you think he meant anything, dear?

MISS THREEGAN. (Extracting long lavender silk stocking from the rubbish.) You know him better than I do.

MISS D. Oh, do be sympathetic, Minnie! I'm sure he does. At least I would be sure if he wasn't always riding with that odious Mrs. Hagan.

MISS T. I suppose so. How does one manage to dance through one's heels first? Look at this—isn't it shameful? (Spreads stocking-heel on open hand for inspection)

MISS D. Never mind that! You can't mend it. Help me with this hateful bodice, I've run the string so, and I've run the string so, and I can't make the fulness come right. Where would you put this? (Waves lilies of the valley.)

MISS T. As high up on the shoulder as possible.

MISS D. Am I quite tall enough? I know it makes May Olger look lop-sided.

MISS T. Yes, but May hasn't your shoulders. Hers are like a hock-bottle.

BEARER. (Rapping at door.) Captain Sahib aya.

MISS D. (Jumping up wildly, and hunting for body, which she has discarded owing to the heat of the day.) Captain Sahib! What Captain Sahib? Oh, good gracious, and I'm only half dressed! Well, I shan't bother.

MISS T. (Calmly.) You needn't. It isn't for us. That's Captain Gadsby. He is going for a ride with Mamma. He generally comes five days out of the seven.

AGONISED VOICE. (From an inner apartment.) Minnie, run out and give Captain Gadsby some tea, and tell him I shall be ready in ten minutes; and, O Minnie, come to me an instant, there's a dear girl!

MISS T. Oh, bother! (Aloud.) Very well, Mamma.

Exit, and reappears, after five minutes, flushed, and rubbing her fingers.

MISS D. You look pink. What has happened?

MISS T. (In a stage whisper.) A twenty-four-inch waist, and she won't let it out. Where are my bangles? (Rummages on the toilet-table, and dabs at her hair with a brush in the interval.)

MISS D. Who is this Captain Gadsby? I don't think I've met him.

MISS T. You must have. He belongs to the Harrar set. I've danced with him, but I've never talked to him. He's a big yellow man, just like a newly-hatched chicken, with an e-normous moustache. He walks like this (imitates Cavalry swagger), and he goes 'Ha-Hmmm!' deep down in his throat when he can't think of anything to say. Mamma likes him. I don't.

MISS D. (Abstractedly.) Does he wax his moustache?

MISS T. (Busy with powder-puff.) Yes, I think so. Why?

MISS D. (Bending oner the bodice and sewing furiously.) Oh, nothing—only—

MISS T. (Sternly.) Only what? Out with it, Emma.

MISS D. Well, May Olger—she's engaged to Mr. Charteris, you know—said—Promise you won't repeat this?

MISS T. Yes, I promise. What did she say?

MISS D. That—that being kissed (with a rush) by a man who didn't wax his moustache was—like eating an egg without salt.

MISS T. (At her full height, with crushing scorn.) May Olger is a horrid, nasty Thing, and you can tell her I said so. I'm glad she doesn't belong to my set—I must go and feed this man! Do I look presentable?

MISS D. Yes, perfectly. Be quick and hand him over to your Mother, and then we can talk. I shall listen at the door to hear what you say to him.

MISS T. 'Sure I don't care. I'm not afraid of Captain Gadsby.

In proof of this swings into drawing-room with a mannish stride followed by two short steps, which produces the effect of a restive horse entering. Misses CAPTAIN GADSBY, who is sitting in the shadow of the window-curtain, and gazes round helplessly.

CAPTAIN GADSBY. (Aside.) The filly, by Jove! 'Must ha' picked up that action from the sire. (Aloud, rising.) Good evening, Miss Threegan.

MISS T. (Conscious that she is flushing.) Good evening, Captain Gadsby. Mamma told me to say that she will be ready in a few minutes. Won't you have some tea? (Aside.) I hope Mamma will be quick. What am I to say to the creature? (Aloud and abruptly.) Milk and sugar?

CAPT. G. No sugar, tha-anks, and very little milk. Ha-Hmmm.

MISS T. (Aside.) If he's going to do that, I'm lost. I shall laugh. I know I shall!

CAPT. G. (Pulling at his moustache and watching it sideways down his nose.) Ha-Hmmm. (Aside.) 'Wonder what the little beast can talk about. 'Must make a shot at it.

MISS T. (Aside.) Oh, this is agonising. I must say something.

BOTH TOGETHER. Have you been—

CAPT. G. I beg your pardon. You were going to say—

MISS T. (Who has been watching the moustache with awed fascination.) Won't you have some eggs?

CAPT. G. (Looking bewilderedly at the tea-table.) Eggs! (A side.) O Hades! She must have a nursery-tea at this hour. S'pose they've wiped her mouth and sent her to me while the Mother is getting on her duds. (Aloud.) No, thanks.

MISS T. (Crimson with confusion.) Oh! I didn't mean that. I wasn't thinking of mou—eggs for an instant. I mean salt. Won't you have some sa—sweets? (Aside.) He'll think me a raving lunatic. I wish Mamma would come.

CAPT. G. (Aside.) It was a nursery-tea and she's ashamed of it. By Jove! She doesn't look half bad when she colours up like that. (Aloud, helping himself from the dish.) Have you seen those new chocolates at Peliti's?

MISS T. No, I made these myself. What are they like?

CAPT. G. These! De-licious. (Aside.) And that's a fact.

MISS T. (Aside.) Oh, bother! he'll think I'm fishing for compliments. (Aloud.) No, Peliti's of course.

CAPT. G. (Enthusiastically.) Not to compare with these. How d'you make them? I can't get my khansamah to understand the simplest thing beyond mutton and fowl.

MISS T. Yes? I'm not a khansamah, you know. Perhaps you frighten him. You should never frighten a servant. He loses his head. It's very bad policy.

CAPT. G. He's so awf'ly stupid.

MISS T. (Folding her hands in her lap.) You should call him quietly and say: 'O khansamah jee!'

CAPT. G. (Getting interested.) Yes? (Aside.) Fancy that little featherweight saying, 'O khansamah jee' to my bloodthirsty Mir Khan!

MISS T. Then you should explain the dinner, dish by dish.

CAPT. G. But I can't speak the vernacular.

MISS T. (Patronizingly.) You should pass the Higher Standard and try.

CAPT. G. I have, but I don't seem to be any the wiser. Are you?

MISS T. I never passed the Higher Standard. But the khansamah is very patient with me. He doesn't get angry when I talk about sheep's topees, or order maunds of grain when I mean seers.

CAPT. G. (Aside, with intense indignation.) I'd like to see Mir Khan being rude to that girl! Hullo! Steady the Buffs! (Aloud.) And do you understand about horses, too?

MISS T. A little—not very much. I can't doctor them, but I know what they ought to eat, and I am in charge of our stable.

CAPT. G. Indeed! You might help me then. What ought a man to give his sais in the Hills? My ruffian says eight rupees, because everything is so dear.

MISS T. Six rupees a month, and one rupee Simla allowance—neither more nor less. And a grass-cut gets six rupees. That's better than buying grass in the bazar.

CAPT. G. (Admiringly.) How do you know?

MISS T. I have tried both ways.

CAPT. G. Do you ride much, then? I've never seen you on the Mall.

MISS T. (Aside.) I haven't passed him more than fifty times. (Aloud.) Nearly every day.

CAPT. G. By Jove! I didn't know that. Ha-Hmmm! (Pulls at his moustache and is silent for forty seconds.)

MISS T. (Desperately, and wondering what will happen next.) It looks beautiful. I shouldn't touch it if I were you. (Aside.) It's all Mamma's fault for not coming before. I will be rude!

CAPT. G. (Bronzing under the tan and bringing down his hand very quickly.) Eh! Wha-at! Oh, yes! Ha! Ha! (Laughs uneasily.) (Aside.) Well, of all the dashed cheek! I never had a woman say that to me yet. She must be a cool hand or else—Ah! that nursery-tea!

VOICE FROM THE UNKNOWN. Tchk! Tchk! Tchk!

CAPT. G. Good Gracious! What's that?

MISS T. The dog, I think. (Aside.) Emma has been listening, and I'll never forgive her!

CAPT. G. (Aside.) They don't keep dogs here. (Aloud.) Didn't sound like a dog, did it?

MISS T. Then it must have been the cat. Let's go into the veranda. What a lovely evening it is!

Steps into veranda and looks out across the hills into sunset. The Captain follows.

CAPT. G. (Aside.) Superb eyes! I wonder that I never noticed them before! (Aloud.) There's going to be a dance at Viceregal Lodge on Wednesday. Can you spare me one?

MISS T. (Shortly.) No! I don't want any of your charity-dances. You only ask me because Mamma told you to. I hop and I bump. You know I do!

CAPT. G. (Aside.) That's true, but little girls shouldn't understand these things. (Aloud.) No, on my word, I don't. You dance beautifully.

MISS T. Then why do you always stand out after half a dozen turns? I thought officers in the Army didn't tell fibs.

CAPT. G. It wasn't a fib, believe me. I really do want the pleasure of a dance with you.

MISS T. (Wickedly.) Why? Won't Mamma dance with you any more?

CAPT. G. (More earnestly than the necessity demands.) I wasn't thinking of your Mother. (Aside.) You little vixen!

MISS T. (Still looking out of the window.) Eh? Oh, I beg your pardon. I was thinking of something else.

CAPT. G. (Aside.) Well! I wonder what she'll say next. I've never known a woman treat me like this before. I might be—Dash it, I might be an Infantry subaltern! (Aloud.) Oh, please don't trouble. I'm not worth thinking about. Isn't your Mother ready yet?

MISS T. I should think so; but promise me, Captain Gadsby, you won't take poor dear Mamma twice round Jakko any more. It tires her so.

CAPT. G. She says that no exercise tires her.

MISS T. Yes, but she suffers afterwards. You don't know what rheumatism is, and you oughtn't to keep her out so late, when it gets chill in the evenings.

CAPT. G. (Aside.) Rheumatism! I thought she came off her horse rather in a bunch. Whew! One lives and learns. (Aloud.) I'm sorry to hear that. She hasn't mentioned it to me.

MISS T. (Flurried.) Of course not! Poor dear Mamma never would. And you mustn't say that I told you either. Promise me that you won't. Oh, Captain Gadsby, promise me you won't!

CAPT. G. I am dumb, or—I shall be as soon as you've given me that dance, and another—if you can trouble yourself to think about me for a minute.

MISS T. But you won't like it one little bit. You'll be awfully sorry afterwards.

CAPT. G. I shall like it above all things, and I shall only be sorry that I didn't get more. (Aside.) Now what in the world am I saying?

MISS T. Very well. You will have only yourself to thank if your toes are trodden on. Shall we say Seven?

CAPT. G. And Eleven. (Aside.) She can't be more than eight stone, but, even then, it's an absurdly small foot. (Looks at his own riding boots.)

MISS T. They're beautifully shiny. I can almost see my face in them.

CAPT. G. I was thinking whether I should have to go on crutches for the rest of my life if you trod on my toes.

MISS T. Very likely. Why not change Eleven for a square?

CAPT. G. No, please! I want them both waltzes. Won't you write them down?

MISS T. I don't get so many dances that I shall confuse them. You will be the offender.

CAPT. G. Wait and see! (Aside.) She doesn't dance perfectly, perhaps, but—

MISS T. Your tea must have got cold by this time. Won't you have another cup?

CAPT. G. No, thanks. Don't you think it's pleasanter out in the veranda? (Aside.) I never saw hair take that colour in the sunshine before. (Aloud.) It's like one of Dicksee's pictures.

MISS T. Yes! It's a wonderful sunset, isn't it? (Bluntly.) But what do you know about Dicksee's pictures?

CAPT. G. I go Home occasionally. And I used to know the Galleries. (Nervously.) You mustn't think me only a Philistine with—a moustache.

MISS T. Don't! Please don't! I'm so sorry for what I said then. I was horribly rude. It slipped out before I thought. Don't you know the temptation to say frightful and shocking things just for the mere sake of saying them? I'm afraid I gave way to it.

CAPT. G. (Watching the girl as she flushes.) I think I know the feeling. It would be terrible if we all yielded to it, wouldn't it? For instance, I might say—

POOR DEAR MAMMA. (Entering, habited, hatted, and booted.) Ah, Captain Gadsby! 'Sorry to keep you waiting. 'Hope you haven't been bored. 'My little girl been talking to you?

MISS T. (Aside.) I'm not sorry I spoke about the rheumatism. I'm not! I'm NOT! I only wish I'd mentioned the corns too.

CAPT. G. (Aside.) What a shame! I wonder how old she is. It never occurred to me before. (Aloud.) We've been discussing 'Shakespeare and the musical glasses' in the veranda.

MISS T. (Aside.) Nice man! He knows that quotation. He isn't a Philistine with a moustache. (Aloud.) Good-bye, Captain Gadsby. (Aside.) What a huge hand and what a squeeze! I don't suppose he meant it, but he has driven the rings into my fingers.

POOR DEAR MAMMA. Has Vermillion come round yet? Oh, yes! Captain Gadsby, don't you think that the saddle is too far forward? (They pass into the front veranda.)

CAPT. G. (Aside.) How the dickens should I know what she prefers? She told me that she doted on horses. (Aloud.) I think it is.

MISS T. (Coming out into front veranda.) Oh! Bad Buldoo! I must speak to him for this. He has taken up the curb two links, and Vermillion hates that. (Passes out and to horse's head.)

CAPT. G. Let me do it.

MISS T. No, Vermillion understands me. Don't you, old man? (Looses curb-chain skilfully, and pats horse on nose and throttle.) Poor Vermillion! Did they want to cut his chin off? There!

CAPTAIN GADSBY watches the interlude with undisguised admiration.

POOR DEAR MAMMA. (Tartly to MISS T.) You've forgotten your guest, I think, dear.

MISS T. Good gracious! So I have! Good-bye. (Retreats indoors hastily)

POOR DEAR MAMMA. (Bunching reins in fingers hampered by too tight gauntlets) Captain Gadsby!

CAPTAIN GADSBY stoops and makes the foot-rest.

POOR DEAR MAMMA blunders, halts too long, and breaks through it.

CAPT. G. (Aside.) Can't hold up eleven stone for ever. It's all your rheumatism. (Aloud.) Can't imagine why I was so clumsy. (Aside.) Now Little Featherweight would have gone up like a bird.

They ride out of the garden. The Captain falls back.

CAPT. G. (Aside.) How that habit catches her under the arms! Ugh!

POOR DEAR MAMMA. (With the worn smile of sixteen seasons, the worse for exchange.) You're dull this afternoon, Captain Gadsby.

CAPT. G. (Spurring up wearily.) Why did you keep me waiting so long?

Et caetera, et caetera, et caetera.

(AN INTERVAL OF THREE WEEKS.)
GILDED YOUTH. (Sitting on railings opposite Town Hall.) Hullo, Gaddy! 'Been trotting out the Gorgonzola! We all thought it was the Gorgon you're mashing.

CAPT. G. (With withering emphasis.) You young cub! What the—does it matter to you?

Proceeds to read GILDED YOUTH a lecture on discretion and deportment, which crumbles latter like a Chinese Lantern. Departs fuming.

(FURTHER INTERVAL OF FIVE WEEKS.)
SCENE.—Exterior of New Simla Library on a foggy evening. MISS THREEGAN and MISS DEERCOURT meet among the 'rickshaws. MISS T. is carrying a bundle of books under her left arm.

MISS D. (Level intonation.) Well?

MISS T. (Ascending intonation.) Well?

MISS D. (Capturing her friend's left arm, taking away all the books, placing books in 'rickshaw, returning to arm, securing hand by the third finger and investigating.) Well! You bad girl! And you never told me.

MISS T. (Demurely.) He—he—he only spoke yesterday afternoon.

MISS D. Bless you, dear! And I'm to be bridesmaid, aren't I? You know you promised ever so long ago.

MISS T. Of course. I'll tell you all about it to-morrow. (Gets into'rickshaw.) O Emma!

MISS D. (With intense interest.) Yes, dear?

MISS T. (Piano.) It's quite true—about—the—egg.

MISS D. What egg?

MISS T. (Pianissimo prestissimo.) The egg without the salt. (Forte.) Chalo ghar ko jaldi, jhampani! (Go home, jhampani.)

THE WORLD WITHOUT

Certain people of importance.

SCENE.—Smoking-room of the Deychi Club. Time, 10.30 P. M. of a stuffy night in the Rains. Four men dispersed in picturesque attitudes and easy-chairs. To these enter BLAYNE of the Irregular Moguls, in evening dress.

BLAYNE. Phew! The Judge ought to be hanged in his own store-godown. Hi, khitmatgar! Poora whiskey-peg, to take the taste out of my mouth.

CURTISS. (Royal Artillery.) That's it, is it? What the deuce made you dine at the Judge's? You know his bandobust.

BLAYNE. 'Thought it couldn't be worse than the Club; but I'll swear he buys ullaged liquor and doctors it with gin and ink (looking round the room). Is this all of you tonight?

DOONE. (P. W. D.) Anthony was called out at dinner. Mingle had a pain in his tummy.

CURTISS. Miggy dies of cholera once a week in the Rains, and gets drunk on chlorodyne in between. 'Good little chap, though. Any one at the Judge's, Blayne?

BLAYNE. Cockley and his memsahib looking awfully white and fagged. 'Female girl—couldn't catch the name—on her way to the Hills, under the Cockleys' charge—the Judge, and Markyn fresh from Simla—disgustingly fit.

CURTISS. Good Lord, how truly magnificent! Was there enough ice? When I mangled garbage there I got one whole lump—nearly as big as a walnut. What had Markyn to say for himself?

BLAYNE. 'Seems that every one is having a fairly good time up there in spite of the rain. By Jove, that reminds me! I know I hadn't come across just for the pleasure of your society. News! Great news! Markyn told me.

DOONE. Who's dead now?

BLAYNE. No one that I know of; but Gaddy's hooked at last!

DROPPING CHORUS. How much? The Devil! Markyn was pulling your leg. Not GADDY!

BLAYNE. (Humming.) 'Yea, verily, verily, verily! Verily, verily, I say unto thee.' Theodore, the gift o' God! Our Phillup! It's been given out up above.

MACKESY. (Barrister-at-Law.) Huh! Women will give out anything. What does accused say?

BLAYNE. Markyn told me that he congratulated him warily—one hand held out, t'other ready to guard. Gaddy turned pink and said it was so.

CURTISS. Poor old Gaddy! They all do it. Who's she? Let's hear the details.

BLAYNE. She's a girl—daughter of a Colonel Somebody.

DOONE. Simla's stiff with Colonels' daughters. Be more explicit.

BLAYNE. Wait a shake. What was her name? Three—something. Three—

CURTISS. Stars, perhaps. Gaddy knows that brand.

BLAYNE. Threegan—Minnie Threegan.

MACKESY. Threegan! Isn't she a little bit of a girl with red hair?

BLAYNE. 'Bout that—from what Markyn said.

MACKESY. Then I've met her. She was at Lucknow last season. 'Owned a permanently juvenile Mamma, and danced damnably. I say, Jervoise, you knew the Threegans, didn't you?

JERVOISE. (Civilian of twenty-five years' service, waking up from his doze.) Eh? What's that? Knew who? How? I thought I was at Home, confound you!

MACKESY. The Threegan girl's engaged, so Blayne says.

JERVOISE. (Slowly.) Engaged—engaged! Bless my soul! I'm getting an old man! Little Minnie Threegan engaged. It was only the other day I went home with them in the Surat—no, the Massilia—and she was crawling about on her hands and knees among the ayahs. 'Used to call me the 'Tick Tack Sahib' because I showed her my watch. And that was in Sixty-seven—no, Seventy. Good God, how time flies! I'm an old man. I remember when Threegan married Miss Derwent—daughter of old Hooky Derwent—but that was before your time. And so the little baby's engaged to have a little baby of her own! Who's the other fool?

MACKESY. Gadsby of the Pink Hussars.

JERVOISE. 'Never met him. Threegan lived in debt, married in debt, and'll die in debt. 'Must be glad to get the girl off his hands.

BLAYNE. Gaddy has money—lucky devil. Place at Home, too.

DOONE. He comes of first-class stock. 'Can't quite understand his being caught by a Colonel's daughter, and (looking cautiously round room) Black Infantry at that! No offence to you, Blayne.

BLAYNE. (Stiffly.) Not much, tha-anks.

CURTISS. (Quoting motto of Irregular Moguls.) 'We are what we are,' eh, old man? But Gaddy was such a superior animal as a rule. Why didn't he go Home and pick his wife there?

MACKESY. They are all alike when they come to the turn into the straight. About thirty a man begins to get sick of living alone—

CURTISS. And of the eternal muttony-chop in the morning.

DOONE. It's dead goat as a rule, but go on, Mackesy.

MACKESY. If a man's once taken that way nothing will hold him. Do you remember Benoit of your service, Doone? They transferred him to Tharanda when his time came, and he married a platelayer's daughter, or something of that kind. She was the only female about the place.

DOONE. Yes, poor brute. That smashed Benoit's chances of promotion altogether. Mrs. Benoit used to ask: 'Was you goin' to the dance this evenin'?'

CURTISS. Hang it all! Gaddy hasn't married beneath him. There's no tar-brush in the family, I suppose.

JERVOISE. Tar-brush! Not an anna. You young fellows talk as though the man was doing the girl an honour in marrying her. You're all too conceited—nothing's good enough for you.

BLAYNE. Not even an empty Club, a dam' bad dinner at the Judge's, and a Station as sickly as a hospital. You're quite right. We're a set of Sybarites.

DOONE. Luxurious dogs, wallowing in—

CURTISS. Prickly heat between the shoulders. I'm covered with it. Let's hope Beora will be cooler.

BLAYNE. Whew! Are you ordered into camp, too? I thought the Gunners had a clean sheet.

CURTISS. No, worse luck. Two cases yesterday—one died—and if we have a third, out we go. Is there any shooting at Beora, Doone?

DOONE. The country's under water, except the patch by the Grand Trunk Road. I was there yesterday, looking at a bund, and came across four poor devils in their last stage. It's rather bad from here to Kuchara.

CURTISS. Then we're pretty certain to have a heavy go of it. Heigho! I shouldn't mind changing places with Gaddy for a while. 'Sport with Amaryllis in the shade of the Town Hall, and all that. Oh, why doesn't somebody come and marry me, instead of letting me go into cholera camp?

MACKESY. Ask the Committee.

CURTISS. You ruffian! You'll stand me another peg for that. Blayne, what will you take? Mackesy is fine on moral grounds. Doone, have you any preference?

DOONE. Small glass Kummel, please. Excellent carminative, these days. Anthony told me so.

MACKESY. (Signing voucher for four drinks.) Most unfair punishment. I only thought of Curtiss as Actaeon being chivied round the billiard tables by the nymphs of Diana.

BLAYNE. Curtiss would have to import his nymphs by train. Mrs. Cockley's the only woman in the Station. She won't leave Cockley, and he's doing his best to get her to go.

CURTISS. Good, indeed! Here's Mrs. Cockley's health. To the only wife in the Station and a damned brave woman!

OMNES. (Drinking.) A damned brave woman!

BLAYNE. I suppose Gaddy will bring his wife here at the end of the cold weather. They are going to be married almost immediately, I believe.

CURTISS. Gaddy may thank his luck that the Pink Hussars are all detachment and no headquarters this hot weather, or he'd be torn from the arms of his love as sure as death. Have you ever noticed the thorough-minded way British Cavalry take to cholera? It's because they are so expensive. If the Pinks had stood fast here, they would have been out in camp a month ago. Yes, I should decidedly like to be Gaddy.

MACKESY. He'll go Home after he's married, and send in his papers—see if he doesn't.

BLAYNE. Why shouldn't he? Hasn't he money? Would any one of us be here if we weren't paupers?

DOONE. Poor old pauper! What has became of the six hundred you rooked from our table last month?

BLAYNE. It took unto itself wings. I think an enterprising tradesman got some of it, and a shroff gobbled the rest—or else I spent it.

CURTISS. Gaddy never had dealings with a shroff in his life.

DOONE. Virtuous Gaddy! If I had three thousand a month, paid from England, I don't think I'd deal with a shroff either.

MACKESY. (Yawning.) Oh, it's a sweet life! I wonder whether matrimony would make it sweeter.

CURTISS. Ask Cockley—with his wife dying by inches!

BLAYNE. Go home and get a fool of a girl to come out to—what is it Thackeray says?—'the splendid palace of an Indian pro-consul.'

DOONE. Which reminds me. My quarters leak like a sieve. I had fever last night from sleeping in a swamp. And the worst of it is, one can't do anything to a roof till the Rains are over.

CURTISS. What's wrong with you? You haven't eighty rotting Tommies to take into a running stream.

DOONE. No: but I'm mixed boils and bad language. I'm a regular Job all over my body. It's sheer poverty of blood, and I don't see any chance of getting richer—either way.

BLAYNE. Can't you take leave?

DOONE. That's the pull you Army men have over us. Ten days are nothing in your sight. I'm so important that Government can't find a substitute if I go away. Ye-es, I'd like to be Gaddy, whoever his wife may be.

CURTISS. You've passed the turn of life that Mackesy was speaking of.

DOONE. Indeed I have, but I never yet had the brutality to ask a woman to share my life out here.

BLAYNE. On my soul I believe you're right. I'm thinking of Mrs. Cockley. The woman's an absolute wreck.

DOONE. Exactly. Because she stays down here. The only way to keep her fit would be to send her to the Hills for eight months—and the same with any woman. I fancy I see myself taking a wife on those terms.

MACKESY. With the rupee at one and sixpence. The little Doones would be little Dehra Doones, with a fine Mussoorie chi-chi anent to bring home for the holidays.

CURTISS. And a pair of be-ewtiful sambhur-horns for Doone to wear, free of expense, presented by—

DOONE. Yes, it's an enchanting prospect. By the way, the rupee hasn't done falling yet. The time will come when we shall think ourselves lucky if we only lose half our pay.

CURTISS. Surely a third's loss enough. Who gains by the arrangement? That's what I want to know.

BLAYNE. The Silver Question! I'm going to bed if you begin squabbling. Thank Goodness, here's Anthony—looking like a ghost.

Enter ANTHONY, Indian Medical Staff, very white and tired.

ANTHONY. 'Evening, Blayne. It's raining in sheets. Whiskey-peg, lao, Khitmatgar. The roads are something ghastly.

CURTISS. How's Mingle?

ANTHONY. Very bad, and more frightened. I handed him over to Fewton. Mingle might just as well have called him in the first place, instead of bothering me.

BLAYNE. He's a nervous little chap. What has he got, this time?

ANTHONY. 'Can't quite say. A very bad tummy and a blue funk so far. He asked me at once if it was cholera, and I told him not to be a fool. That soothed him.

CURTISS. Poor devil! The funk does half the business in a man of that build.

ANTHONY. (Lighting a cheroot.) I firmly believe the funk will kill him if he stays down. You know the amount of trouble he's been giving Fewton for the last three weeks. He's doing his very best to frighten himself into the grave.

GENERAL CHORUS. Poor little devil! Why doesn't he get away?

ANTHONY. 'Can't. He has his leave all right, but he's so dipped he can't take it, and I don't think his name on paper would raise four annas. That's in confidence, though.

MACKESY. All the Station knows it.

ANTHONY. 'I suppose I shall have to die here,' he said, squirming all across the bed. He's quite made up his mind to Kingdom Come. And I know he has nothing more than a wet-weather tummy if he could only keep a hand on himself.

BLAYNE. That's bad. That's very bad. Poor little Miggy. Good little chap, too. I say—

ANTHONY. What do you say?

BLAYNE. Well, look here—anyhow. If it's like that—as you say—I say fifty.

CURTISS. I say fifty.

MACKESY. I go twenty better.

DOONE. Bloated Croesus of the Bar! I say fifty. Jervoise, what do you say? Hi! Wake up!

JERVOISE. Eh? What's that? What's that?

CURTISS. We want a hundred rupees from you. You're a bachelor drawing a gigantic income, and there's a man in a hole.

JERVOISE. What man? Any one dead?

BLAYNE. No, but he'll die if you don't give the hundred. Here! Here's a peg-voucher. You can see what we've signed for, and Anthony's man will come round to-morrow to collect it. So there will be no trouble.

JERVOISE. (Signing.) One hundred, E. M. J. There you are (feebly). It isn't one of your jokes, is it?

BLAYNE. No, it really is wanted. Anthony, you were the biggest poker-winner last week, and you've defrauded the tax-collector too long. Sign!

ANTHONY. Let's see. Three fifties and a seventy—two twenty—three twenty—say four hundred and twenty. That'll give him a month clear at the Hills. Many thanks, you men. I'll send round the chaprassi tomorrow.

CURTISS. You must engineer his taking the stuff, and of course you mustn't—

ANTHONY. Of course. It would never do. He'd weep with gratitude over his evening drink.

BLAYNE. That's just what he would do, damn him. Oh! I say, Anthony, you pretend to know everything. Have you heard about Gaddy?

ANTHONY. No. Divorce Court at last?

BLAYNE. Worse. He's engaged!

ANTHONY. How much? He can't be!

BLAYNE. He is. He's going to be married in a few weeks. Markyn told me at the Judge's this evening. It's pukka.

ANTHONY. You don't say so? Holy Moses! There'll be a shine in the tents of Kedar.

CURTISS. 'Regiment cut up rough, think you?

ANTHONY. 'Don't know anything about the Regiment.

MACKESY. It is bigamy, then?

ANTHONY. Maybe. Do you mean to say that you men have forgotten, or is there more charity in the world than I thought?

DOONE. You don't look pretty when you are trying to keep a secret. You bloat. Explain.

ANTHONY. Mrs. Herriott!

BLAYNE. (After a long pause, to the room generally.) It's my notion that we are a set of fools.

MACKESY. Nonsense. That business was knocked on the head last season. Why, young Mallard—

ANTHONY. Mallard was a candlestick, paraded as such. Think awhile. Recollect last season and the talk then. Mallard or no Mallard, did Gaddy ever talk to any other woman?

CURTISS. There's something in that. It was slightly noticeable now you come to mention it. But she's at Naini Tal and he's at Simla.

ANTHONY. He had to go to Simla to look after a globetrotter relative of his—a person with a title. Uncle or aunt.

BLAYNE. And there he got engaged. No law prevents a man growing tired of a woman.

ANTHONY. Except that he mustn't do it till the woman is tired of him. And the Herriott woman was not that.

CURTISS. She may be now. Two months of Naini Tal work wonders.

DOONE. Curious thing how some women carry a Fate with them. There was a Mrs. Deegie in the Central Provinces whose men invariably fell away and got married. It became a regular proverb with us when I was down there. I remember three men desperately devoted to her, and they all, one after another, took wives.

CURTISS. That's odd. Now I should have thought that Mrs. Deegie's influence would have led them to take other men's wives. It ought to have made them afraid of the judgment of Providence.

ANTHONY. Mrs. Herriott will make Gaddy afraid of something more than the judgment of Providence, I fancy.

BLAYNE. Supposing things are as you say, he'll be a fool to face her. He'll sit tight at Simla.

ANTHONY. 'Shouldn't be a bit surprised if he went off to Naini to explain. He's an unaccountable sort of man, and she's likely to be a more than unaccountable woman.

DOONE. What makes you take her character away so confidently?

ANTHONY. Primum tempus. Gaddy was her first, and a woman doesn't allow her first man to drop away without expostulation. She justifies the first transfer of affection to herself by swearing that it is for ever and ever. Consequently—

BLAYNE. Consequently, we are sitting here till past one o'clock, talking scandal like a set of Station cats. Anthony, it's all your fault. We were perfectly respectable till you came in. Go to bed. I'm off. Good-night all.

CURTISS. Past one! It's past two, by Jove, and here's the khit coming for the late charge. Just Heavens! One, two, three, four, five rupees to pay for the pleasure of saying that a poor little beast of a woman is no better than she should be. I'm ashamed of myself. Go to bed, you slanderous villains, and if I'm sent to Beora to-morrow, be prepared to hear I'm dead before paying my card account!

THE TENTS OF KEDAR

Only why should it be with pain at all,
Why must I 'twixt the leaves of coronal
Put any kiss of pardon on thy brow?
Why should the other women know so much,
And talk together:—Such the look and such

The smile he used to love with, then as now.
Any Wife to any Husband.

SCENE.-A Naini Tal dinner for thirty-four. Plate, wines, crockery, and khitmatgars carefully calculated to scale of Rs. 6000 per mensem, less Exchange. Table split lengthways by bank of flowers.

MRS. HERRIOTT. (After conversation has risen to proper pitch.) Ah! 'Didn't see you in the crush in the drawing-room. (Sotto voce.) Where have you been all this while, Pip?

CAPTAIN GADSBY. (Turning from regularly ordained dinner partner and settling hock glasses.) Good evening. (Sotto voce.) Not quite so loud another time. You've no notion how your voice carries. (Aside.) So much for shirking the written explanation. It'll have to be a verbal one now. Sweet prospect! How on earth am I to tell her that I am a respectable, engaged member of society and it's all over between us?

MRS. H. I've a heavy score against you. Where were you at the Monday Pop? Where were you on Tuesday? Where were you at the Lamonts' tennis? I was looking everywhere.

CAPT. G. For me! Oh, I was alive somewhere, I suppose. (Aside.) It's for Minnie's sake, but it's going to be dashed unpleasant.

MRS. H. Have I done anything to offend you? I never meant it if I have. I couldn't help going for a ride with the Vaynor man. It was promised a week before you came up.

CAPT. G. I didn't know—

MRS. H. It really was.

CAPT. G. Anything about it, I mean.

MRS. H. What has upset you to-day? All these days? You haven't been near me for four whole days— nearly one hundred hours. Was it kind of you, Pip? And I've been looking forward so much to your coming.

CAPT. G. Have you?

MRS. H. You know I have! I've been as foolish as a schoolgirl about it. I made a little calendar and put it in my card-case, and every time the twelve o'clock gun went off I scratched out a square and said: 'That brings me nearer to Pip. My Pip!'

CAPT. G. (With an uneasy laugh.) What will Mackler think if you neglect him so?

MRS. H. And it hasn't brought you nearer. You seem farther away than ever. Are you sulking about something? I know your temper.

CAPT. G. No.

MRS. H. Have I grown old in the last few months, then? (Reaches forward to bank of flowers for menu-card.)

MRS. H. (To partner.) Oh, thanks. I didn't see.

MRS. H. Keeps her arm at full stretch for three seconds.

PARTNER ON LEFT. Allow me. (Hands menu-card.) (Turns right again.) Is anything in me changed at all?

CAPT. G. For Goodness' sake go on with your dinner! You must eat something. Try one of those cutlet arrangements. (Aside.) And I fancied she had good shoulders, once upon a time! What an ass a man can make of himself!

MRS. H. (Helping herself to a paper frill, seven peas, some stamped carrots and a spoonful of gravy.) That isn't an answer. Tell me whether I have done anything.

CAPT. G. (Aside.) If it isn't ended here there will be a ghastly scene somewhere else. If only I'd written to her and stood the racket—at long range! (To Khitmatgar.) Han! Simpkin do. (Aloud.) I'll tell you later on.

MRS. H. Tell me now. It must be some foolish misunderstanding, and you know that there was to be nothing of that sort between us. We, of all people in the world, can't afford it. Is it the Vaynor man, and don't you like to say so? On my honour—

CAPT. G. I haven't given the Vaynor man a thought.

MRS. H. But how d'you know that I haven't?

CAPT. G. (Aside.) Here's my chance and may the Devil help me through with it. (Aloud and measuredly.) Believe me, I do not care how often or how tenderly you think of the Vaynor man.

MRS. H. I wonder if you mean that.—Oh, what is the good of squabbling and pretending to misunderstand when you are only up for so short a time? Pip, don't be a stupid!

Follows a pause, during which he crosses his left leg over his right and continues his dinner.

CAPT. G. (In answer to the thunderstorm in her eyes.) Corns—my worst.

MRS. H. Upon my word, you are the very rudest man in the world! I'll never do it again.

CAPT. G. (Aside.) No, I don't think you will; but I wonder what you will do before it's all over. (To Khitmatgar.) Thorah ur Simpkin do.

MRS. H. Well! Haven't you the grace to apologise, bad man?

CAPT. G. (Aside.) I mustn't let it drift back now. Trust a woman for being as blind as a bat when she won't see.

MRS. H. I'm waiting: or would you like me to dictate a form of apology?

CAPT. G. (Desperately.) By all means dictate.

MRS. H. (Lightly.) Very well. Rehearse your several Christian names after me and go on: 'Profess my sincere repentance.'

CAPT. G. 'Sincere repentance.'

MRS. H. 'For having behaved—'

CAPT. G. (Aside.) At last! I wish to Goodness she'd look away. 'For having behaved'—as I have behaved, and declare that I am thoroughly and heartily sick of the whole business, and take this opportunity of making clear my intention of ending it, now, henceforward, and for ever. (Aside.) If any one had told me I should be such a blackguard—!

MRS. H. (Shaking a spoonful of potato chips into her plate.) That's not a pretty joke.

CAPT. G. No. It's a reality. (Aside.) I wonder if smashes of this kind are always so raw.

MRS. H. Really, Pip, you're getting more absurd every day.

CAPT. G. I don't think you quite understand me. Shall I repeat it?

MRS. H. No! For pity's sake don't do that. It's too terrible, even in fun.

CAPT. G. I'll let her think it over for a while. But I ought to be horse-whipped.

MRS. H. I want to know what you meant by what you said just now.

CAPT. G. Exactly what I said. No less.

MRS. H. But what have I done to deserve it? What have I done?

CAPT. G. (Aside.) If she only wouldn't look at me. (Aloud and very slowly, his eyes on his plate.) D'you remember that evening in July, before the Rains broke, when you said that the end would have to come sooner or later—and you wondered for which of us it would come first?

MRS. H. Yes! I was only joking. And you swore that, as long as there was breath in your body, it should never come. And I believed you.

CAPT. G. (Fingering menu-card) Well, it has. That's all.

A long pause, during which MRS. H. bows her head and rolls the bread-twist into little pellets: G. stares at the oleanders.

MRS. H. (Throwing back her head and laughing naturally.) They train us women well, don't they, Pip?

CAPT. G. (Brutally, touching shirt-stud.) So far as the expression goes. (Aside.) It isn't in her nature to take things quietly. There'll be an explosion yet.

MRS. H. (With a shudder.) Thank you. B-but even Red Indians allow people to wriggle when they're being tortured, I believe. (Slips fan from girdle and fans slowly: rim of fan level with chin.)

PARTNER ON LEFT. Very close to-night, isn't it? 'You find it too much for you?

MRS. H. Oh, no, not in the least. But they really ought to have punkahs, even in your cool Naini Tal, oughtn't they? (Turns, dropping fan and raising eyebrows.)

CAPT. G. It's all right. (Aside.) Here comes the storm!

MRS. H. (Her eyes on the tablecloth: fan ready in right hand.) It was very cleverly managed, Pip, and I congratulate you. You swore—you never contented yourself with merely saying a thing—you swore that, as far as lay in your power, you'd make my wretched life pleasant for me. And you've denied me the consolation of breaking down. I should have done it—indeed I should. A woman would hardly have thought of this refinement, my kind, considerate friend. (Fan-guard as before.) You have explained things so tenderly and truthfully, too! You haven't spoken or written a word of warning, and you have let me believe in you till the last minute. You haven't condescended to give me your reason yet. No! A woman could not have managed it half so well. Are there many men like you in the world?

CAPT. G. I'm sure I don't know. (To Khitmatgar.) Ohe! Simpkin do.

MRS. H. You call yourself a man of the world, don't you? Do men of the world behave like Devils when they do a woman the honour to get tired of her?

CAPT. G. I'm sure I don't know. Don't speak so loud!

MRS. H. Keep us respectable, O Lord, whatever happens! Don't be afraid of my compromising you. You've chosen your ground far too well, and I've been properly brought up. (Lowering fan.) Haven't you any pity, Pip, except for yourself?

CAPT. G. Wouldn't it be rather impertinent of me to say that I'm sorry for you?

MRS. H. I think you have said it once or twice before. You're growing very careful of my feelings. My God, Pip, I was a good woman once! You said I was. You've made me what I am. What are you going to do with me? What are you going to do with me? Won't you say that you are sorry? (Helps herself to iced asparagus.)

CAPT. G. I am sorry for you, if you want the pity of such a brute as I am. I'm awf'ly sorry for you.

MRS. H. Rather tame for a man of the world. Do you think that that admission clears you?

CAPT. G. What can I do? I can only tell you what I think of myself. You can't think worse than that?

MRS. H. Oh, yes, I can! And now, will you tell me the reason of all this? Remorse? Has Bayard been suddenly conscience-stricken?

CAPT. G. (Angrily, his eyes still lowered.) No! The thing has come to an end on my side. That's all. Mafisch!

MRS. H. 'That's all. Mafisch!' As though I were a Cairene Dragoman. You used to make prettier speeches. D'you remember when you said—?

CAPT. G. For Heaven's sake don't bring that back! Call me anything you like and I'll admit it—

MRS. H. But you don't care to be reminded of old lies? If I could hope to hurt you one-tenth as much as you have hurt me to-night—No, I wouldn't—I couldn't do it—liar though you are.

CAPT. G. I've spoken the truth.

MRS. H. My dear Sir, you flatter yourself. You have lied over the reason. Pip, remember that I know you as you don't know yourself. You have been everything to me, though you are—(Fan-guard.) Oh, what a contemptible Thing it is! And so you are merely tired of me?

CAPT. G. Since you insist upon my repeating it—Yes.

MRS. H. Lie the first. I wish I knew a coarser word. Lie seems so ineffectual in your case. The fire has just died out and there is no fresh one? Think for a minute, Pip, if you care whether I despise you more than I do. Simply Mafisch, is it?

CAPT. G. Yes. (Aside.) I think I deserve this.

MRS. H. Lie number two. Before the next glass chokes you, tell me her name.

CAPT. G. (Aside.). I'll make her pay for dragging Minnie into the business! (Aloud.) Is it likely?

MRS. H. Very likely if you thought that it would flatter your vanity. You'd cry my name on the house-tops to make people turn round.

CAPT. G. I wish I had. There would have been an end of this business.

MRS. H. Oh, no, there would not—And so you were going to be virtuous and blase, were you? To come to me and say: 'I've done with you. The incident is clo-osed.' I ought to be proud of having kept such a man so long.

CAPT. G. (Aside.) It only remains to pray for the end of the dinner. (Aloud.) You know what I think of myself.

MRS. H. As it's the only person in the world you ever do think of, and as I know your mind thoroughly, I do. You want to get it all over and—Oh, I can't keep you back! And you're going—think of it, Pip—to throw me over for another woman. And you swore that all other women were—Pip, my Pip! She can't care for you as I do. Believe me, she can't! Is it any one that I know?

CAPT. G. Thank Goodness it isn't. (Aside.) I expected a cyclone, but not an earthquake.

MRS. H. She can't! Is there anything that I wouldn't do for you—or haven't done? And to think that I should take this trouble over you, knowing what you are! Do you despise me for it?

CAPT. G. (Wiping his mouth to hide a smile.) Again? It's entirely a work of charity on your part.

MRS. H. Ahhh! But I have no right to resent it.—Is she better-looking than I? Who was it said—?

CAPT G. No—not that!

MRS. H. I'll be more merciful than you were. Don't you know that all women are alike?

CAPT. G. (Aside.) Then this is the exception that proves the rule.

MRS. H. All of them! I'll tell you anything you like. I will, upon my word! They only want the admiration— from anybody—no matter who—anybody! But there is always one man that they care for more than any one else in the world, and would sacrifice all the others to. Oh, do listen! I've kept the Vaynor man trotting after me like a poodle, and he believes that he is the only man I am interested in. I'll tell you what he said to me.

CAPT. G. Spare him. (Aside.) I wonder what his version is.

MRS. H. He's been waiting for me to look at him all through dinner. Shall I do it, and you can see what an idiot he looks?

CAPT. G. 'But what imports the nomination of this gentleman?'

MRS. H. Watch! (Sends a glance to the Vaynor man, who tries vainly to combine a mouthful of ice pudding, a smirk of self-satisfaction, a glare of intense devotion, and the stolidity of a British dining countenance.)

CAPT. G. (Critically.) He doesn't look pretty. Why didn't you wait till the spoon was out of his mouth?

MRS. H. To amuse you. She'll make an exhibition of you as I've made of him; and people will laugh at you. Oh, Pip, can't you see that? It's as plain as the noonday sun. You'll be trotted about and told lies, and made a fool of like the others. I never made a fool of you, did I?

CAPT. G. (Aside.) What a clever little woman it is!

MRS. H. Well, what have you to say?

CAPT. G. I feel better.

MRS. H. Yes, I suppose so, after I have come down to your level. I couldn't have done it if I hadn't cared for you so much. I have spoken the truth.

CAPT. G. It doesn't alter the situation.

MRS. H. (Passionately.) Then she has said that she cares for you! Don't believe her, Pip. It's a lie—as bad as yours to me!

CAPT. G. Ssssteady! I've a notion that a friend of yours is looking at you.

MRS. H. He! I hate him. He introduced you to me.

CAPT. G. (Aside.) And some people would like women to assist in making the laws. Introduction to imply condonement. (Aloud.) Well, you see, if you can remember so far back as that, I couldn't, in common politeness, refuse the offer.

MRS. H. In common politeness! We have got beyond that!

CAPT. G. (Aside.) Old ground means fresh trouble, (Aloud.) On my honour—

MRS. H. Your what? Ha, ha!

CAPT. G. Dishonour, then. She's not what you imagine. I meant to—

MRS. H. Don't tell me anything about her! She won't care for you, and when you come back, after having made an exhibition of yourself, you'll fine me occupied with—

CAPT. G. (Insolently.) You couldn't while I am alive. (Aside.) If that doesn't bring her pride to her rescue, nothing will.

MRS. H. (Drawing herself up). Couldn't do it? I? (Softening.) You're right. I don't believe I could—though you are what you are—a coward and a liar in grain.

CAPT. G. It doesn't hurt so much after your little lecture—with demonstrations.

MRS. H. One mass of vanity! Will nothing ever touch you in this life? There must be a Hereafter if it's only for the benefit of—But you will have it all to yourself.

CAPT. G. (Under his eyebrows.) Are you so certain of that?

MRS. H. I shall have had mine in this life; and it will serve me right.

CAPT. G. But the admiration that you insisted on so strongly a moment ago? (Aside.) Oh, I am a brute!

MRS. H. (Fiercely.) Will that console me for knowing that you will go to her with the same words, the same arguments, and the—the same pet names you used to me? And if she cares for you, you two will laugh over my story. Won't that be punishment heavy enough even for me—even for me?—And it's all useless. That's another punishment.

CAPT. G. (Feebly.) Oh, come! I'm not so low as you think.

MRS. H. Not now, perhaps, but you will be. Oh, Pip, if a woman flatters your vanity, there's nothing on earth that you would not tell her; and no meanness that you would not do. Have I known you so long without knowing that?

CAPT. G. If you can trust me in nothing else—and I don't see why I should be trusted—you can count upon my holding my tongue.

MRS. H. If you denied everything you've said this evening and declared it was all in fun (a long pause), I'd trust you. Not otherwise. All I ask is, don't tell her my name. Please don't. A man might forget: a woman never would. (Looks up table and sees hostess beginning to collect eyes.) So it's all ended, through no fault of mine—Haven't I behaved beautifully? I've accepted your dismissal, and you managed it as cruelly as you could, and I have made you respect my sex, haven't I? (Arranging gloves and fan.) I only pray that she'll know you some day as I know you now. I wouldn't be you then, for I think even your conceit will be hurt. I hope she'll pay you back the humiliation you've brought on me. I hope—No. I don't. I can't give you up! I must have something to look forward to or I shall go crazy. When it's all over, come back to me, come back to me, and you'll find that you're my Pip still!

CAPT. G. (Very clearly.) 'False move, and you pay for it. It's a girl!

MRS. H. (Rising.) Then it was true! They said—but I wouldn't insult you by asking. A girl! I was a girl not very long ago. Be good to her, Pip. I daresay she believes in you.

Goes out with an uncertain smile. He watches her through the door, and settles into a chair as the men redistribute themselves.

CAPT. G. Now, if there is any Power who looks after this world, will He kindly tell me what I have done? (Reaching out for the claret, and half aloud.) What have I done?

WITH ANY AMAZEMENT

And are not afraid with any amazement.—Marriage service.

SCENE.—A bachelor's bedroom—toilet-table arranged with unnatural neatness. CAPTAIN GADSBY asleep and snoring heavily. Time, 10.30 A. M.—a glorious autumn day at Simla. Enter delicately CAPTAIN MAFFLIM of GADSBY'S regiment. Looks at sleeper, and shakes his head murmuring 'Poor Gaddy.' Performs violent fantasia with hair-brushes on chair-back.

CAPT. M. Wake up, my sleeping beauty! (Roars.)

'Uprouse ye, then, my merry merry men!
It is our opening day!
It is our opening da-ay!'

Gaddy, the little dicky-birds have been billing and cooing for ever so long; and I'm here!

CAPT. G. (Sitting up and yawning.) 'Mornin'. This is awf'ly good of you, old fellow. Most awf'ly good of you. 'Don't know what I should do without you. On my soul, I don't. 'Haven't slept a wink all night.

CAPT. M. I didn't get in till half-past eleven. 'Had a look at you then, and you seemed to be sleeping as soundly as a condemned criminal.

CAPT. G. Jack, if you want to make those disgustingly worn-out jokes, you'd better go away. (With portentous gravity.) It's the happiest day in my life.

CAPT. M. (Chuckling grimly.) Not by a very long chalk, my son. You're going through some of the most refined torture you've ever known. But be calm. I am with you. 'Shun! Dress!

CAPT. G. Eh! Wha-at?

CAPT. M. DO you suppose that you are your own master for the next twelve hours? If you do, of course—(Makes for the door.)

CAPT. G. No! For Goodness' sake, old man, don't do that! You'll see me through, won't you? I've been mugging up that beastly drill, and can't remember a line of it.

CAPT. M. (Overhauling G's uniform.) Go and tub. Don't bother me. I'll give you ten minutes to dress in.

Interval, filled by the noise as of one splashing in the bath-room.

CAPT. G. (Emerging from dressing-room.) What time is it?

CAPT. M. Nearly eleven.

CAPT. G. Five hours more. O Lord!

CAPT. M. (Aside.) 'First sign of funk, that. 'Wonder if it's going to spread. (Aloud.) Come along to breakfast.

CAPT. G. I can't eat anything. I don't want any breakfast.

CAPT. M. (Aside.) So early! (Aloud.) Captain Gadsby, I order you to eat breakfast, and a dashed good breakfast, too. None of your bridal airs and graces with me!

Leads G. downstairs, and stands over him while he eats two chops.

CAPT. G. (Who has looked at his watch thrice in the last five minutes.) What time is it?

CAPT. M. Time to come for a walk. Light up.

CAPT. G. I haven't smoked for ten days, and I won't now. (Takes cheroot which M. has cut for him, and blows smoke through his nose luxuriously.) We aren't going down the Mall, are we?

CAPT. M. (Aside.) They're all alike in these stages. (Aloud.) No, my Vestal. We're going along the quietest road we can find.

CAPT. G. Any chance of seeing Her?

CAPT. M. Innocent! No! Come along, and, if you want me for the final obsequies, don't cut my eye out with your stick.

CAPT. G. (Spinning round.) I say, isn't She the dearest creature that ever walked? What's the time? What comes after 'wilt thou take this woman'?

CAPT. M, You go for the ring. R'clect it'll be on the top of my right-hand little ringer, and just be careful how you draw it off, because I shall have the Verger's fees somewhere in my glove.

CAPT. G. (Walking forward hastily.) D—the Verger! Come along! It's past twelve and I haven't seen Her since yesterday evening. (Spinning round again.) She's an absolute angel, Jack, and She's a dashed deal too good for me. Look here, does She come up the aisle on my arm, or how?

CAPT. M. If I thought that there was the least chance of your remembering anything for two consecutive minutes, I'd tell you. Stop passaging about like that!

CAPT. G. (Halting in the middle of the road.) I say, Jack.

CAPT. M. Keep quiet for another ten minutes if you can, you lunatic; and walk!

The two tramp at five miles an hour for fifteen minutes.

CAPT. G. What's the time? How about that cursed wedding-cake and the slippers? They don't throw 'em about in church, do they?

CAPT. M. In-variably. The Padre leads off with his boots.

CAPT. G. Confound your silly soul! Don't make fun of me. I can't stand it, and I won't!

CAPT. M. (Untroubled.) So-ooo, old horse! You'll have to sleep for a couple of hours this afternoon.

CAPT. G. (Spinning round) I'm not going to be treated like a dashed child. Understand that!

CAPT. M. (Aside) Nerves gone to fiddle-strings. What a day we're having! (Tenderly putting his hand on G's. shoulder) My David, how long have you known this Jonathan? Would I come up here to make a fool of you-after all these years?

CAPT. G. (Penitently.) I know, I know, Jack—but I'm as upset as I can be. Don't mind what I say. Just hear me run through the drill and see if I've got it all right:—

'To have and to hold for better or worse, as it was in the beginning, is now, and ever shall be, world without end, so help me God. Amen.'

CAPT. M. (Suffocating with suppressed laughter) Yes. That's about the gist of it. I'll prompt if you get into a hat.

CAPT. G. (Earnestly) Yes, you'll stick by me, Jack, won't you? I'm awf'ly happy, but I don't mind telling YOU that I'm in a blue funk!

CAPT. M. (Gravely) Are you? I should never have noticed it. You don't LOOK like it.

CAPT. G. Don't I? That's all right. (Spinning round.) On my soul and honour, Jack, She's the sweetest little angel that ever came down from the sky. There isn't a woman on earth fit to speak to Her.

CAPT. M. (Aside.) And this is old Gaddy! (Aloud.) Go on if it relieves you.

CAPT. G. You can laugh! That's all you wild asses of bachelors are fit for.

CAPT. M. (Drawling.) You never WOULD wait for the troop to come up. You aren't quite married yet, y' know.

CAPT. G. Ugh! That reminds me. I don't believe I shall be able to get into my boots. Let's go home and try 'em on! (Hurries forward.)

CAPT. M. 'Wouldn't be in your shoes for anything that Asia has to offer.

CAPT. G. (Spinning round.) That just shows your hideous blackness of soul-your dense stupidity-your brutal narrow-mindedness. There's only one fault about you. You're the best of good fellows, and I don't know what I should have done without you, but-you aren't married. (Wags his head gravely.) Take a wife, Jack.

CAPT. M. (With a face like a wall.) Ya-as. Whose for choice?

CAPT. G. If you're going to be a blackguard, I'm going on—What's the time?

CAPT. M. (Hums.)—'An' since 'twas very clear we drank only ginger-beer,
Faith, there must ha'been some stingo in the ginger.'
Come back, you maniac. I'm going to take you home, and you're going to lie down.

CAPT. G. What on earth do I want to lie down for?

CAPT. M. Give me a light from your cheroot and see.

CAPT. G. (Watching cheroot-butt quiver like a tuning-fork.) Sweet state I'm in!

CAPT. M. You are. I'll get you a peg and you'll go to sleep.

They return and M. compounds a four-finger peg.

CAPT. G. O bus! bus! It'll make me as drunk as an owl.

CAPT. M. Curious thing, 'twon't have the slightest effect on you. Drink it off, chuck yourself down there, and go to bye-bye.

CAPT. G. It's absurd. I shan't sleep. I know I shan't!

Falls into heavy doze at end of seven minutes. CAPT. M. watches him tenderly.

CAPT. M. Poor old Gaddy! I've seen a few turned off before, but never one who went to the gallows in this condition. 'Can't tell how it affects 'em, though. It's the thoroughbreds that sweat when they're backed into double-harness.-And that's the man who went through the guns at Amdheran like a devil possessed of devils. (Leans over G.) But this is worse than the guns, old pal—worse than the guns, isn't it? (G. turns in his sleep, and M. touches him clumsily on the forehead.) Poor, dear old Gaddy! Going like the rest of 'em-going like the rest of 'em—Friend that sticketh closer than a brother—eight years. Dashed bit of a slip of a girl-eight weeks! And-where's your friend? (Smokes disconsolately till church clock strikes three.)

CAPT. M. Up with you! Get into your kit.

CAPT. G. Already? Isn't it too soon? Hadn't I better have a shave?

CAPT. M. NO! You're all right. (Aside.) He'd chip his chin to pieces.

CAPT. G. What's the hurry?

CAPT. M. You've got to be there first.

CAPT. G. To be stared at?

CAPT. M. Exactly. You're part of the show. Where's the burnisher? Your spurs are in a shameful state.

CAPT. G. (Gruffly) Jack, I be damned if you shall do that for me.

CAPT. M. (More gruffly.) Dry up and get dressed! If I choose to clean your spurs, you're under my orders.

CAPT. G. dresses. M. follows suit.

CAPT. M. (Critically, walking round.) M'yes, you'll do. Only don't look so like a criminal. Ring, gloves, fees—that's all right for me. Let your moustache alone. Now, if the ponies are ready, we'll go.

CAPT. G. (Nervously.) It's much too soon. Let's light up! Let's have a peg! Let's—

CAPT. M. Let's make bally asses of ourselves!

BELLS. (Without.)—

'Good—peo—ple—all
To prayers—we call."

CAPT. M. There go the bells! Come on—unless you'd rather not. (They ride off.)

BELLS.—
'We honour the King
And Brides joy do bring—

Good tidings we tell,
And ring the Dead's knell.'

CAPT. G. (Dismounting at the door of the Church.) I say, aren't we much too soon? There are no end of people inside. I say, aren't we much too late? Stick by me, Jack! What the devil do I do?

CAPT. M. Strike an attitude at the head of the aisle and wait for Her. (G. groans as M. wheels him into position before three hundred eyes.)

CAPT. M. (Imploringly.) Gaddy, if you love me, for pity's sake, for the Honour of the Regiment, stand up! Chuck yourself into your uniform! Look like a man! I've got to speak to the Padre a minute. (G. breaks into a gentle perspiration.) If you wipe your face I'll never be your best man again. Stand up! (G. trembles visibly.)

CAPT. M. (Returning.) She's coming now. Look out when the music starts. There's the organ beginning to clack.

Bride steps out of 'rickshaw at Church door. G. catches a glimpse of her and takes heart.

ORGAN.—
'The Voice that breathed o'er Eden,
That earliest marriage day,
The primal marriage-blessing,
It hath not passed away.'

CAPT. M. (Watching G.) By Jove! He is looking well. 'Didn't think he had it in him.

CAPT. G. How long does this hymn go on for?

CAPT. M. It will be over directly. (Anxiously.) Beginning to bleach and gulp? Hold on, Gaddy, and think o' the Regiment.

CAPT. G. (Measuredly.) I say, there's a big brown lizard crawling up that wall.

CAPT. M. My Sainted Mother! The last stage of collapse!

Bride comes up to left of altar, lifts her eyes once to G. who is suddenly smitten mad.

CAPT. G. (To himself again and again.) Little Featherweight's a woman—a woman! And I thought she was a little girl.

CAPT. M. (In a whisper.) Form the halt—inward wheel.

CAPT. G. obeys mechanically and the ceremony proceeds.

PADRE. . . . only unto her as long as ye both shall live?

CAPT. G. (His throat useless.) Ha-hmmm!

CAPT. M. Say you will or you won't. There's no second deal here.

Bride gives response with perfect coolness, and is given away by the father.

CAPT. G. (Thinking to show his learning.) Jack, give me away now, quick!

CAPT. M. You're given yourself away quite enough. Her right hand, man! Repeat! Repeat! 'Theodore Philip.' Have you forgotten your own name?

CAPT. G. stumbles through Affirmation, which Bride repeats without a tremor.

CAPT. M. Now the ring! Follow the Padre! Don't pull off my glove! Here it is! Great Cupid, he's found his voice!

G. repeats Troth in a voice to be heard to the end of the Church and turns on his heel.

CAPT. M. (Desperately.) Rein back! Back to your troop! 'Tisn't half legal yet.

PADRE. . . . joined together let no man put asunder.

CAPT. G. paralysed with fear jibs after Blessing.

CAPT. M. (Quickly.) On your own front—one length. Take her with you. I don't come. You've nothing to say. (CAPT. G. jingles up to altar.)

CAPT. M. (In a piercing rattle meant to be a whisper.)
Kneel, you stiff-necked ruffian! Kneel!

PADRE. . . . whose daughters are ye so long as ye do well and are not afraid with any amazement.

CAPT. M. Dismiss! Break off! Left wheel!
All troop to vestry.

They sign.

CAPT. M. Kiss Her, Gaddy.

CAPT. G. (Rubbing the ink into his glove.) Eh! Wha—at?

CAPT. M. (Taking one pace to Bride.) If you don't, I shall.

CAPT. G. (Interposing an arm.) Not this journey!

General kissing, in which CAPT. G. is pursued by unknown female.

CAPT. G. (Faintly to M.) This is Hades! Can I wipe my face now?

CAPT. M. My responsibility has ended. Better ask Missis Gadsby.

CAPT. G. winces as though shot and procession is Mendelssohned out of Church to house, where usual tortures take place over the wedding-cake.

CAPT. M. (At table.) Up with you, Gaddy. They expect a speech.

CAPT. G. (After three minutes' agony.) Ha-hmmm. (Thunders of applause.)

CAPT. M. Doocid good, for a first attempt. Now go and change your kit while Mamma is weeping over— 'the Missus.' (CAPT. G. disappears. CAPT. M. starts up tearing his hair.) It's not half legal. Where are the shoes? Get an ayah.

AYAH. Missie Captain Sahib done gone band karo all the jutis.

CAPT. M. (Brandishing scabbarded sword.) Woman, produce those shoes! Some one lend me a bread-knife. We mustn't crack Gaddy's head more than it is. (Slices heel off white satin slipper and puts slipper up his sleeve.) Where is the Bride? (To the company at large.) Be tender with that rice. It's a heathen custom. Give me the big bag.

Bride slips out quietly into 'rickshaw and departs towards the sunset.

CAPT. M. (In the open.) Stole away, by Jove! So much, the worse for Gaddy! Here he is. Now Gaddy, this'll be livelier than Amdheran! Where's your horse?

CAPT. G. (Furiously, seeing that the women are out of earshot.) Where the—is my Wife?

CAPT. M. Half-way to Mahasu by this time. You'll have to ride like Young Lochinvar.

Horse comes round on his hind legs; refuses to let G. handle him.

CAPT. G. Oh you will, will you? Get round, you brute-you hog-you beast! Get round!

Wrenches horse's head over, nearly breaking lower jaw; swings himself into saddle, and sends home both spurs in the midst of a spattering gale of Best Patna.

CAPT. M. For your life and your love—ride, Gaddy!—And God bless you!

Throws half a pound of rice at G., who disappears, bowed forward on the saddle, in a cloud of sunlit dust.

CAPT. M. I've lost old Gaddy. (Lights cigarette and strolls off, singing absently):—
'You may carve it on his tombstone, you may cut it on his card,
That a young man married is a young man marred!'

MISS DEERCOURT. (From her horse.) Really, Captain Mafflin! You are more plain spoken than polite!

CAPT. M. (Aside.) They say marriage is like cholera. 'Wonder who'll be the next victim.

White satin slipper slides from his sleeve and falls at his feet. Left wondering.

THE GARDEN OF EDEN

And ye shall be as—Gods!

SCENE.—Thymy grass-plot at back of the Mahasu dak-bungalow, overlooking little wooded valley. On the left, glimpse of the Dead Forest of Fagoo; on the right, Simla Hills. In background, line of the Snows.

CAPTAIN GADSBY, now three weeks a husband, is smoking the pipe of peace on a rug in the sunshine. Banjo and tobacco-pouch on rug. Overhead the Fagoo eagles. MRS. G. comes out of bungalow.

MRS. G. My husband!

CAPT. G. (Lazily, with intense enjoyment.) Eh, wha-at? Say that again.

MRS. G. I've written to Mamma and told her that we shall be back on the 17th.

CAPT. G. Did you give her my love?

MRS. G. No, I kept all that for myself. (Sitting down by his side.) I thought you wouldn't mind.

CAPT. G. (With mock sternness.) I object awf'ly. How did you know that it was yours to keep?

MRS. G. I guessed, Phil.

CAPT. G. (Rapturously.) Lit-tle Featherweight!

MRS. G. I won't be called those sporting pet names, bad boy.

CAPT. G. You'll be called anything I choose. Has it ever occurred to you, Madam, that you are my Wife?

MRS. G. It has. I haven't ceased wondering at it yet.

CAPT. G. Nor I. It seems so strange; and yet, somehow, it doesn't. (Confidently.) You see, it could have been no one else.

MRS. G. (Softly.) No. No one else—for me or for you. It must have been all arranged from the beginning. Phil, tell me again what made you care for me.

CAPT. G. How could I help it? You were you, you know.

MRS. G. Did you ever want to help it? Speak the truth!

CAPT. G. (A twinkle in his eye.) I did, darling, just at the first. But only at the very first. (Chuckles.) I called you—stoop low and I'll whisper—'a little beast.' Ho! Ho! Ho!

MRS. G. (Taking him by the moustache and making him sit up.) 'A—little—beast!' Stop laughing over your crime! And yet you had the—the—awful cheek to propose to me!

CAPT. G. I'd changed my mind then. And you weren't a little beast any more.

MRS. G. Thank you, Sir! And when was I ever?

CAPT. G. Never! But that first day, when you gave me tea in that peach-coloured muslin gown thing, you looked—you did indeed, dear—such an absurd little mite. And I didn't know what to say to you.

MRS. G. (Twisting moustache.) So you said 'little beast.' Upon my word, Sir! I called you a 'Crrrreature,' but I wish now I had called you something worse.

CAPT. G. (Very meekly.) I apologise, but you're hurting me awf'ly. (Interlude.) You're welcome to torture me again on those terms.

MRS. G. Oh, why did you let me do it?

CAPT. G. (Looking across valley.) No reason in particular, but—if it amused you or did you any good— you might—wipe those dear little boots of yours on me.

MRS. G. (Stretching out her hands.) Don't! Oh, don't! Philip, my King, please don't talk like that. It's how I feel. You're so much too good for me. So much too good!

CAPT. G. Me! I'm not fit to put my arm round you. (Puts it round.)

MRS. G. Yes, you are. But I—what have I ever done?

CAPT. G. Given me a wee bit of your heart, haven't you, my Queen?

MRS. G. That's nothing. Any one would do that. They cou—couldn't help it.

CAPT. G. Pussy, you'll make me horribly conceited. Just when I was beginning to feel so humble, too.

MRS. G. Humble! I don't believe it's in your character.

CAPT. G. What do you know of my character, Impertinence?

MRS. G. Ah, but I shall, shan't I, Phil? I shall have time in all the years and years to come, to know everything about you; and there will be no secrets between us.

CAPT. G. Little witch! I believe you know me thoroughly already.

MRS. G. I think I can guess. You're selfish?

CAPT. G. Yes.

MRS. G. Foolish?

CAPT. G. Very.

MRS. G. And a dear?

CAPT. G. That is as my lady pleases.

MRS. G. Then your lady is pleased. (A pause.) D'you know that we're two solemn, serious, grown-up people—

CAPT. G. (Tilting her straw hat over her eyes.) You grown-up! Pooh! You're a baby.

MRS. G. And we're talking nonsense.

CAPT. G. Then let's go on talking nonsense. I rather like it. Pussy, I'll tell you a secret. Promise not to repeat?

MRS. G. Ye—es. Only to you.

CAPT. G. I love you.

MRS. G. Re-ally! For how long?

CAPT. G. For ever and ever.

MRS. G. That's a long time.

CAPT. G. 'Think so? It's the shortest I can do with.

MRS. G. You're getting quite clever.

CAPT. G. I'm talking to you.

MRS. G. Prettily turned. Hold up your stupid old head and I'll pay you for it!

CAPT. G. (Affecting supreme contempt.) Take it yourself if you want it.

MRS. G. I've a great mind to—and I will! (Takes it and is repaid with interest.)

CAPT. G. Little Featherweight, it's my opinion that we are a couple of idiots.

MRS. G. We're the only two sensible people in the world! Ask the eagle. He's coming by.

CAPT. G. Ah! I dare say he's seen a good many sensible people at Mahasu. They say that those birds live for ever so long.

MRS. G. How long?

CAPT. G. A hundred and twenty years.

MRS. G. A hundred and twenty years! O-oh! And in a hundred and twenty years where will these two sensible people be?

CAPT. G. What does it matter so long as we are together now?

MRS. G. (Looking round the horizon.) Yes. Only you and I—I and you—in the whole wide, wide world until the end. (Sees the line of the Snows.) How big and quiet the hills look! D'you think they care for us?

CAPT. G. 'Can't say I've consulted 'em particularly. I care, and that's enough for me.

MRS. G. (Drawing nearer to him.) Yes, now—but afterwards. What's that little black blur on the Snows?

CAPT. G. A snowstorm, forty miles away. You'll see it move, as the wind carries it across the face of that spur, and then it will be all gone.

MRS. G. And then it will be all gone. (Shivers.)

CAPT. G. (Anxiously.) 'Not chilled, pet, are you? 'Better let me get your cloak.

MRS. G. No. Don't leave me, Phil. Stay here. I believe I am afraid. Oh, why are the hills so horrid! Phil, promise me, promise me that you'll always love me.

CAPT. G. What's the trouble, darling? I can't promise any more than I have; but I'll promise that again and again if you like.

MRS. G. (Her head on his shoulder.) Say it, then—say it! N-no—don't! The—the—eagles would laugh. (Recovering.) My husband, you've married a little goose.

CAPT. G. (Very tenderly.) Have I? I am content whatever she is, so long as she is mine.

MRS. G. (Quickly.) Because she is yours or because she is me mineself?

CAPT. G. Because she is both. (Piteously.) I'm not clever, dear, and I don't think I can make myself understood properly.

MRS. G. I understand. Pip, will you tell me something?

CAPT. G. Anything you like. (Aside.) I wonder what's coming now.

MRS. G. (Haltingly, her eyes lowered.) You told me once in the old days—centuries and centuries ago— that you had been engaged before. I didn't say anything—then.

CAPT. G. (Innocently.) Why not?

MRS. G. (Raising her eyes to his.) Because—because I was afraid of losing you, my heart. But now—tell about it—please.

CAPT. G. There's nothing to tell. I was awf'ly old then—nearly two and twenty—and she was quite that.

MRS. G. That means she was older than you. I shouldn't like her to have been younger. Well?

CAPT. G. Well, I fancied myself in love and raved about a bit, and—oh, yes, by Jove! I made up poetry. Ha! Ha!

MRS. G. You never wrote any for me! What happened?

CAPT. G. I came out here, and the whole thing went phut. She wrote to say that there had been a mistake, and then she married.

MRS. G. Did she care for you much?

CAPT. G. No. At least she didn't show it as far as I remember.

MRS. G. As far as you remember! Do you remember her name? (Hears it and bows her head.) Thank you, my husband.

CAPT. G. Who but you had the right? Now, Little Featherweight, have you ever been mixed up in any dark and dismal tragedy?

MRS. G. If you call me Mrs. Gadsby, p'raps I'll tell.

CAPT. G. (Throwing Parade rasp into his voice.) Mrs. Gadsby, confess!

MRS. G. Good Heavens, Phil! I never knew that you could speak in that terrible voice.

CAPT. G. You don't know half my accomplishments yet. Wait till we are settled in the Plains, and I'll show you how I bark at my troop. You were going to say, darling?

MRS. G. I—I don't like to, after that voice. (Tremulously.) Phil, never you dare to speak to me in that tone, whatever I may do!

CAPT. G. My poor little love! Why, you're shaking all over. I am so sorry. Of course I never meant to upset you. Don't tell me anything. I'm a brute.

MRS. G. No, you aren't, and I will tell—There was a man.

CAPT. G. (Lightly.) Was there? Lucky man!

MRS. G. (In a whisper.) And I thought I cared for him.

CAPT. G. Still luckier man! Well?

MRS. G. And I thought I cared for him—and I didn't—and then you came—and I cared for you very, very much indeed. That's all. (Face hidden.) You aren't angry, are you?

CAPT. G. Angry? Not in the least. (Aside.) Good Lord, what have I done to deserve this angel?

MRS. G. (Aside.) And he never asked for the name! How funny men are! But perhaps it's as well.

CAPT. G. That man will go to heaven because you once thought you cared for him. 'Wonder if you'll ever drag me up there?

MRS. G. (Firmly.) 'Shan't go if you don't.

CAPT. G. Thanks. I say, Pussy, I don't know much about your religious beliefs. You were brought up to believe in a heaven and all that, weren't you?

MRS. G. Yes. But it was a pincushion heaven, with hymn-books in all the pews.

CAPT. G. (Wagging his head with intense conviction.) Never mind. There is a pukka heaven.

MRS. G. Where do you bring that message from, my prophet?

CAPT. G. Here! Because we care for each other. So it's all right.

MRS. G. (As a troop of langurs crash through the branches.) So it's all right. But Darwin says that we came from those!

CAPT. G. (Placidly.) Ah! Darwin was never in love with an angel. That settles it. Sstt, you brutes! Monkeys, indeed! You shouldn't read those books.

MRS. G. (Folding her hands.) If it pleases my Lord the King to issue proclamation.

CAPT. G. Don't, dear one. There are no orders between us. Only I'd rather you didn't. They lead to nothing, and bother people's heads.

MRS. G. Like your first engagement.

CAPT.G. (With an immense calm.) That was a necessary evil and led to you. Are you nothing?

MRS. G. Not so very much, am I?

CAPT. G. All this world and the next to me.

MRS. G. (Very softly.) My boy of boys! Shall I tell you something?

CAPT. G. Yes, if it's not dreadful—about other men.

MRS. G. It's about my own bad little self.

CAPT. G. Then it must be good. Go on, dear.

MRS. G. (Slowly.) I don't know why I'm telling you, Pip; but if ever you marry again—(Interlude.) Take your hand from my mouth or I'll bite! In the future, then remember—I don't know quite how to put it!

CAPT. G. (Snorting indignantly.) Don't try. 'Marry again,' indeed!

MRS. G. I must. Listen, my husband. Never, never, never tell your wife anything that you do not wish her to remember and think over all her life. Because a woman—yes, I am a woman—can't forget.

CAPT. G. By Jove, how do you know that?

MRS. G. (Confusedly.) I don't. I'm only guessing. I am—I was—a silly little girl; but I feel that I know so much, oh, so very much more than you, dearest. To begin with, I'm your wife.

CAPT. G. So I have been led to believe.

MRS. G. And I shall want to know every one of your secrets—to share everything you know with you. (Stares round desperately.)

CAPT. G. So you shall, dear, so you shall—but don't look like that.

MRS. G. For your own sake don't stop me, Phil. I shall never talk to you in this way again. You must not tell me! At least, not now. Later on, when I'm an old matron it won't matter, but if you love me, be very good to me now; for this part of my life I shall never forget! Have I made you understand?

CAPT. G. I think so, child. Have I said anything yet that you disapprove of?

MRS. G. Will you be very angry? That—that voice, and what you said about the engagement—

CAPT. G. But you asked to be told that, darling.

MRS. G. And that's why you shouldn't have told me! You must be the judge, and, oh, Pip, dearly as I love you, I shan't be able to help you! I shall hinder you, and you must judge in spite of me!

CAPT. G. (Meditatively.) We have a great many things to find out together, God help us both—say so, Pussy—but we shall understand each other better every day; and I think I'm beginning to see now. How in the world did you come to know just the importance of giving me just that lead?

MRS. G. I've told you that I don't know. Only somehow it seemed that, in all this new life, I was being guided for your sake as well as my own.

CAPT. G. (Aside.) Then Mafflin was right! They know, and we—we're blind—all of us. (Lightly.) 'Getting a little beyond our depth, dear, aren't we? I'll remember, and, if I fail, let me be punished as I deserve.

MRS. G. There shall be no punishment. We'll start into life together from here—you and I—and no one else.

CAPT. G. And no one else. (A pause.) Your eyelashes are all wet, Sweet? Was there ever such a quaint little Absurdity?

MRS. G. Was there ever such nonsense talked before?

CAPT. G. (Knocking the ashes out of his pipe.) 'Tisn't what we say, it's what we don't say, that helps. And it's all the profoundest philosophy. But no one would understand—even if it were put into a book.

MRS. G. The idea! No—only we ourselves, or people like ourselves—if there are any people like us.

CAPT. G. (Magisterially.) All people, not like ourselves, are blind idiots.

MRS. G. (Wiping her eyes.) Do you think, then, that there are any people as happy as we are?

CAPT. G. 'Must be—unless we've appropriated all the happiness in the world.

MRS. G. (Looking towards Simla.) Poor dears! Just fancy if we have!

CAPT. G. Then we'll hang on to the whole show, for it's a great deal too jolly to lose—eh, wife o' mine?

MRS. G. O Pip! Pip! How much of you is a solemn, married man and how much a horrid, slangy schoolboy?

CAPT. G. When you tell me how much of you was eighteen last birthday and how much is as old as the Sphinx and twice as mysterious, perhaps I'll attend to you. Lend me that banjo. The spirit moveth me to yowl at the sunset.

MRS. G. Mind! It's not tuned. Ah! How that jars.

CAPT. G. (Turning pegs.) It's amazingly difficult to keep a banjo to proper pitch.

MRS. G. It's the same with all musical instruments. What shall it be?

CAPT. G. 'Vanity,' and let the hills hear. (Sings through the first and half of the second verse. Turning to MRS. G.) Now, chorus! Sing, Pussy!

BOTH TOGETHER. (Con brio, to the horror of the monkeys who are settling for the night.)—
'Vanity, all is Vanity,' said Wisdom, scorning me—
I clasped my true Love's tender hand and answered
frank and free—ee:—

'If this be Vanity who'd be wise?
If this be Vanity who'd be wise?
If this be Vanity who'd be wi—ise?
(Crescendo.) Vanity let it be!'

MRS. G. (Defiantly to the gray of the evening sky.) 'Vanity let it be!'

ECHO. (From the Fagoo spur.) Let it be!

FATIMA

And you may go into every room of the house and see everything that is there, but into the Blue Room you must not go.—The Story of Blue Beard.

SCENE.—The GADSBYS' bungalow in the Plains. Time, 11 A. M. on a Sunday morning. CAPTAIN GADSBY, in his shirt-sleeves, is bending over a complete set of Hussar's equipment, from saddle to picketing-rope, which is neatly spread over the floor of his study. He is smoking an unclean briar, and his forehead is puckered with thought.

CAPT. G. (To himself, fingering a headstall.) Jack's an ass. There's enough brass on this to load a mule— and, if the Americans know anything about anything, it can be cut down to a bit only. 'Don't want the watering-bridle, either. Humbug!—Half a dozen sets of chains and pulleys for one horse! Rot! (Scratching his head.) Now, let's consider it all over from the beginning. By Jove, I've forgotten the scale of weights! Ne'er mind. 'Keep the bit only, and eliminate every boss from the crupper to breastplate. No breastplate at all. Simple leather strap across the breast—like the Russians. Hi! Jack never thought of that!

MRS. G. (Entering hastily, her hand bound in a cloth.) Oh, Pip, I've scalded my hand over that horrid, horrid Tiparee jam!

CAPT. G. (Absently.) Eh! Wha-at?

MRS. G. (With round-eyed reproach.) I've scalded it aw-fully! Aren't you sorry? And I did so want that jam to jam properly.

CAPT. G. Poor little woman! Let me kiss the place and make it well. (Unrolling bandage.) You small sinner! Where's that scald? I can't see it.

MRS. G. On the top of the little finger. There!—It's a most 'normous big burn!

CAPT. G. (Kissing little finger.) Baby! Let Hyder look after the jam. You know I don't care for sweets.

MRS. G. In-deed?—Pip!

CAPT. G. Not of that kind, anyhow. And now run along, Minnie, and leave me to my own base devices. I'm busy.

MRS. G. (Calmly settling herself in long chair.) So I see. What a mess you're making! Why have you brought all that smelly leather stuff into the house?

CAPT. G. To play with. Do you mind, dear?

MRS. G. Let me play too. I'd like it.

CAPT. G. I'm afraid you wouldn't, Pussy—Don't you think that jam will burn, or whatever it is that jam does when it's not looked after by a clever little housekeeper?

MRS. G. I thought you said Hyder could attend to it. I left him in the veranda, stirring—when I hurt myself so.

CAPT. G. (His eye returning to the equipment.) Po-oor little woman!—Three pounds four and seven is three eleven, and that can be cut down to two eight, with just a lee-tle care, without weakening anything. Farriery is all rot in incompetent hands. What's the use of a shoe-case when a man's scouting? He can't stick it on with a lick—like a stamp—the shoe! Skittles!

MRS. G. What's skittles? Pah! What is this leather cleaned with?

CAPT. G. Cream and champagne and—Look here, dear, do you really want to talk to me about anything important?

MRS. G. No. I've done my accounts, and I thought I'd like to see what you're doing.

CAPT. G. Well, love, now you've seen and—Would you mind?—That is to say—Minnie, I really am busy.

MRS. G. You want me to go?

CAPT. G. Yes, dear, for a little while. This tobacco will hang in your dress, and saddlery doesn't interest you.

MRS. G. Everything you do interests me, Pip.

CAPT. G. Yes, I know, I know, dear. I'll tell you all about it some day when I've put a head on this thing. In the meantime—

MRS. G. I'm to be turned out of the room like a troublesome child?

CAPT. G. No-o. I don't mean that exactly. But, you see, I shall be tramping up and down, shifting these things to and fro, and I shall be in your way. Don't you think so?

MRS. G. Can't I lift them about? Let me try. (Reaches forward to trooper's saddle.)

CAPT. G. Good gracious, child, don't touch it. You'll hurt yourself. (Picking up saddle.) Little girls aren't expected to handle numdahs. Now, where would you like it put? (Holds saddle above his head.)

MRS. G. (A break in her voice.) Nowhere. Pip, how good you are—and how strong! Oh, what's that ugly red streak inside your arm?

CAPT. G. (Lowering saddle quickly.) Nothing. It's a mark of sorts. (Aside.) And Jack's coming to tiffin with his notions all cut and dried!

MRS. G. I know it's a mark, but I've never seen it before. It runs all up the arm. What is it?

CAPT. G. A cut—if you want to know.

MRS. G. Want to know! Of course I do! I can't have my husband cut to pieces in this way. How did it come? Was it an accident? Tell me, Pip.

CAPT. G. (Grimly.) No. 'Twasn't an accident. I got it—from a man—in Afghanistan.

MRS. G. In action? Oh, Pip, and you never told me!

CAPT. G. I'd forgotten all about it.

MRS. G. Hold up your arm! What a horrid, ugly scar! Are you sure it doesn't hurt now? How did the man give it you?

CAPT. G. (Desperately looking at his watch.) With a knife. I came down—old Van Loo did, that's to say—and fell on my leg, so I couldn't run. And then this man came up and began chopping at me as I sprawled.

MRS. G. Oh, don't, don't! That's enough!—Well, what happened?

CAPT. G. I couldn't get to my holster, and Mafflin came round the corner and stopped the performance.

MRS. G. How? He's such a lazy man, I don't believe he did.

CAPT. G. Don't you? I don't think the man had much doubt about it. Jack cut his head off.

MRS. G. Cut—his—head—off! 'With one blow,' as they say in the books?

CAPT. G. I'm not sure. I was too interested in myself to know much about it. Anyhow, the head was off, and Jack was punching old Van Loo in the ribs to make him get up. Now you know all about it, dear, and now—

MRS. G. You want me to go, of course. You never told me about this, though I've been married to you for ever so long; and you never would have told me if I hadn't found out; and you never do tell me anything about yourself, or what you do, or what you take an interest in.

CAPT. G. Darling, I'm always with you, aren't I?

MRS. G. Always in my pocket, you were going to say. I know you are; but you are always thinking away from me.

CAPT. G. (Trying to hide a smile.) Am I? I wasn't aware of it. I'm awf'ly sorry.

MRS. G. (Piteously.) Oh, don't make fun of me! Pip, you know what I mean. When you are reading one of those things about Cavalry, by that idiotic Prince—why doesn't he be a Prince instead of a stable-boy?

CAPT. G. Prince Kraft a stable-boy—Oh, my Aunt! Never mind, dear. You were going to say?

MRS. G. It doesn't matter; you don't care for what I say. Only—only you get up and walk about the room, staring in front of you, and then Mafflin comes in to dinner, and after I'm in the drawing-room I can hear you and him talking, and talking, and talking, about things I can't understand, and—oh, I get so tired and feel so lonely!—I don't want to complain and be a trouble, Pip; but I do—indeed I do!

CAPT. G. My poor darling! I never thought of that. Why don't you ask some nice people in to dinner?

MRS. G. Nice people! Where am I to find them? Horrid frumps! And if I did, I shouldn't be amused. You know I only want you.

CAPT. G. And you have me surely, Sweetheart?

MRS. G. I have not! Pip, why don't you take me into your life?

CAPT. G. More than I do? That would be difficult, dear.

MRS. G. Yes, I suppose it would—to you. I'm no help to you—no companion to you; and you like to have it so.

CAPT. G. Aren't you a little unreasonable, Pussy?

MRS. G. (Stamping her foot.) I'm the most reasonable woman in the world—when I'm treated properly.

CAPT. G. And since when have I been treating you improperly?

MRS. G. Always—and since the beginning. You know you have.

CAPT. G. I don't; but I'm willing to be convinced.

MRS. G. (Pointing to saddlery.) There!

CAPT. G. How do you mean?

MRS. G. What does all that mean? Why am I not to be told? Is it so precious?

CAPT. G. I forget its exact Government value just at present. It means that it is a great deal too heavy.

MRS. G. Then why do you touch it?

CAPT. G. To make it lighter. See here, little love, I've one notion and Jack has another, but we are both agreed that all this equipment is about thirty pounds too heavy. The thing is how to cut it down without weakening any part of it, and, at the same time, allowing the trooper to carry everything he wants for his own comfort—socks and shirts and things of that kind.

MRS. G. Why doesn't he pack them in a little trunk?

CAPT. G. (Kissing her.) Oh, you darling! Pack them in a little trunk, indeed! Hussars don't carry trunks, and it's a most important thing to make the horse do all the carrying.

MRS. G. But why need you bother about it? You're not a trooper.

CAPT. G. No; but I command a few score of him; and equipment is nearly everything in these days.

MRS. G. More than me?

CAPT. G. Stupid! Of course not; but it's a matter that I'm tremendously interested in, because if I or Jack, or I and Jack, work out some sort of lighter saddlery and all that, it's possible that we may get it adopted.

MRS. G. How?

CAPT. G. Sanctioned at Home, where they will make a sealed pattern—a pattern that all the saddlers must copy—and so it will be used by all the regiments.

MRS. G. And that interests you?

CAPT. G. It's part of my profession, y'know, and my profession is a good deal to me. Everything in a soldier's equipment is important, and if we can improve that equipment, so much the better for the soldiers and for us.

MRS.G. Who's 'us'?

CAPT. G. Jack and I; only Jack's notions are too radical. What's that big sigh for, Minnie?

MRS. G. Oh, nothing—and you've kept all this a secret from me! Why?

CAPT. G. Not a secret, exactly, dear. I didn't say anything about it to you because I didn't think it would amuse you.

MRS. G. And am I only made to be amused?

CAPT. G. No, of course. I merely mean that it couldn't interest you.

MRS. G. It's your work and—and if you'd let me, I'd count all these things up. If they are too heavy, you know by how much they are too heavy, and you must have a list of things made out to your scale of lightness, and—

CAPT. G. I have got both scales somewhere in my head; but it's hard to tell how light you can make a headstall, for instance, until you've actually had a model made.

MRS. G. But if you read out the list, I could copy it down, and pin it up there just above your table. Wouldn't that do?

CAPT. G. It would be awf'ly nice, dear, but it would be giving you trouble for nothing. I can't work that way. I go by rule of thumb. I know the present scale of weights, and the other one—the one that I'm trying to work to—will shift and vary so much that I couldn't be certain, even if I wrote it down.

MRS. G. I'm so sorry. I thought I might help. Is there anything else that I could be of use in?

CAPT. G. (Looking round the room.) I can't think of anything. You're always helping me, you know.

MRS. G. Am I? How?

CAPT. G. You are you of course, and as long as you're near me—I can't explain exactly, but it's in the air.

MRS. G. And that's why you wanted to send me away?

CAPT. G. That's only when I'm trying to do work—grubby work like this.

MRS. G. Mafflin's better, then, isn't he?

CAPT. G. (Rashly.) Of course he is. Jack and I have been thinking along the same groove for two or three years about this equipment. It's our hobby, and it may really be useful some day.

MRS. G. (After a pause.) And that's all that you have away from me?

CAPT. G. It isn't very far away from you now. Take care the oil on that bit doesn't come off on your dress.

MRS. G. I wish—I wish so much that I could really help you. I believe I could—if I left the room. But that's not what I mean.

CAPT. G. (Aside.) Give me patience! I wish she would go. (Aloud.) I assure you you can't do anything for me, Minnie, and I must really settle down to this. Where's my pouch?

MRS. G. (Crossing to writing-table.) Here you are, Bear. What a mess you keep your table in!

CAPT. G. Don't touch it. There's a method in my madness, though you mightn't think of it.

MRS. G. (At table.) I want to look—Do you keep accounts, Pip?

CAPT. G. (Bending over saddlery.) Of a sort. Are you rummaging among the Troop papers? Be careful.

MRS. G. Why? I shan't disturb anything. Good gracious! I had no idea that you had anything to do with so many sick horses.

CAPT. G. 'Wish I hadn't, but they insist on falling sick. Minnie, if I were you I really should not investigate those papers. You may come across something that you won't like.

MRS. G. Why will you always treat me like a child? I know I'm not displacing the horrid things.

CAPT. G. (Resignedly.) Very well, then. Don't blame me if anything happens. Play with the table and let me go on with the saddlery. (Slipping hand into trousers-pocket.) Oh, the deuce!

MRS. G. (Her back to G.) What's that for?

CAPT. G. Nothing. (Aside.) There's not much in it, but I wish I'd torn it up.

MRS. G. (Turning over contents of table.) I know you'll hate me for this; but I do want to see what your work is like. (A pause.) Pip, what are 'farcy-buds'?

CAPT. G. Hah! Would you really like to know? They aren't pretty things.

MRS. G. This Journal of Veterinary Science says they are of 'absorbing interest.' Tell me.

CAPT. G. (Aside.) It may turn her attention.

Gives a long and designedly loathsome account of glanders and farcy

MRS. G. Oh, that's enough. Don't go on!

CAPT. G. But you wanted to know—Then these things suppurate and matterate and spread—

MRS. G. Pip, you're making me sick! You're a horrid, disgusting schoolboy.

CAPT. G. (On his knees among the bridles.) You asked to be told. It's not my fault if you worry me into talking about horrors.

MRS. G. Why didn't you say—No?

CAPT. G. Good Heavens, child! Have you come in here simply to bully me?

MRS. G. I bully you? How could I! You're so strong. (Hysterically.) Strong enough to pick me up and put me outside the door and leave me there to cry. Aren't you?

CAPT. G. It seems to me that you're an irrational little baby. Are you quite well?

MRS. G. Do I look ill? (Returning to table.) Who is your lady friend with the big gray envelope and the fat monogram outside?

CAPT. G. (Aside.) Then it wasn't locked up, confound it. (Aloud.) 'God made her, therefore let her pass for a woman.' You remember what farcy-buds are like?

MRS. G. (Showing envelope.) This has nothing to do with them. I'm going to open it. May I?

CAPT. G. Certainly, if you want to. I'd sooner you didn't, though. I don't ask to look at your letters to the Deercourt girl.

MRS. G. You'd better not, Sir! (Takes letter from envelope.) Now, may I look? If you say no, I shall cry.

CAPT. G. You've never cried in my knowledge of you, and I don't believe you could.

MRS. G. I feel very like it to-day, Pip. Don't be hard on me. (Reads letter.) It begins in the middle, without any 'Dear Captain Gadsby,' or anything. How funny!

CAPT. G. (Aside.) No, it's not Dear Captain Gadsby, or anything, now. How funny!

MRS. G. What a strange letter! (Reads.) 'And so the moth has come too near the candle at last, and has been singed into—shall I say Respectability? I congratulate him, and hope he will be as happy as he deserves to be.' What does that mean? Is she congratulating you about our marriage?

CAPT. G. Yes, I suppose so.

MRS. G. (Still reading letter.) She seems to be a particular friend of yours.

CAPT. G. Yes. She was an excellent matron of sorts—a Mrs. Herriott—wife of a Colonel Herriott. I used to know some of her people at Home long ago—before I came out.

MRS. G. Some Colonels' wives are young—as young as me. I knew one who was younger.

CAPT. G. Then it couldn't have been Mrs. Herriott. She was old enough to have been your mother, dear.

MRS. G. I remember now. Mrs. Scargill was talking about her at the Duffins' tennis, before you came for me, on Tuesday. Captain Mafflin said she was a 'dear old woman.' Do you know, I think Mafflin is a very clumsy man with his feet.

CAPT. G. (Aside.) Good old Jack! (Aloud.) Why, dear?

MRS. G. He had put his cup down on the ground then, and he literally stepped into it. Some of the tea spirted over my dress—the gray one. I meant to tell you about it before.

CAPT. G. (Aside.) There are the makings of a strategist about Jack, though his methods are coarse. (Aloud.) You'd better get a new dress, then. (Aside.) Let us pray that that will turn her.

MRS. G. Oh, it isn't stained in the least. I only thought that I'd tell you. (Returning to letter.) What an extraordinary person! (Reads.) 'But need I remind you that you have taken upon yourself a charge of wardship'—what in the world is a charge of wardship?—'which, as you yourself know, may end in Consequences—'

CAPT. G. (Aside.) It's safest to let 'em see everything as they come across it; but 'seems to me that there are exceptions to the rule. (Aloud.) I told you that there was nothing to be gained from rearranging my table.

MRS. G. (Absently.) What does the woman mean? She goes on talking about Consequences—'almost inevitable Consequences' with a capital C—for half a page. (Flushing scarlet.) Oh, good gracious! How abominable!

CAPT. G. (Promptly.) Do you think so? Doesn't it show a sort of motherly interest in us? (Aside.) Thank Heaven, Harry always wrapped her meaning up safely! (Aloud.) Is it absolutely necessary to go on with the letter, darling?

MRS. G. It's impertinent—it's simply horrid. What right has this woman to write in this way to you? She oughtn't to.

CAPT. G. When you write to the Deercourt girl, I notice that you generally fill three or four sheets. Can't you let an old woman babble on paper once in a way? She means well.

MRS. G. I don't care. She shouldn't write, and if she did, you ought to have shown me her letter.

CAPT. G. Can't you understand why I kept it to myself, or must I explain at length—as I explained the farcy-buds?

MRS. G. (Furiously.) Pip, I hate you! This is as bad as those idiotic saddle-bags on the floor. Never mind whether it would please me or not, you ought to have given it to me to read.

CAPT. G. It comes to the same thing. You took it yourself.

MRS. G. Yes, but if I hadn't taken it, you wouldn't have said a word. I think this Harriet Herriott—it's like a name in a book—is an interfering old Thing.

CAPT. G. (Aside.) So long as you thoroughly understand that she is old, I don't much care what you think. (Aloud.) Very good, dear. Would you like to write and tell her so? She's seven thousand miles away.

MRS. G. I don't want to have anything to do with her, but you ought to have told me. (Turning to last page of letter.) And she patronises me, too. I've never seen her! (Reads.) 'I do not know how the world stands with you; in all human probability I shall never know; but whatever I may have said before, I pray for her sake more than for yours that all may be well. I have learnt what misery means, and I dare not wish that any one dear to you should share my knowledge.'

CAPT. G. Good God! Can't you leave that letter alone, or, at least, can't you refrain from reading it aloud? I've been through it once. Put it back on the desk. Do you hear me?

MRS. G. (Irresolutely.) I sh—shan't! (Looks at G'.s eyes.) Oh, Pip, please! I didn't mean to make you angry—'Deed, I didn't. Pip, I'm so sorry. I know I've wasted your time——

CAPT. G. (Grimly.) You have. Now, will you be good enough to go—if there is nothing more in my room that you are anxious to pry into?

MRS. G. (Putting out her hands.) Oh, Pip, don't look at me like that! I've never seen you look like that before and it hu-urts me! I'm sorry. I oughtn't to have been here at all, and—and—and—(sobbing). Oh, be good to me! Be good to me! There's only you—anywhere!

Breaks down in long chair, hiding face in cushions.
CAPT. G. (Aside.) She doesn't know how she flicked me on the raw. (Aloud, bending over chair.) I didn't mean to be harsh, dear—I didn't really. You can stay here as long as you please, and do what you please.

Don't cry like that. You'll make yourself sick. (Aside.) What on earth has come over her? (Aloud.) Darling, what's the matter with you?

MRS. G. (Her face still hidden.) Let me go—let me go to my own room. Only—only say you aren't angry with me.

CAPT. G. Angry with you, love! Of course not. I was angry with myself. I'd lost my temper over the saddlery—Don't hide your face, Pussy. I want to kiss it.

Bends lower, MRS. G. slides right arm round his
neck. Several interludes and much sobbing.
MRS. G. (In a whisper.) I didn't mean about the jam when I came in to tell you—

CAPT. G. Bother the jam and the equipment! (Interlude.)

MRS. G. (Still more faintly.) My finger wasn't scalded at all. I—I wanted to speak to you about—about—something else, and—I didn't know how.

CAPT. G. Speak away, then. (Looking into her eyes.) Eh! Wha—at? Minnie! Here, don't go away! You don't mean?

MRS. G. (Hysterically, backing to portiere and hiding her face in its folds.) The—the Almost Inevitable Consequences! (Flits though portiere as G. attempts to catch her, and bolts herself in her own room.)

CAPT. G. (His arms full of portiere.) Oh! (Sitting down heavily in chair.) I'm a brute—a pig—a bully, and a blackguard. My poor, poor little darling! 'Made to be amused only—?

THE VALLEY OF THE SHADOW

Knowing Good and Evil.

SCENE.—The GADSBYS' bungalow in the Plains, in June. Punkah-coolies asleep in veranda where CAPTAIN GADSBY is walking up and down. DOCTOR'S trap in porch. JUNIOR CHAPLAIN drifting generally and uneasily through the house. Time, 3.40 A. M. Heat 94 degrees in veranda.

DOCTOR. (Coming into veranda and touching G. on the shoulder.) You had better go in and see her now.

CAPT. G. (The colour of good cigar-ash.) Eh, wha-at? Oh, yes, of course. What did you say?

DOCTOR. (Syllable by syllable.) Go—in—to—the—room—and—see—her. She wants to speak to you. (Aside, testily.) I shall have him on my hands next.

JUNIOR CHAPLAIN. (In half-lighted dining-room.) Isn't there any—?

DOCTOR. (Savagely.) Hsh, you little fool!

JUNIOR CHAPLAIN. Let me do my work. Gadsby, stop a minute! (Edges after G.)

DOCTOR. Wait till she sends for you at least—at least. Man alive, he'll kill you if you go in there! What are you bothering him for?

JUNIOR CHAPLAIN. (Coming into veranda.) I've given him a stiff brandy-peg. He wants it. You've forgotten him for the last ten hours and—forgotten yourself too.

G. enters bedroom, which is lit by one night-lamp.

Ayah on the floor pretending to be asleep.

VOICE. (From the bed.) All down the street—such bonfires! Ayah, go and put them out! (Appealingly.) How can I sleep with an installation of the C.I.E. in my room? No—not C.I.E. Something else. What was it?

CAPT. G. (Trying to control his voice.) Minnie, I'm here. (Bending over bed.) Don't you know me, Minnie? It's me—it's Phil—it's your husband.

VOICE. (Mechanically.) It's me—it's Phil—it's your husband.

CAPT. G. She doesn't know me!—It's your own husband, darling,

VOICE. Your own husband, darling.

AYAH. (With an inspiration.) Memsahib understanding all I saying.

CAPT. G. Make her understand me then—quick!

AYAH. (Hand on MRS. G's forehead.) Memsahib! Captain Sahib here.

VOICE. Salma do. (Fretfully.) I know I'm not fit to be seen.

AYAH. (Aside to G.) Say 'marneen" same as breakfash.

CAPT. G. Good-morning, little woman. How are we to-day?

VOICE. That's Phil. Poor old Phil. (Viciously.)
Phil, you fool, I can't see you. Come nearer.

CAPT. G. Minnie! Minnie! It's me—you know me?

VOICE. (Mockingly.) Of course I do. Who does not know the man who was so cruel to his wife—almost the only one he ever had?

CAPT. G. Yes, dear. Yes—of course, of course. But won't you speak to him? He wants to speak to you so much.

VOICE. They'd never let him in. The Doctor would give darwaza bund even if he were in the house. He'll never come. (Despairingly.) O Judas! Judas! Judas!

CAPT. G. (Putting out his arms.) They have let him in, and he always was in the house. Oh, my love—don't you know me?

VOICE. (In a half chant.) 'And it came to pass at the eleventh hour that this poor soul repented.' It knocked at the gates, but they were shut—tight as a plaster—a great, burning plaster. They had pasted our marriage certificate all across the door, and it was made of red-hot iron—people really ought to be more careful, you know.

CAPT. G. What am I to do? (Takes her in his arms.) Minnie! speak to me—to Phil.

VOICE. What shall I say? Oh, tell me what to say before it's too late! They are all going away and I can't say anything.

CAPT. G. Say you know me! Only say you know me!

DOCTOR. (Who has entered quietly.) For pity's sake don't take it too much to heart, Gadsby. It's this way sometimes. They won't recognise. They say all sorts of queer things—don't you see?

CAPT. G. All right! All right! Go away now, she'll recognise me; you're bothering her. She must—mustn't she?

DOCTOR. She will before—Have I your leave to try—?

CAPT. G. Anything you please, so long as she'll know me. It's only a question of—hours, isn't it?

DOCTOR. (Professionally.) While there's life there's hope, y'know. But don't build on it.

CAPT. G. I don't. Pull her together if it's possible. (Aside.) What have I done to deserve this?

DOCTOR. (Bending over bed.) Now, Mrs. Gadsby! We shall be all right to-morrow. You must take it, or I shan't let Phil see you. It isn't nasty, is it?

VOICE. Medicines! Always more medicines! Can't you leave me alone?

CAPT. G. Oh, leave her in peace, Doc!

DOCTOR. (Stepping back,—aside.) May I be forgiven if I've done wrong. (Aloud.) In a few minutes she ought to be sensible; but I daren't tell you to look for anything. It's only—

CAPT. G. What? Go on, man.

DOCTOR. (In a whisper.) Forcing the last rally.

CAPT. G. Then leave us alone.

DOCTOR. Don't mind what she says at first, if you can. They—they—they turn against those they love most sometimes in this.—It's hard, but—

CAPT. G. Am I her husband or are you? Leave us alone for what time we have together.

VOICE. (Confidentially.) And we were engaged quite suddenly, Emma. I assure you that I never thought of it for a moment; but, oh, my little Me!—I don't know what I should have done if he hadn't proposed.

CAPT. G. She thinks of that Deercourt girl before she thinks of me. (Aloud.) Minnie!

VOICE. Not from the shops, Mummy dear. You can get the real leaves from Kaintu, and (laughing weakly) never mind about the blossoms—Dead white silk is only fit for widows, and I won't wear it. It's as bad as a winding sheet. (A long pause.)

CAPT. G. I never asked a favour yet. If there is anybody to listen to me, let her know me—even if I die too!

VOICE. (Very faintly.) Pip, Pip dear.

CAPT. G. I'm here, darling.

VOICE. What has happened? They've been bothering me so with medicines and things, and they wouldn't let you come and see me. I was never ill before. Am I ill now?

CAPT. G. You—you aren't quite well.

VOICE. How funny! Have I been ill long?

CAPT. G. Some days; but you'll be all right in a little time.

VOICE. Do you think so, Pip? I don't feel well and—Oh! what have they done to my hair?

CAPT. G. I d-d-don't know.

VOICE. They've cut it off. What a shame!

CAPT. G. It must have been to make your head cooler.

VOICE. 'Just like a boy's wig. Don't I look horrid?

CAPT. G. Never looked prettier in your life, dear. (Aside.) How am I to ask her to say good-bye?

VOICE. I don't feel pretty. I feel very ill. My heart won't work. It's nearly dead inside me, and there's a funny feeling in my eyes. Everything seems the same distance—you and the almirah and the table—inside my eyes or miles away. What does it mean, Pip?

CAPT. G. You're a little feverish, Sweetheart—very feverish. (Breaking down.) My love! my love! How can I let you go?

VOICE. I thought so. Why didn't you tell me that at first?

CAPT. G. What?

VOICE. That I am going to—die.

CAPT. G. But you aren't! You shan't.

AYAH to punkah-coolie. (Stepping into veranda after a glance at the bed.) Punkah chor do! (Stop pulling the punkah.)

VOICE. It's hard, Pip. So very, very hard after one year—just one year. (Wailing.) And I'm only twenty. Most girls aren't even married at twenty. Can't they do anything to help me? I don't want to die.

CAPT. G. Hush, dear. You won't.

VOICE. What's the use of talking? Help me! You've never failed me yet. Oh, Phil, help me to keep alive. (Feverishly.) I don't believe you wish me to live. You weren't a bit sorry when that horrid Baby thing died. I wish I'd killed it!

CAPT. G. (Drawing his hand across his forehead.) It's more than a man's meant to bear—it's not right. (Aloud.) Minnie, love, I'd die for you if it would help.

VOICE. No more death. There's enough already. Pip, don't you die too.

CAPT. G. I wish I dared.

VOICE. It says: 'Till Death do us part.' Nothing after that—and so it would be no use. It stops at the dying. Why does it stop there? Only such a very short life, too. Pip, I'm sorry we married.

CAPT. G. No! Anything but that, Min!

VOICE. Because you'll forget and I'll forget. Oh, Pip, don't forget! I always loved you, though I was cross sometimes. If I ever did anything that you didn't like, say you forgive me now.

CAPT. G. You never did, darling. On my soul and honour you never did. I haven't a thing to forgive you.

VOICE. I sulked for a whole week about those petunias. (With a laugh.) What a little wretch I was, and how grieved you were! Forgive me that, Pip.

CAPT. G. There's nothing to forgive. It was my fault. They were too near the drive. For God's sake don't talk so, Minnie! There's such a lot to say and so little time to say it in.

VOICE. Say that you'll always love me—until the end.

CAPT. G. Until the end. (Carried away.) It's a lie. It must be, because we've loved each other. This isn't the end.

VOICE. (Relapsing into semi-delirium.) My Church-service has an ivory-cross on the back, and it says so, so it must be true. 'Till Death do us part.'—But that's a lie. (With a parody of G.'s manner.) A damned lie! (Recklessly.) Yes, I can swear as well as Trooper Pip. I can't make my head think, though. That's because they cut off my hair. How can one think with one's head all fuzzy? (Pleadingly.) Hold me, Pip! Keep me with you always and always. (Relapsing.) But if you marry the Thorniss girl when I'm dead, I'll come back and howl under our bedroom window all night. Oh, bother! You'll think I'm a jackal. Pip, what time is it?

CAPT. G. I—I—I can't help it, dear.

VOICE. How funny! I couldn't cry now to save my life. (G. shivers.) I want to sing.

CAPT. G. Won't it tire you? Better not, perhaps.

VOICE. Why? I won't be bothered about. (Begins in a hoarse quaver):—

'Minnie bakes oaten cake, Minnie brews ale,
All because her Johnnie's coming home from the sea.
(That's parade, Pip.)
And she grows red as rose, who was so pale;
And "Are you sure the church-clock goes?" says she.'
(Pettishly.) I knew I couldn't take the last note. How do the bass chords run? (Puts out her hands and begins playing piano on the sheet.)

CAPT. G. (Catching up hands.) Ahh! Don't do that, Pussy, if you love me.

VOICE. Love you? Of course I do. Who else should it be? (A pause.)

VOICE. (Very clearly.) Pip, I'm going now. Something's choking me cruelly. (Indistinctly.) Into the dark—without you, my heart.—But it's a lie, dear—we mustn't believe it.—For ever and ever, living or dead. Don't let me go, my husband—hold me tight.—They can't—whatever happens. (A cough.) Pip—my Pip! Not for always—and—so—soon! (Voice ceases.)

Pause of ten minutes. G. buries his face in the side of the bed while ayah bends over bed from opposite side and feels MRS. G.'s breast and forehead.

CAPT. G. (Rising.) Doctor Sahib ko salaam do.

AYAH. (Still by bedside, with a shriek.) Ai! Ai! Tuta—phuta! My Memsahib! Not getting—not have got!—Pusseena agya! (The sweat has come.) (Fiercely to G.) TUM jao Doctor Sahib ko jaldi! (You go to the doctor.) Oh, my Memsahib!

DOCTOR. (Entering hastily.) Come away, Gadsby. (Bends over bed.) Eh! The Dev—What inspired you to stop the punkah? Get out, man—go away—wait outside! Go! Here, Ayah! (Over his shoulder to G.) Mind, I promise nothing.

The dawn breaks as G. stumbles into the garden.

CAPT. M. (Reining up at the gate on his way to parade and very soberly.) Old man, how goes?

CAPT. G. (Dazed.) I don't quite know. Stay a bit. Have a drink or something. Don't run away. You're just getting amusing. Ha! Ha!

CAPT. M. (Aside.) What am I let in for? Gaddy has aged ten years in the night.

CAPT. G. (Slowly, fingering charger's headstall.) Your curb's too loose.

CAPT. M. So it is. Put it straight, will you? (Aside.) I shall be late for parade. Poor Gaddy.

CAPT. G. links and unlinks curb-chain aimlessly, and finally stands staring towards the veranda.

The day brightens.

DOCTOR. (Knocked out of professional gravity, tramping across flower-beds and shaking G.'s hands.) It's—it's—it's!—Gadsby, there's a fair chance—a dashed fair chance! The flicker, y'know. The sweat, y'know! I saw how it would be. The punkah, y'know. Deuced clever woman that Ayah of yours. Stopped the punkah just at the right time. A dashed good chance! No—you don't go in. We'll pull her through yet I promise on my reputation—under Providence. Send a man with this note to Bingle. Two heads better than one. 'Specially the Ayah! We'll pull her round. (Retreats hastily to house.)

CAPT. G. (His head on neck of M.'s charger.) Jack! I bub—bub—believe, I'm going to make a bub—bub—bloody exhibitiod of byself.

CAPT. M. (Sniffing openly and feeling in his left cuff.) I b-b—believe, I'b doing it already. Old bad, what cad I say? I'b as pleased as—Cod dab you, Gaddy! You're one big idiot and I'b adother. (Pulling himself together.) Sit tight! Here comes the Devil-dodger.

JUNIOR CHAPLAIN. (Who is not in the Doctor's confidence.) We—we are only men in these things, Gadsby. I know that I can say nothing now to help—

CAPT. M. (Jealously.) Then don't say it! Leave him alone. It's not bad enough to croak over. Here, Gaddy, take the chit to Bingle and ride hell-for-leather. It'll do you good. I can't go.

JUNIOR CHAPLAIN. Do him good! (Smiling.) Give me the chit and I'll drive. Let him lie down. Your horse is blocking my cart—please!

CAPT. M. (Slowly without reining back.) I beg your pardon—I'll apologise. On paper if you like.

JUNIOR CHAPLAIN. (Flicking M.'s charger.) That'll do, thanks. Turn in, Gadsby, and I'll bring Bingle back—ahem—'hell-for-leather.'

CAPT. M. (Solus.) It would have served me right if he'd cut me across the face. He can drive too. I shouldn't care to go that pace in a bamboo cart. What a faith he must have in his Maker—of harness! Come hup, you brute! (Gallops off to parade, blowing his nose, as the sun rises.)

(INTERVAL OF FIVE WEEKS.)

MRS. G. (Very white and pinched, in morning wrapper at breakfast table.) How big and strange the room looks, and oh how glad I am to see it again! What dust, though! I must talk to the servants. Sugar, Pip? I've almost forgotten. (Seriously.) Wasn't I very ill?

CAPT. G. Iller than I liked. (Tenderly.) Oh, you bad little Pussy, what a start you gave me!

MRS. G. I'll never do it again.

CAPT. G. You'd better not. And now get those poor pale cheeks pink again, or I shall be angry. Don't try to lift the urn. You'll upset it. Wait. (Comes round to head of table and lifts urn.)

MRS. G. (Quickly.) Khitmatgar, bowarchi-khana see kettly lao. Butler, get a kettle from the cook-house. (Drawing down G.'s face to her own.) Pip dear, I remember.

CAPT. G. What?

MRS. G. That last terrible night.

CAPT. G. Then just you forget all about it.

MRS. G. (Softly, her eyes filling.) Never. It has brought us very close together, my husband. There! (Interlude.) I'm going to give Junda a saree.

CAPT. G. I gave her fifty dibs.

MRS. G. So she told me. It was a 'normous reward. Was I worth it? (Several interludes.) Don't! Here's the khitmatgar.—Two lumps or one, Sir?

THE SWELLING OF JORDAN

If thou hast run with the footmen and they have wearied thee, then how canst thou contend with horses? And if in the land of peace wherein thou trustedst they wearied thee, then how wilt thou do in the swelling of Jordan?

SCENE.—The GADSEYS' bungalow in the Plains, on a January morning. MRS. G. arguing with bearer in back veranda.

CAPT. M. rides up.
CAPT. M. 'Mornin', Mrs. Gadsby. How's the Infant Phenomenon and the Proud Proprietor?

MRS. G. You'll find them in the front veranda; go through the house. I'm Martha just now.

CAPT. M. 'Cumbered about with cares of khitmatgars? I fly.

Passes into front veranda, where GADSBY is watching

GADSBY JUNIOR, aged ten months, crawling about the matting.

CAPT. M. What's the trouble, Gaddy—spoiling an honest man's Europe morning this way? (Seeing G. JUNIOR.) By Jove, that yearling's comin' on amazingly! Any amount of bone below the knee there.

CAPT. G. Yes, he's a healthy little scoundrel. Don't you think his hair's growing?

M. Let's have a look. Hi! Hst! Come here, General Luck, and we'll report on you.

MRS. G. (Within.) What absurd name will you give him next? Why do you call him that?

M. Isn't he our Inspector-General of Cavalry? Doesn't he come down in his seventy-two perambulator every morning the Pink Hussars parade? Don't wriggle, Brigadier. Give us your private opinion on the way the third squadron went past. 'Trifle ragged, weren't they?

G. A bigger set of tailors than the new draft I don't wish to see. They've given me more than my fair share—knocking the squadron out of shape. It's sickening!

M. When you're in command, you'll do better, young 'un. Can't you walk yet? Get my finger and try. (To G.) 'Twon't hurt his hocks, will it?

G. Oh, no. Don't let him flop, though, or he'll lick all the blacking off your boots.

MRS. G. (Within.) Who's destroying my son's character?

M. And my Godson's. I'm ashamed of you, Gaddy. Punch your father in the eye, Jack! Don't you stand it! Hit him again!

G. (Sotto voce.) Put The Butcha down and come to the end of the veranda. I'd rather the Wife didn't hear—just now.

M. You look awf'ly serious. Anything wrong?

G. 'Depends on your view entirely. I say, Jack, you won't think more hardly of me than you can help, will you? Come further this way.—The fact of the matter is, that I've made up my mind—at least I'm thinking seriously of—cutting the Service.

M. Hwhatt?

G. Don't shout. I'm going to send in my papers.

M. You! Are you mad?

G. No—only married.

M. Look here! What's the meaning of it all? You never intend to leave us. You can't. Isn't the best squadron of the best regiment of the best cavalry in all the world good enough for you?

G. (Jerking his head over his shoulder.) She doesn't seem to thrive in this God-forsaken country, and there's The Butcha to be considered and all that, you know.

M. Does she say that she doesn't like India?

G. That's the worst of it. She won't for fear of leaving me.

M. What are the Hills made for?

G. Not for my wife at any rate.

M. You know too much, Gaddy, and—I don't like you any the better for it!

G. Never mind that. She wants England, and The Butcha would be all the better for it. I'm going to chuck. You don't understand.

M. (Hotly.) I understand this. One hundred and thirty-seven new horses to be licked into shape somehow before Luck comes round again; a hairy-heeled draft who'll give more trouble than the horses; a camp next cold weather for a certainty; ourselves the first on the roster; the Russian shindy ready to come to a head at five minutes' notice, and you, the best of us all, backing out of it all! Think a little, Gaddy. You won't do it.

G. Hang it, a man has some duties towards his family, I suppose.

M. I remember a man, though, who told me, the night after Amdheran, when we were picketed under Jagai, and he'd left his sword—by the way, did you ever pay Ranken for that sword?—in an Utmanzai's head—that man told me that he'd stick by me and the Pinks as long as he lived. I don't blame him for not sticking by me—I'm not much of a man—but I do blame him for not sticking by the Pink Hussars.

G. (Uneasily.) We were little more than boys then. Can't you see, Jack, how things stand? 'Tisn't as if we were serving for our bread. We've all of us, more or less, got the filthy lucre. I'm luckier than some, perhaps. There's no call for me to serve on.

M. None in the world for you or for us, except the Regimental. If you don't choose to answer to that, of course—

G. Don't be too hard on a man. You know that a lot of us only take up the thing for a few years and then go back to Town and catch on with the rest.

M. Not lots, and they aren't some of Us.

G. And then there are one's affairs at Home to be considered—my place and the rents, and all that. I don't suppose my father can last much longer, and that means the title, and so on.

M. 'Fraid you won't be entered in the Stud Book correctly unless you go Home? Take six months, then, and come out in October. If I could slay off a brother or two, I s'pose I should be a Marquis of sorts. Any fool can be that; but it needs men, Gaddy—men like you—to lead flanking squadrons properly. Don't you delude yourself into the belief that you're going Home to take your place and prance about among pink-nosed Kabuli dowagers. You aren't built that way. I know better.

G. A man has a right to live his life as happily as he can. You aren't married.

M. No—praise be to Providence and the one or two women who have had the good sense to jawab me.

G. Then you don't know what it is to go into your own room and see your wife's head on the pillow, and when everything else is safe and the house shut up for the night, to wonder whether the roof-beams won't give and kill her.

M. (Aside.) Revelations first and second! (Aloud.) So-o! I knew a man who got squiffy at our Mess once and confided to me that he never helped his wife on to her horse without praying that she'd break her neck before she came back. All husbands aren't alike, you see.

G. What on earth has that to do with my case? The man must ha' been mad, or his wife as bad as they make 'em.

M. (Aside.) 'No fault of yours if either weren't all you say. You've forgotten the tune when you were insane about the Herriott woman. You always were a good hand at forgetting. (Aloud.) Not more mad than men who go to the other extreme. Be reasonable, Gaddy. Your roof-beams are sound enough.

G. That was only a way of speaking. I've been uneasy and worried about the Wife ever since that awful business three years ago—when—I nearly lost her. Can you wonder?

M. Oh, a shell never falls twice in the same place. You've paid your toll to misfortune—why should your wife be picked out more than anybody else's?

G. I can talk just as reasonably as you can, but you don't understand—you don't understand. And then there's The Butcha. Deuce knows where the Ayah takes him to sit in the evening! He has a bit of a cough. Haven't you noticed it?

M. Bosh! The Brigadier's jumping out of his skin with pure condition. He's got a muzzle like a rose-leaf and the chest of a two-year-old. What's demoralised you?

G. Funk. That's the long and the short of it. Funk!

M. But what is there to funk?

G. Everything. It's ghastly.

M. Ah! I see.
You don't want to fight,
And by Jingo when we do,
You've got the kid, you've got the Wife,
You've got the money, too.
That's about the case, eh?

G. I suppose that's it. But it's not for myself. It's because of them. At least I think it is.

M. Are you sure? Looking at the matter in a cold-blooded light, the Wife is provided for even if you were wiped out to-night. She has an ancestral home to go to, money, and the Brigadier to carry on the illustrious name.

G. Then it is for myself or because they are part of me. You don't see it. My life's so good, so pleasant, as it is, that I want to make it quite safe. Can't you understand?

M. Perfectly. 'Shelter-pit for the Orf'cer's charger,' as they say in the Line.

G. And I have everything to my hand to make it so. I'm sick of the strain and the worry for their sakes out here; and there isn't a single real difficulty to prevent my dropping it altogether. It'll only cost me—Jack, I hope you'll never know the shame that I've been going through for the past six months.

M. Hold on there! I don't wish to be told. Every man has his moods and tenses sometimes.

G. (Laughing bitterly.) Has he? What do you call craning over to see where your near-fore lands?

M. In my case it means that I have been on the Considerable Bend, and have come to parade with a Head and a Hand. It passes in three strides.

G. (Lowering voice.) It never passes with me, Jack. I'm always thinking about it. Phil Gadsby funking a fall on parade! Sweet picture, isn't it! Draw it for me.

M. (Gravely.) Heaven forbid! A man like you can't be as bad as that. A fall is no nice thing, but one never gives it a thought.

G. Doesn't one? Wait till you've got a wife and a youngster of your own, and then you'll know how the roar of the squadron behind you turns you cold all up the back.

M. (Aside.) And this man led at Amdheran after Bagal-Deasin went under, and we were all mixed up together, and he came out of the show dripping like a butcher. (Aloud.) Skittles! The men can always open out, and you can always pick your way more or less. We haven't the dust to bother us, as the men have, and whoever heard of a horse stepping on a man?

G. Never—as long as he can see. But did they open out for poor Errington?

M. Oh, this is childish!

G. I know it is, worse than that. I don't care. You've ridden Van Loo. Is he the sort of brute to pick his way—'specially when we're coming up in column of troop with any pace on?

M. Once in a Blue Moon do we gallop in column of troop, and then only to save time. Aren't three lengths enough for you?

G. Yes—quite enough. They just allow for the full development of the smash. I'm talking like a cur, I know: but I tell you that, for the past three months, I've felt every hoof of the squadron in the small of my back every time that I've led.

M. But, Gaddy, this is awful!

G. Isn't it lovely? Isn't it royal? A Captain of the Pink Hussars watering up his charger before parade like the blasted boozing Colonel of a Black Regiment!

M. You never did!

G. Once only. He squelched like a mussuck, and the Troop-Sergeant-Major cocked his eye at me. You know old Haffy's eye. I was afraid to do it again.

M. I should think so. That was the best way to rupture old Van Loo's tummy, and make him crumple you up. You knew that.

G. I didn't care. It took the edge off him.

M. 'Took the edge off him'? Gaddy, you—you—you mustn't, you know! Think of the men.

G. That's another thing I am afraid of. D'you s'pose they know?

M. Let's hope not; but they're deadly quick to spot skrim—little things of that kind. See here, old man, send the Wife Home for the hot weather and come to Kashmir with me. We'll start a boat on the Dal or cross the Rhotang—shoot ibex or loaf—which you please. Only come! You're a bit off your oats and you're talking nonsense. Look at the Colonel—swag-bellied rascal that he is. He has a wife and no end of a bow-window of his own. Can any one of us ride round him—chalk-stones and all? I can't, and I think I can shove a crock along a bit.

G. Some men are different. I haven't the nerve. Lord help me, I haven't the nerve! I've taken up a hole and a half to get my knees well under the wallets. I can't help it. I'm so afraid of anything happening to me. On my soul, I ought to be broke in front of the squadron, for cowardice.

M. Ugly word, that. I should never have the courage to own up.

G. I meant to lie about my reasons when I began, but—I've got out of the habit of lying to you, old man. Jack, you won't?—But I know you won't.

M. Of course not. (Half aloud.) The Pinks are paying dearly for their Pride.

G. Eh! Wha-at?

M. Don't you know? The men have called Mrs. Gadsby the Pride of the Pink Hussars ever since she came to us.

G. 'Tisn't her fault. Don't think that. It's all mine.

M. What does she say?

G. I haven't exactly put it before her. She's the best little woman in the world, Jack, and all that—but she wouldn't counsel a man to stick to his calling if it came between him and her. At least, I think—

M. Never mind. Don't tell her what you told me. Go on the Peerage and Landed-Gentry tack.

G. She'd see through it. She's five times cleverer than I am.

M. (Aside.) Then she'll accept the sacrifice and think a little bit worse of him for the rest of her days.

G. (Absently.) I say, do you despise me?

M. 'Queer way of putting it. Have you ever been asked that question? Think a minute. What answer used you to give?

G. So bad as that? I'm not entitled to expect anything more, but it's a bit hard when one's best friend turns round and—

M. So I have found. But you will have consolations—Bailiffs and Drains and Liquid Manure and the Primrose League, and, perhaps, if you're lucky, the Colonelcy of a Yeomanry Cav-al-ry Regiment—all uniform and no riding, I believe. How old are you?

G. Thirty-three. I know it's—

M. At forty you'll be a fool of a J.P. landlord. At fifty you'll own a bath-chair, and The Brigadier, if he takes after you, will be fluttering the dovecotes of—what's the particular dunghill you're going to? Also, Mrs. Gadsby will be fat.

G. (Limply.) This is rather more than a joke.

M. D'you think so? Isn't cutting the Service a joke? It generally takes a man fifty years to arrive at it. You're quite right, though. It is more than a joke. You've managed it in thirty-three.

G. Don't make me feel worse than I do. Will it satisfy you if I own that I am a shirker, a skrim-shanker, and a coward?

M. It will not, because I'm the only man in the world who can talk to you like this without being knocked down. You mustn't take all that I've said to heart in this way. I only spoke—a lot of it at least—out of pure selfishness, because, because—Oh, damn it all, old man,—I don't know what I shall do without you. Of course, you've got the money and the place and all that—and there are two very good reasons why you should take care of yourself.

G. 'Doesn't make it any the sweeter. I'm backing out—I know I am. I always had a soft drop in me somewhere—and I daren't risk any danger to them.

M. Why in the world should you? You're bound to think of your family—bound to think. Er-hmm. If I wasn't a younger son I'd go too—be shot if I wouldn't!

G. Thank you, Jack. It's a kind lie, but it's the blackest you've told for some time. I know what I'm doing, and I'm going into it with my eyes open. Old man, I can't help it. What would you do if you were in my place?

M. (Aside.) 'Couldn't conceive any woman getting permanently between me and the Regiment. (Aloud.) 'Can't say. 'Very likely I should do no better. I'm sorry for you—awf'ly sorry—but 'if them's your sentiments,' I believe, I really do, that you are acting wisely.

G. Do you? I hope you do. (In a whisper.) Jack, be very sure of yourself before you marry. I'm an ungrateful ruffian to say this, but marriage—even as good a marriage as mine has been—hampers a man's work, it cripples his sword-arm, and oh, it plays Hell with his notions of duty! Sometimes—good and sweet as she is—sometimes I could wish that I had kept my freedom—No, I don't mean that exactly.

MRS. G. (Coming down the veranda.) What are you wagging your head over, Pip?

M. (Turning quickly.) Me, as usual. The old sermon. Your husband is recommending me to get married. 'Never saw such a one-ideaed man!

MRS. G. Well, why don't you? I daresay you would make some woman very happy.

G. There's the Law and the Prophets, Jack. Never mind the Regiment. Make a woman happy. (Aside.) O Lord!

M. We'll see. I must be off to make a Troop Cook desperately unhappy. I won't have the wily Hussar fed on Government Bullock Train shinbones—(Hastily.) Surely black ants can't be good for The Brigadier. He's picking 'em off the matting and eating 'em. Here, Senor Commandante Don Grubbynose, come and talk to me. (Lifts G. JUNIOR in his arms.) 'Want my watch? You won't be able to put it into your mouth, but you can try. (G. JUNIOR drops watch, breaking dial and hands.)

MRS. G. Oh, Captain Mafflin, I am so sorry! Jack, you bad, bad little villain. Ahhh!

M. It's not the least consequence, I assure you. He'd treat the world in the same way if he could get it into his hands. Everything's made to be played with and broken, isn't it, young 'un?

MRS. G. Mafflin didn't at all like his watch being broken, though he was too polite to say so. It was entirely his fault for giving it to the child. Dem little puds are werry, werry feeble, aren't dey, my Jack-in-de-box? (To G.) What did he want to see you for?

G. Regimental shop as usual.

MRS. G. The Regiment! Always the Regiment. On my word, I sometimes feel jealous of Mafflin.

G. (Wearily.) Poor old Jack? I don't think you need. Isn't it time for The Butcha to have his nap? Bring a chair out here, dear. I've got something to talk over with you.

AND THIS IS THE END OF THE STORY OF THE GADSBYS.

What is the moral? Who rides may read.
When the night is thick and the tracks are blind.
A friend at a pinch is a friend indeed;
But a fool to wait for the laggard behind:
Down to Gehenna or up to the Throne
He travels the fastest who travels alone.

White hands cling to the tightened rein,
Slipping the spur from the booted heel,
Tenderest voices cry, 'Turn again,'
Red lips tarnish the scabbarded steel,
High hopes faint on a warm hearth-stone—
He travels the fastest who travels alone.

One may fall but he falls by himself—
Falls by himself with himself to blame;
One may attain and to him is the pelf,
Loot of the city in Gold of Fame;
Plunder of earth shall be all his own
Who travels the fastest and travels alone.

Wherefore the more ye be holpen and stayed—
Stayed by a friend in the hour of toil,
Sing the heretical song I have made—
His be the labour and yours be the spoil.
Win by his aid and the aid of disown—
He travels the fastest who travels alone.

DRAY WARA YOW DEE

For jealousy is the rage of a man: therefore he will not spare in the day of vengeance.—Prov. vi. 34.

Almonds and raisins, Sahib? Grapes from Kabul? Or a pony of the rarest if the Sahib will only come with me. He is thirteen three, Sahib, plays polo, goes in a cart, carries a lady and—Holy Kurshed and the Blessed Imams, it is the Sahib himself! My heart is made fat and my eye glad. May you never be tired! As is cold water in the Tirah, so is the sight of a friend in a far place. And what do you in this accursed land? South of Delhi, Sahib, you know the saying—'Rats are the men and trulls the women.' It was an order? Ahoo! An order is an order till one is strong enough to disobey. O my brother, O my friend, we have met in an auspicious hour! Is all well in the heart and the body and the house? In a lucky day have we two come together again.

I am to go with you? Your favour is great. Will there be picket-room in the compound? I have three horses and the bundles and the horse-boy. Moreover, remember that the police here hold me a horse-thief. What do these Lowland bastards know of horse-thieves? Do you remember that time in Peshawur when Kamal hammered on the gates of Jumrud—mountebank that he was—and lifted the Colonel's horses all in one night? Kamal is dead now, but his nephew has taken up the matter, and there will be more horses amissing if the Khaiber Levies do not look to it.

The Peace of God and the favour of His Prophet be upon this house and all that is in it! Shafizullah, rope the mottled mare under the tree and draw water. The horses can stand in the sun, but double the felts over the loins. Nay, my friend, do not trouble to look them over. They are to sell to the Officer fools who know so many tilings of the horse. The mare is heavy in foal; the gray is a devil unlicked; and the dun— but you know the trick of the peg. When they are sold I go back to Pubbi, or, it may be, the Valley of Peshawur.

O friend of my heart, it is good to see you again. I have been bowing and lying all day to the Officer-Sahibs in respect to those horses; and my mouth is dry for straight talk. Auggrh! Before a meal tobacco is good. Do not join me, for we are not in our own country. Sit in the veranda and I will spread my cloth here. But first I will drink. In the name of God returning thanks, thrice! This is sweet water, indeed— sweet as the water of Sheoran when it comes from the snows.

They are all well and pleased in the North—Khoda Baksh and the others. Yar Khan has come down with the horses from Kurdistan—six and thirty head only, and a full half pack-ponies—and has said openly in the Kashmir Serai that you English should send guns and blow the Amir into Hell. There are fifteen rolls now on the Kabul road; and at Dakka, when he thought he was clear, Yar Khan was stripped of all his Balkh stallions by the Governor! This is a great injustice, and Yar Khan is hot with rage. And of the others: Mahbub Ali is still at Pubbi, writing God knows what. Tugluq Khan is in jail for the business of the Kohat Police Post. Faiz Beg came down from Ismail-ki-Dhera with a Bokhariot belt for thee, my brother, at the closing of the year, but none knew whither thou hadst gone: there was no news left behind. The Cousins have taken a new run near Pakpattan to breed mules for the Government carts, and there is a story in Bazar of a priest. Oho! Such a salt tale! Listen—

Sahib, why do you ask that? My clothes are fouled because of the dust on the road. My eyes are sad because of the glare of the sun. My feet are swollen because I have washed them in bitter water, and my cheeks are hollow because the food here is bad. Fire burn your money! What do I want with it? I am rich and I thought you were my friend; but you are like the others—a Sahib. Is a man sad? Give him money, say the Sahibs. Is he dishonoured? Give him money, say the Sahibs. Hath he a wrong upon his head? Give him money, say the Sahibs. Such are the Sahibs, and such art thou—even thou.

Nay, do not look at the feet of the dun. Pity it is that I ever taught you to know the legs of a horse. Footsore? Be it so. What of that? The roads are hard. And the mare footsore? She bears a double burden, Sahib.

And now I pray you, give me permission to depart. Great favour and honour has the Sahib done me, and graciously has he shown his belief that the horses are stolen. Will it please him to send me to the Thana? To call a sweeper and have me led away by one of these lizard-men? I am the Sahib's friend. I have drunk water in the shadow of his house, and he has blackened my face. Remains there anything more to do? Will the Sahib give me eight annas to make smooth the injury and—complete the insult—?

Forgive me, my brother. I knew not—I know not now—what I say. Yes, I lied to you! I will put dust on my head—and I am an Afridi! The horses have been marched footsore from the Valley to this place, and my eyes are dim, and my body aches for the want of sleep, and my heart is dried up with sorrow and shame. But as it was my shame, so by God the Dispenser of Justice—by Allah-al-Mumit—it shall be my own revenge!

We have spoken together with naked hearts before this, and our hands have dipped into the same dish and thou hast been to me as a brother. Therefore I pay thee back with lies and ingratitude—as a Pathan. Listen now! When the grief of the soul is too heavy for endurance it may be a little eased by speech, and, moreover, the mind of a true man is as a well, and the pebble of confession dropped therein sinks and is no more seen. From the Valley have I come on foot, league by league, with a fire in my chest like the fire of the Pit. And why? Hast thou, then, so quickly forgotten our customs, among this folk who sell their wives and their daughters for silver? Come back with me to the North and be among men once more. Come back, when this matter is accomplished and I call for thee! The bloom of the peach-orchards is upon all the Valley, and here is only dust and a great stink. There is a pleasant wind among the mulberry trees, and the streams are bright with snow-water, and the caravans go up and the caravans go down, and a hundred fires sparkle in the gut of the Pass, and tent-peg answers hammer-nose, and pack-horse squeals to pack-horse across the drift smoke of the evening. It is good in the North now. Come back with me. Let us return to our own people! Come!

Whence is my sorrow? Does a man tear out his heart and make fritters thereof over a slow fire for aught other than a woman? Do not laugh, friend of mine, for your time will also be. A woman of the Abazai was she, and I took her to wife to staunch the feud between our village and the men of Ghor. I am no longer young? The lime has touched my beard? True. I had no need of the wedding? Nay, but I loved her. What saith Rahman: 'Into whose heart Love enters, there is Folly and naught else. By a glance of the eye she hath blinded thee; and by the eyelids and the fringe of the eyelids taken thee into the captivity without ransom, and naught else.' Dost thou remember that song at the sheep-roasting in the Pindi camp among the Uzbegs of the Amir?

The Abazai are dogs and their women the servants of sin. There was a lover of her own people, but of that her father told me naught. My friend, curse for me in your prayers, as I curse at each praying from the Fakr to the Isha, the name of Daoud Shah, Abazai, whose head is still upon his neck, whose hands are still upon his wrists, who has done me dishonour, who has made my name a laughing-stock among the women of Little Malikand.

I went into Hindustan at the end of two months—to Cherat. I was gone twelve days only; but I had said that I would be fifteen days absent. This I did to try her, for it is written: 'Trust not the incapable.' Coming up the gorge alone in the falling of the light, I heard the voice of a man singing at the door of my house; and it was the voice of Daoud Shah, and the song that he sang was 'Dray wara yow dee'—'All three are one.' It was as though a heelrope had been slipped round my heart and all the Devils were drawing it tight past endurance. I crept silently up the hill-road, but the fuse of my matchlock was wetted with the rain, and I could not slay Daoud Shah from afar. Moreover, it was in my mind to kill the woman also. Thus he sang, sitting outside my house, and, anon, the woman opened the door, and I came nearer, crawling on my belly among the rocks. I had only my knife to my hand. But a stone slipped under my foot, and the two looked down the hillside, and he, leaving his matchlock, fled from my anger, because he was afraid for the life that was in him. But the woman moved not till I stood in front of her, crying: 'O woman, what is this that thou hast done?' And she, void of fear, though she knew my thought, laughed, saying: 'It is a little thing. I loved him, and thou art a dog and cattle-thief coming by night.

Strike!' And I, being still blinded by her beauty, for, O my friend, the women of the Abazai are very fair, said: 'Hast thou no fear?' And she answered: 'None—but only the fear that I do not die.' Then said I: 'Have no fear.' And she bowed her head, and I smote it off at the neck-bone so that it leaped between my feet. Thereafter the rage of our people came upon me, and I hacked off the breasts, that the men of Little Malikand might know the crime, and cast the body into the water-course that flows to the Kabul river. Dray wara yow dee! Dray wara yow dee! The body without the head, the soul without light, and my own darkling heart—all three are one—all three are one!

That night, making no halt, I went to Ghor and demanded news of Daoud Shah. Men said: 'He is gone to Pubbi for horses. What wouldst thou of him? There is peace between the villages.' I made answer: 'Aye! The peace of treachery and the love that the Devil Atala bore to Gurel.' So I fired thrice into the gate and laughed and went my way.

In those hours, brother and friend of my heart's heart, the moon and the stars were as blood above me, and in my mouth was the taste of dry earth. Also, I broke no bread, and my drink was the rain of the Valley of Ghor upon my face.

At Pubbi I found Mahbub Ali, the writer, sitting upon his charpoy and gave up my arms according to your Law. But I was not grieved, for it was in my heart that I should kill Daoud Shah with my bare hands thus—as a man strips a bunch of raisins. Mahbub Ali said: 'Daoud Shah has even now gone hot-foot to Peshawur, and he will pick up his horses upon the road to Delhi, for it is said that the Bombay Tramway Company are buying horses there by the truck-load; eight horses to the truck.' And that was a true saying.

Then I saw that the hunting would be no little thing, for the man was gone into your borders to save himself against my wrath. And shall he save himself so? Am I not alive? Though he run northward to the Dora and the snow, or southerly to the Black Water, I will follow him, as a lover follows the footsteps of his mistress, and coming upon him I will take him tenderly—Aho! so tenderly!—in my arms, saying: 'Well hast thou done and well shalt thou be repaid.' And out of that embrace Daoud Shah shall not go forth with the breath in his nostrils. Auggrh! Where is the pitcher? I am as thirsty as a mother-mare in the first month.

Your Law! What is your Law to me? When the horses fight on the runs do they regard the boundary pillars; or do the kites of Ali Musjid forbear because the carrion lies under the shadow of Ghor Kuttri? The matter began across the Border. It shall finish where God pleases. Here, in my own country, or in Hell. All three are one.

Listen now, sharer of the sorrow of my heart, and I will tell of the hunting. I followed to Peshawur from Pubbi, and I went to and fro about the streets of Peshawur like a houseless dog, seeking for my enemy. Once I thought I saw him washing his mouth in the conduit in the big square, but when I came up he was gone. It may be that it was he, and, seeing my face, he had fled.

A girl of the bazar said that he would go to Nowshera. I said: 'O heart's heart, does Daoud Shah visit thee?' And she said: 'Even so.' I said: 'I would fain see him, for we be friends parted for two years. Hide me, I pray, here in the shadow of the window shutter, and I will wait for his coming.' And the girl said: 'O Pathan, look into my eyes!' And I turned, leaning upon her breast, and looked into her eyes, swearing that I spoke the very Truth of God. But she answered: 'Never friend waited friend with such eyes. Lie to

God and the Prophet, but to a woman ye cannot lie. Get hence! There shall be no harm befall Daoud Shah by cause of me.'

I would have strangled that girl but for the fear of your Police; and thus the hunting would have come to naught. Therefore I only laughed and departed, and she leaned over the window-bar in the night and mocked me down the street. Her name is Jamun. When I have made my account with the man I will return to Peshawur and—her lovers shall desire her no more for her beauty's sake. She shall not be Jamun but Ak, the cripple among trees. Ho! Ho! Ak shall she be!

At Peshawur I bought the horses and grapes, and the almonds and dried fruits, that the reason of my wanderings might be open to the Government, and that there might be no hindrance upon the road. But when I came to Nowshera he was gone, and I knew not where to go. I stayed one day at Nowshera, and in the night a Voice spoke in my ears as I slept among the horses. All night it flew round my head and would not cease from whispering. I was upon my belly, sleeping as the Devils sleep, and it may have been that the Voice was the voice of a Devil. It said: 'Go south, and thou shalt come upon Daoud Shah.' Listen, my brother and chiefest among friends—listen! Is the tale a long one? Think how it was long to me. I have trodden every league of the road from Pubbi to this place; and from Nowshera my guide was only the Voice and the lust of vengeance.

To the Uttock I went, but that was no hindrance to me. Ho! Ho! A man may turn the word twice, even in his trouble. The Uttock was no uttock (obstacle) to me; and I heard the Voice above the noise of the waters beating on the big rock, saying: 'Go to the right.' So I went to Pindigheb, and in those days my sleep was taken from me utterly, and the head of the woman of the Abazai was before me night and day, even as it had fallen between my feet. Dray wara yow dee! Dray wara yow dee! Fire, ashes, and my couch, all three are one—all three are one!

Now I was far from the winter path of the dealers who had gone to Sialkot and so south by the rail and the Big Road to the line of cantonments; but there was a Sahib in camp at Pindigheb who bought from me a white mare at a good price, and told me that one Daoud Shah had passed to Shahpur with horses. Then I saw that the warning of the Voice was true, and made swift to come to the Salt Hills. The Jhelum was in flood, but I could not wait, and, in the crossing, a bay stallion was washed down and drowned. Herein was God hard to me—not in respect of the beast, of that I had no care—but in this snatching. While I was upon the right bank urging the horses into the water, Daoud Shah was upon the left; for— Alghias! Alghias!—the hoofs of my mare scattered the hot ashes of his fires when we came up the hither bank in the light of morning. But he had fled. His feet were made swift by the terror of Death. And I went south from Shahpur as the kite flies. I dared not turn aside, lest I should miss my vengeance— which is my right. From Shahpur I skirted by the Jhelum, for I thought that he would avoid the Desert of the Rechna. But, presently, at Sahiwal, I turned away upon the road to Jhang, Samundri, and Gugera, till, upon a night, the mottled mare breasted the fence of the rail that turns to Montgomery. And that place was Okara, and the head of the woman of the Abazai lay upon the sand between my feet.

Thence I went to Fazilka, and they said that I was mad to bring starved horses there. The Voice was with me, and I was not mad, but only wearied, because I could not find Daoud Shah. It was written that I should not find him at Rania nor Bahadurgarh, and I came into Delhi from the west, and there also I found him not. My friend, I have seen many strange things in my wanderings. I have seen Devils rioting across the Rechna as the stallions riot in spring. I have heard the Djinns calling to each other from holes in the sand, and I have seen them pass before my face. There are no Devils, say the Sahibs? They are very wise, but they do not know all things about devils or—horses. Ho! Ho! I say to you who are laughing at my misery, that I have seen the Devils at high noon whooping and leaping on the shoals of the Chenab. And was I afraid? My brother, when the desire of a man is set upon one thing alone, he fears neither God nor Man nor Devil. If my vengeance failed, I would splinter the Gates of Paradise with the butt of my gun, or I would cut my way into Hell with my knife, and I would call upon Those who Govern there for the body of Daoud Shah. What love so deep as hate?

Do not speak. I know the thought in your heart. Is the white of this eye clouded? How does the blood beat at the wrist? There is no madness in my flesh, but only the vehemence of the desire that has eaten me up. Listen!

South of Delhi I knew not the country at all. Therefore I cannot say where I went, but I passed through many cities. I knew only that it was laid upon me to go south. When the horses could march no more, I threw myself upon the earth, and waited till the day. There was no sleep with me in that journeying; and that was a heavy burden. Dost thou know, brother of mine, the evil of wakefulness that cannot break— when the bones are sore for lack of sleep, and the skin of the temples twitches with weariness, and yet—there is no sleep—there is no sleep? Dray wara yow dee! Dray wara yow dee! The eye of the Sun, the eye of the Moon, and my own unrestful eyes—all three are one—all three are one!

There was a city the name whereof I have forgotten, and there the Voice called all night. That was ten days ago. It has cheated me afresh.

I have come hither from a place called Hamirpur, and, behold, it is my Fate that I should meet with thee to my comfort, and the increase of friendship. This is a good omen. By the joy of looking upon thy face the weariness has gone from my feet, and the sorrow of my so long travel is forgotten. Also my heart is peaceful; for I know that the end is near.

It may be that I shall find Daoud Shah in this city going northward, since a Hillman will ever head back to his Hills when the spring warns. And shall he see those hills of our country? Surely I shall overtake him! Surely my vengeance is safe! Surely God hath him in the hollow of His hand against my claiming. There shall no harm befall Daoud Shah till I come; for I would fain kill him quick and whole with the life sticking firm in his body. A pomegranate is sweetest when the cloves break away unwilling from the rind. Let it be in the daytime, that I may see his face, and my delight may be crowned.

And when I have accomplished the matter and my Honour is made clean, I shall return thanks unto God, the Holder of the Scale of the Law, and I shall sleep. From the night, through the day, and into the night again I shall sleep; and no dream shall trouble me.

And now, O my brother, the tale is all told. AHI! AHI! ALGHIAS! AHI!

THE JUDGMENT OF DUNGARA

See the pale martyr with his shirt on fire.—PRINTER'S ERROR.

They tell the tale even now among the groves of the Berbulda Hill, and for corroboration point to the roofless and windowless Mission-house. The great God Dungara, the God of Things as They Are, Most Terrible, One-eyed, Bearing the Red Elephant Tusk, did it all; and he who refuses to believe in Dungara will assuredly be smitten by the Madness of Yat—the madness that fell upon the sons and the daughters of the Buria Kol when they turned aside from Dungara and put on clothes. So says Athon Daze*, who is High Priest of the shrine and Warden of the Red Elephant Tusk. But if you ask the Assistant Collector and Agent in Charge of the Buria Kol, he will laugh—not because he bears any malice against missions, but because he himself saw the vengeance of Dungara executed upon the spiritual children of the Reverend Justus Krenk, Pastor of the Tubingen Mission, and upon Lotta, his virtuous wife.

Yet if ever a man merited good treatment of the Gods it was the Reverend Justus, one time of Heidelberg, who, on the faith of a call, went into the wilderness and took the blonde, blue-eyed Lotta with him. 'We will these Heathen now by idolatrous practices so darkened better make,' said Justus in the early days of his career. 'Yes,' he added with conviction, 'they shall be good and shall with their hands to work learn. For all good Christians must work.' And upon a stipend more modest even than that of an English lay-reader, Justus Krenk kept house beyond Kamala and the gorge of Malair, beyond the Berbulda River close to the foot of the blue hill of Panth on whose summit stands the Temple of Dungara—in the heart of the country of the Buria Kol—the naked, good-tempered, timid, shameless, lazy Buria Kol.

Do you know what life at a Mission outpost means? Try to imagine a loneliness exceeding that of the smallest station to which Government has ever sent you—isolation that weighs upon the waking eyelids and drives you by force headlong into the labours of the day. There is no post, there is no one of your own colour to speak to, there are no roads: there is, indeed, food to keep you alive, but it is not pleasant to eat; and whatever of good or beauty or interest there is in your life, must come from yourself and the grace that may be planted in you.

In the morning, with a patter of soft feet, the converts, the doubtful, and the open scoffers, troop up to the veranda. You must be infinitely kind and patient, and, above all, clear-sighted, for you deal with the simplicity of childhood, the experience of man, and the subtlety of the savage. Your congregation have a hundred material wants to be considered; and it is for you, as you believe in your personal responsibility to your Maker, to pick out of the clamouring crowd any grain of spirituality that may lie therein. If to the cure of souls you add that of bodies, your task will be all the more difficult, for the sick and the maimed will profess any and every creed for the sake of healing, and will laugh at you because you are simple enough to believe them.

As the day wears and the impetus of the morning dies away, there will come upon you an overwhelming sense of the uselessness of your toil. This must be striven against, and the only spur in your side will be the belief that you are playing against the Devil for the living soul. It is a great, a joyous belief; but he who can hold it unwavering for four and twenty consecutive hours, must be blessed with an abundantly strong physique and equable nerve.

Ask the gray heads of the Bannockburn Medical Crusade what manner of life their preachers lead; speak to the Racine Gospel Agency, those lean Americans whose boast is that they go where no Englishman dare follow; get a Pastor of the Tubingen Mission to talk of his experiences—if you can. You will be referred to the printed reports, but these contain no mention of the men who have lost youth and health, all that a man may lose except faith, in the wilds; of English maidens who have gone forth and died in the fever-stricken jungle of the Panth Hills, knowing from the first that death was almost a certainty. Few Pastors will tell you of these things any more than they will speak of that young David of St. Bees, who, set apart for the Lord's work, broke down in utter desolation, and returned half distraught to the Head Mission, crying: 'There is no God, but I have walked with the Devil!'

The reports are silent here, because heroism, failure, doubt, despair, and self-abnegation on the part of a mere cultured white man are things of no weight as compared to the saving of one half-human soul from a fantastic faith in wood-spirits, goblins of the rock, and river-fiends.

And Gallio, the Assistant Collector of the country side, 'cared for none of these things.' He had been long in the district, and the Buria Kol loved him and brought him offerings of speared fish, orchids from the dim moist heart of the forests, and as much game as he could eat. In return, he gave them quinine, and with Athon Daze, the High Priest, controlled their simple policies.

'When you have been some years in the country,' said Gallio at the Krenks' table, 'you grow to find one creed as good as another. I'll give you all the assistance in my power, of course, but don't hurt my Buria Kol. They are a good people and they trust me.'

'I will them the Word of the Lord teach,' said Justus, his round face beaming with enthusiasm, 'and I will assuredly to their prejudices no wrong hastily without thinking make. But, O my friend, this in the mind impartiality-of-creed-judgment-be-looking is very bad.'

'Heigh-ho!' said Gallio, 'I have their bodies and the district to see to, but you can try what you can do for their souls. Only don't behave as your predecessor did, or I'm afraid that I can't guarantee your life.'

'And that?' said Lotta sturdily, handing him a cup of tea.

'He went up to the Temple of Dungara—to be sure he was new to the country—and began hammering old Dungara over the head with an umbrella; so the Buria Kol turned out and hammered HIM rather savagely. I was in the district, and he sent a runner to me with a note saying: "Persecuted for the Lord's sake. Send wing of regiment." The nearest troops were about two hundred miles off, but I guessed what he had been doing. I rode to Panth and talked to old Athon Daze like a father, telling him that a man of his wisdom ought to have known that the Sahib had sunstroke and was mad. You never saw a people more sorry in your life. Athon Daze apologised, sent wood and milk and fowls and all sorts of things; and I gave five rupees to the shrine and told Macnamara that he had been injudicious. He said that I had bowed down in the House of Rimmon; but if he had only just gone over the brow of the hill and insulted Palin Deo, the idol of the Suria Kol, he would have been impaled on a charred bamboo long before I could have done anything, and then I should have had to have hanged some of the poor brutes. Be gentle with them, Padri—but I don't think you'll do much.'

'Not I,' said Justus, 'but my Master. We will with the little children begin. Many of them will be sick—that is so. After the children the mothers; and then the men. But I would greatly that you were in internal sympathies with us prefer.'

Gallio departed to risk his life in mending the rotten bamboo bridges of his people, in killing a too persistent tiger here or there, in sleeping out in the reeking jungle, or in tracking the Suria Kol raiders who had taken a few heads from their brethren of the Buria clan. He was a knock-kneed, shambling young man, naturally devoid of creed or reverence, with a longing for absolute power which his undesirable district gratified.

'No one wants my post,' he used to say grimly, 'and my Collector only pokes his nose in when he's quite certain that there is no fever. I'm monarch of all I survey, and Athon Daze is my viceroy.'

Because Gallio prided himself on his supreme disregard of human life—though he never extended the theory beyond his own—he naturally rode forty miles to the Mission with a tiny brown girl-baby on his saddle-bow.

'Here is something for you, Padri,' said he. 'The Kols leave their surplus children to die. 'Don't see why they shouldn't, but you may rear this one. I picked it up beyond the Berbulda fork. I've a notion that the mother has been following me through the woods ever since.'

'It is the first of the fold,' said Justus, and Lotta caught up the screaming morsel to her bosom and hushed it craftily; while, as a wolf hangs in the field, Matui, who had borne it and in accordance with the law of her tribe had exposed it to die, panted weary and footsore in the bamboo-brake, watching the house with hungry mother-eyes. What would the omnipotent Assistant Collector do? Would the little man in the black coat eat her daughter alive as Athon Daze said was the custom of all men in black coats?

Matui waited among the bamboos through the long night; and, in the morning, there came forth a fair white woman, the like of whom Matui had never seen, and in her arms was Matui's daughter clad in spotless raiment. Lotta knew little of the tongue of the Buria Kol, but when mother calls to mother, speech is easy to follow. By the hands stretched timidly to the hem of her gown, by the passionate gutturals and the longing eyes, Lotta understood with whom she had to deal. So Matui took her child again—would be a servant, even a slave, to this wonderful white woman, for her own tribe would recognise her no more. And Lotta wept with her exhaustively, after the German fashion, which includes much blowing of the nose.

'First the child, then the mother, and last the man, and to the Glory of God all,' said Justus the Hopeful. And the man came, with a bow and arrows, very angry indeed, for there was no one to cook for him.

But the tale of the Mission is a long one, and I have no space to show how Justus, forgetful of his injudicious predecessor, grievously smote Moto, the husband of Matui, for his brutality; how Moto was startled, but being released from the fear of instant death, took heart and became the faithful ally and first convert of Justus; how the little gathering grew, to the huge disgust of Athon Daze; how the Priest of the God of Things as They Are argued subtilely with the Priest of the God of Things as They Should Be, and was worsted; how the dues of the Temple of Dungara fell away in fowls and fish and honeycomb; how Lotta lightened the Curse of Eve among the women, and how Justus did his best to introduce the Curse of Adam; how the Buria Kol rebelled at this, saying that their God was an idle God, and how Justus partially overcame their scruples against work, and taught them that the black earth was rich in other produce than pig-nuts only.

All these things belong to the history of many months, and throughout those months the white-haired Athon Daze meditated revenge for the tribal neglect of Dungara. With savage cunning he feigned friendship towards Justus, even hinting at his own conversion; but to the congregation of Dungara he said darkly: 'They of the Padri's flock have put on clothes and worship a busy God. Therefore Dungara will afflict them grievously till they throw themselves, howling, into the waters of the Berbulda.' At night the Red Elephant Tusk boomed and groaned among the hills, and the faithful waked and said: 'The God of Things as They Are matures revenge against the backsliders. Be merciful, Dungara, to us Thy children, and give us all their crops!'

Late in the cold weather, the Collector and his wife came into the Buria Kol country. 'Go and look at Krenk's Mission' said Gallio. 'He is doing good work in his own way, and I think he'd be pleased if you opened the bamboo chapel that he, has managed to run up. At any rate you'll see a civilised Buria Kol.'

Great was the stir in the Mission. 'Now he and the gracious lady will that we have done good work with their own eyes see, and—yes—we will him our converts in all their new clothes by their own hands constructed exhibit. It will a great day be—for the Lord always,' said Justus; and Lotta said 'Amen.'

Justus had, in his quiet way, felt jealous of the Basel Weaving Mission, his own converts being unhandy; but Athon Daze had latterly induced some of them to hackle the glossy silky fibres of a plant that grew plenteously on the Panth Hills. It yielded a cloth white and smooth almost as the TAPPA of the South Seas, and that day the converts were to wear for the first time clothes made therefrom. Justus was proud of his work.

'They shall in white clothes clothed to meet the Collector and his well-born lady come down, singing "NOW THANK WE ALL OUR GOD." Then he will the Chapel open, and—yes—even Gallio to believe will begin. Stand so, my children, two by two, and—Lotta, why do they thus themselves bescratch? It is not seemly to wriggle, Nala, my child. The Collector will be here and be pained.'

The Collector, his wife, and Gallio climbed the hill to the Mission-station. The converts were drawn up in two lines, a shining band nearly forty strong. 'Hah!' said the Collector, whose acquisitive bent of mind led him to believe that he had fostered the institution from the first. 'Advancing, I see, by leaps and bounds.'

Never was truer word spoken! The Mission was advancing exactly as he had said—at first by little hops and shuffles of shamefaced uneasiness, but soon by the leaps of fly-stung horses and the bounds of maddened kangaroos. From the hill of Panth the Red Elephant Tusk delivered a dry and anguished blare. The ranks of the converts wavered, broke and scattered with yells and shrieks of pain, while Justus and Lotta stood horror-stricken.

'It is the Judgment of Dungara!' shouted a voice. 'I burn! I burn! To the river or we die!'

The mob wheeled and headed for the rocks that over-hung the Berbulda, writhing, stamping, twisting and shedding its garments as it ran, pursued by the thunder of the trumpet of Dungara. Justus and Lotta fled to the Collector almost in tears.

'I cannot understand! Yesterday,' panted Justus, 'they had the Ten Commandments.—What is this? Praise the Lord all good spirits by land and by sea. Nala! Oh, shame!'

With a bound and a scream there alighted on the rocks above their heads, Nala, once the pride of the Mission, a maiden of fourteen summers, good, docile, and virtuous—now naked as the dawn and spitting like a wild-cat.

'Was it for this!' she raved, hurling her petticoat at Justus; 'was it for this I left my people and Dungara—for the fires of your Bad Place? Blind ape, little earthworm, dried fish that you are, you said that I should never burn! O Dungara, I burn now! I burn now! Have mercy, God of Things as They Are!'

She turned and flung herself into the Berbulda, and the trumpet of Dungara bellowed jubilantly. The last of the converts of the Tubingen Mission had put a quarter of a mile of rapid river between herself and her teachers.

'Yesterday,' gulped Justus, 'she taught in the school A,B,C,D.—Oh! It is the work of Satan!'

But Gallio was curiously regarding the maiden's petticoat where it had fallen at his feet. He felt its texture, drew back his shirt-sleeve beyond the deep tan of his wrist and pressed a fold of the cloth against the flesh. A blotch of angry red rose on the white skin.

'Ah!' said Gallio calmly, 'I thought so.'

'What is it?' said Justus.

'I should call it the Shirt of Nessus, but—Where did you get the fibre of this cloth from?'

'Athon Daze,' said Justus. 'He showed the boys how it should manufactured be.'

'The old fox! Do you know that he has given you the Nilgiri Nettle—scorpion—Girardenia heterophylla— to work up? No wonder they squirmed! Why, it stings even when they make bridge-ropes of it, unless it's soaked for six weeks. The cunning brute! It would take about half an hour to burn through their thick hides, and then—!'

Gallio burst into laughter, but Lotta was weeping in the arms of the Collector's wife, and Justus had covered his face with his hands.

'Girardenia heterophylla!'' repeated Gallio. 'Krenk, why didn't you tell me? I could have saved you this. Woven fire! Anybody but a naked Kol would have known it, and, if I'm a judge of their ways, you'll never get them back.'

He looked across the river to where the converts were still wallowing and wailing in the shallows, and the laughter died out of his eyes, for he saw that the Tubingen Mission to the Buria Kol was dead.

Never again, though they hung mournfully round the deserted school for three months, could Lotta or Justus coax back even the most promising of their flock. No! The end of conversion was the fire of the Bad Place—fire that ran through the limbs and gnawed into the bones. Who dare a second time tempt the anger of Dungara? Let the little man and his wife go elsewhere. The Buria Kol would have none of them. An unofficial message to Athon Daze that if a hair of their heads were touched, Athon Daze and the priests of Dungara would be hanged by Gallio at the temple shrine, protected Justus and Lotta from the stumpy poisoned arrows of the Buria Kol, but neither fish nor fowl, honeycomb, salt nor young pig were brought to their doors any more. And, alas! man cannot live by grace alone if meat be wanting.

'Let us go, mine wife,' said Justus; 'there is no good here, and the Lord has willed that some other man shall the work take—in good time—in His own good time. We will go away, and I will—yes—some botany bestudy.'

If any one is anxious to convert the Buria Kol afresh, there lies at least the core of a mission-house under the hill of Panth. But the chapel and school have long since fallen back into jungle.

AT HOWLI THANA

His own shoe, his own head.—Native Proverb.

As a messenger, if the heart of the Presence be moved to so great favour. And on six rupees. Yes, Sahib, for I have three little children whose stomachs are always empty, and corn is now but forty pounds to the rupee. I will make so clever a messenger that you shall all day long be pleased with me, and, at the end of the year, bestow a turban. I know all the roads of the Station and many other things. Aha, Sahib! I am clever. Give me service. I was aforetime in the Police. A bad character? Now without doubt an enemy has told this tale. Never was I a scamp. I am a man of clean heart, and all my words are true. They knew this when I was in the Police. They said: 'Afzal Khan is a true speaker in whose words men may trust.' I am a Delhi Pathan, Sahib—all Delhi Pathans are good men. You have seen Delhi? Yes, it is true that there be many scamps among the Delhi Pathans. How wise is the Sahib! Nothing is hid from his eyes, and he will make me his messenger, and I will take all his notes secretly and without ostentation. Nay, Sahib, God is my witness that I meant no evil. I have long desired to serve under a true Sahib—a virtuous Sahib. Many young Sahibs are as devils unchained. With these Sahibs I would take no service—not though all the stomachs of my little children were crying for bread.

Why am I not still in the Police? I will speak true talk. An evil came to the Thana—to Ram Baksh, the Havildar, and Maula Baksh, and Juggut Ram and Bhim Singh and Suruj Bul. Ram Baksh is in the jail for a space, and so also is Maula Baksh.

It was at the Thana of Howli, on the road that leads to Gokral-Seetarun wherein are many dacoits. We were all brave men—Rustums. Wherefore we were sent to that Thana which was eight miles from the next Thana. All day and all night we watched for dacoits. Why does the Sahib laugh? Nay, I will make a confession. The dacoits were too clever, and, seeing this, we made no further trouble. It was in the hot weather. What can a man do in the hot days? Is the Sahib who is so strong—is he, even, vigorous in that hour? We made an arrangement with the dacoits for the sake of peace. That was the work of the Havildar who was fat. Ho! Ho! Sahib, he is now getting thin in the jail among the carpets. The Havildar said:' Give us no trouble, and we will give you no trouble. At the end of the reaping send us a man to lead before the judge, a man of infirm mind against whom the trumped-up case will break down, Thus we shall save our honour.' To this talk the dacoits agreed, and we had no trouble at the Thana, and could eat melons in peace, sitting upon our charpoys all day long. Sweet as sugar-cane are the melons of Howli.

Now there was an assistant commissioner—a Stunt Sahib, in that district, called Yunkum Sahib. Aha! He was hard-hard even as is the Sahib who, without doubt, will give me the shadow of his protection. Many eyes had Yunkum Sahib, and moved quickly through his district. Men called him The Tiger of Gokral-Seetarun, because he would arrive unannounced and make his kill and, before sunset, would be giving trouble to the Tehsildars thirty miles away. No one knew the comings or the goings of Yunkum Sahib. He had no camp, and when his horse was weary he rode upon a devil-carriage. I do not know its name, but the Sahib sat in the midst of three silver wheels that made no creaking, and drave them with his legs, prancing like a bean-fed horse—thus. A shadow of a hawk upon the fields was not more without noise than the devil-carriage of Yunkum Sahib. It was here: it was there: it was gone: and the rapport was made, and there was trouble. Ask the Tehsildar of Rohestri how the hen-stealing came to be known, Sahib.

It fell upon a night that we of the Thana slept according to custom upon our charpoys, having eaten the evening meal and drunk tobacco. When we awoke in the morning, behold, of our six rifles not one remained! Also, the big Police-book that was in the Havildar's charge was gone. Seeing these things, we were very much afraid, thinking on our parts that the dacoits, regardless of honour, had come by night, and put us to shame. Then said Ram Baksh, the Havildar:' Be silent! The business is an evil business, but it may yet go well. Let us make the case complete. Bring a kid and my tulwar. See you not now, O fools? A kick for a horse, but a word is enough for a man.'

We of the Thana, perceiving quickly what was in the mind of the Havildar, and greatly fearing that the service would be lost, made haste to take the kid into the inner room, and attended to the words of the Havildar. 'Twenty dacoits came,' said the Havildar, and we, taking his words, repeated after him according to custom. 'There was a great fight,' said the Havildar, 'and of us no man escaped unhurt. The bars of the window were broken. Suruj Bul, see thou to that; and, O men, put speed into your work, for a runner must go with the news to The Tiger of Gokral-Seetarun.' Thereon, Suruj Bul, leaning with his shoulder, brake in the bars of the window, and I, beating her with a whip, made the Havildar's mare skip among the melon-beds till they were much trodden with hoof-prints.

These things being made, I returned to the Thana, and the goat was slain, and certain portions of the walls were blackened with fire, and each man dipped his clothes a little into the blood of the goat. Know, O Sahib, that a wound made by man upon his own body can, by those skilled, be easily discerned from a wound wrought by another man. Therefore, the Havildar, taking his tulwar, smote one of us lightly on the forearm in the fat, and another on the leg, and a third on the back of the hand. Thus dealt he with all of us till the blood came; and Suruj Bul, more eager than the others, took out much hair. O Sahib, never was so perfect an arrangement. Yea, even I would have sworn that the Thana had been treated as we said. There was smoke and breaking and blood and trampled earth.

'Ride now, Maula Baksh,' said the Havildar, 'to the house of the Stunt Sahib, and carry the news of the dacoity. Do you also, O Afzal Khan, run there, and take heed that you are mired with sweat and dust on your incoming. The blood will be dry on the clothes. I will stay and send a straight report to the Dipty Sahib, and we will catch certain that ye know of, villagers, so that all may be ready against the Dipty Sahib's arrival.'

Thus Maula Baksh rode and I ran hanging on the stirrup, and together we came in an evil plight before The Tiger of Gokral-Seetarun in the Rohestri tehsil. Our tale was long and correct, Sahib, for we gave even the names of the dacoits and the issue of the fight and besought him to come. But The Tiger made no sign, and only smiled after the manner of Sahibs when they have a wickedness in their hearts. 'Swear ye to the rapport?' said he, and we said: 'Thy servants swear. The blood of the fight is but newly dry upon us. Judge thou if it be the blood of the servants of the Presence, or not.' And he said: 'I see. Ye have done well.' But he did not call for his horse or his devil-carriage, and scour the land as was his custom. He said: 'Rest now and eat bread, for ye be wearied men. I will wait the coming of the Dipty Sahib.'

Now it is the order that the Havildar of the Thana should send a straight report of all dacoities to the Dipty Sahib. At noon came he, a fat man and an old, and overbearing withal, but we of the Thana had no fear of his anger; dreading more the silences of The Tiger of Gokral-Seetarun. With him came Ram

Baksh, the Havildar, and the others, guarding ten men of the village of Howli—all men evil affected towards the Police of the Sirkar. As prisoners they came, the irons upon their hands, crying for mercy—Imam Baksh, the farmer, who had denied his wife to the Havildar, and others, ill-conditioned rascals against whom we of the Thane bore spite. It was well done, and the Havildar was proud. But the Dipty Sahib was angry with the Stunt for lack of zeal, and said 'Dam-Dam' after the custom of the English people, and extolled the Havildar. Yunkum Sahib lay still in his long chair. 'Have the men sworn?' said Yunkum Sahib. 'Aye, and captured ten evildoers,' said the Dipty Sahib. 'There be more abroad in your charge. Take horse—ride, and go in the name of the Sirkar!' 'Truly there be more evil-doers abroad,' said Yunkum Sahib, 'but there is no need of a horse. Come all men with me.'

I saw the mark of a string on the temples of Imam Baksh. Does the Presence know the torture of the Cold Draw? I saw also the face of The Tiger of Gokral-Seeta-run, the evil smile was upon it, and I stood back ready for what might befall. Well it was, Sahib, that I did this thing. Yunkum Sahib unlocked the door of his bath-room, and smiled anew. Within lay the six rifles and the big Police-book of the Thana of Howli! He had come by night in the devil-carriage that is noiseless as a ghoul, and moving among us asleep, had taken away both the guns and the book! Twice had he come to the Thana, taking each time three rifles. The liver of the Havildar was turned to water, and he fell scrabbling in the dirt about the boots of Yunkum Sahib, crying—'Have mercy!'

And I? Sahib, I am a Delhi Pathan, and a young man with little children. The Havildar's mare was in the compound. I ran to her and rode: the black wrath of the Sirkar was behind me, and I knew not whither to go. Till she dropped and died I rode the red mare; and by the blessing of God, who is without doubt on the side of all just men, I escaped. But the Havildar and the rest are now in jail.

I am a scamp? It is as the Presence pleases. God will make the Presence a Lord, and give him a rich Mem-sahib as fair as a Peri to wife, and many strong sons, if he makes me his orderly. The Mercy of Heaven be upon the Sahib! Yes, I will only go to the bazar and bring my children to these so-palace-like quarters, and then—the Presence is my Father and my Mother, and I, Afzal Khan, am his slave.

Ohe, Sirdar-ji! I also am of the household of the Sahib.

GEMINI

Great is the justice of the White Man—greater the power of a lie. —Native Proverb.

This is your English Justice, Protector of the Poor. Look at my back and loins which are beaten with sticks—heavy sticks! I am a poor man, and there is no justice in Courts.

There were two of us, and we were born of one birth, but I swear to you that I was born the first, and Ram Dass is the younger by three full breaths. The astrologer said so, and it is written in my horoscope—the horoscope of Durga Dass.

But we were alike—I and my brother who is a beast without honour—so alike that none knew, together or apart, which was Durga Dass. I am a Mahajun of Pali in Marwar, and an honest man. This is true talk. When we were men, we left our father's house in Pali, and went to the Punjab, where all the people are mud-heads and sons of asses. We took shop together in Isser Jang—I and my brother—near the big well where the Governor's camp draws water. But Ram Dass, who is without truth, made quarrel with me, and we were divided. He took his books, and his pots, and his Mark, and became a bunnia—a money-lender—in the long street of Isser Jang, near the gateway of the road that goes to Montgomery. It was not my fault that we pulled each other's turbans. I am a Mahajun of Pali, and I always speak true talk. Ram Dass was the thief and the liar.

Now no man, not even the little children, could at one glance see which was Ram Dass and which was Durga Dass. But all the people of Isser Jang—may they die without sons!—said that we were thieves. They used much bad talk, but I took money on their bedsteads and their cooking-pots and the standing crop and the calf unborn, from the well in the big square to the gate of the Montgomery road. They were fools, these people—unfit to cut the toe-nails of a Marwari from Pali. I lent money to them all. A little, very little only—here a pice and there a pice. God is my witness that I am a poor man! The money is all with Ram Dass—may his sons turn Christian, and his daughter be a burning fire and a shame in the house from generation to generation! May she die unwed, and be the mother of a multitude of bastards! Let the light go out in the house of Ram Dass, my brother. This I pray daily twice—with offerings and charms.

Thus the trouble began. We divided the town of Isser Jang between us—I and my brother. There was a landholder beyond the gates, living but one short mile out, on the road that leads to Montgomery, and his name was Muhammad Shah, son of a Nawab. He was a great devil and drank wine. So long as there were women in his house, and wine and money for the marriage-feasts, he was merry and wiped his mouth. Ram Dass lent him the money, a lakh or half a lakh—how do I know?—and so long as the money was lent, the landholder cared not what he signed.

The People of Isser Jang were my portion, and the landholder and the out-town was the portion of Ram Dass; for so we had arranged. I was the poor man, for the people of Isser Jang were without wealth. I did what I could, but Ram Dass had only to wait without the door of the landholder's garden-court, and to lend him the money; taking the bonds from the hand of the steward.

In the autumn of the year after the lending, Ram Dass said to the landholder: 'Pay me my money,' but the landholder gave him abuse. But Ram Dass went into the Courts with the papers and the bonds—all correct—and took out decrees against the landholder; and the name of the Government was across the stamps of the decrees. Ram Dass took field by field, and mango-tree by mango-tree, and well by well; putting in his own men—debtors of the out-town of Isser Jang—to cultivate the crops. So he crept up across the land, for he had the papers, and the name of the Government was across the stamps, till his men held the crops for him on all sides of the big white house of the landholder. It was well done; but when the landholder saw these things he was very angry and cursed Ram Dass after the manner of the Muhammadans.

And thus the landholder was angry, but Ram Dass laughed and claimed more fields, as was written upon the bonds. This was in the month of Phagun. I took my horse and went out to speak to the man who makes lac-bangles upon the road that leads to Montgomery, because he owed me a debt. There was in front of me, upon his horse, my brother Ram Dass. And when he saw me, he turned aside into the high crops, because there was hatred between us. And I went forward till I came to the orange-bushes by the landholder's house. The bats were flying, and the evening smoke was low down upon the land. Here met me four men—swashbucklers and Muhammadans—with their faces bound up, laying hold of my horse's bridle and crying out: 'This is Ram Dass! Beat!' Me they beat with their staves—heavy staves bound about with wire at the end, such weapons as those swine of Punjabis use—till, having cried for mercy, I fell down senseless. But these shameless ones still beat me, saying: 'O Ram Dass, this is your interest—well weighed and counted into your hand, Ram Dass.' I cried aloud that I was not Ram Dass but Durga Dass, his brother, yet they only beat me the more, and when I could make no more outcry they left me. But I saw their faces. There was Elahi Baksh who runs by the side of the landholder's white horse, and Nur Ali the keeper of the door, and Wajib Ali the very strong cook, and Abdul Latif the messenger—all of the household of the landholder. These things I can swear on the Cow's Tail if need be, but—Ahi! Ahi!—it has been already sworn, and I am a poor man whose honour is lost.

When these four had gone away laughing, my brother Ram Dass came out of the crops and mourned over me as one dead. But I opened my eyes, and prayed him to get me water. When I had drunk, he carried me on his back, and by byways brought me into the town of Isser Jang. My heart was turned to Ram Dass, my brother, in that hour, because of his kindness, and I lost my enmity.

But a snake is a snake till it is dead; and a liar is a liar till the Judgment of the Gods takes hold of his heel. I was wrong in that I trusted my brother—the son of my mother.

When we had come to his house and I was a little restored, I told him my tale, and he said: 'Without doubt it is me whom they would have beaten. But the Law Courts are open, and there is the Justice of the Sirkar above all; and to the Law Courts do thou go when this sickness is overpast.'

Now when we two had left Pali in the old years, there fell a famine that ran from Jeysulmir to Gurgaon and touched Gogunda in the south. At that time the sister of my father came away and lived with us in Isser Jang; for a man must above all see that his folk do not die of want. When the quarrel between us twain came about, the sister of my father—a lean she-dog without teeth—said that Ram Dass had the right, and went with him. Into her hands—because she knew medicines and many cures—Ram Dass, my brother, put me faint with the beating, and much bruised even to the pouring of blood from the mouth. When I had two days' sickness the fever came upon me; and I set aside the fever to the account written in my mind against the landholder.

The Punjabis of Isser Jang are all the sons of Belial and a she-ass, but they are very good witnesses, bearing testimony unshakingly whatever the pleaders may say. I would purchase witnesses by the score, and each man should give evidence, not only against Nur Ali, Wajib Ali, Abdul Latif and Elahi Baksh, but against the landholder, saying that he upon his white horse had called his men to beat me; and, further, that they had robbed me of two hundred rupees. For the latter testimony, I would remit a little of the debt of the man who sold the lac-bangles, and he should say that he had put the money into my hands, and had seen the robbery from afar, but, being afraid, had run away. This plan I told to my brother Ram Dass; and he said that the arrangement was good, and bade me take comfort and make swift work to be abroad again. My heart was opened to my brother in my sickness, and I told him the names of those whom I would call as witnesses—all men in my debt, but of that the Magistrate Sahib could have no knowledge, nor the landholder. The fever stayed with me, and after the fever, I was taken with colic, and gripings very terrible. In that day I thought that my end was at hand, but I know now that she who gave me the medicines, the sister of my father—a widow with a widow's heart—had brought about my second sickness. Ram Dass, my brother, said that my house was shut and locked, and brought me the big door-key and my books, together with all the moneys that were in my house—even the money that was buried under the floor; for I was in great fear lest thieves should break in and dig. I speak true talk; there was but very little money in the house. Perhaps ten rupees—perhaps twenty. How can I tell? God is my witness that I am a poor man.

One night, when I had told Ram Dass all that was in my heart of the lawsuit that I would bring against the landholder, and Ram Dass had said that he had made the arrangements with the witnesses, giving me their names written, I was taken with a new great sickness, and they put me on the bed. When I was a little recovered—I cannot tell how many days afterwards—I made enquiry for Ram Dass, and the sister of my father said that he had gone to Montgomery upon a lawsuit. I took medicine and slept very heavily without waking. When my eyes were opened, there was a great stillness in the house of Ram Dass, and none answered when I called—not even the sister of my father. This filled me with fear, for I knew not what had happened.

Taking a stick in my hand, I went out slowly, till I came to the great square by the well, and my heart was hot in me against the landholder because of the pain of every step I took.

I called for Jowar Singh, the carpenter, whose name was first upon the list of those who should bear evidence against the landholder, saying: 'Are all things ready, and do you know what should be said?'

Jowar Singh answered: 'What is this, and whence do you come, Durga Dass?'

I said: 'From my bed, where I have so long lain sick because of the landholder. Where is Ram Dass, my brother, who was to have made the arrangement for the witnesses? Surely you and yours know these things!'

Then Jowar Singh said: 'What has this to do with us, O Liar? I have borne witness and I have been paid, and the landholder has, by the order of the Court, paid both the five hundred rupees that he robbed from Ram Dass and yet other five hundred because of the great injury he did to your brother.'

The well and the jujube-tree above it and the square of Isser Jang became dark in my eyes, but I leaned on my stick and said: 'Nay! This is child's talk and senseless. It was I who suffered at the hands of the landholder, and I am come to make ready the case. Where is my brother Ram Dass?'

But Jowar Singh shook his head, and a woman cried: 'What lie is here? What quarrel had the landholder with you, bunnia? It is only a shameless one and one without faith who profits by his brother's smarts. Have these bunnias no bowels?'

I cried again, saying: 'By the Cow—by the Oath of the Cow, by the Temple of the Blue-throated Mahadeo, I and I only was beaten—beaten to the death! Let your talk be straight, O people of Isser Jang, and I will pay for the witnesses.' And I tottered where I stood, for the sickness and the pain of the beating were heavy upon me.

Then Ram Narain, who has his carpet spread under the jujube-tree by the well, and writes all letters for the men of the town, came up and said: 'To-day is the one and fortieth day since the beating, and since these six days the case has been judged in the Court, and the Assistant Commissioner Sahib has given it for your brother Ram Dass, allowing the robbery, to which, too, I bore witness, and all things else as the witnesses said. There were many witnesses, and twice Ram Dass became senseless in the Court because of his wounds, and the Stunt Sahib—the baba Stunt Sahib—gave him a chair before all the pleaders. Why do you howl, Durga Dass? These things fell as I have said. Was it not so?'

And Jowar Singh said: 'That is truth. I was there, and there was a red cushion in the chair.'

And Ram Narain said: 'Great shame has come upon the landholder because of this judgment, and fearing his anger, Ram Dass and all his house have gone back to Pali. Ram Dass told us that you also had gone first, the enmity being healed between you, to open a shop in Pali. Indeed, it were well for you that you go even now, for the landholder has sworn that if he catch any one of your house, he will hang him by the heels from the well-beam, and, swinging him to and fro, will beat him with staves till the blood runs from his ears. What I have said in respect to the case is true, as these men here can testify—even to the five hundred rupees.'

I said: 'Was it five hundred?' And Kirpa Ram, the jat, said: 'Five hundred; for I bore witness also.'

And I groaned, for it had been in my heart to have said two hundred only.

Then a new fear came upon me and my bowels turned to water, and, running swiftly to the house of Ram Dass, I sought for my books and my money in the great wooden chest under my bedstead. There remained nothing: not even a cowrie's value. All had been taken by the devil who said he was my brother. I went to my own house also and opened the boards of the shutters; but there also was nothing save the rats among the grain-baskets. In that hour my senses left me, and, tearing my clothes, I ran to the well-place, crying out for the Justice of the English on my brother Ram Dass, and, in my madness, telling all that the books were lost. When men saw that I would have jumped down the well, they believed the truth of my talk; more especially because upon my back and bosom were still the marks of the staves of the landholder.

Jowar Singh the carpenter withstood me, and turning me in his hands—for he is a very strong man— showed the scars upon my body, and bowed down with laughter upon the well-curb. He cried aloud so that all heard him, from the well-square to the Caravanserai of the Pilgrims: 'Oho! The jackals have quarrelled, and the gray one has been caught in the trap. In truth, this man has been grievously beaten, and his brother has taken the money which the Court decreed! Oh, bunnia, this shall be told for years against you! The jackals have quarrelled, and, moreover, the books are burned. O people indebted to Durga Dass—and I know that ye be many—the books are burned!'

Then all Isser Jang took up the cry that the books were burned—Ahi! Ahi! that in my folly I had let that escape my mouth—and they laughed throughout the city. They gave me the abuse of the Punjabi, which is a terrible abuse and very hot; pelting me also with sticks and cow-dung till I fell down and cried for mercy.

Ram Narain, the letter-writer, bade the people cease, for fear that the news should get into Montgomery, and the Policemen might come down to enquire. He said, using many bad words: 'This much mercy will I do to you Durga Dass, though there was no mercy in your dealings with my sister's son over the matter of the dun heifer. Has any man a pony on which he sets no store, that this fellow may escape? If the landholder hears that one of the twain (and God knows whether he beat one or both, but this man is certainly beaten) be in the city, there will be a murder done, and then will come the Police, making inquisition into each man's house and eating the sweet-seller's stuff all day long.'

Kirpa Ram, the jat, said: 'I have a pony very sick. But with beating he can be made to walk for two miles. If he dies, the hide-sellers will have the body.'

Then Chumbo, the hide-seller, said: 'I will pay three annas for the body, and will walk by this man's side till such time as the pony dies. If it be more than two miles, I will pay two annas only.'

Kirpa Ram said: 'Be it so.' Men brought out the pony, and I asked leave to draw a little water from the well, because I was dried up with fear.

Then Ram Narain said: 'Here be four annas. God has brought you very low, Durga Dass, and I would not send you away empty, even though the matter of my sister's son's dun heifer be an open sore between us. It is a long way to your own country. Go, and if it be so willed, live; but, above all, do not take the pony's bridle, for that is mine.'

And I went out of Isser Jang, amid the laughing of the huge-thighed Jats, and the hide-seller walked by my side waiting for the pony to fall dead. In one mile it died, and being full of fear of the landholder, I ran till I could run no more and came to this place.

But I swear by the Cow, I swear by all things whereon Hindus and Musalmans, and even the Sahibs swear, that I, and not my brother, was beaten by the landholder. But the case is shut and the doors of the Law Courts are shut, and God knows where the baba Stunt Sahib—the mother's milk is not yet dry upon his hairless lip—is gone. Ahi! Ahi! I I have no witnesses, and the scars will heal, and I am a poor man. But, on my Father's Soul, on the oath of a Mahajun from Pali, I, and not my brother, I was beaten by the landholder!

What can I do? The Justice of the English is as a great river. Having gone forward, it does not return. Howbeit, do you, Sahib, take a pen and write clearly what I have said, that the Dipty Sahib may see, and reprove the Stunt Sahib, who is a colt yet unlicked by the mare, so young is he. I, and not my brother, was beaten, and he is gone to the west—I do not know where.

But, above all things, write—so that Sahibs may read, and his disgrace be accomplished—that Ram Dass, my brother, son of Purun Dass, Mahajun of Pali, is a swine and a night-thief, a taker of life, an eater of flesh, a jackal-spawn without beauty, or faith, or cleanliness, or honour!

AT TWENTY-TWO

Narrow as the womb, deep as the Pit, and dark as the heart of a man.—Sonthal Miner's Proverb.

'A weaver went out to reap but stayed to unravel the corn-stalks. Ha! Ha! Ha! Is there any sense in a weaver?'

Janki Meah glared at Kundoo, but, as Janki Meah was blind, Kundoo was not impressed. He had come to argue with Janki Meah, and, if chance favoured, to make love to the old man's pretty young wife.

This was Kundoo's grievance, and he spoke in the name of all the five men who, with Janki Meah, composed the gang in Number Seven gallery of Twenty-Two. Janki Meah had been blind for the thirty years during which he had served the Jimahari Collieries with pick and crowbar. All through those thirty years he had regularly, every morning before going down, drawn from the overseer his allowance of lamp-oil—just as if he had been an eyed miner. What Kundoo's gang resented, as hundreds of gangs had resented before, was Janki Meah's selfishness. He would not add the oil to the common stock of his gang, but would save and sell it.

'I knew these workings before you were born,' Janki Meah used to reply: 'I don't want the light to get my coal out by, and I am not going to help you. The oil is mine, and I intend to keep it.'

A strange man in many ways was Janki Meah, the white-haired, hot-tempered, sightless weaver who had turned pitman. All day long—except on Sundays and Mondays when he was usually drunk—he worked in the Twenty-Two shaft of the Jimahari Colliery as cleverly as a man with all the senses. At evening he went up in the great steam-hauled cage to the pit-bank, and there called for his pony—a rusty, coal-dusty beast, nearly as old as Janki Meah. The pony would come to his side, and Janki Meah would clamber on to its back and be taken at once to the plot of land which he, like the other miners, received from the Jimahari Company. The pony knew that place, and when, after six years, the Company changed all the allotments to prevent the miners from acquiring proprietary rights, Janki Meah represented, with tears in his eyes, that were his holding shifted, he would never be able to find his way to the new one. 'My horse only knows that place,' pleaded Janki Meah, and so he was allowed to keep his land.

On the strength of this concession and his accumulated oil-savings, Janki Meah took a second wife—a girl of the Jolaha main stock of the Meahs, and singularly beautiful. Janki Meah could not see her beauty; wherefore he took her on trust, and forbade her to go down the pit. He had not worked for thirty years in the dark without knowing that the pit was no place for pretty women. He loaded her with ornaments—not brass or pewter, but real silver ones—and she rewarded him by flirting outrageously with Kundoo of Number Seven gallery gang. Kundoo was really the gang-head, but Janki Meah insisted upon all the work being entered in his own name, and chose the men that he worked with. Custom—stronger even than the Jimahari Company—dictated that Janki, by right of his years, should manage these things, and should, also, work despite his blindness. In Indian mines where they cut into the solid coal with the pick and clear it out from floor to ceiling, he could come to no great harm. At Home, where they undercut the coal and bring it down in crashing avalanches from the roof, he would never have been allowed to set foot in a pit. He was not a popular man, because of his oil-savings; but all the gangs admitted that Janki knew all the khads, or workings, that had ever been sunk or worked since the Jimahari Company first started operations on the Tarachunda fields.

Pretty little Unda only knew that her old husband was a fool who could be managed. She took no interest in the collieries except in so far as they swallowed up Kundoo five days out of the seven, and covered him with coal-dust. Kundoo was a great workman, and did his best not to get drunk, because, when he had saved forty rupees, Unda was to steal everything that she could find in Janki's house and run with Kundoo to a land where there were no mines, and every one kept three fat bullocks and a milch-buffalo. While this scheme ripened it was his custom to drop in upon Janki and worry him about the oil-savings. Unda sat in a corner and nodded approval. On the night when Kundoo had quoted that objectionable proverb about weavers, Janki grew angry.

'Listen, you pig,' said he, 'blind I am, and old I am, but, before ever you were born, I was gray among the coal. Even in the days when the Twenty-Two khad was unsunk and there were not two thousand men here, I was known to have all knowledge of the pits. What khad is there that I do not know, from the bottom of the shaft to the end of the last drive? Is it the Baromba khad, the oldest, or the Twenty-Two where Tibu's gallery runs up to Number Five?'

'Hear the old fool talk!' said Kundoo, nodding to Unda. 'No gallery of Twenty-Two will cut into Five before the end of the Rains. We have a month's solid coal before us. The Babuji says so.'

'Babuji! Pigji! Dogji! What do these fat slugs from Calcutta know? He draws and draws and draws, and talks and talks and talks, and his maps are all wrong. I, Janki, know that this is so. When a man has been shut up in the dark for thirty years, God gives him knowledge. The old gallery that Tibu's gang made is not six feet from Number Five.'

'Without doubt God gives the blind knowledge,' said Kundoo, with a look at Unda. 'Let it be as you say. I, for my part, do not know where lies the gallery of Tibu's gang, but I am not a withered monkey who needs oil to grease his joints with.'

Kundoo swung out of the hut laughing, and Unda giggled. Janki turned his sightless eyes towards his wife and swore. 'I have land, and I have sold a great deal of lamp-oil,' mused Janki; 'but I was a fool to marry this child.'

A week later the Rains set in with a vengeance, and the gangs paddled about in coal-slush at the pit-banks. Then the big mine-pumps were made ready, and the Manager of the Colliery ploughed through the wet towards the Tarachunda River swelling between its soppy banks. 'Lord send that this beastly beck doesn't misbehave,' said the Manager piously, and he went to take counsel with his Assistant about the pumps.

But the Tarachunda misbehaved very much indeed. After a fall of three inches of rain in an hour it was obliged to do something. It topped its bank and joined the flood-water that was hemmed between two low hills just where the embankment of the Colliery main line crossed. When a large part of a rain-fed river, and a few acres of flood-water, make a dead set for a nine-foot culvert, the culvert may spout its finest, but the water cannot all get out. The Manager pranced upon one leg with excitement, and his language was improper.

He had reason to swear, because he knew that one inch of water on land meant a pressure of one hundred tons to the acre; and here were about five feet of water forming, behind the railway embankment, over the shallower workings of Twenty-Two. You must understand that, in a coal-mine, the coal nearest the surface is worked first from the central shaft. That is to say, the miners may clear out the stuff to within ten, twenty, or thirty feet of the surface, and, when all is worked out, leave only a skin of earth upheld by some few pillars of coal. In a deep mine where they know that they have any amount of material at hand, men prefer to get all their mineral out at one shaft, rather than make a number of little holes to tap the comparatively unimportant surface-coal.

And the Manager watched the flood.

The culvert spouted a nine-foot gush; but the water still formed, and word was sent to clear the men out of Twenty-Two. The cages came up crammed and crammed again with the men nearest the pit-eye, as they call the place where you can see daylight from the bottom of the main shaft. All away and away up the long black galleries the flare-lamps were winking and dancing like so many fireflies, and the men and the women waited for the clanking, rattling, thundering cages to come down and fly up again. But the out-workings were very far off, and word could not be passed quickly, though the heads of the gangs and the Assistant shouted and swore and tramped and stumbled. The Manager kept one eye on the great troubled pool behind the embankment, and prayed that the culvert would give way and let the water through in time. With the other eye he watched the cages come up and saw the headmen counting the roll of the gangs. With all his heart and soul he swore at the winder who controlled the iron drum that wound up the wire rope on which hung the cages.

In a little time there was a down-draw in the water behind the embankment—a sucking whirlpool, all yellow and yeasty. The water had smashed through the skin of the earth and was pouring into the old shallow workings of Twenty-Two.

Deep down below, a rush of black water caught the last gang waiting for the cage, and as they clambered in, the whirl was about their waists. The cage reached the pit-bank, and the Manager called the roll. The gangs were all safe except Gang Janki, Gang Mogul, and Gang Rahim, eighteen men, with perhaps ten basket-women who loaded the coal into the little iron carriages that ran on the tramways of the main galleries. These gangs were in the out-workings, three-quarters of a mile away, on the extreme fringe of the mine. Once more the cage went down, but with only two Englishmen in it, and dropped into a swirling, roaring current that had almost touched the roof of some of the lower side-galleries. One of the wooden balks with which they had propped the old workings shot past on the current, just missing the cage.

'If we don't want our ribs knocked out, we'd better go,' said the Manager. 'We can't even save the Company's props.'

The cage drew out of the water with a splash, and a few minutes later, it was officially reported that there were at least ten feet of water in the pit's eye. Now ten feet of water there meant that all other places in the mine were flooded except such galleries as were more than ten feet above the level of the bottom of the shaft. The deep workings would be full, the main galleries would be full, but in the high workings reached by inclines from the main roads, there would be a certain amount of air cut off, so to speak, by the water and squeezed up by it. The little science-primers explain how water behaves when you pour it down test-tubes. The flooding of Twenty-Two was an illustration on a large scale.

'By the Holy Grove, what has happened to the air!' It was a Sonthal gangman of Gang Mogul in Number Nine gallery, and he was driving a six-foot way through the coal. Then there was a rush from the other galleries, and Gang Janki and Gang Rahim stumbled up with their basket-women.

'Water has come in the mine,' they said, 'and there is no way of getting out.'

'I went down,' said Janki—'down the slope of my gallery, and I felt the water.'

'There has been no water in the cutting in our time,' clamoured the women. 'Why cannot we go away?'

'Be silent!' said Janki. 'Long ago, when my father was here, water came to Ten—no, Eleven—cutting, and there was great trouble. Let us get away to where the air is better.'

The three gangs and the basket-women left Number Nine gallery and went further up Number Sixteen. At one turn of the road they could see the pitchy black water lapping on the coal. It had touched the roof of a gallery that they knew well—a gallery where they used to smoke their huqas and manage their flirtations. Seeing this, they called aloud upon their Gods, and the Meahs, who are thrice bastered Muhammadans, strove to recollect the name of the Prophet. They came to a great open square whence nearly all the coal had been extracted. It was the end of the out-workings, and the end of the mine.

Far away down the gallery a small pumping-engine, used for keeping dry a deep working and fed with steam from above, was throbbing faithfully. They heard it cease.

'They have cut off the steam,' said Kundoo hopefully. 'They have given the order to use all the steam for the pit-bank pumps. They will clear out the water.'

'If the water has reached the smoking-gallery,' said Janki, 'all the Company's pumps can do nothing for three days.'

'It is very hot,' moaned Jasoda, the Meah basket-woman. 'There is a very bad air here because of the lamps.'

'Put them out,' said Janki; 'why do you want lamps?' The lamps were put out and the company sat still in the utter dark. Somebody rose quietly and began walking over the coals. It was Janki, who was touching the walls with his hands. 'Where is the ledge?' he murmured to himself.

'Sit, sit!' said Kundoo. 'If we die, we die. The air is very bad.'

But Janki still stumbled and crept and tapped with his pick upon the walls. The women rose to their feet.

'Stay all where you are. Without the lamps you cannot see, and I—I am always seeing,' said Janki. Then he paused, and called out: 'Oh, you who have been in the cutting more than ten years, what is the name of this open place? I am an old man and I have forgotten.'

'Bullia's Room,' answered the Sonthal who had complained of the vileness of the air.

'Again,' said Janki.

'Bullia's Room.'

'Then I have found it,' said Janki. 'The name only had slipped my memory. Tibu's gang's gallery is here.'

'A lie,' said Kundoo. 'There have been no galleries in this place since my day.'

'Three paces was the depth of the ledge,' muttered Janki without heeding—'and—oh, my poor bones!— I have found it! It is here, up this ledge. Come all you, one by one, to the place of my voice, and I will count you.'

There was a rush in the dark, and Janki felt the first man's face hit his knees as the Sonthal scrambled up the ledge.

'Who?' cried Janki.

'I, Sunua Manji.'

'Sit you down,' said Janki. 'Who next?'

One by one the women and the men crawled up the ledge which ran along one side of 'Bullia's Room.' Degraded Muhammadan, pig-eating Musahr and wild Sonthal, Janki ran his hand over them all.

'Now follow after,' said he, 'catching hold of my heel, and the women catching the men's clothes.' He did not ask whether the men had brought their picks with them. A miner, black or white, does not drop his pick. One by one, Janki leading, they crept into the old gallery—a six-foot way with a scant four feet from hill to roof.

'The air is better here,' said Jasoda. They could hear her heart beating in thick, sick bumps.

'Slowly, slowly,' said Janki. 'I am an old man, and I forget many things. This is Tibu's gallery, but where are the four bricks where they used to put their huqa fire on when the Sahibs never saw? Slowly, slowly, O you people behind.'

They heard his hands disturbing the small coal on the floor of the gallery and then a dull sound. 'This is one unbaked brick, and this is another and another. Kundoo is a young man—let him come forward. Put a knee upon this brick and strike here. When Tibu's gang were at dinner on the last day before the good coal ended, they heard the men of Five on the other side, and Five worked their gallery two Sundays later—or it may have been one. Strike there, Kundoo, but give me room to go back.'

Kundoo, doubting, drove the pick, but the first soft crush of the coal was a call to him. He was fighting for his life and for Unda—pretty little Unda with rings on all her toes—for Unda and the forty rupees. The women sang the Song of the Pick—the terrible, slow, swinging melody with the muttered chorus that repeats the sliding of the loosened coal, and, to each cadence, Kundoo smote in the black dark. When he could do no more, Sunua Manji took the pick, and struck for his life and his wife, and his village beyond the blue hills over the Tarachunda River. An hour the men worked, and then the women cleared away the coal.

'It is farther than I thought,' said Janki. 'The air is very bad; but strike, Kundoo, strike hard.'

For the fifth time Kundoo took up the pick as the Sonthal crawled back. The song had scarcely recommenced when it was broken by a yell from Kundoo that echoed down the gallery: 'Par hua! Par hua! We are through, we are through!' The imprisoned air in the mine shot through the opening, and the women at the far end of the gallery heard the water rush through the pillars of 'Bullia's Room' and roar against the ledge. Having fulfilled the law under which it worked, it rose no farther. The women screamed and pressed forward. 'The water has come—we shall be killed! Let us go.'

Kundoo crawled through the gap and found himself in a propped gallery by the simple process of hitting his head against a beam.

'Do I know the pits or do I not?' chuckled Janki. 'This is the Number Five; go you out slowly, giving me your names. Ho! Rahim, count your gang! Now let us go forward, each catching hold of the other as before.'

They formed a line in the darkness and Janki led them—for a pit-man in a strange pit is only one degree less liable to err than an ordinary mortal underground for the first time. At last they saw a flare-lamp, and Gangs Janki, Mogul, and Rahim of Twenty-Two stumbled dazed into the glare of the draught-furnace at the bottom of Five: Janki feeling his way and the rest behind.

'Water has come into Twenty-Two. God knows where are the others. I have brought these men from Tibu's gallery in our cutting; making connection through the north side of the gallery. Take us to the cage,' said Janki Meah.

At the pit-bank of Twenty-Two, some thousand people clamoured and wept and shouted. One hundred men—one thousand men—had been drowned in the cutting. They would all go to their homes to-morrow. Where were their men? Little Unda, her cloth drenched with the rain, stood at the pit-mouth calling down the shaft for Kundoo. They had swung the cages clear of the mouth, and her only answer was the murmur of the flood in the pit's eye two hundred and sixty feet below.

'Look after that woman! She'll chuck herself down the shaft in a minute,' shouted the Manager.

But he need not have troubled; Unda was afraid of Death. She wanted Kundoo. The Assistant was watching the flood and seeing how far he could wade into it. There was a lull in the water, and the whirlpool had slackened. The mine was full, and the people at the pit-bank howled.

'My faith, we shall be lucky if we have five hundred hands on the place to-morrow!' said the Manager.

'There's some chance yet of running a temporary dam across that water. Shove in anything—tubs and bullock-carts if you haven't enough bricks. Make them work now if they never worked before. Hi! you gangers, make them work.'

Little by little the crowd was broken into detachments, and pushed towards the water with promises of overtime. The dam-making began, and when it was fairly under way, the Manager thought that the hour had come for the pumps. There was no fresh inrush into the mine. The tall, red, iron-clamped pump-beam rose and fell, and the pumps snored and guttered and shrieked as the first water poured out of the pipe.

'We must run her all to-night,' said the Manager wearily, 'but there's no hope for the poor devils down below. Look here, Gur Sahai, if you are proud of your engines, show me what they can do now.'

Gur Sahai grinned and nodded, with his right hand upon the lever and an oil-can in his left. He could do no more than he was doing, but he could keep that up till the dawn. Were the Company's pumps to be beaten by the vagaries of that troublesome Tarachunda River? Never, never! And the pumps sobbed and panted: 'Never, never!' The Manager sat in the shelter of the pit-bank roofing, trying to dry himself by the pump-boiler fire, and, in the dreary dusk, he saw the crowds on the dam scatter and fly.

'That's the end,' he groaned.' 'Twill take us six weeks to persuade 'em that we haven't tried to drown their mates on purpose. Oh, for a decent, rational Geordie!'

But the flight had no panic in it. Men had run over from Five with astounding news, and the foremen could not hold their gangs together. Presently, surrounded by a clamorous crew, Gangs Rahim, Mogul, and Janki, and ten basket-women, walked up to report themselves, and pretty little Unda stole away to Janki's hut to prepare his evening meal.

'Alone I found the way,' explained Janki Meah, 'and now will the Company give me pension?'

The simple pit-folk shouted and leaped and went back to the dam, reassured in their old belief that, whatever happened, so great was the power of the Company whose salt they ate, none of them could be killed. But Gur Sahai only bared his white teeth and kept his hand upon the lever and proved his pumps to the uttermost.

'I say,' said the Assistant to the Manager, a week later, 'do you recollect Germinal?'

'Yes. 'Queer thing. I thought of it in the cage when that balk went by. Why?'

'Oh, this business seems to be Germinal upside down. Janki was in my veranda all this morning, telling me that Kundoo had eloped with his wife—Unda or Anda, I think her name was.'

'Hillo! And those were the cattle that you risked your life to clear out of Twenty-Two!'

'No—I was thinking of the Company's props, not the Company's men.'

'Sounds better to say so now; but I don't believe you, old fellow.'

IN FLOOD TIME

Tweed said tae Till:
'What gars ye rin sae still?'
Till said tae Tweed:
'Though ye rin wi' speed
An' I rin slaw—
Yet where ye droon ae man
I droon twa.'

There is no getting over the river to-night, Sahib. They say that a bullock-cart has been washed down already, and the ekka that went over a half hour before you came has not yet reached the far side. Is the Sahib in haste? I will drive the ford-elephant in to show him. Ohe, mahout there in the shed! Bring out Ram Pershad, and if he will face the current, good. An elephant never lies, Sahib, and Ram Pershad is separated from his friend Kala Nag. He, too, wishes to cross to the far side. Well done! Well done! my King! Go half way across, mahoutji, and see what the river says. Well done, Ram Pershad! Pearl among elephants, go into the river! Hit him on the head, fool! Was the goad made only to scratch thy own fat back with, bastard? Strike! Strike! What are the boulders to thee, Ram Pershad, my Rustum, my mountain of strength? Go in! Go in!

No, Sahib! It is useless. You can hear him trumpet. He is telling Kala Nag that he cannot come over. See! He has swung round and is shaking his head. He is no fool. He knows what the Barhwi means when it is angry. Aha! Indeed, thou art no fool, my child! Salaam, Ram Pershad, Bahadur! Take him under the trees, mahout, and see that he gets his spices. Well done, thou chiefest among tuskers. Salaam to the Sirkar and go to sleep.

What is to be done? The Sahib must wait till the river goes down. It will shrink to-morrow morning, if God pleases, or the day after at the latest. Now why does the Sahib get so angry? I am his servant.

Before God, I did not create this stream! What can I do? My hut and all that is therein is at the service of the Sahib, and it is beginning to rain. Come away, my Lord. How will the river go down for your throwing abuse at it? In the old days the English people were not thus. The fire-carriage has made them soft. In the old days, when they drave behind horses by day or by night, they said naught if a river barred the way, or a carriage sat down in the mud. It was the will of God—not like a fire-carriage which goes and goes and goes, and would go though all the devils in the land hung on to its tail. The fire-carriage hath spoiled the English people. After all, what is a day lost, or, for that matter, what are two days? Is the Sahib going to his own wedding, that he is so mad with haste? Ho! Ho! Ho! I am an old man and see few Sahibs. Forgive me if I have forgotten the respect that is due to them. The Sahib is not angry?

His own wedding! Ho! Ho! Ho! The mind of an old man is like the numah-tree. Fruit, bud, blossom, and the dead leaves of all the years of the past flourish together. Old and new and that which is gone out of remembrance, all three are there! Sit on the bedstead, Sahib, and drink milk. Or—would the Sahib in truth care to drink my tobacco? It is good. It is the tobacco of Nuklao. My son, who is in service there, sent it to me. Drink, then, Sahib, if you know how to handle the tube. The Sahib takes it like a Musalman. Wah! Wah! Where did he learn that? His own wedding! Ho! Ho! Ho! The Sahib says that there is no wedding in the matter at all? Now is it likely that the Sahib would speak true talk to me who am only a black man? Small wonder, then, that he is in haste. Thirty years have I beaten the gong at this ford, but never have I seen a Sahib in such haste. Thirty years, Sahib! That is a very long time. Thirty years ago this ford was on the track of the bunjaras, and I have seen two thousand pack-bullocks cross in one night. Now the rail has come, and the fire-carriage says buz-buz-buz, and a hundred lakhs of maunds slide across that big bridge. It is very wonderful; but the ford is lonely now that there are no bunjaras to camp under the trees.

Nay, do not trouble to look at the sky without. It will rain till the dawn. Listen! The boulders are talking tonight in the bed of the river. Hear them! They would be husking your bones, Sahib, had you tried to cross. See, I will shut the door and no rain can enter. Wah! Ahi! Ugh! Thirty years on the banks of the ford! An old man am I and—where is the oil for the lamp?

Your pardon, but, because of my years, I sleep no sounder than a dog; and you moved to the door. Look, then, Sahib. Look and listen. A full half kos from bank to bank is the stream now—you can see it under the stars—and there are ten feet of water therein. It will not shrink because of the anger in your eyes, and it will not be quiet on account of your curses. Which is louder, Sahib—your voice or the voice of the river? Call to it—perhaps it will be ashamed. Lie down and sleep afresh, Sahib. I know the anger of the Barhwi when there has fallen rain in the foot-hills. I swam the flood, once, on a night ten-fold worse than this, and by the Favour of God I was released from Death when I had come to the very gates thereof.

May I tell the tale? Very good talk. I will fill the pipe anew.

Thirty years ago it was, when I was a young man and had but newly come to the ford. I was strong then, and the bunjaras had no doubt when I said 'this ford is clear.' I have toiled all night up to my shoulder-blades in running water amid a hundred bullocks mad with fear, and have brought them across losing not a hoof. When all was done I fetched the shivering men, and they gave me for reward the pick of their cattle—the bell-bullock of the drove. So great was the honour in which I was held! But, to-day when the rain falls and the river rises, I creep into my hut and whimper like a dog. My strength is gone from me. I am an old man and the fire-carriage has made the ford desolate. They were wont to call me the Strong One of the Barhwi.

Behold my face, Sahib—it is the face of a monkey. And my arm—it is the arm of an old woman. I swear to you, Sahib, that a woman has loved this face and has rested in the hollow of this arm. Twenty years ago, Sahib. Believe me, this was true talk—twenty years ago.

Come to the door and look across. Can you see a thin fire very far away down the stream? That is the temple-fire, in the shrine of Hanuman, of the village of Pateera. North, under the big star, is the village itself, but it is hidden by a bend of the river. Is that far to swim, Sahib? Would you take off your clothes and adventure? Yet I swam to Pateera—not once but many times; and there are muggers in the river too.

Love knows no caste; else why should I, a Musalman and the son of a Musalman, have sought a Hindu woman—a widow of the Hindus—the sister of the headman of Pateera? But it was even so. They of the headman's household came on a pilgrimage to Muttra when She was but newly a bride. Silver tires were upon the wheels of the bullock-cart, and silken curtains hid the woman. Sahib, I made no haste in their conveyance, for the wind parted the curtains and I saw Her. When they returned from pilgrimage the boy that was Her husband had died, and I saw Her again in the bullock-cart. By God, these Hindus are fools! What was it to me whether She was Hindu or Jain—scavenger, leper, or whole? I would have married Her and made Her a home by the ford. The Seventh of the Nine Bars says that a man may not marry one of the idolaters? Is that truth? Both Shiahs and Sunnis say that a Musalman may not marry one of the idolaters? Is the Sahib a priest, then, that he knows so much? I will tell him something that he does not know. There is neither Shiah nor Sunni, forbidden nor idolater, in Love; and the Nine Bars are but nine little fagots that the flame of Love utterly burns away. In truth, I would have taken Her; but what could I do? The headman would have sent his men to break my head with staves. I am not—I was not—afraid of any five men; but against half a village who can prevail?

Therefore it was my custom, these things having been arranged between us twain, to go by night to the village of Pateera, and there we met among the crops; no man knowing aught of the matter. Behold, now! I was wont to cross here, skirting the jungle to the river bend where the railway bridge is, and thence across the elbow of land to Pateera. The light of the shrine was my guide when the nights were dark. That jungle near the river is very full of snakes—little karaits that sleep on the sand—and moreover, Her brothers would have slain me had they found me in the crops. But none knew—none knew save She and I; and the blown sand of the river-bed covered the track of my feet. In the hot months it was an easy thing to pass from the ford to Pateera, and in the first Rains, when the river rose slowly, it was an easy thing also. I set the strength of my body against the strength of the stream, and nightly I ate in my hut here and drank at Pateera yonder. She had said that one Hirnam Singh, a thief, had sought Her, and he was of a village up the river but on the same bank. All Sikhs are dogs, and they have refused in their folly that good gift of God—tobacco. I was ready to destroy Hirnam Singh that ever he had come nigh Her; and the more because he had sworn to Her that She had a lover, and that he would lie in wait and give the name to the headman unless She went away with him. What curs are these Sikhs!

After that news, I swam always with a little sharp knife in my belt, and evil would it have been for a man had he stayed me. I knew not the face of Hirnam Singh, but I would have killed any who came between me and Her.

Upon a night in the beginning of the Rains, I was minded to go across to Pateera, albeit the river was angry. Now the nature of the Barhwi is this, Sahib. In twenty breaths it comes down from the Hills, a wall three feet high, and I have seen it, between the lighting of a fire and the cooking of a chupatty, grow from a runnel to a sister of the Jumna.

When I left this bank there was a shoal a half mile down, and I made shift to fetch it and draw breath there ere going forward; for I felt the hands of the river heavy upon my heels. Yet what will a young man not do for Love's sake? There was but little light from the stars, and midway to the shoal a branch of the stinking deodar tree brushed my mouth as I swam. That was a sign of heavy rain In the foot-hills and beyond, for the deodar is a strong tree, not easily shaken from the hillsides. I made haste, the river aiding me, but ere I touched the shoal, the pulse of the stream beat, as it were, within me and around, and, behold, the shoal was gone and I rode high on the crest of a wave that ran from bank to bank. Has the Sahib ever been cast into much water that fights and will not let a man use his limbs? To me, my head upon the water, it seemed as though there were naught but water to the world's end, and the river drave me with its driftwood. A man is a very little thing in the belly of a flood. And this flood, though I knew it not, was the Great Flood about which men talk still. My liver was dissolved and I lay like a log upon my back in the fear of Death. There were living things in the water, crying and howling grievously—beasts of the forest and cattle, and once the voice of a man asking for help. But the rain came and lashed the water white, and I heard no more save the roar of the boulders below and the roar of the rain above. Thus I was whirled down-stream, wrestling for the breath in me. It is very hard to die when one is young. Can the Sahib, standing here, see the railway bridge? Look, there are the lights of the mail-train going to Peshawur! The bridge is now twenty feet above the river, but upon that night the water was roaring against the lattice-work and against the lattice came I feet first. But much driftwood was piled there and upon the piers, and I took no great hurt. Only the river pressed me as a strong man presses a weaker. Scarcely could I take hold of the lattice-work and crawl to the upper boom. Sahib, the water was foaming across the rails a foot deep! Judge therefore what manner of flood it must have been. I could not hear. I could not see. I could but lie on the boom and pant for breath.

After a while the rain ceased and there came out in the sky certain new washed stars, and by their light I saw that there was no end to the black water as far as the eye could travel, and the water had risen upon the rails. There were dead beasts in the driftwood on the piers, and others caught by the neck in the lattice-work, and others not yet drowned who strove to find a foothold on the lattice-work— buffaloes and kine, and wild pig, and deer one or two, and snakes and jackals past all counting. Their bodies were black upon the left side of the bridge, but the smaller of them were forced through the lattice-work and whirled down-stream.

Thereafter the stars died and the rain came down afresh and the river rose yet more, and I felt the bridge begin to stir under me as a man stirs in his sleep ere he wakes. But I was not afraid, Sahib. I swear to you that I was not afraid, though I had no power in my limbs. I knew that I should not die till I had seen Her once more. But I was very cold, and I felt that the bridge must go.

There was a trembling in the water, such a trembling as goes before the coming of a great wave, and the bridge lifted its flank to the rush of that coming so that the right lattice dipped under water and the left rose clear. On my beard, Sahib, I am speaking God's truth! As a Mirzapore stone-boat careens to the wind, so the Barhwi Bridge turned. Thus and in no other manner.

I slid from the boom into deep water, and behind me came the wave of the wrath of the river. I heard its voice and the scream of the middle part of the bridge as it moved from the piers and sank, and I knew no more till I rose in the middle of the great flood. I put forth my hand to swim, and lo! it fell upon the knotted hair of the head of a man. He was dead, for no one but I, the Strong One of Barhwi, could have lived in that race. He had been dead full two days, for he rode high, wallowing, and was an aid to me. I laughed then, knowing for a surety that I should yet see Her and take no harm; and I twisted my fingers in the hair of the man, for I was far spent, and together we went down the stream—he the dead and I the living. Lacking that help I should have sunk: the cold was in my marrow, and my flesh was ribbed and sodden on my bones. But he had no fear who had known the uttermost of the power of the river; and I let him go where he chose. At last we came into the power of a side-current that set to the right bank, and I strove with my feet to draw with it. But the dead man swung heavily in the whirl, and I feared that some branch had struck him and that he would sink. The tops of the tamarisk brushed my knees, so I knew we were come into flood-water above the crops, and, after I let down my legs and felt bottom— the ridge of a field—and, after, the dead man stayed upon a knoll under a fig-tree, and I drew my body from the water rejoicing.

Does the Sahib know whither the backwash of the flood had borne me? To the knoll which is the eastern boundary-mark of the village of Pateera! No other place. I drew the dead man up on the grass for the service that he had done me, and also because I knew not whether I should need him again. Then I went, crying thrice like a jackal, to the appointed place which was near the byre of the headman's house. But my Love was already there, weeping. She feared that the flood had swept my hut at the Barhwi Ford. When I came softly through the ankle-deep water, She thought it was a ghost and would have fled, but I put my arms round Her, and—I was no ghost in those days, though I am an old man now.

Ho! Ho! Dried corn, in truth. Maize without juice. Ho! Ho!

[Footnote: I grieve to say that the Warden of Barhwi Ford is responsible here for two very bad puns in the vernacular.—R. K.]

I told Her the story of the breaking of the Barhwi Bridge, and She said that I was greater than mortal man, for none may cross the Barhwi in full flood, and I had seen what never man had seen before. Hand in hand we went to the knoll where the dead lay, and I showed Her by what help I had made the ford. She looked also upon the body under the stars, for the latter end of the night was clear, and hid Her face in Her hands, crying: 'It is the body of Hirnam Singh!' I said: 'The swine is of more use dead than living, my Beloved,' and She said: 'Surely, for he has saved the dearest life in the world to my love. None the less, he cannot stay here, for that would bring shame upon me.' The body was not a gunshot from Her door.

Then said I, rolling the body with my hands: 'God hath judged between us, Hirnam Singh, that thy blood might not be upon my head. Now, whether I have done thee a wrong in keeping thee from the burning-ghat, do thou and the crows settle together.' So I cast him adrift into the flood-water, and he was drawn out to the open, ever wagging his thick black beard like a priest under the pulpit-board. And I saw no more of Himam Singh.

Before the breaking of the day we two parted, and I moved towards such of the jungle as was not flooded. With the full light I saw what I had done in the darkness, and the bones of my body were loosened in my flesh, for there ran two kos of raging water between the village of Pateera and the trees of the far bank, and, in the middle, the piers of the Barhwi Bridge showed like broken teeth in the jaw of an old man. Nor was there any life upon the waters—neither birds nor boats, but only an army of drowned things—bullocks and horses and men—and the river was redder than blood from the clay of the foot-hills. Never had I seen such a flood—never since that year have I seen the like—and, O Sahib, no man living had done what I had done. There was no return for me that day. Not for all the lands of the headman would I venture a second time without the shield of darkness that cloaks danger. I went a kos up the river to the house of a blacksmith, saying that the flood had swept me from my hut, and they gave me food. Seven days I stayed with the blacksmith, till a boat came and I returned to my house. There was no trace of wall, or roof, or floor—naught but a patch of slimy mud. Judge, therefore, Sahib, how far the river must have risen.

It was written that I should not die either in my house, or in the heart of the Barhwi, or under the wreck of the Barhwi Bridge, for God sent down Hirnam Singh two days dead, though I know not how the man died, to be my buoy and support. Hirnam Singh has been in Hell these twenty years, and the thought of that night must be the flower of his torment.

Listen, Sahib! The river has changed its voice. It is going to sleep before the dawn, to which there is yet one hour. With the light it will come down afresh. How do I know? Have I been here thirty years without knowing the voice of the river as a father knows the voice of his son? Every moment it is talking less angrily. I swear that there will be no danger for one hour or, perhaps, two. I cannot answer for the morning. Be quick, Sahib! I will call Ram Pershad, and he will not turn back this time. Is the paulin tightly corded upon all the baggage? Ohe, mahout with a mud head, the elephant for the Sahib, and tell them on the far side that there will be no crossing after daylight.

Money? Nay, Sahib. I am not of that kind. No, not even to give sweetmeats to the baby-folk. My house, look you, is empty, and I am an old man.

Dutt, Ram Pershad! Dutt! Dutt! Dutt! Good luck go with you, Sahib.

THE SENDING OF DANA DA

When the Devil rides on your chest remember the chamar. —Native Proverb.

Once upon a time, some people in India made a new Heaven and a new Earth out of broken tea-cups, a missing brooch or two, and a hair-brush. These were hidden under bushes, or stuffed into holes in the hillside, and an entire Civil Service of subordinate Gods used to find or mend them again; and every one said: 'There are more things in Heaven and Earth than are dreamt of in our philosophy.' Several other things happened also, but the Religion never seemed to get much beyond its first manifestations; though it added an air-line postal service, and orchestral effects in order to keep abreast of the tunes, and choke off competition.

This Religion was too elastic for ordinary use. It stretched itself and embraced pieces of everything that the medicine-men of all ages have manufactured. It approved of and stole from Freemasonry; looted the Latter-day Rosicrucians of half their pet words; took any fragments of Egyptian philosophy that it found in the Encyclopaedia Britannica; annexed as many of the Vedas as had been translated into French or English, and talked of all the rest; built in the German versions of what is left of the Zend Avesta; encouraged White, Gray and Black Magic, including spiritualism, palmistry, fortune-telling by cards, hot chestnuts, double-kernelled nuts and tallow droppings; would have adopted Voodoo and Oboe had it known anything about them, and showed itself, in every way, one of the most accommodating arrangements that had ever been invented since the birth of the Sea.

When it was in thorough working order, with all the machinery, down to the subscriptions, complete, Dana Da came from nowhere, with nothing in his hands, and wrote a chapter in its history which has hitherto been unpublished. He said that his first name was Dana, and his second was Da. Now, setting aside Dana of the New York Sun, Dana is a Bhil name, and Da fits no native of India unless you except the Bengali De as the original spelling. Da is Lap or Finnish; and Dana Da was neither Finn, Chin, Bhil, Bengali, Lap, Nair, Gond, Romaney, Magh, Bokhariot, Kurd, Armenian, Levantine, Jew, Persian, Punjabi, Madrasi, Parsee, nor anything else known to ethnologists. He was simply Dana Da, and declined to give further information. For the sake of brevity and as roughly indicating his origin, he was called 'The Native.' He might have been the original Old Man of the Mountains, who is said to be the only authorised head of the Tea-cup Creed. Some people said that he was; but Dana Da used to smile and deny any connection with the cult; explaining that he was an 'Independent Experimenter.'

As I have said, he came from nowhere, with his hands behind his back, and studied the Creed for three weeks; sitting at the feet of those best competent to explain its mysteries. Then he laughed aloud and went away, but the laugh might have been either of devotion or derision.

When he returned he was without money, but his pride was unabated. He declared that he knew more about the Things in Heaven and Earth than those who taught him, and for this contumacy was abandoned altogether.

His next appearance in public life was at a big cantonment in Upper India, and he was then telling fortunes with the help of three leaden dice, a very dirty old cloth, and a little tin box of opium pills. He told better fortunes when he was allowed half a bottle of whiskey; but the things which he invented on the opium were quite worth the money. He was in reduced circumstances. Among other people's he told the fortune of an Englishman who had once been interested in the Simla Creed, but who, later on, had married and forgotten all his old knowledge in the study of babies and things. The Englishman allowed Dana Da to tell a fortune for charity's sake, and gave him five rupees, a dinner, and some old clothes. When he had eaten, Dana Da professed gratitude, and asked if there were anything he could do for his host—in the esoteric line.

'Is there any one that you love?' said Dana Da. The Englishman loved his wife, but had no desire to drag her name into the conversation. He therefore shook his head.

'Is there any one that you hate?' said Dana Da. The Englishman said that there were several men whom he hated deeply.

'Very good,' said Dana Da, upon whom the whiskey and the opium were beginning to tell. 'Only give me their names, and I will despatch a Sending to them and kill them.'

Now a Sending is a horrible arrangement, first invented, they say, in Iceland. It is a Thing sent by a wizard, and may take any form, but, most generally, wanders about the land in the shape of a little purple cloud till it finds the Sendee, and him it kills by changing into the form of a horse, or a cat, or a man without a face. It is not strictly a native patent, though chamars of the skin and hide castes can, if irritated, despatch a Sending which sits on the breast of their enemy by night and nearly kills him. Very few natives care to irritate chamars for this reason.

'Let me despatch a Sending,' said Dana Da; 'I am nearly dead now with want, and drink, and opium, but I should like to kill a man before I die. I can send a Sending anywhere you choose, and in any form except in the shape of a man.'

The Englishman had no friends that he wished to kill, but partly to soothe Dana Da, whose eyes were rolling, and partly to see what would be done, he asked whether a modified Sending could not be arranged for—such a Sending as should make a man's life a burden to him, and yet do him no harm. If this were possible, he notified his willingness to give Dana Da ten rupees for the job.

'I am not what I was once,' said Dana Da, 'and I must take the money because I am poor. To what Englishman shall I send it?'

'Send a Sending to Lone Sahib,' said the Englishman, naming a man who had been most bitter in rebuking him for his apostasy from the Tea-cup Creed. Dana Da laughed and nodded.

'I could have chosen no better man myself,' said he. 'I will see that he finds the Sending about his path and about his bed.'

He lay down on the hearth-rug, turned up the whites of his eyes, shivered all over and began to snort. This was Magic, or Opium, or the Sending, or all three. When he opened his eyes he vowed that the Sending had started upon the war-path, and was at that moment flying up to the town where Lone Sahib lives.

'Give me my ten rupees,' said Dana Da wearily, 'and write a letter to Lone Sahib, telling him, and all who believe with him, that you and a friend are using a power greater than theirs. They will see that you are speaking the truth.'

He departed unsteadily, with the promise of some more rupees if anything came of the Sending.

The Englishman sent a letter to Lone Sahib, couched in what he remembered of the terminology of the Creed. He wrote: 'I also, in the days of what you held to be my backsliding, have obtained Enlightenment, and with Enlightenment has come Power.' Then he grew so deeply mysterious that the recipient of the letter could make neither head nor tail of it, and was proportionately impressed; for he fancied that his friend had become a 'fifth-rounder.' When a man is a 'fifth-rounder' he can do more than Slade and Houdin combined.

Lone Sahib read the letter in five different fashions, and was beginning a sixth interpretation when his bearer dashed in with the news that there was a cat on the bed. Now if there was one thing that Lone Sahib hated more than another, it was a cat. He scolded the bearer for not turning it out of the house. The bearer said that he was afraid. All the doors of the bedroom had been shut throughout the morning, and no real cat could possibly have entered the room. He would prefer not to meddle with the creature.

Lone Sahib entered the room gingerly, and there, on the pillow of his bed, sprawled and whimpered a wee white kitten; not a jumpsome, frisky little beast, but a slug-like crawler with its eyes barely opened and its paws lacking strength or direction—a kitten that ought to have been in a basket with its mamma. Lone Sahib caught it by the scruff of its neck, handed it over to the sweeper to be drowned, and fined the bearer four annas.

That evening, as he was reading in his room, he fancied that he saw something moving about on the hearth-rug, outside the circle of light from his reading-lamp. When the thing began to myowl, he realised that it was a kitten—a wee white kitten, nearly blind and very miserable. He was seriously angry, and spoke bitterly to his bearer, who said that there was no kitten in the room when he brought in the lamp, and real kittens of tender age generally had mother-cats in attendance.

'If the Presence will go out into the veranda and listen,' said the bearer, 'he will hear no cats. How, therefore, can the kitten on the bed and the kitten on the hearth-rug be real kittens?'

Lone Sahib went out to listen, and the bearer followed him, but there was no sound of any one mewing for her children. He returned to his room, having hurled the kitten down the hillside, and wrote out the incidents of the day for the benefit of his co-religionists. Those people were so absolutely free from superstition that they ascribed anything a little out of the common to Agencies. As it was their business to know all about the Agencies, they were on terms of almost indecent familiarity with Manifestations of every kind. Their letters dropped from the ceiling—unstamped—and Spirits used to squatter up and down their staircases all night; but they had never come into contact with kittens. Lone Sahib wrote out the facts, noting the hour and the minute, as every Psychical Observer is bound to do, and appending the Englishman's letter because it was the most mysterious document and might have had a bearing upon anything in this world or the next. An outsider would have translated all the tangle thus: 'Look out! You laughed at me once, and now I am going to make you sit up.'

Lone Sahib's co-religionists found that meaning in it; but their translation was refined and full of four-syllable words. They held a sederunt, and were filled with tremulous joy, for, in spite of their familiarity with all the other worlds and cycles, they had a very human awe of things sent from Ghost-land. They met in Lone Sahib's room in shrouded and sepulchral gloom, and their conclave was broken up by a clinking among the photo-frames on the mantelpiece. A wee white kitten, nearly blind, was looping and writhing itself between the clock and the candlesticks. That stopped all investigations or doublings. Here was the Manifestation in the flesh. It was, so far as could be seen, devoid of purpose, but it was a Manifestation of undoubted authenticity.

They drafted a Round Robin to the Englishman, the backslider of old days, adjuring him in the interests of the Creed to explain whether there was any connection between the embodiment of some Egyptian God or other [I have forgotten the name] and his communication. They called the kitten Ra, or Toth, or Tum, or something; and when Lone Sahib confessed that the first one had, at his most misguided instance, been drowned by the sweeper, they said consolingly that in his next life he would be a 'bounder,' and not even a 'rounder' of the lowest grade. These words may not be quite correct, but they accurately express the sense of the house.

When the Englishman received the Round Robin—it came by post—he was startled and bewildered. He sent into the bazar for Dana Da, who read the letter and laughed. 'That is my Sending,' said he. 'I told you I would work well. Now give me another ten rupees.'

'But what in the world is this gibberish about Egyptian Gods?' asked the Englishman.

'Cats,' said Dana Da with a hiccough, for he had discovered the Englishman's whiskey bottle. 'Cats, and cats, and cats! Never was such a Sending. A hundred of cats. Now give me ten more rupees and write as I dictate.'

Dana Da's letter was a curiosity. It bore the Englishman's signature, and hinted at cats—at a Sending of Cats. The mere words on paper were creepy and uncanny to behold.

'What have you done, though?' said the Englishman; 'I am as much in the dark as ever. Do you mean to say that you can actually send this absurd Sending you talk about?'

'Judge for yourself,' said Dana Da. 'What does that letter mean? In a little time they will all be at my feet and yours, and I—O Glory!—will be drugged or drunk all daylong.'

Dana Da knew his people.

When a man who hates cats wakes up in the morning and finds a little squirming kitten on his breast, or puts his hand into his ulster-pocket and finds a little half-dead kitten where his gloves should be, or opens his trunk and finds a vile kitten among his dress-shirts, or goes for a long ride with his mackintosh strapped on his saddle-bow and shakes a little squawling kitten from its folds when he opens it, or goes out to dinner and finds a little blind kitten under his chair, or stays at home and finds a writhing kitten under the quilt, or wriggling among his boots, or hanging, head downwards, in his tobacco-jar, or being mangled by his terrier in the veranda,—when such a man finds one kitten, neither more nor less, once a day in a place where no kitten rightly could or should be, he is naturally upset. When he dare not murder his daily trove because he believes it to be a Manifestation, an Emissary, an Embodiment, and half a dozen other things all out of the regular course of nature, he is more than upset. He is actually distressed. Some of Lone Sahib's co-religionists thought that he was a highly favoured individual; but many said that if he had treated the first kitten with proper respect—as suited a oth-Ra-Tum-Sennacherib Embodiment—all this trouble would have been averted. They compared him to the Ancient Mariner, but none the less they were proud of him and proud of the Englishman who had sent the Manifestation. They did not call it a Sending because Icelandic magic was not in their programme.

After sixteen kittens, that is to say after one fortnight, for there were three kittens on the first day to impress the fact of the Sending, the whole camp was uplifted by a letter—it came flying through a window-from the Old Man of the Mountains—the Head of all the Creed—explaining the Manifestation in the most beautiful language and soaking up all the credit of it for himself. The Englishman, said the letter, was not there at all. He was a backslider without Power or Asceticism, who couldn't even raise a table by force of volition, much less project an army of kittens through space. The entire arrangement, said the letter, was strictly orthodox, worked and sanctioned by the highest Authorities within the pale of the Creed. There was great joy at this, for some of the weaker brethren seeing that an outsider who had been working on independent lines could create kittens, whereas their own rulers had never gone beyond crockery—and broken at best—were showing a desire to break line on their own trail. In fact, there was the promise of a schism. A second Round Robin was drafted to the Englishman, beginning: 'O Scoffer,' and ending with a selection of curses from the Rites of Mizraim and Memphis and the Commination of Jugana, who was a 'fifth-rounder,' upon whose name an upstart 'third-rounder' once traded. A papal excommunication is a billet-doux compared to the Commination of Jugana. The Englishman had been proved, under the hand and seal of the Old Man of the Mountains, to have appropriated Virtue and pretended to have Power which, in reality, belonged only to the Supreme Head. Naturally the Round Robin did not spare him.

He handed the letter to Dana Da to translate into decent English. The effect on Dana Da was curious. At first he was furiously angry, and then he laughed for five minutes.

'I had thought,' he said, 'that they would have come to me. In another week I would have shown that I sent the Sending, and they would have discrowned the Old Man of the Mountains who has sent this Sending of mine. Do you do nothing. The time has come for me to act. Write as I dictate, and I will put them to shame. But give me ten more rupees.'

At Dana Da's dictation the Englishman wrote nothing less than a formal challenge to the Old Man of the Mountains. It wound up: 'And if this Manifestation be from your hand, then let it go forward; but if it be from my hand, I will that the Sending shall cease in two days' time. In that day there shall be twelve kittens and thenceforward none at all. The people shall judge between us.' This was signed by Dana Da, who added pentacles and pentagrams, and a crux ansata, and half a dozen swastikas, and a Triple Tau to his name, just to show that he was all he laid claim to be.

The challenge was read out to the gentlemen and ladies, and they remembered then that Dana Da had laughed at them some years ago. It was officially announced that the Old Man of the Mountains would treat the matter with contempt; Dana Da being an Independent Investigator without a single 'round' at the back of him. But this did not soothe his people. They wanted to see a fight. They were very human for all their spirituality. Lone Sahib, who was really being worn out with kittens, submitted meekly to his fate. He felt that he was being 'kittened to prove the power of Dana Da,' as the poet says.

When the stated day dawned, the shower of kittens began. Some were white and some were tabby, and all were about the same loathsome age. Three were on his hearth-rug, three in his bath-room, and the other six turned up at intervals among the visitors who came to see the prophecy break down. Never was a more satisfactory Sending. On the next day there were no kittens, and the next day and all the other days were kittenless and quiet. The people murmured and looked to the Old Man of the Mountains for an explanation. A letter, written on a palm-leaf, dropped from the ceiling, but every one except Lone Sahib felt that letters were not what the occasion demanded. There should have been cats, there should have been cats,—full-grown ones. The letter proved conclusively that there had been a hitch in the Psychic Current which, colliding with a Dual Identity, had interfered with the Percipient Activity all along the main line. The kittens were still going on, but owing to some failure in the Developing Fluid, they were not materialised. The air was thick with letters for a few days afterwards. Unseen hands played Gluck and Beethoven on finger-bowls and clock-shades; but all men felt that Psychic Life was a mockery without materialised Kittens. Even Lone Sahib shouted with the majority on this head. Dana Da's letters were very insulting, and if he had then offered to lead a new departure, there is no knowing what might not have happened.

But Dana Da was dying of whiskey and opium in the Englishman's godown, and had small heart for honours.

'They have been put to shame,' said he. 'Never was such a Sending. It has killed me.'

'Nonsense,' said the Englishman, 'you are going to die, Dana Da, and that sort of stuff must be left behind. I'll admit that you have made some queer things come about. Tell me honestly, now, how was it done?'

'Give me ten more rupees,' said Dana Da faintly, 'and if I die before I spend them, bury them with me.' The silver was counted out while Dana Da was fighting with Death. His hand closed upon the money and he smiled a grim smile.

'Bend low,' he whispered. The Englishman bent.

'Bunnia—Mission-school—expelled—box-wallah (peddler)—Ceylon pearl-merchant—all mine English education—out-casted, and made up name Dana Da—England with American thought-reading man and—and—you gave me ten rupees several times—I gave the Sahib's bearer two-eight a month for cats—little, little cats. I wrote, and he put them about—very clever man. Very few kittens now in the bazar. Ask Lone Sahib's sweeper's wife.'

So saying, Dana Da gasped and passed away into a land where, if all be true, there are no materialisations and the making of new creeds is discouraged.

But consider the gorgeous simplicity of it all!

ON THE CITY WALL

Then she let them down by a cord through the window; for her house was upon the town-wall, and she dwelt upon the wall.—Joshua ii. 15.

Lalun is a member of the most ancient profession in the world. Lilith was her very-great-grandmamma, and that was before the days of Eve as every one knows. In the West, people say rude things about Lalun's profession, and write lectures about it, and distribute the lectures to young persons in order that Morality may be preserved. In the East where the profession is hereditary, descending from mother to daughter, nobody writes lectures or takes any notice; and that is a distinct proof of the inability of the East to manage its own affairs.

Lalun's real husband, for even ladies of Lalun's profession in the East must have husbands, was a big jujube-tree. Her Mamma, who had married a fig-tree, spent ten thousand rupees on Lalun's wedding, which was blessed by forty-seven clergymen of Mamma's church, and distributed five thousand rupees in charity to the poor. And that was the custom of the land. The advantages of having a jujube-tree for a husband are obvious. You cannot hurt his feelings, and he looks imposing.

Lalun's husband stood on the plain outside the City walls, and Lalun's house was upon the east wall facing the river. If you fell from the broad window-seat you dropped thirty feet sheer into the City Ditch. But if you stayed where you should and looked forth, you saw all the cattle of the City being driven down to water, the students of the Government College playing cricket, the high grass and trees that fringed the river-bank, the great sand bars that ribbed the river, the red tombs of dead Emperors beyond the river, and very far away through the blue heat-haze, a glint of the snows of the Himalayas.

Wali Dad used to lie in the window-seat for hours at a time watching this view. He was a young Muhammadan who was suffering acutely from education of the English variety and knew it. His father had sent him to a Mission-school to get wisdom, and Wali Dad had absorbed more than ever his father or the Missionaries intended he should. When his father died, Wali Dad was independent and spent two years experimenting with the creeds of the Earth and reading books that are of no use to anybody.

After he had made an unsuccessful attempt to enter the Roman Catholic Church and the Presbyterian fold at the same time (the Missionaries found him out and called him names, but they did not understand his trouble), he discovered Lalun on the City wall and became the most constant of her few admirers. He possessed a head that English artists at home would rave over and paint amid impossible surroundings—a face that female novelists would use with delight through nine hundred pages. In reality he was only a clean-bred young Muhammadan, with pencilled eye-brows, small-cut nostrils, little feet and hands, and a very tired look in his eyes. By virtue of his twenty-two years he had grown a neat black beard which he stroked with pride and kept delicately scented. His life seemed to be divided between borrowing books from me and making love to Lalun in the window-seat. He composed songs about her, and some of the songs are sung to this day in the City from the Street of the Mutton-Butchers to the Copper-Smiths' ward.

One song, the prettiest of all, says that the beauty of Lalun was so great that it troubled the hearts of the British Government and caused them to lose their peace of mind. That is the way the song is sung in the streets; but, if you examine it carefully and know the key to the explanation, you will find that there are three puns in it—on 'beauty,' 'heart,' and 'peace of mind,'—so that it runs: 'By the subtlety of Lalun the administration of the Government was troubled and it lost such and such a man.' When Wali Dad sings that song his eyes glow like hot coals, and Lalun leans back among the cushions and throws bunches of jasmine-buds at Wali Dad.

But first it is necessary to explain something about the Supreme Government which is above all and below all and behind all. Gentlemen come from England, spend a few weeks in India, walk round this great Sphinx of the Plains, and write books upon its ways and its works, denouncing or praising it as their own ignorance prompts. Consequently all the world knows how the Supreme Government conducts itself. But no one, not even the Supreme Government, knows everything about the administration of the Empire. Year by year England sends out fresh drafts for the first fighting-line, which is officially called the Indian Civil Service. These die, or kill themselves by overwork, or are worried to death or broken in health and hope in order that the land may be protected from death and sickness, famine and war, and may eventually become capable of standing alone. It will never stand alone, but the idea is a pretty one, and men are willing to die for it, and yearly the work of pushing and coaxing and scolding and petting the country into good living goes forward. If an advance be made all credit is given to the native, while the Englishmen stand back and wipe their foreheads. If a failure occurs the Englishmen step forward and take the blame. Overmuch tenderness of this kind has bred a strong belief among many natives that the native is capable of administering the country, and many devout Englishmen believe this also, because the theory is stated in beautiful English with all the latest political colour.

There be other men who, though uneducated, see visions and dream dreams, and they, too, hope to administer the country in their own way—that is to say, with a garnish of Red Sauce. Such men must exist among two hundred million people, and, if they are not attended to, may cause trouble and even break the great idol called Pax Britannic, which, as the newspapers say, lives between Peshawur and Cape Comorin. Were the Day of Doom to dawn to-morrow, you would find the Supreme Government 'taking measures to allay popular excitement' and putting guards upon the graveyards that the Dead might troop forth orderly. The youngest Civilian would arrest Gabriel on his own responsibility if the Archangel could not produce a Deputy Commissioner's permission to 'make music or other noises' as the license says.

Whence it is easy to see that mere men of the flesh who would create a tumult must fare badly at the hands of the Supreme Government. And they do. There is no outward sign of excitement; there is no confusion; there is no knowledge. When due and sufficient reasons have been given, weighed and approved, the machinery moves forward, and the dreamer of dreams and the seer of visions is gone from his friends and following. He enjoys the hospitality of Government; there is no restriction upon his movements within certain limits; but he must not confer any more with his brother dreamers. Once in every six months the Supreme Government assures itself that he is well and takes formal acknowledgment of his existence. No one protests against this detention, because the few people who know about it are in deadly fear of seeming to know him; and never a single newspaper 'takes up his case' or organises demonstrations on his behalf, because the newspapers of India have got behind that lying proverb which says the Pen is mightier than the Sword, and can walk delicately.

So now you know as much as you ought about Wali Dad, the educational mixture, and the Supreme Government.

Lalun has not yet been described. She would need, so Wali Dad says, a thousand pens of gold and ink scented with musk. She has been variously compared to the Moon, the Dil Sagar Lake, a spotted quail, a gazelle, the Sun on the Desert of Kutch, the Dawn, the Stars, and the young bamboo. These comparisons imply that she is beautiful exceedingly according to the native standards, which are practically the same as those of the West. Her eyes are black and her hair is black, and her eyebrows are black as leeches; her mouth is tiny and says witty things; her hands are tiny and have saved much money; her feet are tiny and have trodden on the naked hearts of many men. But, as Wali Dad sings: 'Lalun is Lalun, and when you have said that you have only come to the Beginnings of Knowledge.'

The little house on the City wall was just big enough to hold Lalun, and her maid, and a pussy-cat with a silver collar. A big pink and blue cut-glass chandelier hung from the ceiling of the reception room. A petty Nawab had given Lalun the horror, and she kept it for politeness' sake. The floor of the room was of polished chunam, white as curds. A latticed window of carved wood was set in one wall; there was a profusion of squabby pluffy cushions and fat carpets everywhere, and Lalun's silver huqa, studded with turquoises, had a special little carpet all to its shining self. Wali Dad was nearly as permanent a fixture as the chandelier. As I have said, he lay in the window-seat and meditated on Life and Death and Lalun— specially Lalun. The feet of the young men of the City tended to her doorways and then—retired, for Lalun was a particular maiden, slow of speech, reserved of mind, and not in the least inclined to orgies which were nearly certain to end in strife. 'If I am of no value, I am unworthy of this honour,' said Lalun. 'If I am of value, they are unworthy of Me.' And that was a crooked sentence.

In the long hot nights of latter April and May all the City seemed to assemble in Lalun's little white room to smoke and to talk. Shiahs of the grimmest and most uncompromising persuasion; Sufis who had lost all belief in the Prophet and retained but little in God; wandering Hindu priests passing southward on their way to the Central India fairs and other affairs; Pundits in black gowns, with spectacles on their noses and undigested wisdom in their insides; bearded headmen of the wards; Sikhs with all the details of the latest ecclesiastical scandal in the Golden Temple; red-eyed priests from beyond the Border, looking like trapped wolves and talking like ravens; M. A.'s of the University, very superior and very voluble—all these people and more also you might find in the white room. Wali Dad lay in the window-seat and listened to the talk.

'It is Lalun's salon' said Wali Dad to me, 'and it is electic—is not that the word? Outside of a Freemason's Lodge I have never seen such gatherings. There I dined once with a Jew-a Yahoudi!' He spat into the City Ditch with apologies for allowing national feelings to overcome him. 'Though I have lost every belief in the world,' said he, 'and try to be proud of my losing, I cannot help hating a Jew. Lalun admits no Jews here.'

'But what in the world do all these men do?' I asked.

'The curse of our country,' said Wali Dad. 'They talk. It is like the Athenians—always hearing and telling some new thing. Ask the Pearl and she will show you how much she knows of the news of the City and the Province. Lalun knows everything.'

'Lalun,' I said at random—she was talking to a gentleman of the Kurd persuasion who had come in from God-knows-where—'when does the 175th Regiment go to Agra?'

'It does not go at all,' said Lalun, without turning her head. 'They have ordered the 118th to go in its stead. That Regiment goes to Lucknow in three months, unless they give a fresh order.'

'That is so,' said Wali Dad without a shade of doubt. 'Can you, with your telegrams and your newspapers, do better? Always hearing and telling some new thing,' he went on. 'My friend, has your God ever smitten a European nation for gossiping in the bazars? India has gossiped for centuries—always standing in the bazars until the soldiers go by. Therefore—you are here today instead of starving in your own country, and I am not a Muhammadan—I am a Product—a Demnition Product. That also I owe to you and yours: that I cannot make an end to my sentence without quoting from your authors.' He pulled at the huqa and mourned, half feelingly, half in earnest, for the shattered hopes of his youth. Wali Dad was always mourning over something or other—the country of which he despaired, or the creed in which he had lost faith, or the life of the English which he could by no means understand.

Lalun never mourned. She played little songs on the sitar, and to hear her sing, 'O Peacock, cry again,' was always a fresh pleasure. She knew all the songs that have ever been sung, from the war-songs of the South that make the old men angry with the young men and the young men angry with the State, to the love-songs of the North where the swords whinny-whicker like angry kites in the pauses between the kisses, and the Passes fill with armed men, and the Lover is torn from his Beloved and cries, Ai, Ai, Ai! evermore. She knew how to make up tobacco for the huqa so that it smelt like the Gates of Paradise and wafted you gently through them. She could embroider strange things in gold and silver, and dance softly with the moonlight when it came in at the window. Also she knew the hearts of men, and the heart of the City, and whose wives were faithful and whose untrue, and more of the secrets of the Government Offices than are good to be set down in this place. Nasiban, her maid, said that her jewellery was worth ten thousand pounds, and that, some night, a thief would enter and murder her for its possession; but Lalun said that all the City would tear that thief limb from limb, and that he, whoever he was, knew it.

So she took her sitar and sat in the window-seat and sang a song of old days that had been sung by a girl of her profession in an armed camp on the eve of a great battle—the day before the Fords of the Jumna ran red and Sivaji fled fifty miles to Delhi with a Toorkh stallion at his horse's tail and another Lalun on his saddle-bow. It was what men call a Mahratta laonee, and it said:—

Their warrior forces Chimajee
Before the Peishwa led,
The Children of the Sun and Fire
Behind him turned and fled.
And the chorus said:—

With them there fought who rides so free
With a sword and turban red,

The warrior-youth who earns his fee
At peril of his head.

'At peril of his head,' said Wali Dad in English to me. 'Thanks to your Government, all our heads are protected, and with the educational facilities at my command'—his eyes twinkled wickedly—'I might be a distinguished member of the local administration. Perhaps, in time, I might even be a member of a Legislative Council.'

'Don't speak English,' said Lalun, bending over her sitar afresh. The chorus went out from the City wall to the blackened wall of Fort Amara which dominates the City. No man knows the precise extent of Fort Amara. Three kings built it hundreds of years ago, and they say that there are miles of underground rooms beneath its walls. It is peopled with many ghosts, a detachment of Garrison Artillery and a Company of Infantry. In its prime it held ten thousand men and filled its ditches with corpses.

'At peril of his head,' sang Lalun again and again.

A head moved on one of the Ramparts—the gray head of an old man—and a voice, rough as shark-skin on a sword-hilt, sent back the last line of the chorus and broke into a song that I could not understand, though Lalun and Wali Dad listened intently.

'What is it?' I asked. 'Who is it?'

'A consistent man,' said Wali Dad. 'He fought you in '46, when he was a warrior-youth; refought you in '57, and he tried to fight you in '71, but you had learned the trick of blowing men from guns too well. Now he is old; but he would still fight if he could.'

'Is he a Wahabi, then? Why should he answer to a Mahratta laonee if he be Wahabi—or Sikh?' said I.

'I do not know,' said Wali Dad. 'He has lost, perhaps, his religion. Perhaps he wishes to be a King. Perhaps he is a King. I do not know his name.'

'That is a lie, Wali Dad. If you know his career you must know his name.'

'That is quite true. I belong to a nation of liars. I would rather not tell you his name. Think for yourself.'

Lalun finished her song, pointed to the Fort, and said simply: 'Khem Singh.'

'Hm,' said Wali Dad. 'If the Pearl chooses to tell you the Pearl is a fool.'

I translated to Lalun, who laughed. 'I choose to tell what I choose to tell. They kept Khem Singh in Burma,' said she. 'They kept him there for many years until his mind was changed in him. So great was the kindness of the Government. Finding this, they sent him back to his own country that he might look upon it before he died. He is an old man, but when he looks upon this country his memory will come. Moreover, there be many who remember him.'

'He is an Interesting Survival,' said Wali Dad, pulling at the huqa. 'He returns to a country now full of educational and political reform, but, as the Pearl says, there are many who remember him. He was once a great man. There will never be any more great men in India. They will all, when they are boys, go whoring after strange gods, and they will become citizens—"fellow-citizens"—"illustrious fellow-citizens." What is it that the native papers call them?'

Wali Dad seemed to be in a very bad temper. Lalun looked out of the window and smiled into the dust-haze. I went away thinking about Khem Singh who had once made history with a thousand followers, and would have been a princeling but for the power of the Supreme Government aforesaid.

The Senior Captain Commanding Fort Amara was away on leave, but the Subaltern, his Deputy, had drifted down to the Club, where I found him and enquired of him whether it was really true that a political prisoner had been added to the attractions of the Fort. The Sub-altern explained at great length, for this was the first time that he had held Command of the Fort, and his glory lay heavy upon him.

'Yes,' said he, 'a man was sent in to me about a week ago from down the line—a thorough gentleman whoever he is. Of course I did all I could for him. He had his two servants and some silver cooking-pots, and he looked for all the world like a native officer. I called him Subadar Sahib; just as well to be on the safe side, y'know. "Look here, Subadar Sahib," I said, "you're handed over to my authority, and I'm supposed to guard you. Now I don't want to make your life hard, but you must make things easy for me. All the Fort is at your disposal, from the flagstaff to the dry ditch, and I shall be happy to entertain you in any way I can, but you mustn't take advantage of it. Give me your word that you won't try to escape, Subadar Sahib, and I'll give you my word that you shall have no heavy guard put over you." I thought the best way of getting at him was by going at him straight, y'know; and it was, by Jove! The old man gave me his word, and moved about the Fort as contented as a sick crow. He's a rummy chap—always asking to be told where he is and what the buildings about him are. I had to sign a slip of blue paper when he turned up, acknowledging receipt of his body and all that, and I'm responsible, y'know, that he doesn't get away. Queer thing, though, looking after a Johnnie old enough to be your grandfather isn't it? Come to the Fort one of these days and see him?'

For reasons which will appear, I never went to the Fort while Khem Singh was then within its walls. I knew him only as a gray head seen from Lalun's window—a gray head and a harsh voice. But natives told me that, day by day, as he looked upon the fair lands round Amara, his memory came back to him and, with it, the old hatred against the Government that had been nearly effaced in far-off Burma. So he raged up and down the West face of the Fort from morning till noon and from evening till the night, devising vain things in his heart, and croaking war-songs when Lalun sang on the City wall. As he grew more acquainted with the Subaltern he unburdened his old heart of some of the passions that had withered it. 'Sahib,' he used to say, tapping his stick against the parapet, 'when I was a young man I was one of twenty thousand horsemen who came out of the City and rode round the plain here. Sahib, I was the leader of a hundred, then of a thousand, then of five thousand, and now!'—he pointed to his two servants. 'But from the beginning to to-day I would cut the throats of all the Sahibs in the land if I could. Hold me fast, Sahib, lest I get away and return to those who would follow me. I forgot them when I was in Burma, but now that I am in my own country again, I remember everything.'

'Do you remember that you have given me your Honour not to make your tendance a hard matter?' said the Subaltern.

'Yes, to you, only to you, Sahib,' said Khem Singh. 'To you because you are of a pleasant countenance. If my turn comes again, Sahib, I will not hang you nor cut your throat.'

'Thank you,' said the Subaltern gravely, as he looked along the line of guns that could pound the City to powder in half an hour. 'Let us go into our own quarters, Khem Singh. Come and talk with me after dinner.'

Khem Singh would sit on his own cushion at the Subaltern's feet, drinking heavy, scented anise-seed brandy in great gulps, and telling strange stories of Fort Amara, which had been a palace in the old days, of Begums and Ranees tortured to death—aye, in the very vaulted chamber that now served as a Mess-room; would tell stories of Sobraon that made the Subaltern's cheeks flush and tingle with pride of race, and of the Kuka rising from which so much was expected and the foreknowledge of which was shared by a hundred thousand souls. But he never told tales of '57 because, as he said, he was the Subaltern's guest, and '57 is a year that no man, Black or White, cares to speak of. Once only, when the anise-seed brandy had slightly affected his head, he said: 'Sahib, speaking now of a matter which lay between Sobraon and the affair of the Kukas, it was ever a wonder to us that you stayed your hand at all, and that, having stayed it, you did not make the land one prison. Now I hear from without that you do great honour to all men of our country and by your own hands are destroying the Terror of your Name which is your strong rock and defence. This is a foolish thing. Will oil and water mix? Now in '57—'

'I was not born then, Subadar Sahib,' said the Subaltern, and Khem Singh reeled to his quarters.

The Subaltern would tell me of these conversations at the Club, and my desire to see Khem Singh increased. But Wali Dad, sitting in the window-seat of the house on the City wall, said that it would be a cruel thing to do, and Lalun pretended that I preferred the society of a grizzled old Sikh to hers.

'Here is tobacco, here is talk, here are many friends and all the news of the City, and, above all, here is myself. I will tell you stories and sing you songs, and Wali Dad will talk his English nonsense in your ears. Is that worse than watching the caged animal yonder? Go to-morrow, then, if you must, but to-day such and such an one will be here, and he will speak of wonderful things.'

It happened that To-morrow never came, and the warm heat of the latter Rains gave place to the chill of early October almost before I was aware of the flight of the year. The Captain commanding the Fort returned from leave and took over charge of Khem Singh according to the laws of seniority. The Captain was not a nice man. He called all natives 'niggers,' which, besides being extreme bad form, shows gross ignorance.

'What's the use of telling off two Tommies to watch that old nigger?' said he.

'I fancy it soothes his vanity,' said the Subaltern. 'The men are ordered to keep well out of his way, but he takes them as a tribute to his importance, poor old wretch.'

'I won't have Line men taken off regular guards in this way. Put on a couple of Native Infantry.'

'Sikhs?' said the Subaltern, lifting his eyebrows.

'Sikhs, Pathans, Dogras—they're all alike, these black vermin,' and the Captain talked to Khem Singh in a manner which hurt that old gentleman's feelings. Fifteen years before, when he had been caught for the second time, every one looked upon him as a sort of tiger. He liked being regarded in this light. But he forgot that the world goes forward in fifteen years, and many Subalterns are promoted to Captaincies.

'The Captain-pig is in charge of the Fort?' said Khem Singh to his native guard every morning. And the native guard said: 'Yes, Subadar Sahib,' in deference to his age and his air of distinction; but they did not know who he was.

In those days the gathering in Lalun's little white room was always large and talked more than before.

'The Greeks,' said Wali Dad who had been borrowing my books, 'the inhabitants of the city of Athens, where they were always hearing and telling some new thing, rigorously secluded their women—who were fools. Hence the glorious institution of the heterodox women—is it not?—who were amusing and not fools. All the Greek philosophers delighted in their company. Tell me, my friend, how it goes now in Greece and the other places upon the Continent of Europe. Are your women-folk also fools?'

'Wali Dad,' I said, 'you never speak to us about your women-folk and we never speak about ours to you. That is the bar between us.'

'Yes,' said Wali Dad, 'it is curious to think that our common meeting-place should be here, in the house of a common—how do you call her?' He pointed with the pipe-mouth to Lalun.

'Lalun is nothing but Lalun,' I said, and that was perfectly true. 'But if you took your place in the world, Wali Dad, and gave up dreaming dreams—'

'I might wear an English coat and trouser. I might be a leading Muhammadan pleader. I might be received even at the Commissioner's tennis-parties where the English stand on one side and the natives on the other, in order to promote social intercourse throughout the Empire. Heart's Heart,' said he to Lalun quickly, 'the Sahib says that I ought to quit you.'

'The Sahib is always talking stupid talk,' returned Lalun with a laugh. 'In this house I am a Queen and thou art a King. The Sahib'—she put her arms above her head and thought for a moment—'the Sahib shall be our Vizier—thine and mine, Wali Dad—because he has said that thou shouldst leave me.'

Wali Dad laughed immoderately, and I laughed too. 'Be it so,' said he. 'My friend, are you willing to take this lucrative Government appointment? Lalun, what shall his pay be?'

But Lalun began to sing, and for the rest of the time there was no hope of getting a sensible answer from her or Wali Dad. When the one stopped, the other began to quote Persian poetry with a triple pun in every other line. Some of it was not strictly proper, but it was all very funny, and it only came to an end when a fat person in black, with gold pince-nez, sent up his name to Lalun, and Wali Dad dragged me into the twinkling night to walk in a big rose-garden and talk heresies about Religion and Governments and a man's career in life.

The Mohurrum, the great mourning-festival of the Muhammadans, was close at hand, and the things that Wali Dad said about religious fanaticism would have secured his expulsion from the loosest-thinking Muslim sect. There were the rose-bushes round us, the stars above us, and from every quarter of the City came the boom of the big Mohurrum drums. You must know that the City is divided in fairly equal proportions between the Hindus and the Musalmans, and where both creeds belong to the fighting races, a big religious festival gives ample chance for trouble. When they can—that is to say when the authorities are weak enough to allow it—the Hindus do their best to arrange some minor feast-day of their own in time to clash with the period of general mourning for the martyrs Hasan and Hussain, the heroes of the Mohurrum. Gilt and painted paper presentations of their tombs are borne with shouting and wailing, music, torches, and yells, through the principal thoroughfares of the City, which fakements are called tazias. Their passage is rigorously laid down beforehand by the Police, and detachments of Police accompany each tazia, lest the Hindus should throw bricks at it and the peace of the Queen and the heads of Her loyal subjects should thereby be broken. Mohurrum time in a 'fighting' town means anxiety to all the officials, because, if a riot breaks out, the officials and not the rioters are held responsible. The former must foresee everything, and while not making their precautions ridiculously elaborate, must see that they are at least adequate.

'Listen to the drums!' said Wali Dad. 'That is the heart of the people—empty and making much noise. How, think you, will the Mohurrum go this year? I think that there will be trouble.'

He turned down a side-street and left me alone with the stars and a sleepy Police patrol. Then I went to bed and dreamed that Wali Dad had sacked the City and I was made Vizier, with Lalun's silver huqa for mark of office.

All day the Mohurrum drums beat in the City, and all day deputations of tearful Hindu gentlemen besieged the Deputy Commissioner with assurances that they would be murdered ere next dawning by the Muhammadans. 'Which,' said the Deputy Commissioner, in confidence to the Head of Police, 'is a pretty fair indication that the Hindus are going to make 'emselves unpleasant. I think we can arrange a little surprise for them. I have given the heads of both Creeds fair warning. If they choose to disregard it, so much the worse for them.'

There was a large gathering in Lalun's house that night, but of men that I had never seen before, if I except the fat gentleman in black with the gold pince-nez. Wali Dad lay in the window-seat, more bitterly scornful of his Faith and its manifestations than I had ever known him. Lalun's maid was very busy cutting up and mixing tobacco for the guests. We could hear the thunder of the drums as the processions accompanying each tazia marched to the central gathering-place in the plain outside the City, preparatory to their triumphant re-entry and circuit within the walls. All the streets seemed ablaze with torches, and only Fort Amara was black and silent.

When the noise of the drums ceased, no one in the white room spoke for a time. 'The first tazia has moved off,' said Wali Dad, looking to the plain.

'That is very early,' said the man with the pince-nez.

'It is only half-past eight.' The company rose and departed.

'Some of them were men from Ladakh,' said Lalun, when the last had gone. 'They brought me brick-tea such as the Russians sell, and a tea-urn from Peshawur. Show me, now, how the English Memsahibs make tea.'

The brick-tea was abominable. When it was finished Wali Dad suggested going into the streets. 'I am nearly sure that there will be trouble to-night,' he said. 'All the City thinks so, and Vox Populi is Vox Dei, as the Babus say. Now I tell you that at the corner of the Padshahi Gate you will find my horse all this night if you want to go about and to see things. It is a most disgraceful exhibition. Where is the pleasure of saying "Ya Hasan, Ya Hussain," twenty thousand times in a night?'

All the processions—there were two and twenty of them—were now well within the City walls. The drums were beating afresh, the crowd were howling 'Ya Hasan! Ya Hussain!' and beating their breasts, the brass bands were playing their loudest, and at every corner where space allowed, Muhammadan preachers were telling the lamentable story of the death of the Martyrs. It was impossible to move except with the crowd, for the streets were not more than twenty feet wide. In the Hindu quarters the shutters of all the shops were up and cross-barred. As the first tazia, a gorgeous erection ten feet high, was borne aloft on the shoulders of a score of stout men into the semi-darkness of the Gully of the Horsemen, a brickbat crashed through its talc and tinsel sides.

'Into thy hands, O Lord?' murmured Wali Dad profanely, as a yell went up from behind, and a native officer of Police jammed his horse through the crowd. Another brickbat followed, and the tazia staggered and swayed where it had stopped.

'Go on! In the name of the Sirkar, go forward!' shouted the Policeman; but there was an ugly cracking and splintering of shutters, and the crowd halted, with oaths and growlings, before the house whence the brickbat had been thrown.

Then, without any warning, broke the storm—not only in the Gully of the Horsemen, but in half a dozen other places. The tazias rocked like ships at sea, the long pole-torches dipped and rose round them while the men shouted: 'The Hindus are dishonouring the tazias! Strike! Strike! Into their temples for the faith!' The six or eight Policemen with each tazia drew their batons, and struck as long as they could in the hope of forcing the mob forward, but they were overpowered, and as contingents of Hindus poured into the streets, the fight became general. Half a mile away where the tazias were yet untouched the drums and the shrieks of 'Ya Hasan! Ya Hussain!' continued, but not for long. The priests at the corners of the streets knocked the legs from the bedsteads that supported their pulpits and smote for the Faith, while stones fell from the silent houses upon friend and foe, and the packed streets bellowed: 'Din! Din! Din!' A tazia caught fire, and was dropped for a flaming barrier between Hindu and Musalman at the corner of the Gully. Then the crowd surged forward, and Wali Dad drew me close to the stone pillar of a well.

'It was intended from the beginning!' he shouted in my ear, with more heat than blank unbelief should be guilty of. 'The bricks were carried up to the houses beforehand. These swine of Hindus! We shall be gutting kine in their temples to-night!'

Tazia after tazia, some burning, others torn to pieces, hurried past us and the mob with them, howling, shrieking, and striking at the house doors in their flight. At last we saw the reason of the rush. Hugonin, the Assistant District Superintendent of Police, a boy of twenty, had got together thirty constables and was forcing the crowd through the streets. His old gray Police-horse showed no sign of uneasiness as it was spurred breast-on into the crowd, and the long dog-whip with which he had armed himself was never still.

'They know we haven't enough Police to hold 'em,' he cried as he passed me, mopping a cut on his face. 'They know we haven't! Aren't any of the men from the Club coming down to help? Get on, you sons of burnt fathers!' The dog-whip cracked across the writhing backs, and the constables smote afresh with baton and gun-butt. With these passed the lights and the shouting, and Wali Dad began to swear under his breath. From Fort Amara shot up a single rocket; then two side by side. It was the signal for troops.

Petitt, the Deputy Commissioner, covered with dust and sweat, but calm and gently smiling, cantered up the clean-swept street in rear of the main body of the rioters. 'No one killed yet,' he shouted. 'I'll keep 'em on the run till dawn! Don't let 'em halt, Hugonin! Trot 'em about till the troops come.'

The science of the defence lay solely in keeping the mob on the move. If they had breathing-space they would halt and fire a house, and then the work of restoring order would be more difficult, to say the least of it. Flames have the same effect on a crowd as blood has on a wild beast.

Word had reached the Club and men in evening-dress were beginning to show themselves and lend a hand in heading off and breaking up the shouting masses with stirrup-leathers, whips, or chance-found staves. They were not very often attacked, for the rioters had sense enough to know that the death of a European would not mean one hanging but many, and possibly the appearance of the thrice-dreaded Artillery. The clamour in the City redoubled. The Hindus had descended into the streets in real earnest and ere long the mob returned. It was a strange sight. There were no tazias—only their riven platforms—and there were no Police. Here and there a City dignitary, Hindu or Muhammadan, was vainly imploring his co-religionists to keep quiet and behave themselves—advice for which his white beard was pulled. Then a native officer of Police, unhorsed but still using his spurs with effect, would be borne along, warning all the crowd of the danger of insulting the Government. Everywhere men struck aimlessly with sticks, grasping each other by the throat, howling and foaming with rage, or beat with their bare hands on the doors of the houses.

'It is a lucky thing that they are fighting with natural weapons,' I said to Wali Dad, 'else we should have half the City killed.'

I turned as I spoke and looked at his face. His nostrils were distended, his eyes were fixed, and he was smiting himself softly on the breast. The crowd poured by with renewed riot—a gang of Musalmans hard-pressed by some hundred Hindu fanatics. Wali Dad left my side with an oath, and shouting: 'Ya Hasan! Ya Hussain!' plunged into the thick of the fight where I lost sight of him.

I fled by a side alley to the Padshahi Gate where I found Wali Dad's house, and thence rode to the Fort. Once outside the City wall, the tumult sank to a dull roar, very impressive under the stars and reflecting great credit on the fifty thousand angry able-bodied men who were making it. The troops who, at the Deputy Commissioner's instance, had been ordered to rendezvous quietly near the fort, showed no signs of being impressed. Two companies of Native Infantry, a squadron of Native Cavalry and a company of British Infantry were kicking their heels in the shadow of the East face, waiting for orders to march in. I am sorry to say that they were all pleased, unholily pleased, at the chance of what they called 'a little fun.' The senior officers, to be sure, grumbled at having been kept out of bed, and the English troops pretended to be sulky, but there was joy in the hearts of all the subalterns, and whispers ran up and down the line: 'No ball-cartridge—what a beastly shame!' 'D'you think the beggars will really stand up to us?' ''Hope I shall meet my money-lender there. I owe him more than I can afford.' 'Oh, they won't let us even unsheathe swords.' 'Hurrah! Up goes the fourth rocket. Fall in, there!'

The Garrison Artillery, who to the last cherished a wild hope that they might be allowed to bombard the City at a hundred yards' range, lined the parapet above the East gateway and cheered themselves hoarse as the British Infantry doubled along the road to the Main Gate of the City. The Cavalry cantered on to the Padshahi Gate, and the Native Infantry marched slowly to the Gate of the Butchers. The surprise was intended to be of a distinctly unpleasant nature, and to come on top of the defeat of the Police who had been just able to keep the Muhammadans from firing the houses of a few leading

Hindus. The bulk of the riot lay in the north and north-west wards. The east and south-east were by this time dark and silent, and I rode hastily to Lalun's house for I wished to tell her to send some one in search of Wali Dad. The house was unlighted, but the door was open, and I climbed upstairs in the darkness. One small lamp in the white room showed Lalun and her maid leaning half out of the window, breathing heavily and evidently pulling at something that refused to come.

'Thou art late—very late,' gasped Lalun without turning her head. 'Help us now, O Fool, if thou hast not spent thy strength howling among the tazias. Pull! Nasiban and I can do no more! O Sahib, is it you? The Hindus have been hunting an old Muhammadan round the Ditch with clubs. If they find him again they will kill him. Help us to pull him up.'

I put my hands to the long red silk waist-cloth that was hanging out of the window, and we three pulled and pulled with all the strength at our command. There was something very heavy at the end, and it swore in an unknown tongue as it kicked against the City wall.

'Pull, oh, pull!' said Lalun at the last. A pair of brown hands grasped the window-sill and a venerable Muhammadan tumbled upon the floor, very much out of breath. His jaws were tied up, his turban had fallen over one eye, and he was dusty and angry.

Lalun hid her face in her hands for an instant and said something about Wali Dad that I could not catch.

Then, to my extreme gratification, she threw her arms round my neck and murmured pretty things. I was in no haste to stop her; and Nasiban, being a handmaiden of tact, turned to the big jewel-chest that stands in the corner of the white room and rummaged among the contents. The Muhammadan sat on the floor and glared.

'One service more, Sahib, since thou hast come so opportunely,' said Lalun. 'Wilt thou'—it is very nice to be thou-ed by Lalun—'take this old man across the City—the troops are everywhere, and they might hurt him for he is old—to the Kumharsen Gate? There I think he may find a carriage to take him to his house. He is a friend of mine, and thou art—more than a friend—therefore I ask this.'

Nasiban bent over the old man, tucked something into his belt, and I raised him up, and led him into the streets.

In crossing from the east to the west of the City there was no chance of avoiding the troops and the crowd. Long before I reached the Gully of the Horsemen I heard the shouts of the British Infantry crying cheeringly: 'Hutt, ye beggars! Hutt, ye devils! Get along! Go forward, there!' Then followed the ringing of rifle-butts and shrieks of pain. The troops were banging the bare toes of the mob with their gun-butts—for not a bayonet had been fixed. My companion mumbled and jabbered as we walked on until we were carried back by the crowd and had to force our way to the troops. I caught him by the wrist and felt a bangle there—the iron bangle of the Sikhs—but I had no suspicions, for Lalun had only ten minutes before put her arms round me. Thrice we were carried back by the crowd, and when we made our way past the British Infantry it was to meet the Sikh Cavalry driving another mob before them with the butts of their lances.

'What are these dogs?' said the old man.

'Sikhs of the Cavalry, Father,' I said, and we edged our way up the line of horses two abreast and found the Deputy Commissioner, his helmet smashed on his head, surrounded by a knot of men who had come down from the Club as amateur constables and had helped the Police mightily.

'We'll keep 'em on the run till dawn,' said Petitt. 'Who's your villainous friend?'

I had only time to say:' The Protection of the Sirkar!' when a fresh crowd flying before the Native Infantry carried us a hundred yards nearer to the Kumharsen Gate, and Petitt was swept away like a shadow.

'I do not know—I cannot see—this is all new to me!' moaned my companion. 'How many troops are there in the City?'

'Perhaps five hundred,' I said.

'A lakh of men beaten by five hundred—and Sikhs among them! Surely, surely, I am an old man, but—the Kumharsen Gate is new. Who pulled down the stone lions? Where is the conduit? Sahib, I am a very old man, and, alas, I—I cannot stand.' He dropped in the shadow of the Kumharsen Gate where there was no disturbance. A fat gentleman wearing gold pince-nez came out of the darkness.

'You are most kind to my old friend,' he said suavely. 'He is a landholder of Akala. He should not be in a big City when there is religious excitement. But I have a carriage here. You are quite truly kind. Will you help me to put him into the carriage? It is very late.'

We bundled the old man into a hired victoria that stood close to the gate, and I turned back to the house on the City wall. The troops were driving the people to and fro, while the Police shouted, 'To your houses! Get to your houses!' and the dog-whip of the Assistant District Superintendent cracked remorselessly. Terror-stricken bunnias clung to the stirrups of the cavalry, crying that their houses had been robbed (which was a lie), and the burly Sikh horsemen patted them on the shoulder, and bade them return to those houses lest a worse thing should happen. Parties of five or six British soldiers, joining arms, swept down the side-gullies, their rifles on their backs, stamping, with shouting and song, upon the toes of Hindu and Musalman. Never was religious enthusiasm more systematically squashed; and never were poor breakers of the peace more utterly weary and footsore. They were routed out of holes and corners, from behind well-pillars and byres, and bidden to go to their houses. If they had no houses to go to, so much the worse for their toes.

On returning to Lalun's door I stumbled over a man at the threshold. He was sobbing hysterically and his arms flapped like the wings of a goose. It was Wali Dad, Agnostic and Unbeliever, shoeless, turbanless, and frothing at the mouth, the flesh on his chest bruised and bleeding from the vehemence with which he had smitten himself. A broken torch-handle lay by his side, and his quivering lips murmured, 'Ya Hasan! Ya Hussain!' as I stooped over him. I pushed him a few steps up the staircase, threw a pebble at Lalun's City window and hurried home.

Most of the streets were very still, and the cold wind that comes before the dawn whistled down them. In the centre of the Square of the Mosque a man was bending over a corpse. The skull had been smashed in by gun-butt or bamboo-stave.

'It is expedient that one man should die for the people,' said Petitt grimly, raising the shapeless head. 'These brutes were beginning to show their teeth too much.'

And from afar we could hear the soldiers singing 'Two Lovely Black Eyes,' as they drove the remnant of the rioters within doors.

Of course you can guess what happened? I was not so clever. When the news went abroad that Khem Singh had escaped from the Fort, I did not, since I was then living this story, not writing it, connect myself, or Lalun, or the fat gentleman with the gold pince-nez, with his disappearance. Nor did it strike me that Wali Dad was the man who should have convoyed him across the City, or that Lalun's arms round my neck were put there to hide the money that Nasiban gave to Khem Singh, and that Lalun had used me and my white face as even a better safeguard than Wali Dad who proved himself so untrustworthy. All that I knew at the time was that, when Fort Amara was taken up with the riots, Khem Singh profited by the confusion to get away, and that his two Sikh guards also escaped.

But later on I received full enlightenment; and so did Khem Singh. He fled to those who knew him in the old days, but many of them were dead and more were changed, and all knew something of the Wrath of the Government. He went to the young men, but the glamour of his name had passed away, and they were entering native regiments of Government offices, and Khem Singh could give them neither pension, decorations, nor influence—nothing but a glorious death with their backs to the mouth of a gun. He wrote letters and made promises, and the letters fell into bad hands, and a wholly insignificant subordinate officer of Police tracked them down and gained promotion thereby. Moreover, Khem Singh was old, and anise-seed brandy was scarce, and he had left his silver cooking-pots in Fort Amara with his nice warm bedding, and the gentleman with the gold pince-nez was told by those who had employed him that Khem Singh as a popular leader was not worth the money paid.

'Great is the mercy of these fools of English!' said Khem Singh when the situation was put before him. 'I will go back to Fort Amara of my own free will and gain honour. Give me good clothes to return in.'

So, at his own time, Khem Singh knocked at the wicket-gate of the Fort and walked to the Captain and the Subaltern, who were nearly gray-headed on account of correspondence that daily arrived from Simla marked 'Private.'

'I have come back, Captain Sahib,' said Khem Singh.

'Put no more guards over me. It is no good out yonder.'

A week later I saw him for the first time to my knowledge, and he made as though there were an understanding between us.

'It was well done, Sahib,' said he, 'and greatly I admired your astuteness in thus boldly facing the troops when I, whom they would have doubtless torn to pieces, was with you. Now there is a man in Fort Ooltagarh whom a bold man could with ease help to escape. This is the position of the Fort as I draw it on the sand—'

But I was thinking how I had become Lalun's Vizier after all.

Born in Bombay on 30th December 1865, Joseph Rudyard Kipling wrote short stories, poems and novels, a body of work whose reputation is in constant flux as his presentations and interpretations of empire are viewed within the changing context of empirical absolution in the twentieth century. Having spent the first five years of his life in India he felt a natural affinity for the country, though his upbringing had a distinctly colonial taste flavour. He was born in the Bombay Presidency of British India to Lockwood Kipling, an English art teacher and illustrator who took a position as professor of architectural sculpture in the Jeejeebhoy School of Art and Alice MacDonald, spoken of by the Viceroy of India that "dullness and Mrs Kipling cannot exist in the same room". Though their presence in India was principally artistic and educational, rather than political, the company they kept and the establishments in which they they kept it indicate an existence very much benefitting from the British Empire. Lockwood would later go on to assume a position as curator of the Lahore Museum, while working on various illustrations for Rudyard's writing, and various decorations for the Victoria and Albert museum in London. Much of his work, then, was coloured by the empire, whether in service to or benefitting from, and it was into this distinctly British experience of India that Rudyard was born.

Lockwood and Alice had met and fallen in love at Rudyard Lake in Rudyard, Staffordshire, and their affections for the area were so great they chose to refer to the lake in naming their first-born. Alice came from a family of four sisters, all of whose marriages were significant and well-arranged; moreover, Rudyard's most famous relative was Stanley Baldwin, Conservative Prime Minister on three occasions in the 1920s and 1930s. Kipling's sense of belonging in Bombay is found in 'To the City of Bombay' in the dedication to Seven Seas, a collection of poems published in 1900, which reads

> Mother of Cities to me,
> For I was born in her gate,
> Between the palms and the sea,
> Where the world-end steamers wait.

His parents considered themselves Anglo-Indians, and he would later assume this classification although he did not live there long. His first five years, which he describes as days of "strong light and darkness", ended when he and his three-year-old sister Alice were removed to Southsea, Plymouth, to board with Captain Pryse Agar Holloway and his wife Mrs Sarah Holloway, a couple who cared for the children of couples born in British India. They were there for six years and Kipling would later recall their time there with horror, describing incidents of cruelty and neglect and wondering whether it was these which speeded up his literary maturity, for "it made me give attention to the lies I soon found it necessary to tell: and this, I presume, is the foundation of literary effort".

Alice's time, by contrast, was relatively comfortable, Mrs Holloway hoping that she would marry her son, though this ambition would not come to fruition. They did have relatives in England, a maternal aunt Georgiana and her husband who lived in Fulham, London, in a house at which they spent a month each Christmas and which Kipling later described as "a paradise which I verily believe saved me". Their mother returned in 1877 and removed them from their custody with the Holloways. A year later he gained admission to the United Services College at Westward Ho! in Devon, a recently established school with the intention of readying boys for military service in the British Army. His time here was fraught physically, though emotionally it proved fruitful for he began several firm friendships with other boys at the school. Moreover, he found in it inspiration for the setting of his series of schoolboy stories,

Stalky and Co, begun in 1899. Meanwhile, his sister Alice had returned to Southsea and was boarding with Florence Garrard, with whom he fell in love and on whom he modeled Maisie in his first novel, The Light That Failed, published in 1891. At sixteen he was found lacking in the academic perspicacity necessary to undertake a scholarship to Oxford University, his parents meanwhile lacking the wherewithal to finance him therein. As such his father sought a job for him in Lahore, Punjab, where he was now a museum curator. The position he found for his son was as assistant editor of the Civil and Military Gazette, a small local newspaper. Kipling left for India on 20th September 1882, arriving in Bombay on 18th October. "There were yet three or four days" rail to Lahore, where my people lived. After these, my English years fell away, nor ever, I think, came back in full strength".

The Gazette appeared six days of the week, year-round save for a short break at both Christmas and Easter. Its editor Stephen Wheeler was diligent but Kipling's writing was insatiable, and he came to consider the paper his "mistress and most true love". In the summer of 1883 Kipling visited Shimla, the colonial hill-station and summer capital of British India which was then called Simla. Chosen by the British owing to its resemblance of English climate and scenery (as far as was possible in India), it became the seat of the Viceroy of India for the six months on the plains which were too hot for the British temperament, and subsequently became a "centre of power as well as pleasure". Lockwood was asked to serve in the Church there, and his family became yearly visitors while Kipling himself would take his annual leave here from 1885-88. The value of this time is evident from the regularity with which Simla appears in his writing for the Gazette, which in his journals he describes the time as

> "pure joy—every golden hour counted. It began in heat and discomfort, by rail and road. It ended in the cool evening, with a wood fire in one's bedroom, and next morn —thirty more of them ahead!—the early cup of tea, the Mother who brought it in, and the long talks of us all together again."

In 1886, his Departmental Ditties appeared, his first collection of verse, and brought with it a change of editor; Kay Robinson, Wheeler's replacement, was in favour of Kipling's creativity and granted him more freedom in that respect, even asking him to write short stories to appear in the newspaper. The vivacity of his writing was captured in a description of him by an ex-colleague at the Gazette, saying he "never knew such a fellow for ink - he simply revelled in it, filling up his pen viciously, and then throwing the contents all over the office, so that it was almost dangerous to approach him". While in Lahore, he had thirty-nine stories published in the Gazette between November 1886 and June 1887. Most of these are compiled in Plain Tales from the Hills, his first collection of prose, which was published in January 1888 in Calcutta, shortly after his 22nd birthday. In November 1887, he transferred from the Gazette to its much larger sister newspaper, The Pioneer, based in Allahabad. The pace of his writing remained, and in 1888 he published six collections of stories, Soldiers Three, The Story of the Gadsbys, In Black and White, Under the Deodars, The Phantom Rickshaw and Wee Willie Winkie, composed of some 41 stories. In addition, his position as The Pioneer's special correspondent in the Western region of Rajputna, he wrote many sketches which were plater compiled in Letters of Marque and published in From Sea to Sea and OTher Sketches, Letters of Travel.

A dispute in 1889 saw him discharged from The Pioneer, though by now he had been considering his future and sold the rights to his six volumes of stories for £200 and a small royalty, while the Plain Tales fetched £50, along with six months' salary from The Pioneer in lieu of notice. Using the money to undertake a pilgrimage to London, the literary centre of the British Empire, he left India on 9th March 1889, travelling via Rangoon, San Francisco, Hong Kong and Japan, then through the United States writing articles for The Pioneer which were also included in From Sea to Sea and Other Sketches, Letters of Travel. Arriving in England at Liverpool on October 1889, London and his literary début there beckoned.

His first task was to find a place to live, and he eventually settled on quarters in Villiers Street, Strand. The next two years saw several stories accepted by various magazine editors, the publication of the novel The Light That Failed, a nervous breakdown, the collaboration with Wolcott Balestier on the novel (uncharacterstically misspelt) The Naulhaka, and in 1891, following his doctors' advice, he embarked on a further sea voyage, travelling to South Africa, Australia, New Zealand and also returning to India. His plans to spend Christmas with his family were cut short on the news of Balestier's sudden death from typhoid fever, prompting an immediate return to London. Before he left, he had proposed to Balestier's sister Caroline Starr Balestier, with whom he had been having a hushed romance for just over a year. Back in London, Life's Handicap was published in 1891, a collection of short stories whose subject was the British in India, and British India. On 18th January 1892 aged 26 he married Caroline in the midst of an epidemic of influenza. Caroline was given away by Henry James, the famous and celebrated American author.

Honeymooning in Japan, they travelled via Vermont, America, to visit the Balestier estate, and upon arrival in Yokahama they found that their bank, The New Oriental Banking Corporation, had failed, though this loss did not deter them and they returned to Vermont, Caroline now pregnant with their first child. Renting a cottage on a farm for $10 per month, they lived a spartan existence and were "extraordinarily and self-centredly content". The named the residence Bliss Cottage, and it was here that the child was born, named Josephine, "in three foot of snow on the night of 29th December 1892. Her Mother's birthday being the 31st and mine the 30th we congratulated her on her sense of the fitness of things." While here, Kipling had his first ideas for the Jungle Books. Shortly after Josephine was born the couple moved in pursuit of more space and comfort, buying ten acres overlooking the Connecticut River from Caroline's brother. The house they built there was inspired by the Mughul architecture he encountered in Lahore, and was named Naulakha (this time correctly spelt) in honour of Wolcott. His literary output in four years here included the Jungle Books, a collection of short stories entitled The Day's Work, the novel Captain Courageous and a plethora of poetry, of which most notably the volume The Seven Seas and his Barrack-Room Ballads. Meanwhile, he enjoyed correspondence with the many children who wrote to him about the Jungle Books.

In between this writing, Kipling took regular visitors. Most notably Arthur Conan Doyle came, bringing golf clubs and staying for two days to give Kipling an extended golf lesson. Kipling enjoyed the game so much that he continued to play, even in winter with special red balls, though he found that the ice would lead to drives travelling two miles as they slid "down the long slope to the Connecticut River". Elsie, the couple's second daughter, was born in February 1896, and by this time it is thought that their marriage had lost its original spark of spontaneity and descended into routine, though they remained loyal to one another. By now, failed arbitration between the United States and England over a border dispute involving British Guiana incited Anglo-American tensions which, in May 1896, resulted in a confrontation between Kipling and Caroline's brother, resulting in his arrest and, in the hearing which followed, the destruction of Kipling's private life, leaving him exhausted and miserable and leading to their return to England.

They had settled Torquay, Devon, by September 1896, and he remained socially present and literarily productive. The success of his writing had brought him fame, and he had responded with a sense of duty to include in his writing elements of political persuasion, most notably in his two poems Recessional and The White Man's Burden, which caused controversy when they were published in 1897 and 1899 respectively. Many considered them anthemic to the empire, propaganda for the imperial mindset so prevalent in the Victoria era. Their first son, John, was born in August 1887. Another journey to South Africa began a tradition of wintering there, which continued until 1908. His reputation as Poet of the Empire saw him well-received by politicians in the Cape Colony, and he started the newspaper The Friend for Lord Roberts and the British troops in Bloemfontein. Back in England, they moved to Rottingdean, East Sussex, in 1897, and in 1902 he bought Bateman's, a house built in 1630, which was his home from until his death in 1936. Kim was published in 1902, after which he collected material for Just So Stories for Little Children, published a year later. Both he and Josephine developed pneumonia while visiting the United States, from which she later died.

This decade proved his most successful, being awarded the Nobel Prize for Literature in 1907, the prize citation reading "in consideration of the power of observation, originality of imagination, virility of ideas and remarkable talent for narration which characterise the creations of this world-famous author". He was the first English-language recipient. At the award ceremony in Switzerland, Carl David af Wirsén praised Kipling and the English literary tradition:

> The Swedish Academy, in awarding the Nobel Prize in Literature this year to Rudyard
> Kipling, desires to pay a tribute to the literature of England, so rich in manifold
> glories, and to the greatest genius in the realm of narrative that that country has
> produced in our times.

Following this achievement, Kipling published Rewards and Fairies, which contained If, voted Britain's favourite poem in a BBC opinion poll in 1995. He turned down several recommendations for knighthood and was considered for Poet Laureate, though this position was never offered to him.

The sense of perseverance, honour and stoicism in If prevailed in many of his opinions, including that on the First World War. Writing in The New Army in Training in 1915, he scorned those who refused conscription, considering

> ....what will be the position in years to come of the young man who has deliberately
> elected to outcaste himself from this all-embracing brotherhood? What of his family,
> and, above all, what of his descendants, when the books have been closed and the
> last balance struck of sacrifice and sorrow in every hamlet, village, parish, suburb,
> city, shire, district, province, and Dominion throughout the Empire?

This attitude saw him encourage his son, John, to go to war, and he was promptly killed at the Battle of Loos in September 1915, aged 18. Last seen during the battle stumbling blindly through the mud, screaming in agony after an exploding shell had ripped his face apart, Kipling would write "If any question why we died / Tell them, because our fathers lied", perhaps betraying the guilt he felt at encouraging his son to go to war and finding him a position in the Irish Guards through his friendship with commander-in-chief Lord Roberts, for whom he had established The Friend in Bloemfontein. His death inspired much of Kipling's successive writing, notably My Boy Jack and a two-volume history of the Irish Guards, considered one of the finest examples of regimental history. Ironically, though his writing and his political position had arguably cost John his life, after the war he became friends with a French soldier whose copy of Kim, kept in his breast pocket, had stopped a bullet and saved his life. For a while the book and the soldier's Croix de Guerre were with Kipling, presented as tokens of gratitude, and they remained in contact, though when Kipling learned of the soldier's child he insisted on returning both book and medal.

He kept writing until 1930, though at a considerably slower pace, and to less success. His death, already once incorrectly announced early by a magazine in a premature obituary (and to which he responded "I've just read that I am dead. Don't forget to delete me from your list of subscribers") came on 18th January 1936, at the age of 70, from a perforated duodenal ulcer. His coffin was carried by, among others, his cousin the Prime Minister Stanley Baldwin, and his marble casket covered by a Union flag. He was cremated at Golders Green Crematorium in Northwest London and his ashes are buried at Poets' Corner in Westminster Abbey, alongside the graves of both Charles Dickens and Thomas Hardy. In conjunction with various earthly memorials which commemorate him, alongside his extensive writing, he has a crater on Mercury named after him. The question of memorial and monument is much-addressed in English Literature and, as various great authors and poets have agreed before Kipling's time, his memory lives on more vivaciously set in his words, far longer and better represented than it could set in stone.

Rudyard Kipling - A Concise Bibliography

Books
(These are collections of, or single short stories except as noted)
The City of Dreadful Night (1885, short story)
Departmental Ditties (1886, poetry)
Plain Tales from the Hills (1888)
Soldiers Three (1888)
The Story of the Gadsbys (1888)
In Black and White (1888)
Under the Deodars (1888)
The Phantom 'Rickshaw and other Eerie Tales (1888)
Wee Willie Winkie and Other Child Stories (1888)
Life's Handicap (1891)
The Light that Failed (1891, novel)
American Notes (1891, non-fiction)
Barrack-Room Ballads (1892, poetry)
The Naulahka: A Story of West and East (1892) (with Wolcott Balestie)
Many Inventions (1893)
The Jungle Book (1894)
Mowgli's Brothers" (short story)
Kaa's Hunting" (short story)
Tiger! Tiger!" (short story)
The White Seal" (short story)
Rikki-Tikki-Tavi" (short story)
Toomai of the Elephants" (short story)
Her Majesty's Servants" (originally titled "Servants of the Queen") (short story)
The Second Jungle Book (1895)
How Fear Came" (short story)
The Miracle of Purun Bhagat" (short story)
Letting in the Jungle" (short story)
The Undertakers" (short story)

The King's Ankus" (short story)
Quiquern" (short story)
Red Dog" (short story)
The Spring Running" (short story)
Captains Courageous (1896, novel)
The Seven Seas (1896, poetry)
The Day's Work (1898)
A Fleet in Being (1898)
Stalky & Co. (1899)
From Sea to Sea and Other Sketches, Letters of Travel (1899, non-fiction)
Kim (1901, novel)
The Five Nations (1903, poetry)
Just So Stories for Little Children (1902)
Traffics and Discoveries (1904, 24 collected short stories)
With the Night Mail (1905, A Story of 2000 A.D)
Puck of Pook's Hill (1906)
The Brushwood Boy (1907)
Actions and Reactions (1909)
A Song of the English (1909) with W. Heath Robinson (illustrator)
Rewards and Fairies (1910)
A History of England (1911, non-fiction) with Charles Robert Leslie Fletcher
Songs from Books (1912)
As Easy as A.B.C. (1912, Science-fiction short story)
The Fringes of the Fleet (1915, non-fiction)
Sea Warfare (1916, non-fiction)
A Diversity of Creatures (1917)
The Years Between (1919, poetry)
Land and Sea Tales for Scouts and Guides (1923)
The Irish Guards in the Great War (1923, non-fiction)
Debits and Credits (1926)
A Book of Words (1928, non-fiction)
Thy Servant a Dog (1930)
Limits and Renewals (1932)
Tales of India: the Windermere Series (1935)
Something of Myself (1937, autobiography)
The Muse among the Motors (poetry) "The Elephant's Child" (fiction)

Autobiographies and Speeches
A Book of Words (1928)
Something of Myself (1937)

Short Story Collections
Quartette (1885) – with his father, mother, and sister
Plain Tales from the Hills (1888)
Soldiers Three, The Story of the Gadsbys, In Black and White (1888)
The Phantom 'Rickshaw and other Eerie Tales (1888)

Under the Deodars (1888)
Wee Willie Winkie and Other Child Stories (1888)
Life's Handicap (1891)
Many Inventions (1893)
The Jungle Book (1894)
The Second Jungle Book (1895)
The Day's Work (1898)
Life's Handicap (1899)
Stalky & Co. (1899)
Just So Stories (1902)
Traffics and Discoveries (1904)
Puck of Pook's Hill (1906)
Actions and Reactions (1909)
Abaft the Funnel (1909)
Rewards and Fairies (1910)
The Eyes of Asia (1917)
A Diversity of Creatures (1917)
Land and Sea Tales for Scouts and Guides (1923)
Debits and Credits (1926)
Thy Servant a Dog (1930)
Limits and Renewals (1932)

Military Collections
A Fleet in Being (1898)
France at War (1915)
The New Army in Training (1915)
Sea Warfare (1916)
The War in the Mountains (1917)
The Graves of the Fallen (1919)
The Irish Guards in the Great War (1923)
Poetry collections by Kipling[edit]
Schoolboy Lyrics (1881)
Echoes (1884) – with his sister, Alice ('Trix')
Departmental Ditties (1886)
Barrack-Room Ballads (1890)
The Seven Seas (1896)
An Almanac of Twelve Sports (1898, with illustrations by William Nicholson)
The Five Nations (1903)
Collected Verse (1907)
Songs from Books (1912)
The Years Between (1919)
Rudyard Kipling's Verse: Definitive Edition (1940)

Travel Writing
From Sea to Sea – Letters of Travel: 1887–1889 (1899)
Letters of Travel: 1892–1913 (1920)

Souvenirs of France (1933)
Brazilian Sketches: 1927 (1940)

Collected Works
The Outward Bound Edition (1897–1937, 36 volumes)
The Edition de Luxe (1897–1937, 38 volumes)
The Bombay Edition (1913–38, 31 volumes)
The Sussex Edition (1937–39, 35 volumes)
The Burwash Edition (1941, 28 volumes)

Poems
Departmental Ditties and Other Verses (1886)
Barrack Room Ballads (1889, republished with additions at later times)
The Seven Seas and Further Barrack-Room Ballads (In various editions 1891–96)
The Five Nations (with some new and some reprinted and revised poems, 1903)
Twenty-two original 'Historical Poems' (1911)
Songs from Books (1912)
The Years Between (1919)

Posthumous Collections
Rudyard Kipling's Verse: Definitive edition.
A Choice of Kipling's Verse, edited by T.S.Eliot.

In addition Kipling wrote and published many hundreds of poems too numerous to include here.